FRONTIER JUSTICE
AN ALASKAN TALE

C. MARCHI

Cover Photo: Cie Marchi, Alaska

Other Books by C. Marchi

<u>*Children's Books*</u>
You Can Grow Old with Me
A Raven's Call

<u>*Humor*</u>
*"Honey, Throw Me A Bone"— A Fun Guide to
Intimacy*

<u>*Non-Fiction*</u>
Burned Out — Chelan County Fires 2015

THE NORTHERN TERRITORY IMPOSES
ITS OWN GRIEVANCE SYSTEM KNOWN AS
FRONTIER JUSTICE. ALASKA IS A PLACE
WHERE EVERY MAN IS JUDGE, WHERE
CONVICTIONS ARE HARSH AND WHERE
EXECUTIONS GO UNNOTICED.

EUREKA

Dayton Pass Alcoholic Rehabilitation Center stretched out beyond the Alaskan timberline. Annoyed, Bryan scanned the adjacent hexagon shaped state prison. *Five years, two months, seven days, then twelve weeks of rehab,* he thought. He scratched his whiskers wondering which was more contemptible—a jail cell shared with Magpie, a stunted loose-lipped, despicable informant or the nurses in the sterile corridors of rehab. In contrast to Magpie, Bryan's lanky physique gave him the edge and dominant quell rights. He had no liberties in rehab.

Prison was more satisfying, especially the night of the slicing. Bryan placed a pillow over Magpie's face, allowed the struggle to subside, and then slit the jailhouse talker's wrist. Blood splattered the concrete floor. Bryan eagerly reached for the dripping mid-air beads; the taste settled his nerves. He licked the sweet tincture from the gushing wound. Suddenly he realized Magpie's value, released the pillow and slapped him into consciousness. Magpie gasped, screaming out his first breath. Bryan jumped into bed completely satiated knowing small plastic bags filled with ninety-proof whiskey would arrive by noon. While incarcerated he had managed forceful manipulation for his daily alcohol rations—weaker inmates had to become industrious, a trait that saved their lives and manhood. Key to his addiction, his drunken companion, Magpie, purveyed the alcohol that kept Bryan sane.

As the guards bolted through the iron door, Bryan faked a wet dream. His smile was authentic enough: entertained by stifling Magpie, thrilled by the sampling of warm blood, and more importantly, secure knowing that the covert delivery of his liquid gold would continue. That was two years, three months and eleven days into his prison sentence.

Looking out of the Eagle Motel, the grungy window vibrated with each tap of Bryan's finger. An idiosyncrasy he had developed—a clear indicator of his rising temper. Unfortunately, he did not devise this warning signal before murdering his drinking buddy, the day a bloody beer changed Bryan's life, and unexpectedly altered the lives of many.

The tapping continued on the Susitna Sunday newspaper advertisement dated July 18, 1974. Bryan read the half-dozen listings*: For sale: Ford studded tires, rims...Must sell: Riverboat...Paula in the Pass—satisfaction guaranteed...For rent: Cozy mountain cabin....* He contemplated over his thirst for gratification or the prospect of peace. His prison work detail netted him twenty-nine hundred dollars. After five years, two months, seven days and twelve weeks of rehab masturbation was a bore. Paula sounded nice. He tapped harder as his denim zipper bulged. He dialed the phone.

Running his fingers through his wavy black hair, Bryan lit a cigarette. He waited impatiently, tapping his thumb, for someone to answer. Six rings later, a deep voice came through the receiver, "Hurks."

Finally, Bryan thought as he released a puff of smoke. "I'm looking for J.T.?"

"Hey, Jess. It's for you," the throaty man hollered, slamming down the receiver causing Bryan's wrist to flinch away from his ear. "Tealand here. Who's this?"

"I'm callin' about the cabin. Is it still available?"

"Are you lookin' for a place in the bush?" Tealand asked.

"Anyplace but the city—it's got to be clean and quiet."

"It's clean. There's no toilet or running water."

Airwaves crackled as Bryan thought for a moment. "I've lived with less. What else?"

"George Creek runs all year—that's where you'll haul water. There's an outhouse with all the Styrofoam trimmings. You'll want to add lime to break down the solid waste and reduce the uric acid odor. You heat with wood. That means you gotta cut it, too. There's a propane cook stove and a propane refrigerator, a bed and a few standard furnishings. Showers cost fifty cents. I've got two washers and dryers; fifty cents for a wash load and seventy-five cents to dry it."

"Sounds reasonable, what mile post?" Bryan asked with more interest, still tapping his pen on the morning paper.

"Thirty-eight miles northeast of Hurricane County—mile post three hundred twenty. You got a four-by-four?"

"I've a Chevy half-ton with four-wheel drive on the fly. Get much snow up there?" *What a dumb question*, Bryan thought as the words flew from his mouth.

Tealand laughed and said, "It's nothing a shovel won't cure. You're not one of those city boys, are you? It takes a real man to live out here. If you're afraid of a little snow, then stay south."

Bryan recalled the few times he actually felt fear: the afternoon he signed over his children to his ex-wife, the night he killed his best friend and the twelve weeks of sobriety. Discounting the bad memories, he asked, "How many people live nearby? Like I said, I like it quiet."

"You'll find it out here. There's not many that'll brave the uncertain winters," Tealand laughed suspiciously.

Tealand's tone curled Bryan's neck hairs. Apprehensive he asked, "I need to take a look before I decide?"

"Don't mind at all. Nevertheless, it's a long drive just for a look. Can you make it out here tomorrow?"

"I can be there by mid-afternoon."

"If you don't rent it, I'll charge you twenty-five bucks for a night's stay," Tealand said.

"That sounds fair enough."

"Cash."

"No problem," Bryan said aggravated. His fingers drummed on the marred tabletop.

Bryan took the more detailed directions, hung up the phone and then lit another cigarette. Nervously, he tapped away on the table. Immersed in a daydream, he thought about a cabin tucked far away from the highway, far from his therapy group, and far from his former lifestyle. He fantasized about the smell of burning wood on a fall day while freshly ground coffee brewed in its pot. Picturing interior shadows bouncing off the cabin walls as kerosene lanterns lit the room, he was sure peace was achievable—a new beginning. Beating his friend to death was his calling card for change. The courts called it manslaughter, but Bryan knew it was murder.

The chemical smell of a burning cigarette filter drew Bryan out of his potential utopia. Allowing the filter to burn until extinguished, his gaze cleared eliciting his memory of where he was—in the heart of downtown Dayton Pass, Alaska, inside a dumpy motel where tacky curtains hung from a filthy window overlooking the four-block township. The studio was a grim sight. Its worn-out ash cabinets and food stained orange shag carpet cheapened the attempted décor. The wallpaper with country farm scenes had turned brown from a blend of road dust and cigarette smoke. *I won't miss this place*, Bryan thought as he poured hot water over instant coffee. He lit his last cigarette, took two puffs and pinched out the burning end into a chipped ceramic ashtray. "Another stinking habit that I've got to quit," he said disgusted.

Deep crow's feet around his eyes reflected back from the window as he looked down on the decaying town. It was as run down as its patrons. Worse yet, it was a dry borough. Bryan glanced over at his previous residence. The town's two primary attractions were the barbed wire, grey concrete block habitats and the impersonal hallways of rehabilitation. "Hell town, USA," Bryan said softly. He chuckled recalling his futile expectations for reprieve from prison when he entered rehab. Immediately the wretched, cloned staff members confiscated his last two plastic whiskey containers. They forced their psychology on him, irritating him every day: 'Do this. Don't do that. How do you feel today, Mr. Smith?'

"Like crap, Nurse Jackson. How does anyone feel going cold turkey?" Nurse Jackson was a grey haired, overweight nurse with a spinal hump just below her neck. Instead of treating patients kindly, she verbally tormented them. Her disparaging words contradicted the psychologists', always delivered behind closed doors and without witnesses, allowing her abuse to continue for over twenty-three years.

Fifteen years of drinking had taken its toll, but Bryan finished the mandatory court ordered twelve weeks. Rehab was tough mentally and physically. However, not as taxing as living with seeing your only friend lying dead on a sleazy tavern floor, murder was daunting enough, prison and rehab only hardened the brutal image. Routinely he cursed the nurses for imparting rules, the meetings with shrinks and the bland food. Deep down, he knew they probably had saved his life though he would never admit that he had learned from their strategies. *A straight life can't be harder than five years, two months, seven days and twelve weeks of rehab,* Bryan thought as he reached for his empty Camel pack.

Early the next morning, Bryan packed his entire life into a cardboard box. His assets consisted of three shirts, two pair blue jeans, four pairs of mismatched grey socks, a flashlight, his steel-toed army issue boots, gloves, a wool hat and three faded photographs of his family. Folding a red winter coat, he placed it over the box then easily carried his belongings out of the drab efficiency. Without looking back, he tossed his room key on the registration counter and then walked outside to his precious brown Chevy pick-up truck.

After placing the box on the passenger seat, he looked up and down the street of the dry county. Bryan lit his first cigarette of the day, inhaled thoroughly enjoying the tobacco taste, and then slowly exhaled. *What a dump,* he thought discerning the muted street colors and dilapidated buildings.

Morning fog made the town look even more deserted. Bryan knew otherwise. He felt the wet, stagnate air penetrating his clothes, prompting his memory of rehab and the nurses' uniforms pressed to perfection. County jail and rehab's adjacent dwellings' bare essence suffocated him. He flicked the cigarette into the road gutter, climbed into his spotless truck then drove over to PJ's Garage.

Obviously proud of his freshly starched uniform, embroidered nametag and matching cap, the attendant asked, "How can I help you?"

"Fill 'er up and check the oil," Bryan said perturbed.

Acknowledging the order, the attendant began pumping the gasoline. As he walked past the open truck window, he asked, "So where you headed?"

Bryan rolled his eyes, tapping his thumb on the steering wheel then huffed, "North. Look…Peter, I'm in a hurry."

"Everyone is," Peter said checking the dipstick, wiping it twice. Slamming down the hood, its tether recoiled. Bryan's nerves cringed; he was sure damage to his precious truck would cause another murder. Peter filled the tanks. "The oil's fine. Thirty-seven dollars for the fuel."

Bryan paid the gas bill, grumbling out the window, "They get you comin' and goin'."

"Yes, Sir," Peter said with a smile counting the cash.

Bryan rolled onto the Alaskan Highway. *Highway 1* read the black and white sign with an illustration of the Big Dipper stamped in the center. Driving past the road sign, he thought, *One road in and one road out.* He settled in for the six-hour drive toward Hurricane County.

The Alaska Railroad bestowed the small county of Hurricane County with its name. In 1923, a train named *Hurricane* was one of the fastest trains in America—traveling at a rate of 74 miles per hour. It was a passenger flag stop with spectacular easterly views of Denali. Gold miners quietly transported their riches as incoming thieves chose less laborious methods, robbing unprotected miners. Eventually, *Hurricane* prohibited guns and knives from its route. Conductors often lost their lives implementing the ban. Wealthy men became a part of the Alaskan tundra as they discreetly slipped below the fast-moving rail system. Bandits gleaned their riches, paying off railroad executives, creating a profitable and deadly business.

Bryan turned on the radio to help pass the time. As he cruised along, he felt his sense of freedom returning. A slight smile turned the corners of his lips upward. Feeling proud and strong, he had successfully escaped the clutches of society. His fingers thumped hard on the steering wheel as the music blasted the cab. Maintaining a constant speed, reducing wear on the Chevy's engine, he slowed down for only small town speed zones. By the time his speed decreased, he had already passed through the one-block townships.

The timberline was an odd sight. Freezing winters hampered tree heights, leaving groups of miniature spruce. Yet the birch trees managed to thrive. After hours of driving, the trees became sparser.

Only the low and hardy tundra plants consistently accompanied Bryan as he moved north. Streaks of pink and purple laced the earth's floor. Drawn to the vast mountains paralleling his course, Bryan sped past without noticing the tundra's beauty.

He drove along the two-lane highway stretch observing the clouds ahead. A breeze separated the veils, opening the sky, exposing the Great One. "Denali," Bryan whispered. This huge landmass sprung up out of nowhere. Compelled by the view, he pulled over, stepped outside of the cab and peed. In awe, he felt fortunate to see the mountain in her glory. From the highest 20,320-foot mountain peak to her braided rivers below, it was an extraordinary piece of land.

Constantly covered with snow, glaciers formed in Denali's crevasses, building ancient slabs of compressed ice. Faithfully, the slabs retreated and advanced while scarring the earth below. Bryan stood near the tundra witnessing Denali's cloud formations, assembling slowly then cloaking, once again, the isolated landmass. He felt small and insignificant compared to the majestic power of the mountain. An eighteen-wheeler suddenly blew past Bryan scaring him back into reality. Once settled back into his truck, he pulled onto *Highway 1*. As he drove, Denali's partially hidden landscaped held his attention; the mountain's clouds moved toward him as he passed the 284th mile marker.

Shifting in the bench seat, Bryan reached for his half-empty cigarette pack. *This is one long-ass drive,* he thought. *WELCOME TO HURRICANE COUNTY* read the next road sign. *It's about time,* he thought extinguishing a cigarette, thinking back to his last welcoming party. The *Dayton Pass Prison* residents certainly had their own unique way of greeting a new inmate. The thought of his first day in prison made him shudder. It nauseated him when the other male inmates whistled, making vividly crude remarks. That was all behind him now, though in the back of his mind he was not convinced that he had fully recovered.

OL' CHARLIE'S

Strobe lights pulsed ahead. As Bryan drove closer, he read the flashing letters, *HURKS CAFÉ.* That was his cue. He steered off the paved highway into a gravel parking lot. There were no definitive spaces identified, so he haphazardly parked sideways, making sure that no one would damage his truck. The long drive had crimped his legs and back reminding him of his prison cot. Day after day, his body ached from the over used, metal spring mattress. Apparently, poor bedding was another systematic punishment used by those running detention centers. Looking crippled, he stepped out of the truck, stretched his legs and aching back, lit a cigarette then walked over to the café entrance. Gas pumps and garbage containers lined the side of the parking lot. A rusty blue and white U.S. mailbox sat near the front door. The café had seen better days, moldy logs and a sagging metal roof caused Bryan to wonder about his safety as he entered.

Filled with arctic memorabilia, this was a typical Alaskan trading post. Tarnished photographs hung crooked on the walls. Painted gold pans indiscriminately placed around the café depicted vibrant color schemes of log cabins next to rivers, the Aurora Borealis and various wildlife scenes. Smaller gold pans were fashioned into tacky clocks. Proudly displayed moose antlers hung above the entrance with a child's hand-written sign that read, *Not for Sale*. Native jewelry and beaded hair clips arranged in a dusty glass cabinet awaited purchase, reviving their original luster and purpose. A faded Alaskan map dominated the far wall. Aisles stored basic food staples, candy and automobile supplies. Refrigerated drinks and a dusty multi-shelved magazine rack offered the three past issues of *National Geographic* and a two-year-old *Guide to Denali*. Paperback books and greeting cards spun in their carousel stands.

Several native patrons looked Bryan over, silently judging his demeanor and wardrobe. Immediately feeling uncomfortable in the unfamiliar store, he hastily sat down at the lunch counter.

"I'm Max. What can I get you? Coffee?"

Bryan turned around to face a six-foot five, strawberry blonde bearded man. "Sure, coffee and a menu." Max tipped his faded baseball cap, exposing his bald scalp with deep red patches. *Psoriasis or frostbite*, Bryan thought.

"Comin' right up," Max said cheerfully. "Cream? Sugar?"

"Black." Bryan scanned the four-item menu. "Give me a cheese bison burger and fries," he said as Max poured his coffee. *More spots on his hands and forearms, definitely psoriasis,* Bryan thought hoping Max would wash his hands before touching his food.

"Sure thing, Mister," Max said disappearing behind the partitioned kitchen. Without scrubbing his hands, he dropped home fries into a metal basket then into boiling grease. They sizzled as their skins browned. Through an open window, he asked, "So, you just passin' through?"

Tapping his thumb, Bryan looked up from his coffee, "I'm heading east toward George Creek. Maybe rent a cabin for a year, that is if I can handle the heavy snowfall." Hoping Max would take a hint and stop asking questions Bryan added, "I'm just lookin' for peace and quiet."

"You'll be staying up at Jess Tealand's place. Don't worry about the snow. It's nothing a shovel won't cure." Max snickered as he flipped the bison burger, adding American cheese.

Bryan nodded. "So I've heard."

Max piled hot fries into a blue and white paper-lined basket added the burger then served his customer. "Order up," he said with a big smile showing off his tarnished, crooked teeth.

"As far as the quiet goes, I remember the days when my life was peaceful. That's all you need in this world is solitude. Take it from me. I've a wife and four kids—hardly a moment's rest, noise all the time. That's not to say they're unruly, just always busy."

"No peace? Not even when they're in school?" Bryan asked.

Max laughed. "You must be new to the bush. There aren't any schools this far north. The wife home schools the kids. It's been that way from the beginning of time. What you see right here is as close to society as you're going get—without driving three hundred miles either direction. My supplies often come in late. Fuel, too. Sometimes the tanks go dry, and that's hell on my pocketbook. Kids gotta eat, ya know. There's no peace if they're complaining. Enjoy your meal."

"Thanks." Adventurously, Bryan took his first bite of bison. It was tasteless, over cooked and dry, causing him to gulp down his coffee. Next, he added several squirts of catsup to the bun. Finishing his lunch, he motioned for the bill.

"That'll be $ 7.85."

From his pants pocket, Bryan dug out a crumpled ten-dollar bill. "Keep the change. Feed your kids."

"Thanks," Max said. "Oh, and I'll take your money for the gas. You are gonna fill up before heading northeast, right?"

Bryan gave Max a crooked smile. "As a matter of fact, I am." He handed Max a wrinkled twenty-dollar bill.

Max's grin widened as he placed the cash into his breast pocket. "Appreciate your business, friend. Oh, and don't go hurting yourself either. There aren't any doctors in Hurricane."

"Thanks for the warning, Max." *I wish he had warned me about the coffee*, Bryan thought. His stomach cramped and growled as the bitter coffee descended into his intestines.

After refueling the truck, he slid back inside the cab, eager to view his potential new home, hoping it was acceptable living conditions. He was confident that the isolation would cure him permanently. Searching through his coat pockets, he found the directions that Tealand had provided the day before. After carefully reading them, Bryan pointed his vehicle northeast then drove through the town of Hurricane.

Deserted, the four-block miner's town felt ghostly as if mortal deaths ceased commerce, yet prosperity lingered as a phantom memory. Wooden buildings weathered and greyed, their timbers split and dried, now perfect for kindling. Glacial winds had blown off a majority of the abandoned storefront signs. Boarded windows added to the mystic and mystery of this forsaken town. Dirt from the one lane, unpaved thoroughfare swirled as the wind lifted it, carrying it off to its new location. Leaves rustled over the avenue, skipping across the muted ground, some hid beneath broken signs that harbored years of crisp, dry foliage. The howling winds spooked even Bryan. He shivered. *Prison*, he thought.

He turned left at the dilapidated Nugget Inn. Its covered porch sagged, nearly resting on the boardwalk below. Continuing onward a quarter of a mile, he saw a "Y" in the road. Per the instructions, he stayed to the right, which led him onto River Road. The desolate sight of the Knikinek Glacier River glistened on the left. Warned about native spirits kidnapping white souls, he cautiously looked into the distance, ignoring his unsettled nerves. As if driving on buried carcasses, Bryan maneuvered over what felt like crushed bone and talisman, a queer sensation. Undeniably, the desiccated road disturbed his senses.

The truck sprang upward then downward, jostling Bryan in his seat. Pothole after pothole, he tried to avoid driving into the craters. Where there was an absence of potholes, washboard patterns rippled the dusty road, wreaking havoc on the shock absorbers. Worse yet, Hurk's coffee weighed heavily on Bryan's bladder. Finally, he stopped to relieve himself.

Standing in the midst of a widespread valley, he unzipped his pants. For the second time that day, he felt insignificant. Millions of years ago, compressed snow once owned this U-shaped valley. He imagined the terrain covered with aqua-blue ice, for centuries freezing the land beneath. The glacier's movement carved the mountain contour, leaving scored and crushed rocks and earthly moraines—byproducts of the advancing and receding glaciers. The ancient river ways forced the valley wider.

Bryan's thoughts turned to the original homesteaders. What was it like to break trail through the virgin territory and streams? How strenuous would it have been to pack in one's family and supplies? Imagine, walking mile after mile. With each new step, another mountain pass with glorious views beckoned the brave souls. *In this spacious and desolate wilderness, how did they decide where to build their homes, where to raise their families?* he thought.

Now driving, Bryan tried to remember the last time he had had a home. His wife left him years ago, taking the kids. Drinking caused the split he was sure. He loved his family, but alcohol throttled him toward divorce court. It was easier to drink than to love. With life pressures lifted, family burdens diminished. Paradoxically, he missed his two kids more than anything, even more than a fifth of whiskey. The bottle had suffocated his logic and devotion. *How could I call them mine? No contact or support for twelve years...or was it thirteen years? The last fifteen years were just a blur. Why did it matter now anyway?* he thought knowing he could never go back.

His self-induced shame was a life sentence, an isolation cell that protected his offspring and occasionally society.

Bryan checked his odometer, calculating the mileage. *Only twenty-three miles left,* he thought. A cozy mountain cabin, tranquility and a dry county awaited—at least two of the three waited.

River Road continued, paralleling the south side of the Knikinek Glacier. High water levels moved fast around raised sandbars. In July, the glacier recedes, competing with the warm earth below its mass, dissolving century old compressed snow layers into icy water. Dead trees floated down through the twisted canal—a pattern that changed with each season. Tree limbs and brush drifted onto the ever-rising silt mounds.

A large bird soared above Bryan. White crown feathers led its outstretched wings. Bald eagles had always impressed him. Slowing to watch the king of Alaskan birds gracefully career overhead, he recalled someone once telling him that eagles signify freedom. *Perfect timing,* he thought, thankful for the omen.

Nearing mile twenty-two, Bryan saw a crowd of people gathered around a rectangular plywood building. The washed-out green-grey paint and red trim devalued the aging dwelling. The people were reaching for and grabbing at a white woman standing near the red front door. Her large breasts swayed as she handed out something that Bryan could not make out. A wooden sign hung on the exterior wall. It read, *Ravens*. An eighteen-foot totem pole stood to the right of the only door. Dressing the top of the totem was a raven's head. Just below the faded head, black and grey wings spread three-feet on both sides. Underneath the wings were three ill-defined faces. It was obvious that the totem pole had stood there for many years. The totem's red paint had faded to dusty pink. The solid blues and whites paled to dusty greys. Black paint had turned grey.

Rolling down his window, the group's clamor increased. Approaching Ravens, Bryan saw mostly Native Alaskans. They spoke in foreign dialects. White people gathered, isolating themselves from the natives. Both engaged in trading possessions, vying for the best deal. The blonde woman standing above the crowd smiled as a native man handed her a moose leg wrapped in butcher paper. Furs and baskets made their way up to her, as well. In turn, she exchanged bottles of clear or amber liquid—bottles of booze.

"Shit, a bar?" Bryan said distressed, checking his odometer. One mile from the cabin, in the middle of nowhere, his adversary had followed him north.

His mind raced to control his thirst. A strong urge tugged at Bryan to pull over, to drive south, to have a drink, to check back into to rehab. Wrestling internally caused his ears to ring, eyes to blur and head to throb. Drooling, he desperately wanted to trade his beloved truck for a bottle; his liver screamed for the beneficial trade. Need overcame want; he needed the liquid poison—every body cell craved the toxic medicine. Frantically, he barreled past Ravens, praying that his foot would not depress the brakes. His angelic conscience shouted, *Eagle…freedom, peace…no more alcohol.*

The potent surge persisted for another half mile. Bryan quickly recited the twelve steps for recovery—repeatedly, the words flowed easily. Finally, through logic, his mind settled. His cravings followed suit. Easing off the accelerator, the RPM's decreased lessening the engine's stress and Bryan's. Wiping the sweat from his brow, stifling his inner voices, he drove smoothly into Jess Tealand's driveway.

Hidden from sight, a dog barked continuously. Bryan shook his head, realizing his panic had caused him to overlook the inclined slope. Cottonwood and spruce trees towered above Tealand's two-story home. River Road not only increased in elevation, it stopped at the base of a lush, densely forested mountain range.

From the left fender, he saw black Labrador growling up at him. Bryan cracked the window then ordered a firm, "Get back. Get back, now." The dog persisted, confining him to his vehicle. Cautious, Bryan slightly opened the truck door. The dog rushed in, lunging for

Bryan's ankle. He kicked the dog's snout then slammed the truck door closed. Inside the cab, Bryan heard a whistle.

The sound came from a short, stocky black haired man who was standing on the porch. "Mat-Su, come. Come on, boy." The dog obeyed, giving Bryan an indignant look then disappeared as the patchy-bearded man approached the truck.

"Jess Tealand. I own this place. Are you here for the cabin? Bryan, right?"

Bryan nodded, slipped out of the truck, shook Tealand's hand and said, "Killer dog, huh?"

"Mat-Su? He's a great watchdog. He doesn't like trespassers— that's when he bites."

"Mat-Su, what kind of a name is that?"

"It's short for Matanuska-Susitna—a glacier and a river. My wife named him."

"Of course," Bryan said. *What was she thinking?* he thought.

"Let's walk up to Ol' Charlie's, so I can fill you in."

"Sounds good. I need to stretch my legs," Bryan said as he turned to lock his truck.

Tealand chuckled. "No need locking things. Folks 'round here are fairly honest."

"Fairly?" Bryan locked his rig, placed the keys in his pants pocket then followed Tealand out of the parking area.

"Ol' Charlie's cabin is about a half mile up Tundra Rose Lane," Tealand said. "There are only a few others living up on this side of the canyon."

Bryan felt the kinks in his calves relax, as the two men briskly walked up the sloping terrain. The fresh air revived Bryan's weary eyes and cleared his head. The sun shone on his back. The warmth on his shoulders lessened his stress, though his defensive posture remained intact, as trust was not innate.

Occasionally, he looked up at the dense forest. Cottonwood trees leaned toward Tundra Rose Lane. Their lime green leaves contrasted against the competing evergreens. Willow trees grew abundantly. Scattered throughout the rugged landscape Devil's Claw plants flourished, just waiting to prick unwelcome intruders. Alder berry trees had propagated the forest with their many seedlings. Purple asters sprung up from out of the parched soil, softening the more prominent forest occupants.

Bryan heard a rustling sound. He checked for signs of wind, but saw no moving foliage. "What's that noise? It's getting louder."

"Oh, that's the creek—*George Creek*. It's just up the road," Tealand said. He raised his voice. "It gets noisy this time of year, what with the echoing canyon and summer run-off. That's where you'll be retrieving your water. But, if there's a mudslide, which is inevitable, you can get your water at Tealand's."

They stood at the edge of the road amazed by the flowing gush of water. The sound was similar to standing next to a waterfall. Rocks moved underneath the rapid currents and white water bubbled to the surface. They both felt the creek rumble as the water passed through the silver culvert, only to hurl itself to freedom on the opposite side of Tundra Rose Lane. Pools of water laced its decent, showing its clarity. Suddenly, Bryan wanted a cold glass of water. He swallowed dryly.

Tealand hollered, "Come on. We're about halfway there."

Bryan nodded absorbing the northern atmosphere, expecting redemption, hoping rehabilitation cured him from his unacceptable childhood and adult conduct—society and his demeanor would never become cohesive relatives, but with professional therapy, Bryan endeavored toward positive life changes.

The men continued walking up Tundra Rose Lane. The sounds of the roaring creek tapered off. As Bryan hiked up a short, steep L-shaped driveway, he heard his lungs exhausting themselves. Reluctant to partake in the jailhouse gym, reducing his exposure to feisty, sexual predators and lethal inmates, he now cursed himself.

The least he could have done was to walk around the barbwire perimeter.

"In case you weren't counting, it's the third driveway on the left. Two others live between you and the creek. Another lives above Ol' Charlie's."

A milled two-sided log cabin with a silver metal roof came into view. The trim was painted pale yellow. A small deck lay in front and on the right side of the cabin, skinny debarked logs were used for the railing. The cabin's foundation was constructed of four large spruce logs that pressed into the ground. A mustard yellow colored outhouse stood to the left of the log cabin with its door ajar; fortunately, a vent pipe stretched above its silver metal roofing.

They climbed the short stack of pine stairs to the front door. The door was obviously handmade from thick pine logs, placed vertically with metal hinges. The steel creaked when Tealand opened it. Similar to the outside, the inside was also timeworn and rustic. The back wall made from river rock dominated the small cabin. A cast iron barrel woodstove sat in the center of the rounded rock hearth.

The cabin was cold and uninviting. The kitchen lined the right wall. A square table sat against the far wall between the woodstove and the propane cook stove. The living room consisted of a dusty brown and yellow couch and a matching reclining chair. A mahogany end table separated the two furnishings. Behind the old chair was an even smaller bedroom with a single-size bed and a closet that hid behind a cloth door. The material was faded and worn, yet it added to the bucolic atmosphere. Attached to the closet wall was a brass candlestick holder with a half-burned green candle in its cup. A glass lantern filled with orange kerosene sat alone on top of a cherry wood dresser. The rear window above the bed had a water stained hand drawn curtain. He peaked inside the closet then tested two of the cherry wood drawers. To Bryan, the room seemed dark.

"Did Ol' Charlie build this place?"

Tealand looked downward. Uncomfortable he said, "Well, no. Old Charlie used to live here. He'd been here for years. Then one day, he just up and disappeared. He went out for a walk, I reckon, and no one's seen him since. Most this stuff's his. He had no family, so we just kept it thinking that he might show up. But it's been four or five months now."

A queer feeling came over Bryan. Accustomed to liars, he felt that Tealand was hiding something. "Did the cops search for him?"

Tealand chuckled. "Troopers don't come this far north. Trapper and I got together this past spring and looked. But after the hard winter, we couldn't even find a bone." "The Trappers?" Bryan asked.

"No, Trapper," Tealand said. "He lives above you—back in the canyon." Tealand pointed to the right. "The locals call him Trapper, because that's what he does. He traps animals, kills and eats them then trades what's left. No one knows his real name, so "Trapper" fits just fine. He's a recluse." Testing Bryan's fear, Tealand continued in a demonic voice, "You can hear his gunshots or an animal squealing—sometimes in the middle of the night." He leveled his eyes with Bryan's. Terror gleamed from his retina, cruelty played inside his mind—a game he could switch on and off, randomly and frequently.

Desensitized, Bryan did not flinch. Fear was manageable, especially since he had lived with it most of his life. Gunfire during the night was nothing compared to a raging, drunk stepfather whose main callous late night goal was to beat his mother, scaring him and his brother into submission; becoming model citizens was not the result for these children. Both learned the power of fear, learned how to dominate and control a loved one's survival, and they became empowered by violence. After strangling his wife to death, Bryan's brother placed a .357 pistol to his own temple, pulled the trigger, leaving their bedroom walls, carpet and furnishings with a blood splattered mess of burnt hair, brain tissue and bone. The 1.59-inch bullet obliterated his brother's head.

Accustomed to having the upper hand, Tealand knew how to abuse the weak. His first test on Bryan proved futile. Achieving no emotional reaction to his backwoods scare tactic, Tealand plotted the best method in which to frighten this man from the south. Reeling his attention back to business at hand, he paused for a second. "So, you interested in renting? Rent is seventy-five dollars a month—three months in advance. You provide your own heat, but you're welcome to use what's left of Ol' Charlie's wood stack."

Bryan thought for a moment. "What if Old Charlie comes back?"

Tealand chuckled mischievously. "He's not coming back. He's dead."

Startled by the blunt remark, Bryan paused. Guardedly he said, "His demise works for me. I'll take it."

"Great. Let's go back to Tealand's. You *do* have the two hundred twenty-five bucks, right?"

Perturbed, Bryan walked through the heavy door and said, "Yeah, I've got it."

MOUNTAIN POWER

"I got ya, ya little rodent," Trapper said as he watched his prey fall from a spruce tree. "You'll be soup tonight—nice and fresh. Think I'll start on a new pair of gloves, too."

Stroking the squirrel's limp figure, Trapper wrapped a leather string around its half-missing head and tossed the dead carcass over his shoulder then continued to hike through the woods looking for his next kill.

Within the forest, cottonwood trees stood tall. The Sitka evergreens provided shelter for the hunted. Blueberries, highbush cranberries and blackberries were in full bloom. Wild roses scattered throughout, colored the forest various shades of pink as their stalks grew weapons.

Upwind, Trapper stopped to nibble on his favorite blueberry bush. With blue stained lips, he popped another berry into his mouth. He froze and listened. He heard a branch snap and then another. Without moving, Trapper quietly drew in a slow deep nasal breath. The air smelled of skunk. The pungent scent blended contradictory with the blueberries. Stealthily, he moved toward the stench.

Intuition nagged at him to trade his rifle for a forty-four-magnum pistol. Skillfully, he aimed the shorter, powerful weapon. He thought, *Are you hungry? Me, too.*

The snapping sounds closed in. Motionless, Trapper waited in silence.

Suddenly from behind, a brown woolly arm swatted Trapper to the ground, spinning him face up. His eyes widened as a golden-brown bear wildly dug her claws into his layered clothing, ripping them to shreds. Growling hideously, displaying her sharp fangs, she slashed open Trapper's left arm. The fangs penetrated deep into his bicep. He cried out from the brutal attack, struggling as the grizzly continued scraping bloody flesh, then muscle, clawing down to human bone.

Standing eight-feet high the grizzly stretched, steadying herself for another blow. Trapper cut her off with a hollow-tip bullet that burned through her right shoulder. The echo of pain roared through the forest. Trapper seized the nanosecond of opportunity and rolled away. Once on his feet, he ran as fast as he could.

Sprinting, cradling his mauled arm, he hid behind a double-trunk birch tree. Turning to face his death, he single-handedly propped the heavy pistol between the two trees, focusing steady aim on the raging bear.

Fifty-feet away the bear stopped, reared up and broadcasted an ominous growl while rigorously shaking her enormous blood splattered head. Her pink mouth foamed around her lethal, bloody fangs. She reared up again, announcing her warning to all forest dwellers, snarling even louder as she lashed out with her healthy arm toward Trapper. As soon as the animal reached full pitch and height, Trapper pulled the trigger. The bullet soared through the air, entering the roof of the grizzly's mouth. Then, silence. For a moment, the bear froze in mid-air. Her heavy, crippled body dropped to the Alaskan soil. Blood poured from the partially blasted-off skull, leaving her with one open brown eye as she sank further into death, groaning faintly and twitching as her blood drained onto the forest floor.

Sliding down the side of his thin wooden protector, Trapper said with bravado, "Hollow points'll get ya every time."

Wearily and with weak knees, Trapper rose and cautiously approached the bear. Standing over the stilled bear, he kicked her to make sure she was dead. The bear's fur rippled as Trapper's kick bounced off the colossal giant. She was dead indeed. Satisfied, Trapper began to assess the dead grizzly's value. *Meat for the winter and a hefty price for the hide*, he thought. Trapper's eyes moved toward his feet. Blood streamed down his legs, soaking the shredded blue fibers. His left arm throbbed and his abdominal muscles stung. He was seriously injured.

Widespread pain became rampant as he performed triage on his own body. With a clawed torso and both quadriceps gashed, surges of pain raced through his wounds. He spat on the bear and said, "Lucky you're a big one, because I'm gonna be out of commission for a few weeks." Though he knew it would take well over a month to heal.

Sitting down, leaning against the grizzly bear, he took off what was left of his shirt. Using his teeth and right hand, he tied a makeshift sling around his minced left arm. With his belt knife, he cut off several remaining pant strips. Groaning in agony, he tied the soiled cloth around the red rivers spewing down his legs. Shakily, the virtually naked man stood up, leaving his stomach to bleed freely.

Adrenaline flowed as Trapper grabbed branches and piles of leaves then placed them over the slain grizzly. "I'll skin ya later and have ya over for dinner," he said triumphantly.

Drained and shaken, Trapper walked back to where the attack started. He rustled through the disturbed groundcover locating his first victim. "Soup tonight," he said to the mangled squirrel. Using his rifle as a cane, he staggered toward home.

Blurry-eyed, he knocked on a bright red door. A dog barked inside. As the door opened, Trapper fell helplessly inside.

"Gentleman, get down. Get off him," Ruby said in a huff to her loyal German Shepherd. "Trap, are you all right? What got ya? Can you get up?"

Trapper moaned. Barely able to sit up, he felt an arm slide under and around his body. It pulled at him. Grunting, Ruby said, "Jeez Trap, you gotta help me some."

Trapper recognized Ruby's voice. He waited for his vision to clear. Incapable of standing, dependent and vulnerable, he eased himself into the arms of his neighbor.

The pair struggled, as Ruby guided him to her bed. "Now lie still while I look you over. God Trap, it must have been a big one," she said as she scanned his gouges muddled with dirt. In the past, Ruby and Trapper rarely spoke. He being a recluse and a stubborn man, Ruby generally felt contempt for him and for his abrasive style of living.

Trapper fell unconscious. "Don't pass out on me now, Trap. Stay awake." Ruby received no response. She held up the dead rodent. "Well, it looks like I got the day's catch—one broken man and one flattened squirrel. I can't make soup out of the man, so in the pot you go." She tossed the squirrel into the sink, placed creek water into a teapot then went to work on Trapper.

She pinned strands of blonde hair away from her blue eyes, eyes that showed thirty-eight-years of stress from a whore's lifestyle, a lifestyle that she inherited twenty-two-years ago. Next, she added a protective apron, tying it just below her large breasts. Bloodstained cloth hit the newspaper-lined floor as she carefully unwrapped each strip of denim. She took a pair of scissors and cut off what was left of Trapper's pants. He lay naked and scarred in the dim cottonwood cabin. "Most of the men that stay in my bed are at least *half* alive," Ruby said with a chuckle.

She jumped up to quiet the whistling teapot. After filling a ceramic basin with hot water, she sat next to Trapper and dabbed his wounds clean. Most of the bleeding had stopped, but his tall, lean body was still streaked. For an hour, Ruby wiped, rinsed and then wiped again. Her hands absorbed the battlefield gore, turning them as red as her front door.

Ruby was amazed to see the deep scores in Trapper's skin. Cleansing the wounds, she noticed how gentle her neighbor appeared, even with blood droplets still in his brown beard his features were like Jesus—peaceful and content. *With an almighty attitude to go with it, too*, she thought with a smirk.

She placed a mixture of comfrey and stinging nettle on top of each wound, gently secured them with a clean frayed cotton shirt, then sat back to examine her patient. "There, that'll fix you for now."

Hours passed as Ruby continued to nurse Trapper. She watched for signs of fever or infection. As Trapper slowly regained consciousness, Ruby leaned over the bed and asked softly, "How are you feeling?"

Trying to sit up, Trapper grabbed his left arm, moaning in agony, "My arm…"

Ruby sat down next to him. "Stay still, Trap. You're beat up pretty badly. You'll have to stay here at least until morning."

"How long have I been out?"

"Four hours." She handed him a glass tumbler full of whiskey. "Here drink this. It'll kill the pain."

With his good arm, Trapper pushed himself up just enough to swallow the medicine. In one chug, it was gone. Trapper's face turned red from the rush of alcohol. He sank back into the bed, drifting into a deep slumber.

"Night Trap," Ruby whispered blowing out the candle near his bedside.

Relieved to see him sleeping, she cut through the squirrel fur and removed its guts. She soaked the rich, dark meat in water. Next, she added canned tomatoes, spices and dehydrated vegetables. Startled by a knock on the door, Ruby quickly washed her hands. As she reached for a hand towel, the knock sounded again. She dashed over to the door, hoping the knock did not wake Trapper. "Who's out there?"

A slurred voice resonated back, "Ruby, it's me. I gotta see ya."

"I've got company. Come back tomorrow."

"But Ruby, I need ya tonight. I got cash," the man said pleading.

"Didn't I just say that I have company? Come back tomorrow. I mean it. Get out of here. Take your drunken butt home and bug your wife."

"Ah, Ruby," the voice said trailing off.

Ruby returned to the kitchen and the squirrel meat. Her concoction began to simmer on the stove, filling the small cabin with a delicious aroma. She sat down at her half-round table, where she read by candlelight. Engulfed in a murder mystery, she sat on edge waiting for the next victim and for clues as to who was doing the killing. Her ears tuned into her sleeping neighbor and her simmering soup. When she approached the final chapter, Ruby began to tire. Her eyelids became heavy as she tried to read further. The book's crescendo neared conclusion. The pot lid clanked as its contents rose in temperature. "Damn," Ruby spouted, closing the book, irritated by the interruption.

Removing the moist lid, she stirred then sampled the squirrel soup. She reached for the black pepper and cayenne, added two shakes of each, stirred and sipped the broth again. *That's better. It'll be perfect tomorrow,* she thought replacing the lid and turning off the burner. The rich smell of squirrel meat and spices permeated the small cabin.

Quietly, Ruby slowly peeled back Trapper's thin blanket and examined each bandage. Pleased to find that there were no fresh bloodstains nor were there any signs of infection, she felt Trapper's forehead. It felt normal, there was no rise in body temperature. She covered him up with the blanket then climbed into the loft above and fell asleep.

Ruby awoke late the next morning. The log cabin was quiet as usual. Mornings were her favorite time of the day. She descended the steep ladder then pushed open the kitchen window. The sound of the creek came rushing in, and she inhaled the morning dew.

She peeked around into her tiny bedroom where Trapper lay peacefully. Pleased, her morning ritual commenced. She brewed freshly ground coffee, hiked up to the outhouse, relieved herself, and then walked down to the creek. Relying on his master's routine, Gentleman took the lead, guiding Ruby safely around the uncertain Alaskan forest. Standing before the fast-moving creek, she pulled up her cotton nightdress above her knees and squatted. She cupped her hands, scooped up a palm full of ice-cold water and splashed her face, twice, wiping away the sleepers from her eyes. And like every other morning, she kneeled down, placed her mouth in the rushing spring water and took in a refreshing gulp. She tossed the cold water around in her mouth, spitting it out over her shoulder. Her morning ritual ended with filling two sterilized five-gallon plastic paint containers with water then struggled with the weighty containers back to the cottonwood log cabin. The smell of coffee filled the cabin. Ruby poured herself a cup, built a fire in the narrow woodstove and placed a pot of creek water on its top. She placed the soup on the woodstove next to the water then sat down to finish the paperback novel.

After two cups of coffee, Ruby made her second visit to the plywood outhouse. As she relieved herself, she looked through the stained-glass window—a yellow crescent moon with a purple sky. She looked down at her red roofed cabin with its vertical and horizontal logs, thinking how adorable the house was with all of the matching red trim and arctic relics. As the sun shone down on the barely alive purple and blue lobelia flowers, she realized that winter was on its way. No amount of water could save the blossoms now. Clearly, it was time to begin stocking food and other winter staples. *Another winter, when will I ever leave this place,* she thought sighing as she closed the outhouse door.

Meanwhile, Trapper eased himself up to the edge of the bed and memories of yesterday's events came flooding back. Grabbing his left arm, he tried to stop the burning pain and relentless throbbing. Slowly, he unraveled the bloodstained bandage that Ruby had so carefully wrapped. The original white garment had turned brown as it advanced closer to the wound, closer to the pain. Trapper shivered. His arm looked like a raw, ground chuck steak. The unsightly flesh motivated him toward an open whiskey bottle. Swallowing an eighth of its contents, the alcohol raced through his veins, numbing Trapper's affliction.

As Ruby entered the cabin, she was pleased to see Trapper sitting up or at least slumped on the edge of the bed. "Good morning, Trap. How are you? Hungry?"

His head swam for a moment, blurring his eyesight as he sat up. He replied, "I'm skunked. That bear messed me up good. Is that squirrel soup I smell?"

Ruby walked over to Trapper and tucked him back into bed. "Rest, I'll fix you a bowl. I hope you don't mind, but I skinned and gutted your catch. I haven't had squirrel soup for some time now."

After sipping a spoonful of broth, Trapper complimented the cook. Ruby had used an unusual mix of spices, reviving Trapper's taste buds and causing him to rethink his own mundane soup recipe. "When I was young, Mama cooked a large pot of squirrel soup once a week. It was so delicious, her customers traded her for it," Ruby chuckled. "I remember she used to call the male traders *'Pa.'* I greeted them as if they were my real father. Can you believe that?

Somehow, I knew though that none of them planted the paternal seed. Sometimes they'd stay all week or just for the night, drinking and laughing until dawn. I was so young then. It took me until my teens to realize how Mama acquired our supplies." Ruby looked up and sighed, "I guess things haven't changed much, except there's no little one to feed." The small cabin became silent. Trapper was thankful that Ruby stopped her incessant talking, a trait that she was well known for.

Several spoonfuls later, Trapper broke the silence, "Luckily, you had a mom. My old man kicked me out when I was fourteen. Apparently, I wasn't refined enough for him—hunting and trading is all I know."

With an empty bowl in hand, Ruby half smiled. "Did you get enough?"

Trapper nodded, "Thanks."

Ruby removed the rest of his arm bandages. With warm water, she cleaned off the green herbal antiseptic, replaced it with a fresh comfrey and stinging nettle compress and then rewrapped the swollen arm with a clean strip of cotton material. Next, she confined the arm to a sling. She gently took Trapper's unmarred arm and pulled him up to the side of the bed. "Can you stand up?"

Trapper looked down at his clean feet, shrieking after scanning the unfamiliar orange and green flora embroidered cotton shirt. "I think so." Wearily, he rose.

"Can you make it to the outhouse?"

Trapper nodded then eased his way through the front door, inhaling short agonizing breaths. With each step, his knees felt weak as he climbed the steep ninety-yard trail. He stopped halfway to catch his breath. Gentleman waited near his side. Turning to look down the incline, he watched George Creek flow downstream, absorbing the forest surroundings. In the distance, he heard several chimes dancing in the morning breeze. They were handcrafted—some from colored glass, some ceramic and several made from bone and driftwood.

Each piece chimed differently. Trapper noticed a spoon quartet clanking in a nearby tree; its fork conductor centered itself amongst the choir. Unwilling to hike further, he peed on a watermelon bush, wilting it.

Despite his pain, he was grateful to be alive, surmising that his superb physical conditioning would expedite his recovery. Slowly he walked through Ruby's arctic entry, sat on her bed, reassessed his injuries, and devoured another shot of whiskey, waiting for his pain to subside, even if relief was temporary.

"That'll kill the pain, Trap. Just take it easy. I have business to attend to. Do you think you can hike back to your cabin?"

"Yes Ruby, I'll be fine."

"I'll give you some comfrey and aloe for your wounds. Do you have enough wood chopped for a few days? You really should rest."

"I need to skin my kill before it rots."

"Now wait a minute. You're not in any shape to pack out a grizzly. There's no way you can do it with just one arm. Let me get some help. Maybe Jess or Derek will lend a hand."

Angry, Trapper said, "I don't need anyone's help. I can manage just fine. I *have* all these years."

Knowing his stubborn ways, Ruby said, "Have it your way. If you're ready, I'll gather your belongings and the herbs. The soup will hold you over for a few days."

"I'm ready when you are. Except...I could use some pants."

Leaving Gentleman inside the cabin, the pair hiked past the outhouse. Over her shoulder, Ruby carried Trapper's gear. They followed George Creek up an even steeper slope. This windy trail was old and hardly used. Devil's Claw lunged out at the trespassers, occasionally pricking them. The forest was thick with watermelon bushes, purple asters and lush green ferns. Spruce, birch and cottonwood trees grew to great heights, their heavy limbs stretched out like camouflaged skeletons. The companion alders rooted deeply into the soil, quietly suffocating the dense ground moss, secretly reproducing, demanding territory.

The canyon began to close in on Ruby and Trapper. The pass narrowed, the sound of running water and tumbling rocks deafened the hikers. In a distant clearing, Trapper's cabin provided a break in the foliage. The green metal roof reflected the morning's sunlight. Trapper struggled, climbing steeper and steeper.

Hides hung near the cabin like laundry set out to dry. Proudly displayed above the front door was a sizable moose rack. Mounted on the gable end walls were several other beheaded animal antlers. Metal traps dangled from the eaves. Their rusty jaw hinges waiting to snap shut, surprising the unsuspecting, then starving them to death. An axe glistened in the sunlight. Next to the front door hung a wooden bow without its arrows, lessening its visual impact. *His name suits him,* Ruby thought.

She had visited Trapper's log cabin only a dozen times. She grew apprehensive, hoping for an invitation to enter his personal space. They walked up the single-sided spruce log steps, Trapper leading the way, steering himself back into seclusion.

The canyon echoed the raging creek water. As they stood on the deck, suddenly Trapper turned and said, "Leave my gear." Then, he disappeared behind the rough-hewn door.

Stunned, Ruby dropped the hunting gear, smashing her big toe. "Ouch—you ungrateful bastard," she said with disdain. Once off the deck she looked back offended by the arrogant and mysterious man. *The King of his hill,* she thought spitting on his property.

Lost in thoughts of all the selfish men she had known, Ruby slipped through the dense foliage, deciding to take a direct route home. The trail did not parallel the creek. It led to the Shack where Hoss lived— an insane, dirty, aging man set in the ways of old timers when women stayed home, produced baby after baby and doted on the man. Somehow, Hoss had convinced her mother, Golda, that his lifestyle was better than whoring and that he would provide for her, giving her what she needed to feel like a *real* woman. Being so young, Ruby never quite understood their relationship, nor did Golda have time to answer her questions. To this day, Ruby was convinced that Hoss had killed her mother.

Golda's death was a day that she remembered intensely. It was too much of a coincidence that a tree should happen to fall in the creek where Golda was bathing. Hoss denied the evidence, stating that hollow cottonwood trees fell haphazardly—their stout craggy trunks disguised weak, porous interiors.

On that fatal day, she heard Golda's terrifying and final cry as a chainsaw revved in the distance. Ruby ran toward Hoss' shack. George Creek turned red, and Ruby followed the color to its source. Unaware of her presence, Hoss grinned with amusement on the bank's edge, causing Ruby to shiver with a sickening feeling. Instinctually she knew she was now alone—her mother's blood raced past their cabin, dumping into the glacier-fed river merging with the teal-green water below, turning it brown. What she remembered most was Golda's petite body lying under a cottonwood tree, crushed; each bone fused, melding with the creek's timeworn boulders.

The sound of a chainsaw snapped Ruby back into the present. She gasped, instantly changing her direction. The overgrown trail slowed her pace. The chainsaw rumbled louder. Hoss sprang into view. Ruby's fright suffocated her breath. Wild with discovery, Hoss' eyes glistened viciously.

"I was just about to cut down a tree when I saw your blonde streaks pass through my forest," Hoss said seething with malice. "You know, you should be more careful. Nasty things can happen to nosy neighbors." His oversized hand grabbed Ruby by one arm. "Come see what I'm building." Ruby struggled, causing Hoss to tighten his grip. Penetrating her bicep muscle, breaking capillaries, bruises formed beneath Ruby's opaque skin.

The chainsaw roared louder than George Creek as he led Ruby toward its edge. "I'm gonna have electricity yet," Hoss yelled. He tugged Ruby closer. Surprised by his strength, Ruby obeyed recalling the red creek water as her mother bled to death. "Look blonde bitch, I'm stacking the logs high—forcing the water hard. Power, give me power!" Hoss spread his arms wide, revving his weapon, allowing Ruby a window for freedom.

She yanked herself free and ran down the hillside paralleling the creek. With Golda's distorted body firmly etched in her mind, she yelled back with a commanding voice, "You crazy son-of-a-bitch. You're not killin' me today." Finally reaching her outhouse, she raced to the red front door. Glancing over her shoulder, witnessing Hoss rev his weapon, her wits sharpened, she swiftly locked herself inside.

Her oversized German Shepherd barked, following Ruby to her rifle. She checked its cargo and stepped outside. Hoss was gone. Gentleman's piercing bark turned to a subtle whine. "It's okay Gentleman," she said stroking him on the head. Once inside, she maneuvered around her dog then lunged for a narrow bookshelf; Ruby had spotted an open pack of cigarettes. By the third puff, her terror diminished. Shaken, she endured the rest of the day analyzing the bizarre men living above her.

RAVENS

Bryan spent the first month milling about Ol' Charlie's cabin. His new routine became regularly stoking the fire, in the afternoon becoming over heated, dressing and undressing for outhouse visits and evenings with candlelight and kerosene.

At 11 AM, Bryan awoke to a chilling forty-one degrees. The crisp air was a sure sign that winter was on its way. Winter in northern Alaska was not something he was looking forward to. Time spent isolated would add him to the list of those who responded positively to jail and addiction treatment. Not convinced that either remedy was effective, he was at least attempting to garner a somewhat society approved lifestyle.

Stepping outside in unlaced black army boots and a flannel shirt that covered his baggy, dingy briefs, he lit a cigarette, located Old Charlie's snow shovel, and then entered the outdoor commode. The Styrofoam with its circular cutout eliminated the cold as Bryan sat on it, though morning dew dampened its surface, making the seat uncomfortable for the first few seconds.

Once back inside, Bryan shed the skimpy wardrobe then began his morning routine. Even though it was near noon, he still needed to build a fire and make coffee. A slice of toasted white bread smothered with butter and strawberry jam would suffice for breakfast, and another cigarette would complete his morning meal.

As he finished placing the third log in the chamber, his head started to throb. As he slowly stood upright, his neck tensed, his ears rang in high-pitched tones and his eyes distorted. Another migraine was well on its way. Now that he was off the bottle, his headaches had taken on a completely new meaning—no quick or easy pressure relief valve, no instant alcohol addiction cure.

Bryan scoured the kitchen for aspirin and coffee. "Damn," he said tossing the empty coffee container across the room. Disappointed, he added two layers of clothing then walked toward Tealand's. The chilly fresh air and clear sky relaxed him some. The sun shined brightly, warming his face as he briskly strolled down Tundra Rose Lane. Even with a splitting headache, he enjoyed the sun's heat.

George Creek was two hundred feet away, and the sound of cascading water bounced off the canyon walls, growing louder as Bryan approached, enhancing the brutal migraine pain. A culvert diverted the water under the road. He felt the powerful rumble and pondered the brown water. *A landside*, he thought. A flicker of light caught Bryan's attention. "Gold!" he exclaimed.

Excited, he climbed down the short levee. Bare handed, he scooped up a handful of rocks from the icy water. Examining the green, red, and mostly plain grey rocks, Bryan moved up the creek to find what he was looking for—quartz. Tucked nicely under a shallow log waterfall, the white rock stood out among the muted ones. Anxious to discover the riches that lay beneath, his heart beat faster. Finally, his luck was changing. Into his fifth step, his foot lost traction. He slid off the log into the freezing water both his riches and luck floated downstream. Before becoming fully submerged, he reached for a boulder, though not before both boots had become soaked. His blue jeans and left side absorbed the frigid water. Hastily, he pushed himself away from the boulder. Embarrassed by his greed and botched fortune, he shook off the incident.

He was halfway between Tealand's and Ol' Charlie's. His head was still hammering away inside, and his wet clothes clung to his body. The cold and soggy sensation reminded him of the night of the murder, as his best friend's blood soaked through Bryan's favorite shirt, seeping through the heavy cotton material, adhering to his warm skin.

Disgusted, he walked back to the cabin and removed the wet clothes. Standing naked in front of the woodstove his body warmed, drying quickly as the migraine worsened. After dressing, he decided to drive down Tundra Rose Lane, trying to forget his inadequate life, shameless decisions, and clumsy mistakes. Massaging his forehead, Bryan parked his precious rig. Hastily bolting through Tealand's door, he wished for a shot of whiskey.

"You son-of-a-bitch, keep your hands off Anna Rose," a man yelled knocking Tealand to the vinyl floor. Satisfied, the man stomped outside.

The regulars were in awe of the strike. The late morning brawl would become the afternoon's conversation. They snickered as they drank their coffee.

"Who was that?" Bryan asked, assisting Tealand to his feet.

Tealand pushed him aside. "Get away from me. What do you want?"

Bryan stammered, "Coffee. I'm out of coffee, and I have a splitting headache."

"Tell me about it," Tealand said rubbing his jaw, discounting his humiliating defeat. He poured Bryan a cup of coffee. "Sit down."

Bryan sat down, chuckling to himself. *Glad I'm not the only idiot around here,* he thought. Suddenly his misfortune appeared not so bleak. He sat erect, smirking at the disjointed man before him.

Noticing Bryan's enjoyment Tealand grouchily said, "Better place your wood order in at Hurks before it's too late."

"Yeah, the mornings are getting colder each day," Bryan said anxiously.

Tealand chuckled. "Don't worry. You can get most anything from Hurks. If Max doesn't have it, he'll order it. I wouldn't wait too much longer. We never know how soon or how hard winter's going to hit until we're right smack in the middle of it."

Bryan stood up. "Thanks for the coffee. Can I buy a can of coffee and a bottle of aspirin? My head's killing me."

"I'll sell you some coffee, but the aspirin you'll have to get elsewhere. I don't trust city folks. You never know what they put in those quick-fix drugs. Go see Ruby. She'll fix that headache."

The locals laughed, knowing first-hand that Ruby would take care of his ailments, pains and loneliness. Ruby would welcome the newest trader in town with open arms and sprawled legs.

Tealand motioned for quiet. The locals obeyed. "She's the closest thing we got to a doctor around here. Her cabin's the first driveway past the creek. Look for the red roof. She takes cash or trade. Go see her. She'll make you forget all about those aches and pains." Tealand and his customers laughed in unison.

Inside jokes annoyed Bryan. Tapping his finger on the counter, he waited irritably as Tealand slowly counted back his change. The coffee was expensive which annoyed him even further. Without acknowledging the locals, Bryan made a quick exit.

Thankful to be outside, he lit a cigarette, inhaled deeply, allowing the smoke to saturate his lungs. This eased his tension, but not the jack hammers inside his head. Painfully he drove toward the raging creek. The noise of summer's last push to exhaust George Creeks' tributaries edged Bryan closer to insanity—the migraine overwhelmed his nervous system, obliterating all rational thinking. The drive up Tundra Rose Lane could not end fast enough.

The vibrant red color scheme settled beneath the forest; Ruby's vertical log cabin resembled an illustration from a children's fairy tale. Bryan half expected a big bad wolf to appear in the twisted driveway. Death by a wolf was a pleasant thought, knowing the migraine would perish as well, leaving Bryan with his intended purpose for moving north—peace.

Two drags into another cigarette, Bryan pinched off the butt end extinguishing it, placing it strategically on an exposed rock, leaving it behind for later. He knocked on the door. Gentleman barked inside. Impatiently waiting, he read a bumper sticker at the top of the door. It read, *Altered States.* He thought, *What am I doing here?* Before he could turn around to leave, Ruby opened the door, holding Gentleman by his red collar. Her blonde hair was uncombed and pointing in all directions. Below her blue eyes, black makeup smudges partially concealed the dark circles around her eyes. Traces of cheap red lipstick lined her dehydrated, cracked white lips. *Definitely not Little Red Riding Hood,* Bryan thought.

"Who the hell are you? What do you want? Gentleman, shush."

"Tealand said you might be able to help get rid of my headache. My name's Bryan, Bryan Smith. I moved into Ol' Charlie's about a month ago." He extended his right hand. Ruby accepted it.

"I heard we had a city boy living nearby. Come in. Excuse the mess. I had a little too much fun last night."

Ruby led Bryan through the arctic entryway and pointed to a chair. "Sit down. It's okay, Gentleman, lie down." Bryan and Gentleman sat in opposite corners, watching each other suspiciously.

With her back toward Bryan, Ruby combed her hair. "Do you have a hangover, too? I don't recall seeing you at Ravens last night." Abruptly, Ruby turned around causing Gentleman to snarl.

Alarmed, Bryan sat straight up and said, "I get migraines. Hey, aren't you the woman I saw a few weeks ago trading liquor?"

"So, what, I own Ravens," Ruby said irritated, wiping the mascara smudges from below her eyes.

"Oh nothing, I just realized who you were. Don't be offended."

"Well, Mr. Smith, it looks as though you need a lesson on wilderness living. But first, let's see about that headache." Ruby poured boiling water into a dainty gold-rimmed, pink porcelain teacup. A light brown twig floated to the top. "I don't trust synthetic drugs. Wait a few minutes, and then slowly drink the tea."

Bryan peered over the teacup. "Uh Ruby, what is this?"

She laughed. "Haven't you ever seen an herb? It's white willow bark. It's nature's aspirin, a natural pain reliever. Believe me. Now, stop looking at me as if I'm some kind of witch—hocus-pocus doesn't work for me. My mother handed down over forty recipes for many ailments. She died when I was sixteen."

Bryan tried to say something intelligent. "That's too bad. I mean…"

"Oh, go on take a sip. What do you think is in the manmade aspirin? Don't you want your head to stop pounding? White Willow tea is the quickest, most effective antidote or you can just chew on the twig." Ruby handed him a half dozen brown sticks. "These are for later." "Okay Ruby, I believe you." He braved his first sip. "Not bad. A little bitter, though."

"Would you like a shot of whiskey? It makes for a wonderful sweetener." Eye level with Bryan, Ruby stood shaking the bottle, unknowingly ready to rematerialize her new neighbor's addiction.

Bryan said, "That's what I really need. Your so-called medicine tastes like shit. But I'll pass."

"Have it your way."

Anxiety stricken, Bryan tried to ignore the whiskey. The slosh of the bottle's content called to him, beckoned reminiscent times, harbored his familiar lifestyle and was an instant pain reliever. With dwindling resistance, Bryan spouted, "How much do I owe you?" He just wanted to leave—desire was beginning to overtake resistance.

Turning back toward Ruby, he suddenly felt her glare penetrating his clothes. Uncomfortable, he shifted in his chair. Ruby took another step forward, reached for Bryan's top shirt button, unbuttoned it and whispered, "This one's on the house. I usually take my services out in trade. Some pay me cash and some pay in gold. If you like, I can please you for the same barter." Ruby's trained hand slid down, like a slithering snake, beneath the unbuttoned shirt, taking her prey's breath away. "But like I said, this one's on the house. I wouldn't want to frighten you on your first visit. That wouldn't be neighborly." Ruby swept her hand across Bryan's chest,

39

snaking her hand out of the cotton shirt then lightly scoring his neck with her painted red fingernails, sensuously gliding them upward to stroke his hair. Bryan's neck hairs reacted, sending a shiver down his spine. She laughed wickedly as she sat down, striking the whiskey bottle on the table.

Astonished, Bryan casually buttoned his shirt. Completely uncomfortable with this uninhibited medicine woman, ignoring her advances and needing to change the subject he said, "I'm curious, some guy punched Tealand his morning. I caught the tail end of the conversation. The next thing I knew, Tealand was on the floor."

"Was this guy over six-foot tall, sandy-brown hair and really handsome?"

"Well, I guess a woman would think him good looking. And yes, he was tall. Do you know him?"

"I know everyone around here. Derek's his name. The women call him the *Hunk of Hurricane County*. He works for the widow Sara. Together, they maintain the Sutton homestead property. The Sutton family owns the land that we all live on. Jess rents the cabins for Sara's mom, Dorothy. She's a widow, too."

"Why would Derek hit Tealand? I thought this was peaceful country living?"

Ruby laughed. "You've a lot to learn. Out here in northern Alaska, we take care of our own grievances. I'm sure Derek had his reasons. From what I've seen of him, he appears tame. He rarely drinks, and I don't see him mingling with the locals. He works hard. Sara's lucky. Like I said, Sara's a widow, living in the homestead cabin with her two kids. Dorothy couldn't stomach the homestead cabin after old George passed away. She lives in the Quonset hut just below the homestead."

Bryan sipped his tea with one eye on the whiskey bottle. Contemplating sweetening the witches brew, sweetening his day, desperately eliminating the migraine in half the time.

Ruby continued rambling, "Now Dorothy, she's always complaining. She's been unhappy for a long time. I noticed her moods changing after her husband's death. She talks about everyone—even bad mouths her own daughters. Get that old broad alone, and you'll receive an earful. I think she's a little nutty upstairs, if you know what I mean. She's a creature of old habits, spouting off whether we request her opinion or not. Nevertheless, she's had a hard life. Dorothy married young, birthed two daughters right away, homesteaded what property George left behind, and still she manages to make life miserable for everyone. Her youngest, Anna Rose followed suit, marrying Jess when she was eighteen—no kids though. I doubt that she'll ever have any either. That marriage was a mistake from the beginning. I knew it as soon as Jess changed the café name from Sutton's to Tealand's."

"Like you said, it sounds like Dorothy had a hard but an interesting life. Why was it a mistake for Anna Rose to marry Tealand?" Bryan asked.

"Let's just say that Jess has the upper hand in their marriage. He keeps the family business running. Surprisingly, his crude methods have yet to sway customers away. In that respect, I'm glad that Anna Rose has food and shelter."

Bryan nodded. The smell of whiskey was driving him crazy. His mouth drooled, salivating for the malted barley. Abruptly he said, "I've got to go. My fire's probably stone cold." He stood up, as did his host. Ruby followed close behind as Bryan walked through the arctic entry.

"Nice meeting you, Mr. Smith. Come back anytime. I'm either here or at Ravens." Ruby seductively scanned him from head to toe.

Without making eye contact, Bryan waved good-bye. He briskly walked to his truck then backed it down Ruby's twisted driveway.

RESTLESS NATIVES

A low-pressure system had moved in overnight. It had an overpowering influence on Bryan; his migraine had returned. He conducted his morning chores in agony. With each step, his head throbbed, and he was sure it was going to explode—a comforting thought.

Blurry eyed, he sat down, struck a match and then lit the end of a cigarette. Impatiently waiting for the willow bark to turn brown as it seeped in hot water, he tapped his fingers. He distracted himself by checking his shopping list. It read:

10 gal. kerosene, lantern
Propane
T.P. (1 case),P.T. (1 case)
dried peas, 4 lbs carrots
soap (5)

case canned corn
potatoes (20 lb.)
cornmeal, rice (10 lb.)
powdered milk, flour,
sugar (5 lb.)
butter (8 lb.)
beef/moose canned
bacon coffee (lots)
paper, pen/pencil
cards, book(s)
puzzle
matches
5 cords wood
Styrofoam
lime

Bryan sipped Ruby's migraine tea. The bitterness rolled over his tongue, thankfully paralyzing his taste buds. He checked the supply list for any missing items. Thirty minutes later, his headache subsided. He gathered his list, coat and cash. Before heading out to his truck, he loaded the woodstove with seasoned birch.

Fall leaves laced Tundra Rose Lane, coloring the road with brilliant yellows, lime-green with splashes of red. As Bryan drove over the leaves, they dispersed under the truck then flocked back together as swiftly as the truck moved through, coalescing along the roadside as if someone was rolling up a multi-colored carpet. Fall had begun. In just two to three weeks, the foliage would be gone. Winter was closing in fast. The clouds above darkened. Bryan sensed their heavy load.

He felt another surge of panic as Ravens came into view. Squirming in the seat, his grip tightened around the steering wheel. Stepping down on the accelerator, he tried to block out the images of the whiskey residing inside the bar. Ravens flashed by on his right side. Bryan looked, for an instant, into the rear-view mirror. The faded totem pole projected back his uneasiness. It called out to him, *"Just one...just one for old times. Trust me."*

The truck slammed into a pothole, the shock absorbers compressed unevenly, rigorously bouncing Bryan. The taste of whiskey covered his upper lip. "How sweet it is," he said reminiscing. The poison leached into his bloodstream, and he began to feel the imaginary high.

As he gained distance from Ravens, he relaxed some. His awakened taste buds simmered. The cravings passed as he proceeded. Fortunately, the winter would limit his travels down this unrefined roadway, a roadway full of potholes, washboard and temptation. Snow would eventually cover up his path. However, it would not disguise his addiction. Ravens would be easily accessible, the hard winter would test his sobriety, and failure was just a heavy cloud away.

As Hurks Café neared, Bryan visualized his business running smoothly. Just outside the phantom town of Hurricane, fall leaves scattered across the road. Occasionally, the wind lifted them high, elevating the dry, weightless foliage toward the overcast sky. Then, like a sweeping broom, it recklessly discarded them in every direction. Their radiant hues danced haphazardly in the silent passage, eventually joining their colorless elders beneath the boardwalk. *Creepy town,* Bryan thought.

Two native women carrying grocery bags walked through the desolate town. Fearing possible rejection, Bryan waved anyway. The women stiffened, yielding. Suddenly, an ensemble of leaves wrapped the women in color, cloaking them from sight.

The multicolored whirlwind spooked Bryan. Now, he was certain the town was haunted; spirits and natives went hand and hand, myths and legends had created remarkable tales. Disbelieving these jailhouse stories supplied by native inmates, Bryan hastily drove into Hurks parking lot. Much to his surprise, the lot was overflowing with vehicles.

Several native children played a game of tag. One young girl darted across the gravel lot. Bryan tried to dodge her, but her attention was behind her. Her inconsistent stride caused the two to bump into each other. Startled, she held her dark brown eyes wide open as she faced the unknown white man.

Bryan smiled, patted her shoulder and sent her on her playful way. His stomach tightened as memories of his own children came flooding back. His shoulders slumped. By now, they must have forgotten about him.

"Hey, Bryan Smith," Ruby hollered from across the parking lot. "Perfect timing, can I catch a ride back to Ravens with you? I've got a few bags and oh, Gentleman's with me, too." Ruby dumped two full brown bags into Bryan's arms. "Would you be a dear and put these in your truck? It's okay to hitch a ride, right?"

"Sure," Bryan said reluctantly.

Ruby led Bryan back to his truck. She whistled over her shoulder. Gentleman leapt off Hurks porch, racing to his caretaker's side. "Come on boy…jump." The shepherd flew effortlessly across the tailgate that Bryan had barely finished lowering. Excited to be on the move again, Gentleman wagged his tail, howling at Ruby with a slight grin. Once her dog settled down, Ruby wiped the dust from her hands then headed back into Hurks.

Fortunately for Bryan, a native man stopped to talk with her. She stalled the man with her persistent chatter. Thankful for the distraction, Bryan continued into the café.

Patrons monopolized the trading post. The bustle seemed out of place. Bryan felt as if the city had moved north. A teenage boy staffed the order line. Max sweated behind the grill. A tall, overweight redhead woman managed the hot food orders and the cash register— undoubtedly Max's wife.

Scanning the narrow aisles, the shelves were nearly empty. This tossed Bryan's nervous system into another panic. Finding only a few items on his list caused him to head directly to the order line.

"Hello, I'm Bryan Smith. I'd like to place an order."

Without making eye contact, the gangly teenage boy nodded. Ill-mannered, he tugged on his long red hair. Obviously tired, bored, and perturbed, he thought his life sucked; having to turn down an offer to ride four-wheelers and climbing up the glacier with his friends heightened his gruff posture. Working for his parents netted him a sour attitude and contemptible distaste for servicing the public. He longed to attend the University of Alaska in Anchorage, leaving behind the bush lifestyle. Bars and frolicking with young girls occupied his mind.

"Been busy today, huh?" Bryan asked the teenager.

Nico glared at him and said, "I've never seen you before."

"I've been living near Tealand's since July. Is there any firewood available or are you sold out?"

Without looking up, Nico pointed to the sign above his mother's head. Bryan followed the boy's index finger just below Max's wife. The sign was handmade. The handwritten letters declined as they stretched further across the board. The sign read: Ten-inch firewood: Cords available – 3.

"Can I pay for the remaining cords and order two more?" Bryan asked.

"That's why I'm here," Nico said with resistance.

"Nico, be polite," his mother scolded.

"Whatever, Lorraine."

"It's *Mother*, to you."

"Whatever."

Bryan's thumb tapped on the counter, as he gave the teenager a dirty look.

"Tealand has an order going out this week. You can pick it up there. It won't cost you anything for delivery."

"Can you deliver it to Ol' Charlie's cabin?"

"Cost you twenty-five bucks."

"It's less than a half mile from Tealand's."

"I'm saving for college—twenty-five bucks."

"Smartass, deliver it to Ol' Charlie's cabin and order these supplies," Bryan said handing him the list. *Punk kid*, he thought. Walking over to the lunch counter his mood calmed, realizing that the wood delivery and the excessive charge saved his pickup struts and wheel alignment.

Once seated, he grabbed an abandoned newspaper. This was his first outside news since arriving in Hurricane County. He ordered lunch then immediately began catching up on world events.

Humans destroying the earth, destroying themselves and murdering family or friends captured the headlines. Peace and love slogans from the people received a deafened ear by the government. The Republicans obsessed over building more war toys and frivolously spending the taxpayer's money. The thirty-seventh President announces his resignation, the first resignation in the history of the United States of America. The Watergate scandal had inundated the news for months prior to President Nixon's official public announcement. *What a mess—nothing but bad news,* Bryan thought.

A scuffle distracted him from the newspaper. Down an aisle, two young boys shoved each other. The shorter of the two fell to the ground while the older one tossed three quarters to the cash register then raced off with a small green box. The fallen boy jumped to his feet, brushing off the tussle. His face turned red over the lost battle. He sternly looked at Bryan and asked, "What are ya lookin' at, Mister?"

Bryan quietly turned around. *Why do we need other countries for war when there's always one in our own backyards?* he thought. His children, his drinking, and the loss of his friendships drifted through his mind. The years of self-abuse had separated him from the norm, and had disconnected him from being a father. Surely, life's intent toward struggle, defeat with alienating consequences could not be the master plan, though Bryan knew no other method.

Lorraine plopped Bryan's order down in front of him. "Do you want catsup or mustard with your burger?"

"Catsup," he said without looking up from the sports page.

"Comin' up." She reached under the counter and grabbed a bottle of catsup. "It's been pretty crazy around here the last few weeks. That was the fourth fight this week. What folks will fight over, amazes me. I've seen bloody noses over matches, puzzles, and can you believe a pack of gum?"

Bryan half smiled as Lorraine fondled the catsup bottle. His senses searched for a match. No magic, nothing stirred him, although she did have a nice smile.

"It's every man for himself. I've seen men being beaten over a cigarette," he said.

Bryan recalled a greasy, muscular inmate who pummeled his face over a single non-filtered cigarette. After the beating, he considered quitting, though after the bruises had disappeared it made sense to concede to his bad habit. He resigned himself to lung cancer and cirrhosis of the liver. Smoking calmed his nerves.

Shaking off the unpleasant memory, he dove into his muskox burger and scooped in a few fries. Filling his stomach in record time, he placed a wrinkled ten-dollar bill on the counter then walked outside. He heard Lorraine's voice behind him, "Thanks. Come again."

Bryan arrived at his truck without incident. When he neared it, he noticed the bed was nearly full. "Ruby," he said offended. As he turned around, he glimpsed Ruby running toward him, waving frantically.

"You weren't gonna leave without me, were you?" Ruby teased short of breath.

"Not today," he said grinning.

"Are you sure that's your real name? Smith sounds so…generic."

"That's what it says on my birth certificate."

"You're running from something. Tell me what it is. I promise not to tell anyone. I can tell you're running—I sense it. I'm good at sensing what people need, especially men." Ruby said boasting.

"Get in, Ruby," Bryan said dryly.

Without missing a beat, Ruby tossed a brown bag full of groceries into the cab. "Are you ready to head back to Ravens? I sure could use a drink. As soon as I unload these supplies, I'll have that drink.

There are thirty-five cases of whiskey and vodka in back for the coming winter. I'll give you a bottle for the ride. Is that a fair trade, Bryan Smith—if that *is* your real name?" Ruby chuckled.

The two drove through Hurricane in silence. Bryan turned onto River Road and asked, "So you own Ravens?"

"Owner, operator, you name it, I do it," she said with a sensuous smile. She slid over into the middle of the bench-style seat.

Bryan's face reddened. He cracked the window, allowing the cool air to calm his senses. "Superwoman, huh?" he asked uncomfortably.

"I do what's necessary. Golda left me this business. Believe me it pays for itself. I've plenty of customers. What the hell would I do anyway? I'm living in the bush...alone. I've plans though. One day, I'll sell it all and move to the city—where life is less challenging. I'll find a good man, marry him and have a few kids."

"And live happily ever after? Now, that's an illusion. Marriage is enough of a demand without the kids. The payoff for both is bittersweet."

"Well, that's my plan. I'm getting tired of serving drunks and petty traders. I want a real life."

"Don't you feel badly about polluting the natives with liquor?"

"Hell no. They were drinking before I was born. Why should I care?"

"But you do agree that the white man has destroyed their heritage?"

"That's bullshit. Look Bryan, the natives are free to drink, free to think, and free to believe in anything they wish—just like the rest of us. I'm not upsetting the natural order of anyone's life. We'll all destroy ourselves eventually."

"Some of us will take out a few others along the way," Bryan said slanting a reproachful look toward Ruby and discounting murdering his friend.

"Why should I live your sanctimonious way, Mr. Smith? My life is what I know—service. I think you've been cooped up in Ol'

Charlie's too long. You need a companion." Ruby's eyes sparkled flirtatiously.

Eager to change the subject, Bryan asked, "Speaking of Ol' Charlie, just what happened to him? Was his body ever found?"

"Nope. I'm sure by now the crows have cleaned the flesh off his old bones. The old man probably just got lost. I saw him last at Ravens. A storm came in, and I offered him a cot. He refused. As a regular, he drank heavily. Worst-case scenario, the locals put him out of his misery. He often swindled them. Only Ol' Charlie knows what happened that night. And it doesn't look as though he'll be telling his side of the story."

"Looks like we've got company," Bryan said, spotting a bull moose up the road. He slowed the vehicle to a crawl. Gentleman growled. Enhancing her vista point, Ruby slid back to the passenger seat.

The huge animal lumbered onto the road and seemed content on staying. Bryan and Ruby patiently admired the male hulk; antlers extended five-feet across; suspended flesh draped exposing the weighty mass. The bull entangled himself in an alder bush. Bloody velvet pieces of flesh hit the ground, leaving a meal for the arctic fox. Nearer to the rutting season, the bull scraped and sharpened the impressive bone structure. Finally, strolling off the road, he enmeshed himself in another alder bush.

"Can't beat Mother Nature," Ruby said.

Bryan nodded. With each pothole, the partitioned off bottles danced, luring his attention to the back of the truck. He squirmed nervously, hearing the call of the totem pole, *"...Just one...trust me...."*

Ruby directed him to park tailgate first toward the entrance staircase. "Lend me a hand?" she asked. Deep down Bryan knew his dormant obsession had crept back. It was as if the whiskey had hands that, quickly and unannounced, reached behind his head, grabbed his conscience, reviving his dependency. Unwillingly, he agreed to offload his adversary.

Bottles rattled inside their cardboard boxes. Bryan tried to ignore the contents, a difficult task since the bar reeked of booze. It took great concentration to stay focused and maintain his senses until the final case. He stood alone in the storeroom, facing his enemy.

"Bryan, take two bottles as payment for helping me out," Ruby yelled out from behind the bar, triggering Bryan's subconscious. *Permission granted*, he thought.

Two bottles clanked together as he lifted them from the box. *My bottles, I earned them. An hour with Ruby, plus physical labor, I deserve a good stiff drink. Just one drink won't hurt*, he thought. Twisting off the cap, he gulped down a shot, then another. Instantly, his body relaxed, and his mind began to spin. "Man, that feels good," he said with a sigh.

"What feels good, Mr. Smith?" Ruby said entering the storeroom and grabbing his butt. "I'm better than any whiskey. Let me—"

"Hey Ruby, you open?" One of three native men yelled from inside the bar.

"You made it through the door, didn't you?" Ruby said curtly as she stepped back into the bar area. "Hey Wally, Jeff, Eddie, you up to no good I suppose. What'll it be today?"

The trio sat down. "Bring us a bottle," Wally ordered.

Twenty minutes later, three shot glasses touched in another toast. Old jokes surrounded the table. The merry mouths opened wide with laughter, revealing tar stained teeth—some of which were missing. Their loud muse continued as they ordered a second bottle.

Bryan quieted them when he staggered out holding two whiskey bottles—one half-empty and the other full.

"Hey Ruby, you got a man locked in the storeroom? What…didn't he pay you? Well…he's breakin' out," Wally said causing the others to laugh.

Ruby came to Bryan's side. "Bryan's staying at Ol' Charlie's for the winter. So, lighten up, boys."

Eddie eyed Bryan's bottles. "Come join us."

With a clouded mind, Bryan looked at Ruby, then looked at the boisterous table. Uncertain if friend or foe had requested his company, he was confident that the bottle welcomed him. Securely gripping his best friend, he ingested the venom.

Ruby raised an eyebrow. "Take your chances."

Hoping for the best, Bryan loosely swung out the empty chair and sat among the men. After all, they were drinkers, happy drunks, with amiable personalities.

"Treat him right," Ruby said.

"Some days, listening to you is just like being at home," Wally said waving off Ruby.

"I'll cut you off right now, Wally. Behave."

He waved her off again. Eddie and Jeff laughed knowing that Ruby was more like Wally's mother than his wife.

Hours passed. The tavern filled to its capacity. Drunk and engaged in sparring conversations, Bryan swerved out of his chair. "I gotta go," he said slurred. His abrupt movements caused him to waiver, and the sensation of slow motion scrambled his synaptic transmissions. Enjoying his stupor, his new drinking buddies howled. Bryan staggered to the front door. Perplexed, trying to focus, he asked, "Ruby, where's my rig?"

"Left, Bryan, to your left," she replied disenchanted.

Pitch black surrounded the tavern. Only four wooden steps separated Bryan from his pride and joy. He searched each jean pocket, but the keys eluded him. As his vacant mind swirled, he stooped, looking down at the floorboard. Clumsily, he hit his head on the south end of the steering wheel, rattling the keys in the ignition. As he fired up the engine, he grinned. Disregarding the warnings of driving while intoxicated, he proceeded down the broken road. A solar wind storm hovered in the night's sky.

Wide bands of pink and green rays flashed behind the moving vehicle. They filled the rearview mirror, dodging Bryan's every glance. Frustrated, he risked looking over his shoulder. The truck swerved, Bryan corrected. The night dancers dispersed their colorful silk-like scarves caressing the Alaskan sky. Bryan hit another pothole and veered right. He maneuvered the truck successfully back to the center of River Road. *Only one mile to go*, he thought relaxing. His mind began to wander unconsciously as he depressed the accelerator.

Again, the rearview mirror caught Bryan's attention. The erratic beams vanished leaving him to search out their beauty. The mysterious particles concealed themselves in the black atmosphere. Baffled by their covert dance, Bryan stared into the narrow mirror. The front tires plunged into another pothole, rippled through washboard bouncing the truck out of control and off the road, hitting a spruce tree. Simultaneously, Bryan's face slammed into the steering wheel, snapping his neck backward causing his head to bang hard against the back window. The damage was minimal, yet noticeable. Bryan passed out.

THE TRAP

The following day, Bryan woke with a migraine—the worst kind of head pain: blurring his vision, scattering his nervous system, annihilating his memory. His mouth was dry and tacky, sinuses swelled with unimaginable pressure, causing his face to throb. Rubbing his neck, he sat up in the twin bed. Even with his slow movements, his head hammered away. He lay back down on the soft pillow. The pressure overwhelmed him, and he fell unconscious again.

Eight hours had passed. The chilly cabin awoke Bryan. The sunshine had turned into the glow of a full moon. Sitting up in bed, he tried to recall the past events. He had no recollection of driving home. With a nauseous stomach, his hangover enhanced a migraine, spinning blank memories into the abyss of lost time—another celebration gone awry.

Lighting the kerosene lantern near the bedroom door, attempting not to disturb his head, he lowered himself to one knee in front of the woodstove. The trip downward churned his stomach. His rotten gut demanded his full attention. He lunged toward the kitchen sink, and then vomited, losing the last of his good time. Rehabilitation nurses chanted the twelve steps inside Bryan's clouded mind. "Give it a rest, Nurse Jackson," he said hoping to silence the voices.

He waited for his body to stabilize, and then rinsed the acid from his mouth. The hand mirror sitting on the kitchen windowsill reflected a black and blue half-moon shaped bruise. Gingerly, he touched around his eye, examining his yellow-brown cheekbone. Ignoring self-examination of his alcoholism, he turned the mirror around to reflect Alaska's landscape.

"Okay now, what's the last thing I remember?" He contemplated with a pounding headache. "Did I fight with the natives? We drank a lot. Shit, I can't remember anything." Bryan caught a chill, not sure that he even wanted to remember. Crazy things had happened in the past, so there was no telling what occurred. Blackouts had been his pattern, a convenient method for forgetting his addictive and lonely existence. He built a fire then placed a water-filled iron kettle on top of the woodstove. What he needed most was warmth, and Ruby's headache remedy. *God, I miss Magpie's deliveries*, he thought.

The shame of drinking consumed Bryan. He had let himself down again. Even moderation had failed him. The nurses from rehab screamed out in his head the details motivating an alcoholic. The thought of returning to the sterile corridors strengthened his confidence. It became apparent that booze would always have a grip on him. He promptly made another pact never to drink again.

With the woodstove door open, Bryan watched the kindling burst into flames. The fire began to blaze, snapping and popping, squeezing into combustion. Once it completely caught fire, he placed a porous cottonwood log on top. It too blistered into fuel. Minutes later, the kettle began to boil and steam rose from its spout. He knew the recovery routine quite well—a half-dozen crackers and small amounts of water would sway his nauseated stomach back into balance. The heat soothed his aching muscles as he sat staring into the open woodstove, an hour of futile recollection passed. Mother Nature beckoned Bryan out into the much-needed fresh air.

Pleased to sit upon a clean piece of Styrofoam, he relaxed in the dark, moist surroundings. The butt end of cigarette glowed red; the rising burnt tobacco smoke diffused the outhouse odor. Bryan placed a cup of grey, powdered lime down the eight-foot earthen, composting hole. As he reached for his pants, branches rustled against the outhouse, the plywood box shook. Panic set in. With his pants around his knees, Bryan awkwardly ran back into the cabin. Quickly locking the door behind him, he hollered as he pulled up his pants, "Who's out there?"

Head hammering, out of breath and alarmed, Bryan peaked out the front window. Alder and willow branches swayed back and forth. There was more than one trespasser. Retrieving a loaded gun, darting back to the window, his body tensed. Sweat surfaced below his nose, dripping between his lips, tasting like whiskey. Salivating, he wanted more. His addiction returned to every cell, every memory—good and bad. His liver craved the fermented sweet caramel. *It's me or them. They die first. Who will care?* he thought. His mind fluttered from self-terror to the wilderness intruder. Bryan prepared himself to kill, again. Waiting in the shadows, he cursed, wishing for a porch light.

Leaves fell to the ground, as branches shoved to one side. Suddenly, an oversized head with deep black eyes bolted through the brush, emerging with pride. Startled, Bryan jumped backward. His discovery spun him into laughter. The alleged perpetrator was a bull moose nibbling his way toward winter.

"I could really use a drink now," he said laughing. Hysteria relieved his tension. *How ridiculous I must look*, he thought. Humor brought tears to his eyes, thankful that no one had witnessed his ridiculous paranoid behavior. Magpie would have ridden him relentlessly, teasing him until he was released.

With cold water, Bryan splashed his face clean. Humiliated, he sipped his tea then placed three more logs in the iron stove. Walking back into his tiny bedroom, he crawled underneath the dingy white sheets, covered himself with the soft blue blanket and drifted off into a deep slumber.

****

That afternoon, Trapper returned to his cabin carrying the hindquarter of a moose. It had been a long day of hunting, and he was pleased with the size of his kill. Even with depleted energy, Trapper's work was just beginning as he prepared the meat for curing. Wrapping individual body parts with cloth, he hung them out to dry Next, he scraped blood and connective tissue from the hide, soaking it intermittently. The hollow haired animal proved to be effective for repelling moisture. Later on, Trapper would convert the hide into a new rain cape. Walking by the dried bear hide, he proudly smiled, knowing that he would feast on these Alaskan delicacies during the coming winter.

A short distance from his cabin, Trapper unloaded his gear into a log shed. Sensing an intruder, he quickly turned around. There was no one in sight, though he felt as if the grizzly had come back to life, haunting his ego, taunting him, waiting to return the cruel murderous favor. With elevated awareness, he turned his attention toward his recent kill.

Two rabbits had also crossed Trapper's path today. Engaging the bow, he heard the whisper of the arrow's breeze. The faint squeal of the rabbit's surprise and pain shaded the forest. Now, in one tug, Trapper removed the arrows lodged in each of the rabbits. Blood stained the supple fur of the grey hares. He gutted, stripped and dressed them for dinner. At least one would make it to the dinner table tonight. The other would be frozen, adding variety to meals during the lengthy winter.

On his way back to the cabin, Trapper again sensed someone watching. As he glanced upward, he noticed that the front door was ajar. Adrenaline quickened his pace as he rushed through the broken door. Someone had ransacked his cabin.

Dry food covered the butcher-block counter top. The freezer door stood wide open; a year's worth of work was gone. The contents of Trapper's oak desk were scattered throughout the tiny living room.

In a fury, Trapper raced to his trading cache—an old army trunk filled with antique hunting gear and collectables such as knives, compasses and wood carving tools. Suspended from the latch was the lock. "Empty," he said as he slammed down the trunk top, breaking the hinges. Next, he bolted up the steep wooden staircase. In two giant steps, he stood above a steel compartment. Normally hidden from site, the box was now exposed. Worse, it was empty. Thirty-three river and rock mined gold nuggets were missing.

Trapper was devastated. Now, there was nothing. *I won't survive the coming winter,* he thought. "I'll get you, you bastards," he yelled. Keenly, he traced back the trespassers' steps, searching the bedroom, the living room and the washroom.

Frustrated, Trapper emerged from the cluttered cabin. His usual hunting ritual had begun. Outside, looking for clues, he towered over the deck's edge. "There," he said. Unfamiliar tire patterns marked the driveway. The wide tread imprint clearly stuck out. Trapper followed them down to Tundra Rose Lane.

Just as he passed Ol' Charlie's driveway, his luck faded. The sun set below the horizon. "Damn it," he said. "Just don't rain tonight. Please don't rain." With his back toward the descending rays, he hiked back onto the deck. "Full moon, I should've known. Bastards, I'll get you."

The silhouette of the jagged peaks caught Trapper's sight. He watched the velvet sky blacken, delaying his return to the breached cabin. Repulsed, he went inside. The door bounced back open as the contorted faceplate lay arched on the hardwood floor. Upsetting him more was the perfectly square, fragmented door that took him weeks to construct. Like splintered kindling, the damaged artisanship tore through Trapper's sense of pride.

Early the next morning, he skipped his regular morning coffee and headed out on the trail. The weather favored him. The tracks remained identifiable. *Hunting humans is easier than bears. Humans always leave something behind. They lack the discipline to be good thieves*, he thought quickening his pace to where dusk had previously left him standing to fume all night.

A wide swing track led to Ol' Charlie's cabin. Confident the trespasser was a persuasive grip away, Trapper blindly hurdled up the short L-shaped gravel driveway.

He pounded repeatedly on the heavy door. Bryan was inside unconscious. Trapper twisted the locked doorknob. He looked through the window. Nothing moved. "Damn," he whispered jumping from the waist-high porch. Dropping to the ground landing on one knee, he memorized the truck's tread pattern. The rubber was dissimilar to the tracks found near his cabin. Mistaken, angry and frustrated, Trapper continued with his pursuit. *Can't kill the wrong man... yes, I can*, he thought not caring if he executed the innocent. Blood was blood, and he was the only one bleeding now. In the great North, cases of mistaken identity frequently went unnoticed. The vast landscape was a perfect location for the dead, a weapon for the undiscoverable; the unexplored terrain was an ideal hiding place for the murdered.

Trapper followed the tire tracks down past George Creek and Tealand's, leading him onto River Road. Moisture raised the imprints creating hard, definitive patterns though the clusters had muddled into two distinct treads. "A three-wheeler, shit, it could be anyone," he said, realizing that Bryan's tires had intertwined with the thieves' three-wheeler tracks.

Ten yards further up, Trapper saw where Bryan's truck swerved into the tree, jumbling the two tread patterns together. River Road returned to dust. "Damn drunks," he said disgusted.

Trapper's anger sent him racing back toward Tealand's. He shoved open the door in such a fury that the local patrons' facial expressions dropped in terror. Tealand jumped to his feet. Anna Rose left the room.

"Which one of you stole my gold, furs and food?" Trapper yelled scanning the room. Astonished, Trapper's voice had them pinned back in their seats. No one spoke. "Who was it? Which one of you drunken fools broke up my cabin or was it all of you? I want some answers." Trapper slammed his fist down on a table causing the white porcelain cups to rattle against their saucers.

Tealand scrambled bravely to Trapper's side. "Calm down. No one here has the balls to steal from you. How much did you lose?"

Trapper took in a deep breath. "I lost everything." He lunged toward the blank faces, leaning in with the ferocity of a mad man. "I followed the tracks down to River Road—so it must be one of you." No one flinched.

Tealand asked nervously, "Give it up guys? Does anyone know anything about this?"

The patrons held their breath, shaking their heads. Fearing Trapper's violent behavior, aware of his masterful hunts, the locals remained quiet, concealing any hint of mischievous or guilty conduct.

"Sorry Trap, it doesn't look like anyone here knows anything. What can we do?" Tealand asked trying to pacify the crazed recluse. Trapper's fist connected with the table again. Everyone jumped. "I'll get you...you dried up drunken local yokels. I'll kill all of you if that's what it takes." With bloodshot eyes, he faced each person in the room, glaring death into their souls. He turned and stormed outside, slamming the door behind him.

The hunt wasn't over yet. Trapper was an expert tracker. Those old goats had lost their conspirator skills many moons ago. He would find his thief. The longer it took the harsher the punishment.

THE ACCUSED

Two days into the search, Trapper's cabin remained in disarray, and he remained livid over the incident. At a quarter past ten in the morning, he had all he could stand. Determined to produce the thieves, he gulped down the last of his coffee, tossed the cup into the sink; it shattered against the white porcelain. As he charged out of the cabin, the front door fell from its hinges.

Rage guided him to Ruby's cabin. Surely, she would know something. He firmly knocked on the door hollering, "Ruby, you in there? It's Trapper. I need to talk to you." Over Gentleman's barking, Trapper's finely tuned ears heard faint sounds of movement inside. He pounded on the door. "Ruby, I know you're in there. Open up or I'll break down this trashy red door."

Half-dressed, Ruby swung open the door. She hollered, "What the hell do you want? I'm with a customer. What makes you think you can come over here, practically knocking down my door, yelling at the top of your lungs, and so damn early at that?" She slammed the door in Trapper's face.

"Ruby, this is important. Some bastard destroyed my cabin. You gotta know who did it. Ruby, open up now," he yelled.

She did open up, taking aim. Ruby's double barrel shot gun pressed against Trapper's gut. "Look Trap, I've had enough of your selfishness. Who do you think you are anyway? You don't own the world. You're not God. Did you ever think it was your regal attitude that got you ripped off? Huh? You sit up on your hill thinking you're Jesus Christ—condemning everyone—you self-righteous, self-centered bastard. I don't know about your precious belongings and at this point, I wouldn't tell you if I did." Ruby slammed closed the door.

Trapper kicked the door. "Whore." His anger riled him down her crooked driveway. "Just wait 'til she needs help. I'll get her. I'll get all of them." He kicked a rock out of his path, feeling smothered by the neighborhood. "This is bullshit. I can't trust anyone. When I find out who did this, there'll be bloodshed."

Furious, he entered his cabin. Retaliation began as he loaded a 357 pistol, smirking as each silver bullet slid into its chamber.

Minutes later, he parked his 1969 Ford pickup truck at Ravens. A blue tarp covered the bed of a newer white truck. Trapper sensed that he was closing in on the thief. He untied two corners of the tarp, abruptly flung it backward, revealing a new gas generator.

"Shithead sold my goods for this?" Trapper said. He stomped into the bar. Daylight hampered his vision. The tavern patrons spoke loudly. The smell of old smoke and liquor repulsed him, reminding him of his filthy smelling, drunk parents whom he despised.

Over the crowd, he yelled, "Who owns the white Chevy—the one with the generator in the back?"

The patrons quieted to a low murmur. Accustomed to Trapper's outbursts, they stilled themselves waiting for his retaliation, hoping it did not ruin their time for cocktails and socializing.

A drunk man stood up, slurring his words, "Hey man, what are ya doin' snoopin' around my rig?" It was Wally.

Trapper's eyes needed more time to adjust to the dim hall. Instinctively, he swiftly moved toward the slurred voice. "Who wants to know?"

"Me. What 'cha gonna do about it?" Wally asked as Trapper's sight adjusted.

"You busted up my cabin and took everything. Drunken old man, I'm here to settle the score."

The tavern fell silent. A native Alaskan bravely defended his friend. "Leave Wally alone. He was with me the last few days."

"Yeah right, like I'm going to believe you. Natives stick up for one another. You cheat, steal and lie together. Didn't your Mommies teach you any respect? Come on." Trapper picked up old man Wally by his flannel shirt collar. "You're comin' with me."

Wally squirmed, retaliating by slapping Trapper's face. Trapper punched him back. Stunned, Wally staggered sideways. Trapper landed another hard right fist onto Wally's weathered face. Wally fell to the dank carpet.

Trapper readied for his next blow. Just before he lowered his heavy black boot to Wally's head, someone dragged Trapper backward against his will. Two stern-faced native men flanked Trapper, pinning him to the wall. His back slammed up against it, shaking the flimsy building. As he struggled to free himself, his head connected with the sheetrock causing his vision to blur.

With great force, Trapper lunged forward, dropping to one knee, landing on the accused, punching Wally's swollen cheek. Trapper controlled justice being served. He reeled back for the next strike.

The two men scrambled to halt Trapper's next assault. Latching onto his arms, they jerked him to his feet, dragged him to the door and then shoved him outside. Trapper tumbled down the steps. Gravel embedded his hands as he slid to a stop. Painfully, he landed on his pistol. Natives gathered at the door.

"Don't come back, white man. We've had enough of your accusations. You're wrong about this. Stay away," one native man said.

"Fuck you. You'll all pay for this. I know you're in this together. Thieves, all of you—you'll pay." Standing, Trapper dusted himself off. His hands stung as he gripped the Ford pickup truck's steering wheel. By striking and accusing the natives, he felt like the winner as he barreled past Ravens and then Tealand's.

Satisfaction replaced his rage though it was short lived. The pain of losing his supplies lingered deep within, transporting his anger back to the surface. Gnawing at his upper lip, he vowed to remain watchful for any human errors, waiting for his prey to slip up. Then, he would move in for the kill. *North, I need to move further north,* he thought as he sped past Ol' Charlie's cabin, leaving behind a haze of dust.

Looking up at his violated log cabin, he recalled the summer he erected it. He hauled the water from George Creek to mix cement then stacked concrete blocks, weighing thirty-five pounds each, ten high for the basement. While the sap was still running, Trapper cut down forty-eight trees, knowing they would peel easily. Like a banana, he stripped the bark from the timbers then used a mixture of bleach and water to treat the logs, preventing mold. Implementing a lateral scribe technique, Trapper meticulously rolled each log atop its predecessor, insulating, chinking and chaffing with precision. Tying off to the ridge log, he belayed downward to retrieve each piece of green metal roofing then struggled with the oversized plank, raising and attaching each piece to the ridge and gable supports. Construction of this magnitude traditionally required a crew of men, but Trapper accomplished this feat as a single individual. Ready to assess the damage, he entered the cabin.

****

Ruby always enjoyed her walk to Ravens. The twenty-two-minute walk permitted her time to transition out of her service mode, allowing for self-nurturing. Days, weeks, months and years blurred, meshing collectively, as if time granted by Mother Earth became surreal.

Ravens rectangular building was visible now. She dreamed of the day when she exchanged the porch light for the big city lights—even though opportunities diminished as she aged, she would not relinquish her fantasy.

Standing underneath that single burning bulb outside of her mother's legacy, she slid her hand down into her blue jean pant pocket, and began rubbing a small, palm-sized jade stone. As it warmed to her touch, she uttered a wish then sighed heavily. Taking in another deep breath, she entered her hand-me-down tavern and the lifestyle that came with it.

"Ruby, I'm glad you're here," Russell said. Her native right-hand man was tall, with high-bronzed cheekbones and shimmering black waist length braided hair. He worked for trade, but never for booze. His duties included heavy lifting, bar-back organizing and cleaning, and managing the till while Ruby tended to other affairs. He was her eyes and ears when she was away. Trustworthy and abstinent, Russell provided the necessary physical strength to operate Ravens. Public relations with the natives increased his worth; all gossip filtered through him—Ruby's advantage, yet a mind-numbing experience for Russell.

"What's going on?" Ruby asked.

Russell detailed the morning brawl. Ruby rushed to Wally's side. "Are you okay? Let me see." She carefully removed the bundle of melting ice from Wally's face. "It looks bad. Damn it, Trapper! Why didn't someone come get me?"

"Wally said he was fine," Russell said while counting empty bottles. Scuffles were commonplace. Complacent, Russell had ignored the disturbance.

Tilting her head in disgust she asked, "Are you kidding me? Have you seen the swelling?" Russell shrugged, ignoring her, discounting the incident. Swiftly, in disbelief, she turned back toward Wally.

"Why'd he hit me, Ruby? I didn't wreck his place."

Wally didn't need to confess his innocence. Ruby was convinced that Trapper was out of his mind. Fortunately, earlier she was able to scare him off, though Wally regrettably had absorbed Trapper's fury. "Wally, give me your keys. Russell'll drive me home. I'll bring back comfrey and white willow herbs."

"I'm okay. Don't bother. I'm just an old man."

"Your face is badly bruised. The herbs'll speed the healing and relieve your pain. Come on, it's the least I can do. The keys...." Ruby held out her hand.

Reluctantly, Wally handed over the keys. Ruby tossed them to Russell. She looked down at Wally, patted him lightly on the shoulder, indicating she would return.

He said, "I didn't take from any white man. I was just sittin' here when he jumped all over me."

"I know you wouldn't steal, Wally. If the pain gets too bad, sip on this...on the house." She handed him a bottle of whiskey. "Come on, Russell."

During their short drive, Ruby explained her morning encounter with Trapper. She was completely aggravated by the time she retrieved the herbal remedies. As she exited her cabin, she was surprised to see Trapper and Russell arguing nose-to-nose. She hurried over to the men. "What the hell's going on, Trapper?"

"I knew you and the natives were in on the heist. You whore. You betrayed your own kind for this native scrap."

Ruby pushed Russell backward. Now, she was under Trapper's nose. "You son-of-a-bitch, you think you have it all figured out. You don't know shit. You accused an old man of breaking up your place, but you have no proof. You're crazy. You give white people a bad name."

"That old man has my gold, and you know it. This generator is proof enough. And you were in on it the whole time. I want my stuff back, and I want it now."

"His generator is no proof that I or anyone else stole your belongings. You're a fool. I don't have time for your blind accusations. Why don't you get your facts straight before pounding on a helpless old man? And get off my property, you psychopath."

Ruby pushed Trapper aside. She and Russell jumped into the borrowed truck. Russell gave Trapper an evil eye then spat on the ground narrowly missing Trapper's boot. "White trash," Russell said then gunned the truck down the curved driveway.

Trapper stood alone with his heated temper boiling to the surface. "I'm coming to get you—all of you," Trapper yelled waving his arms frantically.

"That jerk, who does he think he is?" Ruby asked rhetorically.

Back inside Ravens, Wally allowed Ruby to nurse him. It was not the first time Ruby assumed maternal responsibilities for Wally nor would it be the last. As a healer and compassionate person, Ruby frequently doted on her sickly patrons, perhaps facilitating relief was karmic or perhaps her inability to admit fault, blaming herself for intrinsic genocide—supplying distilled beverages as the eventual cause of death.

She compassionately ordered him to drink the white willow tea. "I'm so sorry that this happened to you. Will you ever forgive me?"

Wally said with a half-smile, "Trapper's to blame. Next time he wrongfully accuses me of stealing, I *will* rob him blind. That white bastard better stay away from me."

"Trapper's on his high horse again, sitting alone, fuming. His hatred will transfer stomach cancer to his rotting soul, and will be his demise," Ruby said, secretly releasing her statement as a toxic prayer. Knowing the truth about cancer being the disease of hatred, she internalized a speedy, fatal bout for Trapper.

White willow reduced Wally's facial swelling, calming his nerves as well. Suddenly Ruby remembered the jade stone as it warmed in her pocket. She dug it out, handed it over to Wally, and said with a caring smile, "It's Russian jade. Golda found it long ago. It'll help heal your wounds. And if you're lucky, it'll bring you prosperity." Ruby winked, hoping the peace offering would ease the old man's pain, simultaneously relieving her sense of guilt. Together they smiled. "What a morning," she said with a heavy sigh.

****

In the four days it took him to sober up, Bryan hardly noticed the drop in outside temperature; the crisp, dry air withheld moisture from the living. Looking up at the heavy dark clouds, an indication of impending snowfall, he felt panic with a surge of alarming dread, knowing that winter was hours away, and that he desperately needed to retrieve his supplies.

He recalled that Hurk's was delivering his firewood. *It should be here by now*, he thought. He checked outside, sure enough, Hurks delivered three cords of wood, placing it directly behind his rig. Shaking his head in disbelief, perturbed by the wood's placement, he was not looking forward to the extra physical labor, though he was relieved knowing that he was not going to freeze to death during the long Alaskan winter.

He patted the hood of his truck. To him the truck was a dear friend—his only constant. Then, he noticed the damaged bumper and headlight. Both were creased. He gasped. This was the first real damage he had ever caused his beloved truck. He fumed at the thought of being miles from a repair shop. Pleated metal and missing paint scarred his impeccable maintenance track record. Now, he worried about rust having its way with the damaged metal. This was worse than murdering his best friend, oxidized metal; no repair shop and winter unfolding stirred his need to drink. The thought turned his stomach. He relinquished both scenarios, shaking his head in disbelief. *It's happening again,* he thought.

Walking down Tundra Rose Lane, the past events came into perspective. He remembered the last few semi-conscious moments before passing out. Dismayed by his behavior, he stopped at the creek and picked up a red stone. He held it tightly, making himself a promise—never to drink again. With renewed commitment, he threw the rock into the moving water. Instantly, he felt lighter. This time he had learned his lesson though his subconscious mocked his intentions for a sober lifestyle. *Humility is a great teacher*, he thought overriding his inner voice. Depressed, he returned to Ol' Charlie's cabin to stack the firewood properly.

Sweaty and cold, he turned his attention toward a hot shower. Drawing in a deep breath, looking toward the sky, he said a silent prayer of gratitude. A bald eagle soared above the northern Alaska sky seemingly acknowledging his prayer. Once again, Bryan felt a genuine sense of freedom as he strolled down to Tealand's.

Entering the driveway, he picked up a stick and encouraged Mat-Su to play fetch. Mat-Su didn't need much coaxing. His tail went around and around while his back legs moved from side to side. Bryan chuckled. Today, he shared the dog's enthusiasm. With full force, he threw the stick into the air then disappeared behind Tealand's front door.

"Morning," Bryan said.

The morning chatter broke off immediately. Bryan felt the thick, oppressive tension as he looked around at the sun-worn faces glowing with contempt, realizing integration was impossible, and at this point co-mingling with the locals was unappealing.

Tealand said, "Hey Bryan, I see Trapper found his man. He sure messed you up, though I'm surprised you're still living. You should know better than to come up here in the middle of nowhere and start ripping off people—especially Trapper. You're one lucky bastard. No one messes with him."

Astonished, Bryan said, "Now just a minute, Tealand. What are you talkin' about?"

The room filled with whispered accusations. One patron started to laugh in disbelief. Tealand fostered the local patron's opinion, taunting Bryan with allegations of thievery.

Finally, it dawned on Bryan. "Oh, my eye. Trapper didn't punch me. I haven't even met the guy." A low roar of laughter broke out, perturbing Bryan. "I'm innocent. I just need a shower. Let me clean up in peace."

Tealand said dryly, "Okay Bryan Smith, clear the air. Tell us what or who are you running from?"

As if on trial, Bryan raised his right arm half-mast. "Okay, my real name is Bryan Smith. I am not running from anything or anyone. I have committed no crime. What gives you people the right to place me on trial? Give me the damn shower key. Stop all of this bullshit."

"What 'cha running from, boy. Delinquent, corruption, misconduct, what's your muse?" Tealand asked.

Frustrated, Bryan exploded. "I'm an alcoholic. Is that a crime? I got drunk at Ravens a few days ago and crashed my truck into a tree. And as you can see, I lost." Embarrassed by his confession, he boldly reached around Tealand for the shower key.

Tealand caught him by the wrist and pulled him close, staring into his angry eyes. "Are you tellin' the truth? If you're not…we'll take care of you. That black eye could be just the beginning." As Tealand

71

finished his threat, he sniffed and straightened. "You do smell rancid—smells like an old whore house saloon."

Accustom to participating in random sex and drinking whiskey the locals came alive, applauding the good old days. Old age, lack of gold and an absence of truthful promises had diminished not only their chances for sexual encounters, but eradicated Hurricane County's brothels.

"Join the crowd, Bryan Smith. We're all a bunch of alcoholics. We're sorry for the hassle. Go on and take that shower. Man, you need it. No charge," Tealand said.

Bryan looked around the room. "Assholes," he said with disdain, feeling chastised.

Steam filled the shower stall as he cranked up the hot water. *Alone at last*, he thought. After almost a week of not showering, he washed the whiskey and the sour smell from his naked body, adding a fresh scent by scrubbing with a lavender bar soap, taking full advantage of the free hot water. Twenty minutes later, he casually walked toward Tealand. The ends of his shoulder length hair dripped onto his forest green and black flannel shirt.

"Look Bryan, we owe you one. We pressed the truth out of you. We're sorry. We didn't mean to pry," Tealand said.

"Yes, we did. That's what we do," one local spouted.

Bryan turned around. As they tried to mitigate their territory, all of the locals had the same damn expression—vacant black eyes that looked over swollen, red noses. "Later," Bryan said, storming out the door, glad to be free and alone. *Northern prison, northern jerks, I can't get away from drunks. God, my life sucks*, he thought.

His wet hair chilled his neck as he entered Ol' Charlie's cabin. Dropping his toiletries by the front door disgusted by its association with Tealand's, he looked at his watch; amazingly, it was already two thirty. Bryan's blithe mood had disappeared so quickly. Feeling heavy, yet somehow relieved, his alcoholism disgraced him again, now his secret was out. Weary from the accusations and humiliation, he took a nap.

INNOCENT VICTIMS

Beneath the dried blood rose a fresh knot. Jess missed the old mark by half an inch. Anna Rose's left eye swelled again. Jess' shove to the floor was abrupt and forceful though the pain was familiar. This round added a cracked rib to the injury report. It did not matter. The gnawing heartache caused by an abusive husband hurt more.

Anna Rose's petite body trembled as her sister placed an ice pack over her eye. "You have to do something about this. He's going to kill you. You've already lost one baby. Don't let him take you, too. You can move in with us. I'll take care of him if he tries anything. Come on, Sis, say you'll leave Jess," Sara said concerned.

"I can't. You know he'll hunt me down if I leave." Anna Rose whimpered while her battered body shook.

Sara carefully held her little sister close. "This is going to hurt. Try not to move." Sara lifted the speckled bloodstained shirt then tightly wrapped Anna Rose's purple torso, disgusted with her brother-in-law while fearing for her sister's life. "Try to sleep. I'll get Ruby."

Frightened to be alone, Anna Rose said faintly, "Give me a rifle."
"Derek's on watch. Don't worry. Just try to rest. Think about
what I said because nothing is going to change. He's never going
to change." With a gentle sweep of her fingertip, Sara brushed
Anna Rose's damp forehead bangs, leaving her sister's long black
hair to sweep across the pillow.

A meek groan came from Anna Rose indicating that she would
rest. She closed her eyes confident that Derek would guard her.
Passed out as usual, Jess would wait until the day after the beating
to apologize; this comforted Anna Rose into slumber.

Two hours passed before she awoke. Sara and Ruby hurried to her
side. Instantly, Anna Roses' injuries caused her severe discomfort.

"Let Ruby have a look," Sara said.

Anna Rose agonized as she slowly lifted her arms. Ruby applied a
comfrey pack to the bruised rib cage then placed a second pack on
Anna Rose's swollen eye.

"Dear Anna Rose, you'll be bedridden for several weeks. Your last
bruises haven't even healed yet," Ruby said disturbed, glancing up
at Sara. "Have you been taking the herbs that I gave you?"

Frightened and confused, Anna Rose nodded with her head hung
low. The beatings came more frequent as Jess' drinking habits
increased; alcohol was a major influence that commanded his fits of
rage. Places for Anna Rose to hide became elusive.

"Look at me. There's nothing to be embarrassed about. I've known
you before you were born. Leave Jess, Anna Rose. It's the right thing
to do. I'd like to rip that drunken fool's head off, break his legs and
blacken his eyes." Ruby looked up. "By the power vested in me,
Karma seize this opening, this well of destruction, this wounded man
scratches the earth, beaconing your reprisal. Jess Tealand deserves
your wrath. Make him feel Anna Rose's pain."

"Stop, Ruby. You're scaring me," Anna Rose said.

"Don't worry, dear. These things have a way of taking care of
themselves. Sleep," Ruby ordered.

Sara handed her sister a cup of tea. "It's Ruby's special blend. Drink it slowly and between sips be sure to inhale its aroma. It'll clear your sinuses and help you to rest. Ruby's orders."

Ruby gently stroked Anna Rose's leg as her patient sipped the prescribed medicine. Soon the cup was empty, and Anna Rose was fast asleep.

Sara and Ruby retreated outside. Derek whittled a spruce branch, eavesdropping impassively, unaffected by the emotions of the women he served.

"This time it's gone too far. He's going to pay for this. When are the beatings going to stop, after he's broken all of her bones?" Ruby asked rhetorically.

"Ruby calm down, you'll wake Anna Rose."

With a stern low tone, Ruby said, "I don't want to calm down. I want to kick Jess' ass. I am so mad I might just hire someone to do it. We have to do something before he takes her away from us—permanently."

"I know. What can we do? He'll kill all of us if he has to. I never did trust him. I knew he was a brute. Oh, if only Anna Rose had listened." Sara began to whimper.

After a few quiet moments, Ruby said, "This time...your Mom deserves to know."

Sara wiped away her tears, nodding. Ruby led the way to a fate neither woman would enjoy nor live down—a fate so severe the prospects of going to hell seemed more tolerable, less harsh than an old woman's scorn.

Dorothy's eleven hundred square-foot Quonset hut rested seven hundred yards below the homestead cabin. Routinely, the inside temperature rose above eighty degrees. The woodstove was large enough to heat two homes of the same size. Dorothy's packrat habits had developed over the years from living a hard life, living without luxuries or delicacies while raising two girls alone. The children's father, her beloved husband, George, died when the girls were in their early teens. An annual subsistence fishing outing took his life, took the life out of Dorothy, who was once a warm, kind-hearted woman.

The three-person crew had slammed into an unseen river sandbar. George's body took flight over the starboard side of the twenty-foot vessel. The dense murky silt-filled river lodged into every seam, every pocket, and every orifice. George sunk quickly, innocently taking Dorothy's amiable personality down to the depths of Alaska's untamed origins, where bodies and souls became unrecoverable.

Dorothy said curtly, "Well Ruby, I haven't seen you for a while. I suppose you've been keepin' the boys happy."

"Dorothy, you're looking mawkish as usual. I see you've been packing in more junk." The familiar jousting bored Ruby. She nudged Sara.

"Mom, I've got something to tell you, and you're not going to like it."

"What is it, Sara? Are you knocked up?"

Irritated Ruby said, "Can you please just shut up and listen?"

"No, I'm not pregnant. It's Anna Rose."

"What has Anna Rose got herself into this time?"

"Jess has been beating her. She's at the homestead cabin with cracked ribs and another black eye," Sara said.

"What do you mean 'another black eye'?" Dorothy said enraged. "You mean the three of you have been lying to me? You're always up to something hateful. How long has this been going on? I want the truth."

Ruby stepped forward. "Calm down, old woman. This is hard enough for Sara without a tongue lashing from you."

"Hush, both of you. Let me explain, Mother, and we'll be on our way. I don't want to leave Anna Rose for too long."

The three women sat around the table as Sara told her sister's side of the beatings. Before Sara had time to finish, Dorothy's stiff body was heading for the door.

"Momma, Anna Rose is resting." Sara's words came too late as Dorothy had raced outside, forgetting her cane, hiking up the hill toward the homestead cabin and toward her youngest daughter. It was as if Dorothy had taken Jess' beating as well—her heart bled for her daughter, her maternal instincts bruised as her mind cracked, snapping with violent avenging schemes.

Ruby grabbed Sara by the arm. "Let her go. She has to see for herself. Dorothy is a hardened fool, but that is her last-born child lying on your couch."

Dorothy's stern attitude dissolved with one look at her baby daughter. "That jackass," she whispered. Not touching Anna Rose, leaving her undisturbed, Dorothy stomped out of the cabin.

Derek paid her no attention as she stormed towards Anna Rose's home. He felt empathy for the Sutton women, felt nothing for Jess Tealand. Over the years witnessing Dorothy's wrath, he knew Tealand could not compete with her abrasive nature. Constantly her disparaging words far outweighed, and were far more painful, than Tealand's fist.

She threw open Tealand's door and yelled, "Jess Tealand where are you?" The house was quiet. "Foolish man." As adrenaline subsided, her arthritic legs began to ache. She slowed her pace as she returned to the Quonset hut.

Sitting next to the woodstove, she rubbed her kneecaps; adrenaline once again pulsed through her aging body. Immediately, Dorothy began her interrogation. "Did he make her lose the baby?"

Sara nodded shamefully. Realizing her mother's disappointment, she felt insubordinate as a daughter, disconnected, and felt more like a criminal; withholding evidence, a co-conspirator, Anna Rose's accomplice. Guilt overwhelmed her.

"How many times has he beaten her?"

"Five times, maybe six with varying degrees of bodily damage."

"Rotten kids. You've kept this well-hidden."

"Mamma, he beats her in places you wouldn't normally see—she hides the bruises under her clothes. She tries to hide it from me, but I always catch her."

"How long has this been going on?"

"It started about a year after the wedding."

Dorothy's internal temperature sweltered. "I'm gonna kill him when he sobers up. He'll suffer greatly. I'll beat him slowly until he cries out for mercy," Dorothy said reprimanding as tears stung both corners of her eyes. The watery solution blurred her vision.

Ruby put her arms around her. Dorothy pushed her aside. "Get away, Ruby. If you hadn't sold him the whiskey this wouldn't have happened."

"We've been through this before. I didn't make him drink, and I certainly didn't make him beat up Anna Rose. He makes his own choices."

"You provided the weapon, you harlot. You're just like your mother—wicked and wild. You don't give a damn that you hurt others as long as you get paid."

"Momma, Ruby's right. Jess is a cruel and violent man. So please stop blaming Ruby. She's not the problem. Besides, we need to be here for Anna Rose."

Dorothy cast Ruby a scornful look. "Okay, for now. But if that poison wasn't available—"

"Mamma, stop this bantering."

"Okay old woman, I promise not to sell, trade or give Jess any liquor from now on. Will that satisfy you?" Ruby asked.

"The damage is done, but I'll accept your promise. Don't break it, Ruby, or that'll be the end of Ravens."

"You better watch your step, old woman. Spout your next threat toward Max because Hurks will become his next supplier."

"Hush, both of you. Let's check on Anna Rose," Sara said. The three women finally agreed on something then scrambled out of the overheated Quonset hut.

FATAL OFFERINGS

Chilly air awoke Dorothy from her vengeful dreams. A light powder of snow had carpeted the homestead. As she walked through the arctic entry, she put on her winter boots, trading her cane for a ski pole.

The door slammed behind her as she entered Tealand's home. She yelled, "Jess? Where are you? Jess?" Dorothy headed upstairs to the bedroom. Her arthritic hips and knees felt like a rusty hinge, unable to move fluidly, the pain set deeply into her bones. Anna Rose's injuries fueled her to power up the incline. "Jess, are you in there?" Still there was no reply.

"I'm comin' in." Stepping across the bedroom threshold, the hallway light shone on Jess' face. His oily hair stood straight up in the back. His facial hair was scruffy and matted. His head throbbed. Blurry-eyed, he shook off the sight of his mother-in-law standing in his bedroom—a nightmare in progress, one he would never forget or forgive.

"What do you want? Get out of my room. You have no right," Jess said defiantly.

Taking two steps forward, she pressed her silver metal sword into his chest. She hissed, "Listen to me, you no good drunk and wife beater. If you ever touch my daughter again…I'll kill you." Firmly, she pressed the dagger further into his breastbone.

Jess' eyes widened. His heart skipped a beat. His head hammered as his blood pressure rose. Anger and hatred surfaced.

"Anna Rose has two cracked ribs by way of your destructive hands. If you raise even an eyebrow to my child, I'll kill you. If I see her lifting one finger for you in the next few months, I'll break both of your legs so badly that you won't be able to walk 'til summer. Then, we'll see who has the upper hand around here. Weasel. Only weak men beat women. You have no power, no control and no conscience. Jess Tealand, had I known before, I would have slain you long ago." Dorothy shoved the ski pole even deeper into the frightened man's chest. Staring into his wide eyes, she slightly released her stake and said, "Oh, and if I ever hear or see you drinking, I'll set your booze ablaze."

Dorothy spotted a half-empty whiskey bottle on the nightstand. Grabbing its neck, she shoved the bottle into Jess' face, pressing downward on her aluminum dagger then threw the poison across the bedroom. The glass bottle shattered, splattering its contents in every direction. Her body blocked most of the incoming light as she walked through the framed door. She looked back and whispered, "Consider yourself a dead man." With a demonic look upon her face, she quietly shut the door.

Jess heard the stomping of the ski pole as Dorothy descended the staircase. Relieved, he sank back into bed, passing out for another five hours.

Four days later, Tealand's dishes piled high in the kitchen sink. Leftover food and crusty utensils sat on the table. Jess had had little business. Without the morning clientele, the store was empty and melancholy. Jess had no one with whom to commiserate.

Finally, Tealand approached the homestead driveway. A cluster of chickens haphazardly crossed in front of him. They squawked, dispersing beneath his feet. The clamor caused Derek to promptly drop his hammer and walk over to Tealand.

"You're trespassing, Tealand. Sara doesn't want you around here. You'll have to leave," Derek said firmly.

Furious, Jess said, "I've come for Anna Rose. You can't stop me. She's my property."

Derek glared into Jess' eyes. "Anna Rose is resting. I suggest you disappear before Miss Sara comes out shootin'."

Jess laughed, shoving Derek aside. "Sara doesn't have the balls to shoot me. Anna Rose is my wife. I need her back at the house."

A bullet soared over the men. "No balls, huh? I just grew a pair. I'll shoot you dead if you come one step closer," Sara said holding steady aim.

"You won't shoot. What would Anna Rose think of you if you killed her husband? She would hate you forever. Come now, let me see my wife."

Sara cocked the rifle. "The next bullet's yours if you don't get off my land."

"What's going on?" Anna Rose asked from behind the cabin door.

"Just a trespasser," Sara said convincingly.

"I thought I heard Jessy's voice." Anna Rose emerged from behind her sister. "Jessy, you look awful."

Jess started his routine, speaking lovingly and compassionately, yet his tainted tongue and breath released fecal and sour odors. "Anna Rose, I need you. I've been thinking about you. I'm sorry about what happened. I promise it won't happen again. Please come home. I really miss you."

"Don't listen to him, Anna Rose," Sara said aiming the rifle at Jess. "He says that after every beating."

Dishonestly, Jess pleaded, "You know how much I need you. I love you. I'm sorry if I hurt you. I promise this is the last time. I swear."

Fed up with his lies and noticing the compassion in her sister's eyes, quickly Sara said, "Next time will you kill her? We all know there *will* be a next time. You play on her kindness every time. Anna Rose, don't fall for it. Don't go back to him. Remember your pain, your ribs, your black eyes and your bruised arms."

"I need you, Anna Rose. Come home. I love you."

Sara saw Anna Rose falling further into the same trap. "I'm going to shoot. Get out of here, Jess." Sara took careful aim. Jess' chest cavity gleamed in the rifle's scope.

Softly Anna Rose said, "Sis, release the gun." Sara remained steadfast. "Lower the gun, Sara."

Sara lowered the rifle for an instant, then without warning raised it above Jess' head, pulling the trigger. Simultaneously, Jess and Derek ducked. Anna Rose gasped.

"If you ever touch her again, Jess Tealand, I'll hunt you down and shoot you between the eyes. Do you hear me? Now, get off my property," Sara said fuming.

"I think we should let Anna Rose decide," Jess said. "You know how much I love you. Let's try to have that baby you always wanted." Jess had used this effective bluff before, a ploy certain to work, as he knew Anna Rose's weaknesses. Her desire for children and a happy home was not in Jess' future. Secretly, he maintained his deceit, allowing him to control, taunt and beat his meek wife of eight years.

"Anna Rose, don't forget how you lost your first child. He lied then too. Where will it stop, Anna Rose?" Sara knew her words cut deeply into her sister, but Anna Rose's pain was all she had left to bargain with.

Memories of the dead fetus came flooding back. On that day, Anna Rose held the tiny undeveloped baby in the palm of her bloody hands. The sight of her dead baby engraved her memories; her mind scarred by unacceptable violence. The slaughtering of a helpless embryo was unforgivable. Tears began to drip down her face, as her heartache returned. Now, her ribs restricted every breath. Painfully, she sighed heavily.

"Anna Rose, I've apologized many times for the baby. When will you forgive me? We can try again, but you have to come home. Let's start over. I promise never to hurt you again. I love you," Jess said pleading, lying and trying to control the outcome.

Anna Rose stabilized herself. "Jessy, I need some time to think. I should stay here—at least until my ribs mend."

Jess hollered, "You'll come home this instant. I need you back at the house."

Jess' tone weakened Anna Rose's knees. She grabbed for Sara's arm. "Not now, Jessy, I need to rest. You can't take care of me and the store. I'm no good to you now. I'd just be in your way." She walked back into the cabin, collapsing on the couch.

"It's the law, Anna Rose. You're my wife. Come home this instant," Jess yelled.

Derek abruptly grabbed Jess' arm. Sara aimed her weapon, sighting in on Jess' forehead. Derek escorted him off the property. "Stay off Miss Sara's land. She'll kill you. She's mad enough to do it." Derek shoved Jess into Tundra Rose Lane.

****

Ruby's hopes for the winter auction were high. She anticipated profitable barters, stock piling rare and expensive artifacts, her method for a northern Alaska savings account.

A crowd of Caucasians and Alaskan Natives formed in front of Ravens—whites mingled with whites, natives socialized among natives. Occasionally, the two not so different worlds met, agreeably, sharing experiences and trading goods before the auction started. Each group chatted in their native tongues while showing off their favorite exchangeable items. Furs, ropes, traps, lanterns and herbs hung from the traders' arms. Some carried pouches filled with gold.

"It's time," Ruby said to Russell. They stood on the narrow porch. "Today, whiskey and vodka are available. Now, who'll trade with me?" Ruby asked.

The crowd rumbled with excitement as Ruby enjoyed her fantasy that they were cheering for her. All they really wanted was the booze. Hopeful to become the first trader, each person showed his prized possessions. Their trade offerings were valuable, arriving in limited quantities and frequency. As usual, Ruby was quick to make the trades.

"Two bottles for the beaver pelt," she said in her auctioneer's voice: "One bottle of vodka for the lantern, earn another bottle if it comes with kerosene...one whiskey for the pound of moose jerky...two bottles for your gold dust, Frankie. What's your gold weight, Bobby? Two ounces, wow you've been workin' that mine. I'll trade you ten bottles—your choice of whiskey, vodka or a combination." Russell busied himself with the exchanges just as quickly as Ruby committed to the barter.

Two native women stretched out two different blankets: one yellow and green with an eagle pattern; one red and black with a raven pattern; both birds had outstretched wings; both highly respected birds. Ruby recognized the artisanship as high quality.

Enamored by the unique pattern and knowing its true value, she said, "Five bottles for the blanket."

One of the women flashed her free hand three times. Ruby countered, "Ten bottles." Again, the brown hand showed a count of fifteen. Reluctantly, Ruby conceded. "Okay, fifteen bottles, ladies." The three women happily exchanged items, completing the trade.

Another native woman pulled out an impeccable six-inch baleen basket. She had intricately woven the whale's upper jaw elastic fringe into a shiny black basket. A horn shaped bone topped the masterpiece. It took another fifteen bottles to seal the deal.

The standard fur gloves, hats and fur slippers sold for one bottle each. Ruby was pleased to see the slippers; they would make a nice gift for Russell. She also collected Alaskan jade, a few small gold nuggets, gold dust and a little cash. She turned no one away and was satisfied as the auction closed.

The crowd dispersed. Russell returned to serving the regular customers while Ruby took inventory. She was counting the furs when Russell came through the material covered doorway.

"I saw Trapper hiding behind the totem pole."

Ruby's brow raised, her eyes widened and she stopped counting. "Do you think he's going to make trouble?"

"Trap's got a temper. He could do just about anything. My sense is that he was checking out the traders' goods to see if anything was his. If it was, I'm sure he would've already made a scene or clobbered someone."

"I agree, keep an eye out anyway. These are for you." Ruby handed him a large pair of doll sheep skinned slippers. "I hope they fit." Russell smiled. "Thanks. Oh, one more thing, some of the locals heard about Anna Rose. They're offering to, you know, put Tealand out of his misery. They're serious. And of course, they have a price." Ruby relished a good trade. Her eyes sparkled with enthusiasm.

A clamor came from the lounge. Instantly, Russell stepped out of the makeshift office. Ruby waited for his report.

Several patrons stood unified, protectively controlling their environment, ready to defend their rights. Wide-eyed, Trapper appeared in front of Russell.

With authority, Russell said, "Trapper, you're banned from Ravens. Get out."

"Fuck you. I'm not leaving until I speak with Ruby."

Ruby forced open the curtain. "What do you want? I told you never show your face in here again. Get out." She nodded to Russell, giving him permission to remove Trapper from Ravens.

Russell firmly grabbed Trapper by the arm. Trapper resisted, breaking Russell's grip.

"Get your hands off me. Ruby, we need to talk…privately."

Ruby glanced over to Russell. He shrugged, unclear about Trappers' intentions. Ruby looked at Trapper. He appeared to be sulking. The bar fell silent while Ruby decided. Due to Trapper's demeanor, Ruby consented to the request. "Okay, but make it quick. I've got a lot of work to do." She pointed him through the curtain.

"I'll be right here if you need me, Ruby," Russell said sternly. She winked with approval and thanks.

Trapper and Ruby sat down among the new treasures. Trapper assessed what items he could put to good use. His mind scanned the inventory. He calculated the highest-valued articles; trading for survival had become more than necessary, a meager winter was sure to ensue. Shame gnawed at his gut, self-worth displaced, subservient posturing was not innate for this ego-based man.

"I really don't have time for any of your pompous, holier-than-thou allegations. So, state your business and be on your way."

"I'm in a bind. In order to make it through the winter, I need fuel and food. Those thieves took everything, Ruby, and at the worst possible time. I'm embarrassed even to ask you, but can you loan me some supplies? I'll repay you in trade or whatever you want—a moose, work, whatever you need. I give you my word."

Ruby thoroughly enjoyed watching him stew. She realized it took Trapper courage to come down off his perch and ask for help. Nevertheless, she maintained a stern, distrusting demeanor. She allowed Trapper to feel ostracized and detested which increased her bartering leverage.

"What good is your word? How can I be sure you'll pay me back? What collateral do you offer?"

Trapper's shoulders slumped further to the ground. "Ruby, they took everything—all I have *is* my word. My situation is life threatening. I could die this winter. I'm sure you wouldn't like to clean up the mess—a dead corpse is full of bugs, gaseous bloating and decay. Nothing you really want to clean up."

"That's a little over the top, Trapper, even for you. And, for future reference, I'd be happy to scatter your decaying corpse throughout the forest. That's where you belong. Stop wasting my time."

"The situation warrants repayment by means of extreme measures. This is what I offer you."

"Really, what did you have in mind?"

"I heard about Anna Rose. She's far too good for Tealand. I'm sure you're just as angry. I'm offering to lend a hand or fist. Disposal of waste, even human waste, can be resolved quickly."

Ruby knew that Trapper would take care of the matter impeccably, leaving no traces for Anna Rose's suspicion.

"Your loyalties have changed? You no longer believe that I stole your belongings—me and my native friends?"

"At the time, I was furious and ready to kill. I don't know who robbed me. All I know is that I'll starve or freeze to death this winter."

Ruby was stunned. The appearance of begging for forgiveness was a first for Trapper. Delighted, she took control of his fate. Playing the upper hand slowly, silently, she stalled her decision.

Finally, she said, "Your word and your loyalty will be collateral enough—breaking either makes me a fool. Break either promise and

I'll finish you. It took guts to come in here and ask for help. You've shown humility."

"I don't need your threats. And don't expect this to happen again—ever," Trapper said, stiffening and returning to his authentic self.

Ruby chuckled, enjoying Trapper's unfamiliar conduct for his unique-to-him circumstances. She paused withholding her terms and conditions. "Discretion, your lifelong silence, your impeccable skills for permanent removal and disposal are essential. These are my stipulations—non-negotiable." Trapper nodded.

"What specifically do you need?"

Trapper's body straightened. Relieved, he exhaled then picked up a bundle of furs, a jar of raw Alaskan jade and the two locally crafted native blankets. "I can trade these for wood and food staples. Used sparingly, the provisions should last approximately four months."

"That sounds good to me. That'll save me a trip into Talkeetna." Ruby paused for a long moment. "I'm sure you are aware of the consequences of this trade; the price is high and the benefits outweigh any remorse. I suspect this barter will be easier on you than on me. Again, discretion and your lifelong silence are of the utmost importance."

WITNESS

Decisions and their consequences can ruin a person's life. Life would not be life without pleasure and pain. Hurdles come and go. Moments of joy come and go even faster. People grow to know one another. A person dies and another person takes his place. In life, what can one really hold onto? Ruby thought.

Her decision had consequences. The possibility of losing a childhood friend whom she had watched grow up tormented Ruby. A walk on the tundra was what she needed to clear her conscience, to keep the suffering to a minimum. She placed her wool hat and gloves in her winter jacket, nodded to Russell as she disappeared behind Ravens.

Shale and sheets of ice scored the towering landmarks of Alaska's jagged mountains. The Eklutna Twin Peaks towered above the slowly moving glacial river. Ruby sat toward the south in the tundra near the edge of a frozen kettle pond—a pond created by caving glaciers. Warming to the sun's rays, she became a part of the landscape, nothing moved except her lungs breathing cold air in and out.

A blonde-bellied arctic fox stood alone on the frozen pond. The cloudless sky enhanced her handsome coat and full downy red tail. Her breath condensed, vaporizing into thin air.

For Ruby, it was a blessing to see the playful fox in her curious mood. Lightheartedly, the fox scanned the center of the unnamed pond, expressing many newborn behaviors. The fox stood on her hind legs, arching her thin spine then pounced on her target, causing Ruby to smile.

Again, the fox rose on her back legs, curving her body. Next, she pressed her shoulder and pointed ear into the clean snow. Her body heat melted the frozen crystals, allowing cleansing of the ear and jowls. Whimsically, she slid half of herself through the snow, pushing and pushing; she swiveled from side to side taking extra time with her back strap. Moisturizing her dry skin, she endeavored to battle the arid season.

Unable to allow herself the luxury of a prolonged underside warming, she sprang to her feet, shook the ice crystals from her thick fur and stood motionless, yielding to a pungent aroma. A female moose had interrupted her afternoon delight. The moose stood near the south edge of the pond, sensing the fox and Ruby.

Familiar with this giant species, the fox had witnessed their massive physics gliding through heavy snow. She knew that they posed no immediate danger—unless provoked. The fox raised her snout, sniffed the passing air then repositioned herself, looking around once for reassurance.

Daringly, the fox decided to circle around the moose to hunt in the south where the temperatures were sure to be higher and food more plentiful. The fox pranced off to claim her next meal.

Meanwhile, Ruby watched the female moose emerge from behind the willows. Gracefully the moose tugged on the thin branches surrounding the pond. She stripped the bark from a willow tree. The exposed branch instantly browned—the sheath that protected the willow would remain open throughout the harsh Alaskan winter. The benign movements of the moose were magnificent as she stepped around the snow-covered reservoir, nudging another alder bush, nibbling away at its frozen bud.

From out of the thickets, suddenly a spiked mass of bone appeared. To the crystallized landscape of Alaska, the male moose proudly displayed his weapon of choice. A protector of his species, his crown was a testament to his vigilant alliance.

Today there was no bloodshed, no threat, only the calm of the day ensuring peace in their world.

Ruby did not have the luxury to feel warmth; bloodshed was inevitable. The Alaskan spirit had sent her a message. What Ruby had just observed, confirmed her decision. In her world, there would be only one witness, a psychopath—Ruby's weapon of choice. As a protector of unrelenting humans, she was now ready to accept the consequences of her wretched decision.

SNOWSCAPES

"I'm heading to Hurks before the storm breaks. Did you replace the emergency gear in my truck, like I told you?" Tealand asked sternly.

"Of course, I did. Will I see you for dinner?" Anna Rose asked lovingly.

"I'll eat at Hurks." Tealand plucked his coat from the rack, pecked Anna Rose on the cheek and was gone. The few late afternoon customers followed close behind him—no doubt heading to Ravens for their evening shot. Ruby would see to it that they had more than one drink. She profited by fortifying livers with booze.

Anna Rose took this rare silence to change her bandages. Her bruised ribs and eye, now yellow, hurt less each day. Jessy had lightened her chore load and had been kinder than usual. Anna Rose now believed in the possibility of a happy and fulfilling life. Imagining the laughter of children running through the house, she pictured Jessy's surprise when their children jumped onto his lap for story time. *He's changing*, she thought.

Tealand's door chimes interrupted Anna Rose's daydream. Reluctantly, she headed for the cash register.

"Good afternoon, Mr. Smith," Anna Rose said with a smile.

"Mrs. Tealand, good afternoon. How are you?" Bryan asked.

"Just fine, thank you. What can I do for you?"

"I need a hot shower and something to read. Do you have any paperbacks, a newspaper or a magazine?"

"We sure do. I loan them out. I keep a checkout list, so they come back here when you're finished reading them. Okay?"

"I didn't realize you were Tealand's librarian, too."

Anna Rose smiled. "I enjoy reading. What are you interested in— romance, westerns, classics, outdoor survival or mysteries? We have some of each."

"From the looks of that cloud outside, I may need a survival course. Do you have any suggestions on how to endure a lonely winter?" Bryan asked.

Anna Rose blushed. "Mr. Smith, I'm sure you can manage just fine."

"With your years of experience, I'm sure you can teach me a few secrets, right?"

"I see that loneliness has caught up with you, Mr. Smith."

"I'm far from lonely."

"So, what'll it be…a romance novel?"

"I prefer live romance. You select the titles for me."

"You're so trusting."

"Someone as beautiful as you could never lead the weary astray."

Anna Rose felt her ears burn with embarrassment.

"You might consider a cold shower, today Mr. Smith," Anna Rose said as she briskly walked to the hall closet.

Bryan chuckled as he watched her petite frame move from site. *A little filly in the woods, needing some TLC—an easy target,* he thought aroused by the prospect.

Drops of water fell to his shirt collar as he returned to the cash register. The fresh scent of his aftershave filtered through Tealand's store.

"So, what did you find?" Bryan asked.

Lifting her head, Anna Rose honed in on Bryan's intoxicating fragrance. Aroused, she blushed. Quick to ignore her awakened senses, deadened from eight years of marriage to a drunk whose only bedroom function was to snore reeking of whiskey. Nervous, hoping to hide her embarrassment, she rattled off, "I hope there's something here you'll enjoy. I got caught up in this one." She flashed the title past Bryan. "It's been a long time since I read it. I remember how entranced I was then. I think even you'll become captivated by it."

"I'm already captivated," Bryan said, staring into Anna Rose's fluorite green eyes.

Even with stirred senses, Anna Rose dodged his flirtatious words "The book is about—"

"Don't tell me what happens. I've a feeling I'll be doing a lot of reading this winter*." As much reading as I did when I was in my cozy jail cell*, he thought.

"These novels will keep you company."

"That's what I'm looking for." He winked at Anna Rose and paid for the shower. "Thanks."

Before Bryan exited, Anna Rose said, "If you need to hear another voice, you're welcome here anytime—for the company that is."

"I generally keep to myself. But I'm sure I'll need the local librarian's assistance." He glided back to Anna Rose, cupped his hand next to her tarnished eye and said, "How could anyone strike such an exquisite creature?" He turned and walked out the door, smirking. *Another great line from another great book—thanks Magpie*, he thought.

Anna Rose flushed with surprise. It had been years since Jessy's last compliment. She returned to her chores, completing them with sheer glee, feeling aloof, yet more poised, fully accepting Bryan's unanticipated comment. Alas, her posture sank forlornly, devoid of true completeness, as reality inundated her surroundings. *It's not Jessy's way,* she thought sadly.

As Bryan walked home, Anna Rose's delicate features crept into his mind: her tender smile, her unusual translucent green eyes and thick black eyelashes had a special appeal, as did her glistening long black hair.

Water droplets froze to his shirt collar as he lit his fifth cigarette of the day. Exhaling he noticed the weather had turned ugly. Heavy dark clouds covered the sky. The low-pressure system pushed Bryan into depression. Gloomy, he missed his criminal acquaintances and he craved the bottle more each day. The more he thought about the whiskey, the more he thought that he could actually taste it. He felt lightheaded rolling the imaginary sweet sugar over his tongue. *I'm not going backwards,* he thought. He gathered four logs from the wood stack, stepped inside Ol' Charlie's cabin then placed one birch log in the metal chamber. The dry wood ignited sending sparks flying. Easing into the warmth of the glowing embers, he blurred his eyes as the flames grew. His hair quickly thawed, and his face turned red from the heat. Closing the cast iron door, he mentally prepared for a long winter, unsure if he could survive without liquor.

****

"Damn, this truck gives me nothing but trouble," Tealand said disgusted. Forced to park the 1967 Dodge pickup, he calculated his distance from Hurks to be fifteen miles west. Lifting the hood, steam rolled out, blasting his face. Stepping backward, he waved clear the heated vapor and the damage became obvious. The radiator hose had a hole in it. "Shit," Tealand exclaimed. He proceeded to retrieve electrical tape from his emergency toolbox. Placing an old sock over the radiator cap, he released its remaining pressure. A final stream of liquid gushed out, turning the sock lime green. Tealand searched behind the truck seat for his emergency water jug. "Son-of-a-bitch," he spouted as he shook the empty container. "I'm gonna kill that bitch."

As he scoured the truck for extra clothing, two inches of snow accumulated above the windshield wiper. A lightweight jacket and a pair of cotton work gloves added little protection. Tealand was now at the mercy of the unforgiving Great North. "No good woman. I'm gonna finish you off when I get home," he said enraged.

Disturbed, he settled into a steady pace, walking toward the native village—eight miles to the southwest. Tealand recounted how frequently rude he was to the natives. Karma was not in his belief system, nor was coincidental fate. Regardless of his discriminating attitude toward people of color, Tealand would demand refuge. Fortunately, the natives believed in both karma and coincidental fate, confidently and without hesitation, Tealand would use their own spirituality against them.

In just thirty minutes, the snow settled over the glacier-carved valley. Black clouds covered the distant mountain peaks. Temperatures dipped well below freezing. Tealand's situation became life threatening. He yelled to the heavens above, "You're not taking me out like this—black bastard clouds. I'm gonna kill that bitch—worthless wife."

The thought of wolves tearing at his limbs and eagles plucking at his eyeballs caused him to quicken his pace. Fifteen minutes later, he was still over six miles from shelter. The wind blew snow over his tracks. Soon whiteout conditions took charge. Covered in wet garments, Tealand's hope for survival diminished.

The sudden ray of headlights shined through the raging snowstorm. A truck swerved, striking Tealand. His right arm snapped, exposing bone, as he plunged into the heavy snowfall. The truck continued east.

The soft groundcover was no comfort as his body came to a rest. His clothes absorbed moisture, further soaking his thin protective layer. Quickly and painfully, he brushed himself off and returned to River Road, leaving his broken arm to dangle. His pace slowed. Help was only ninety minutes away. He continued to engage his mind even though each step closer to survival was excruciatingly painful. Knowing that his life had the potential to end, he persevered, trudging through the calf-high snow, contemplating punishing Anna Rose: a fist to the abdominals, another punch to the lower back and hamstrings. *That'll put her in her place. That'll teach her. She'll never disobey again,* he thought.

Cradling his broken arm, he walked with an uneven gait. Hope struck when Tealand saw another set of headlights shining through his stride. Immediately, he turned, waving with his left arm. He shouted, "Wait. Help. Help me." The truck throttled its horsepower, hitting Tealand again. He flew mid-air into the swirl of white powder. The vehicle abruptly stopped.

Black army boots merged with the heavy snowfall as the driver exited the truck, then hoisted Tealand to his feet. "This one's for Anna Rose," he said lifting his gloved hand then punched Tealand between the eyes. Tealand fell backward. His nasal passage filled with fragmented bones. Wearily, Tealand staggered to his feet. Another fist came hurling at him. "That one's for me."

Tealand collapsed unconscious into winter's first significant snowfall. Blood solidified into red ice crystals, ruining its pristine essence—evidence hid beneath its layers.

The driver moved fast, tying one end of a rope to the truck bed and the other end to himself then quickly strapped on his snowshoes. He lifted Tealand's limp body over his shoulder then hiked perpendicular to the road. With the added weight, he struggled in the knee-high snow. Three hundred feet into the blizzard, he felt a solid tug at his waist. He dropped Tealand's lifeless body then covered it with snow. "Just the way the coyotes like it—flash frozen," he said kicking the body. Using the rope, he guided himself back to his truck. He never looked back.

Just three hundred feet away from River Road, a human snowscape evolved. Beneath Alaska's artistry, shallow breathing aspired to persevere though the harsh elements quickly suffocated all hopes. Restful sleep came easily as the white cocoon offered both warmth and mortality.

****

With an open book resting on her lap, Anna Rose awoke. She checked the clock. It was three in the morning. She looked out the front window. Snow had filled Tealand's driveway. Panic took over when she realized Jessy had not returned home. Without thinking, she grabbed her coat and Mat-Su. Bravely they stepped outside, sinking into the deep snow as they stepped off the porch. Anna Rose followed in Mat-Su's narrow trail. A whirlpool of snow clouded their visibility.

"Good boy, Mat-Su, we're almost there." Safely on Sara's porch, Anna Rose knocked on the door.

"Who's there?" Sara asked sleepily.

"It's me, Sara. Let me in." Anna Rose and Mat-Su entered the overheated cabin, shaking off the snow.

"What are you doing out in this storm? It must be two o'clock in the morning."

"It's after three."

"Did Jess attack you again?" Sara asked groggy.

"No. Jessy hasn't made it home yet. I'm worried sick. Something's terribly wrong. I can feel it."

"You could've lost your way without a flashlight."

"I wasn't thinking. I'm scared." Anna Rose began to cry withholding her secret, knowing that her defiance could have cost Jessy his life.

"Jess probably just waited out the storm at Hurks. You know Max'll put him up. He's fine. He's probably sleeping off a good drunk. Be thankful. He'll be home safely tomorrow. Let's get these wet clothes off of you. I'll make chamomile tea. Mat-Su, come sit by the fire." Anna Rose and Mat-Su followed Sara's orders. Soon both were warm and dry, safe from the howling snowstorm though Anna Rose struggled with concealing her disobedience. Thankfully, Sara was too sleepy to read her sister's anxiety.

"It's going to be a long winter," Sara said peering out the kitchen window. "Looks like four to five-feet already with more coming."

"Sis, something's not right. I just wish I knew if Jessy made it to Hurks." *I'll be found guilty of murder. I'll be thrown in jail. I'll have to leave Tealand's, my family...what'll become of me,* she thought sending her mind into overdrive. Still she held her secret close, not ready to divulge her error, her uncharacteristic behavior, though in the far reaches of her mind her silence created a convenient solution, releasing her from future brutality.

"Jess has lived up here all of his life. He's smart enough to let the storm pass before traveling back home. Everything's fine. Wait and see. Here's your tea. Drink it, and then get some rest. Lord knows when Jess does return, he'll be a hung-over, hungry bear. How are your ribs?"

"Still sore, I picked up several books for Bryan, and wham, I thought I cracked them again."

"Bryan, huh?"

"He came in for a shower and the books."

"So, tell me, what's this guy like? Did he really rip off Trapper?"
"I don't think so. Jessy and the guys grilled him about his past. Bryan blurted out that he's an alcoholic. I like him. He's a flirt, though."

Sara smiled, sipping her tea hoping that Anna Rose noticed that other possibilities for a healthy relationship existed. Maybe this Bryan Smith would be the catalyst for Anna Rose's personal growth, relieving the family and all of Hurricane County of the grief that Jess had caused by beating their beloved Anna Rose.

The woodstove warmed the cabin residents back to sleep. They rested peacefully as doom neared the homestead door though destiny had already collaborated with Mother Nature.

Snow accumulated to five-feet during the early morning hours, the winds fell silent. Anna Rose stirred restlessly on the couch. Before drifting back to sleep, she prayed for Jessy's safe journey home, and her freedom, knowing that she would never survive in prison.

The metal edges of a snowplow's blade scraped the homestead driveway. Its reverse signal beeped obnoxiously, waking everyone.

"What time is it?" Sara asked.

"Nine thirty-three," Anna Rose answered.

Sara hollered drowsily, "Kids?"

Sara's nine-year-old son, Mathew cried out, "Mommy, Mommy, can I go out and play?"

Rubbing her eyes, Georgina looked out the front window. Holding back the blue and white calico curtain she said, "Look at all the snow."

"Duh, Georgina it's winter," Mathew said all knowing.

"Give her a break…she's only seven years old." Sara scolded.

"Put on your snowsuits, gloves and hats. You two can play, nicely, for a while. How does blueberry pancakes sound for breakfast?"

"Pancakes, yes," the children replied excitedly.

"I'm going home to check on Jessy. If the plow made it through, he should be home now," Anna Rose said.

"Bring him over for coffee and pancakes. I'll send the kids to get Mom. We'll celebrate the first of many snowfalls."

Smiling, Anna Rose said, "Great idea. I'll ask Jessy. We'll be right back. I'll help cook."

"Breakfast is in one hour," Sara said firmly.

"Okay," Anna Rose said as she closed the front door.

Anna Rose took in her surroundings. The crisp air and white blanket of snow revived her spirits. Georgina and Mathew had a good start on a snowman. Sharing in their delight, Anna Rose happily walked home.

"If you have time, breakfast at Sara's in an hour," Anna Rose yelled over the snowplow truck's engine.

"Thanks," the driver said and continued to push the snow aside on Tundra Rose Lane.

Anna Rose didn't wait for the driver to plow out her driveway. She and Mat-Su made their own trail, every few feet they struggled through the mound of snow. It was an endeavor; she felt her muscles stretching, tearing away from her ribs. Out of breath, she stopped. Caught up in the morning excitement, she realized she forgot to notice if Jessy's truck was on the road. There were no vehicles parked between the two properties. Her stomach wrenched her emotions. *I'm going to jail for murdering my husband*, she thought.

Back on River Road, her hopes shattered. There was no sign of Jessy. From a distance, she saw a truck heading her way. She waited anxiously. It was Derek. Running, she waved him down. Panic stricken, she asked, "Have you seen Jessy?"

Derek meekly said, "No, but I did see his truck on the roadside."

"Was he in it? Did you see him walking? Where are you coming from? Hurks? Did you see him there?" Anna Rose asked frantically without allowing Derek to respond.

"Get in Anna Rose," Derek said bleakly as he opened the passenger door. Anna Rose got in the truck. Derek sped into Sara's partially plowed driveway, overturning and compressing the remaining heavy snowfall with his four-wheel drive truck. Before Derek halted the vehicle, Anna Rose jumped out. Desperate for answers and the comfort of family, she bolted into the homestead cabin, crying.

Anna Rose was sobbing in Sara's arms when Derek entered the cabin. Grim-faced, eyes looking downward, uncomfortable with delivering dreadful news, Derek did not offer information until spoken too.

"Derek, what happened?" Sara asked confused.

"The storm caught me by surprise. After loading the last of the supplies, I decided to stay at Hurks. This morning, about fifteen miles east of Hurks, I saw Tealand's truck. The hood was up. I checked the cab...."

"Ravens?" Sara asked hopeful.

"He would've been closer to Hurks. I'm sorry, Anna Rose," Derek said without emotion.

His words sounded so final. Anna Rose burst into tears. "I knew something was wrong," she said trying to catch her breath.

"Don't worry little sister. We'll form a search party. Maybe one of the natives picked him up. We'll find him soon enough, Anna Rose. Trust me."

"What's going on here?" Dorothy asked after entering the cabin. "Anna Rose, why are you crying?"

"Jess is missing, Mom. We're gathering a search party," Sara said assembling her winter gear.

"I knew it was going to be a good day."

"Mother," Sara scolded. Anna Rose buried her face into a silky, royal blue pillow, sobbing.

Sara immediately regretted handing her sister off to their cruel mother. "Let's get going, Derek. Round up everyone that you can. Check with Trapper. Just in case, we'll have Ruby open Ravens. Stop by Old Charlie's place; see if Mr. Smith is willing to join us. We need all the people we can find. Break out the snowshoes. We have only three hours of daylight left. Mom, you watch the kids and Anna Rose—be kind. Make pancakes for breakfast, and keep the coffee hot. I've a feeling it's going to be a long day."

Derek sped up the hill dropping off Sara near Trapper's driveway. She laced her snowshoes and began the six-hundred-yard incline to Trapper's front door. Derek parked behind the unmanned plow truck. It was parked in Ruby's driveway entrance way. Derek strapped on his snowshoes and began his short trek, snickering as he hiked up to the red door. *Way to trade for labor, Ruby—a good trade for both,* he thought.

Sara knocked on Trapper's door. "Trap, it's Sara. I need your help."

The door cracked open. Half of Trapper's bearded face filled the slight opening. "What do you want?"

"Trap, Jess is missing. We need help. Will you come?"

"Damn neighbors," Trapper said as he shut the door.

Half-startled by Trapper's attitude, she knew it was a gamble even to ask her distant and solitary neighbor for assistance. She was three quarters down the snow-covered driveway when she heard shuffling above and behind her. She stopped to look back. Much to her surprise, Trapper was snowshoeing downhill in a heavy, hand sown moose fur cape, packing a rifle.

"Thanks Trap. I knew you couldn't be that cold blooded."

Trapper grumbled an inaudible remark. Skillfully he accelerated, passing Sara, grumpy as usual, disturbed by having his personal space invaded.

"We're meeting down at Old Charlie's. Derek, Ruby and hopefully Mr. Smith will join us," Sara said.

Derek retrieved Ruby and with her came the keys to Ravens. He hurried to Sara's side, leaving Ruby and the plow driver behind. Derek and Sara walked up to Ol' Charlie's cabin and knocked on the door.

"Mr. Smith, are you in there?" Sara hollered. "We need help."

Bryan peaked out the window. *The lynching crew is here, sent by Judge Jess Tealand himself,* he thought. With a loaded gun in hand, he opened the door. "What's going on? I haven't done anything wrong. What do you want?"

"We need your help. Jess Tealand is missing. Can you join in the search?" Sara asked.

Bryan stood his ground, scanning the pleading faces at his front door then reluctantly said, "I'll get dressed." As he closed the door, his thoughts turned obsessive. *What if this is a trick? Tealand isn't missing. Are they here to finish me off, like Old Charlie?* he thought wishing for one of Magpie's weekly deliveries.

The pair had stepped off the deck and headed down the short driveway. Still leery, Bryan grabbed Ol' Charlie's rifle and extra bullets. He stepped out into the cold air, removed Ol' Charlie's snowshoes hanging from the exterior cabin wall. Paranoid, he joined the group of strangers.

"Glad you could make it, Mr. Smith. Do you know everyone here?" Sara asked.

"Well, no," Bryan said as he stretched out his right hand. "You must be Trapper. I'm Bryan."

Trapper took the hand giving it a firm, single handshake but said nothing. Standoffish was his customary greeting, a ploy to remain reclusive and mysterious to all he met, especially toward strangers from southern Alaska. Trapper avoided Ruby's line of sight.

Sara commanded everyone's attention. "Here's what we got. Derek found Jess' abandoned rig on River Road. Obviously, Jess is missing. Ruby, we need to check Ravens first. If he's not there, and I doubt that he is, we'll drive out to his rig. We can search the area from there. Let's get going."

Bryan anxiously waited, allowing his fate to play out or was it their fate he was plotting? He and Trapper jumped in the back of Derek's truck. Unsuccessful at Ravens, Derek drove on toward Jess' truck.

Unable to face conviction, possibly a life sentence imposed by her dear friend Anna Rose, Ruby remained behind. Presumably, Trapper completed his trade agreement. The locals were sure to know something, so she waited for the morning patrons—a legitimate excuse, swaying the evidence elsewhere. Her conscience filled with sadness and guilt; sadness solely for Anna Rose's suffering; guilt from taking charge of an abusive, possibly fatal situation. Vowing to rid herself of both feelings in a short time period, she felt time was too precious to waste on the inevitable, justice was served appropriately and it was time to move forward for all involved.

Watching Trapper intently, Bryan tapped his fingers on his gun. Derek abruptly stopped the truck causing Bryan's head to strike the cab window. Trapper immediately jumped out and started to canvass the site. Bryan followed, rubbing the back of his head, feeling awkward and uneasy as if he was in the wrong place at the wrong time, and with people he clearly did not trust. Nor did they trust him.

Three-feet of snow separated Jess' truck hood from the windshield in a perfect V-shaped pattern. Snowdrifts turned the engine white. Firmly packed snow surrounded the vehicle where the plow had made its early morning pass. Free of snow the driver's side window exposed the empty truck cab. There was no evidence of vandalism.

"Radiator fluid," Trapper said examining the road beneath Jess' rig. "There's a trail of green fluid ending at the tailpipe."

Sara looked at Derek. Wide-eyed and fearful, she knew that Jess probably died from hypothermia. There was only one hope left—the native village of the Eagle clan.

Trapper broke the silence. "I reckon Jess has met his fate. Let's go home." Relieved that his neighborly duties had ended, his trade somehow complete, he laced up his snowshoes.

Ignoring Trapper's callous comment, Sara said, "There's no sense in searching the area on snowshoes today. The storm would've buried Jess by dawn—that search will have to wait until spring. There's one more option. The natives may have housed him. Maybe he's still with them—possibly he's waiting for the road to be cleared."

"He's gone, Sara. Drop it. The wild animals will feast on his freeze-dried flesh come spring," Trapper said. Emphatically relieved by the undetected body of Jess Tealand, hiding a waste of a human, heavy snowfall had worked its magic. Pleased and undisturbed, Trapper disconnected himself from Tealand's associations.

Perturbed and not willing to surrender, Sara said, "Look Trapper, I'm inclined to agree. Lord knows Jess Tealand isn't worth all this effort, but for Anna Rose's sake, we must continue."

"I'm heading back. Maybe a snow hare will cross my path." Trapper turned to trek east. Walking a few paces, he turned around and said, "You're right, Sara, Tealand ain't worth fussing over." With his rifle resting on his shoulder, Trapper continued to snowshoe home.

Sara shook her head in disbelief. "Jump in boys. We're wasting daylight. We'll have to hike into the village. Hopefully, they'll forgive the intrusion." Sara fired up Derek's pickup while the men followed her orders.

She drove west for ten miles then turned south. The snowplow had cleared one mile of unpaved road on Pearl Street. Sara abruptly stopped the truck, jumped out, rushed to the tailgate and removed her snowshoes. "Put on your gear, Mr. Smith. It's about a mile hike." Sara noticed Bryan's apprehension. "You are coming, right?"

"Shouldn't I stay with the truck? I mean with the natives so close, will it be safe?"

Without glancing away from her snowshoe laces, Sara said, "Nothing to worry about there. There's too much snow, even for them to shovel. They won't be going too far until the road is cleared. Hardy as they may be, they're probably hung over from last night's drunk. And it's late enough, so they've probably started drinking again. Well, not all of them, but they'll wait lazily for the plow to finish." Sara tugged one last time on her snowshoe laces and skillfully began her trek south into native territory. Derek followed close behind.

Inexperienced on snowshoes, Bryan tilted from side to side losing his balance, only to recover at the last second before falling. Sara and Derek's laughter provoked Bryan to light a cigarette.

"Mr. Smith, the city's made you lethargic—your lungs are weak. If you get lost, you'll never make it in the bush. Stay close. City folks," Sara said shaking her head. Derek smiled in agreement.

Flicking the cigarette into the snow, Bryan quietly released the gun's safety. Fearing another stint in jail for double homicide, he would have to plead self-defense.

In the distance, smoke plumed weaving out and around the snow covered village. Silver metal roofing topped plywood lodges. Native women carried firewood on their backs then disappeared behind rustic doors. Young children hustled pails of snow into dilapidated dwellings. Teenagers piled mounds of snow in designated areas. Outside wood-burning barrels warmed conversing tribal members— mostly men, as tribal women kept to their daily routines of cooking and educating the children. Three raised wooden boats slept inverted until spring—nets and spears receiving shelter beneath the concave vessels. Eagerly awaiting their next expedition, the clan's work dogs rested in their respective plywood doghouses. The lively village routinely accommodated the Elders while Uncles disciplined their sisters' offspring. An ancient lifestyle delivered by a Raven, who transported the three ocean pearls that created indigenous Alaskans. As their heritage flourished, various clans tamed the merciless North with persistence and devoted spiritual connections.

Bryan was the only one out of breath, as the trio stood beneath an arched overhead entrance sign, which neither could read. Native words stretched across a two-sided spruce tree supported by two twenty-foot spruce pillars; snow draped over the carved eagle wings spanning three-feet on each side, denoting the clan's crest. Animal carvings decorated the massive pillars, surely describing the history of the tribe. The village entrance was the most attractive structure of their community.

The presence of the white hikers stopped the bustling village. Immediately, children summoned an Elder. An aged man wearing a red cloth cape walked toward the three searchers. Furs swung from his chest. Fine black beadwork adorned the cape's bright red trim. His sleeve fringe, an indication of high regard, glided with him as he approached the unwanted trespassers.

"Why have you come here?" the Elder asked sternly.

Traditionally, men negotiated with men, Sara stepped aside allowing Derek to speak. "Old man Kurtz, we apologize for the intrusion. We're looking for a man lost in last night's storm. We found his truck about eight miles northeast of here. We thought one of your people might've provided him with shelter."

Kurtz looked toward the majestic North, searching and connecting with the four directions. Inhaling the frigid dry air, Kurtz shot his words through Bryan, penetrating the white man's soul. "Only the dead knows who violently took his life. A spineless white man murdered a cruel, malicious white man—the Great Spirit offers both nothing in return, no redemption, no atonement, nothing. *You* remember where you left him," Kurtz said with authority, garnering his insight through Bryan, then turned and walked back to the village, leaving the trio dumbfounded.

Swiftly facing Bryan, Sara's glare penetrated his marrow. The guilt on his face told her everything she needed to know—guilty as charged, old man Kurtz spoke the truth. Sara was confident and no longer curious; she rested on Kurtz' sacred knowledge.

Shocked by the notion that he killed Tealand, Bryan tried to exude innocence, a trait that eluded him, especially around those liberally tossing accusations his way. *Proclaim your innocence once incarcerated or at the gates of hell,* he thought. At this moment, the latter condemnation welcomed him, as a jail cell was a continuous form of torment for a dismal future.

A small crowd gathered near the village foyer. Kurtz addressed the group. After the crowd dispersed, he turned around to ensure that the trio had departed. They had.

The northern Alaskan afternoon sun dropped behind the horizon, leaving behind a shadowed mountain backdrop. The frigid air condensed, then immediately vaporized. Sounds of scored snow and Bryan's heavy breathing paced the searchers back to Derek's truck.

With heated disdain, Sara scowled at Bryan, prodding for a confession. Slowly she diverted her eyes toward Derek and asked, "Derek, what do you think old man Kurtz meant by all that?"

Derek said idly, "Ken Kurtz thinks he has a direct link with Great Spirits. He knows all and sees all. The old man has lost it. He doesn't know what he's talking about. Just forget it."

"Mr. Smith, what do you think he meant?" Sara asked with persecuting eyes.

"I don't know. Maybe he had something to do with Tealand's disappearance. Maybe Jess did make it to the village. Maybe old man Kurtz is lying. After all, they are a clan. Their bloodlines run thick." The local lynching crew had turned on him. With Bryan's suspicions confirmed, he believed that old man Kurtz had it in for him, too.

"Forget it, Sara," Derek said. "Jess probably tried to walk to Hurks and got hypothermia. We'll find him in the spring." Derek's voice became compassionate. "I know Anna Rose will be upset, but the end result is the same—Jess hasn't been found. I'll tell Anna Rose, if it's too difficult for you."

Sara shook off his suggestion. "No. I'll tell her myself. This'll break her heart. She so badly wanted their marriage to work out. Even though he is, or was, a no-good wife beating bastard, she'll still be devastated."

"She's better off without him," Derek said.

She agreed and jumped in the truck. Derek followed her lead as a passenger while Bryan hopped into the truck bed.

Sara drove in silence, the moderate speed allowed her to procrastinate. Her inevitable conversation with Anna Rose would be more than uncomfortable. Suddenly, she swerved the truck into Ravens.

"Why are we stopping here?" Derek asked.

"Ruby's my last chance before I speak with Anna Rose. A shot of whiskey'll steady my nerves, as well." Indifferent, Derek nodded knowing the truth was buried, leaving only formalities to establish Tealand as a cruel memory.

The candlelit tavern was almost empty. Only a few regulars had made their way through the heavy snowpack. Bryan headed straight for the bar and ordered a shot of whiskey straight up. His nerves wavered from the stressful accusations. Derek sat down in a far dark corner while Sara headed for Ruby's office.

"Ruby?" Sara said.

"I'm back here. Come in."

"We're still searching for Jess. Did the locals say anything?"

"No. No one's seen him. The locals aren't talking. What did you find out?"

Sara repeated the eerie speech told by old man Kurtz, emphasizing his piercing theory, indicating Bryan as the murderer. Befuddled, Sara sought Ruby's opinion.

"He is an elder, Sara. He was born with an uncanny spiritual connection," Ruby said.

Despondently, Sara asked, "I don't know what to believe. How am I going to tell Anna Rose?"

"It'll be tough. The words will come, dear. Anna Rose is a woman now. She'll get through this. You can't protect her forever. I'll offer a cash reward for information. Money is always a good motivator. Would you like me to tell Anna Rose?"

"No." Sara paused, saddened. "Will you come with me? We both could use your support."

Ruby agreed. Heavy hearted, ushering their true sentiments regarding Jess' fatality to the back of their minds, together they left the dingy office.

Derek's feet hit the floor as soon as Sara opened the curtain door. He followed the women to the only exit. Bryan continued staring into his drink. His final chance to consume the booze had arrived. Slowly, he picked up the brown poison, smelled its intoxicating aroma and then slammed the shot glass on the bar. "Thanks anyway, barkeep. I quit drinking. This was just a test." Russell nodded indifferently thinking how many times he had heard that line.

"Oh, what the hell...." Bryan downed the shot then walked out of Ravens confident, relaxed, knowing the poison could be his last celebration. The cold air caught his breath. He sighed, feeling as though he had passed another sobriety test—consuming only one shot of whiskey placed him at the top of recovery. Two or more shots would have hurled him back into rehab. Darkness settled his mood. For the first time in many years, he was actually proud of himself, an unfamiliar spark stirred within, as Russell rolled his eyes.

"Get with it, Mr. Smith. Are you comin' or not?" Sara asked impatiently.

His concern turned toward his persecutors. Their chilling posturing alarmed him. Watching his back by day had become necessary. He decided to sleep with Ol' Charlie's rifle next to his bed—loaded with the safety disengaged.

Anna Rose paced the hardwood flooring, awaiting her fate. Without success, Dorothy had tried to calm her youngest, the more sensitive, less courageous daughter.

The mantel clock chimed three o'clock, as the search party entered the homestead cabin. Their grim appearance mobilized Anna Rose's emotions.

"Where's Jessy? What did you find out? Tell me, what happened?" Anna Rose asked shakily.

Ruby gently guided her to sit on the dark blue couch. "Calm down, Anna Rose. We'll tell you everything. Try to stay calm."

Anna Rose obeyed Ruby, but whimpered some. The sight of the searchers told the story, and she knew she would never see her husband again. Instinctually, she knew it twelve hours ago. Maintaining her silence was wrong, too. For the first time in her marriage, she tried to defy her husband, lying caused his death, lying caused her heart to break, shattering her life though she was free.

Free from his brutal beatings and harsh treatment. Torn by her behavior, she broke down.

The details revealed Jess' fate. Tears filled everyone's eyes. Inside their bedroom, the children listened, as another husband was lost to Alaska's harsh elements. Soon memories would dissipate in their hearts, leaving only a scribbled notation on the Sutton family tree.

Ruby drew Anna Rose close. Dorothy soothingly patted her leg. Their sorrow saturated the homestead cabin. Everyone grieved for the shattered widow, secretly approving of Jess Tealand's demise.

Anna Rose became overwhelmed with emotions. Derek shifted uncomfortably near the door, then cautiously gave his condolences and rushed outside. Bryan deserted the widows, too. The much needed fresh air filled their lungs, relaxing the men.

As he lit a cigarette, without warning, Sara grabbed Bryan's arm. She took in a deep breath and said, "If you had anything to do with this, Mr. Smith, I will personally take care of you." Her tone was retaliatory and convincing, unnerving both Bryan and Derek.

"I didn't—"

Interrupting him, Sara abruptly released his arm, "I never did like city folks." She returned to the cabin, leaving the men to find their way home in the dark.

Tears continued to flow. Each of the women took turns holding and consoling the young widow. Two hours passed. Anna Rose's emotions finally began to settle. Once Anna Rose quieted, Ruby hugged her then excused herself to prepare one of her herbal remedies. Ruby could not take the pain away, but could ease Anna Rose into slumber. Ruby was hopeful that in time Anna Rose's world would recover. Internally, Ruby prayed for Trapper's silence.

Ruby replaced Sara on the couch. Sara went into her children's bedroom. Comforting her children with childish words, she explained the day's events, answered their questions then wiped their tears. She assured them that Jess was safe in heaven and that Anna Rose would recover from the loss.

Near the woodstove, Dorothy sat in the family rocking chair. For the last hundred years, the heavy oak chair bestowing *The Man of the North* carving had rocked each Sutton infant to sleep. As it rocked back and forth, its distinctive creak reminded Dorothy of when her two girls were babies. In some respects, life was easier then; their cabin filled with four happy occupants. Now, the Sutton homestead sheltered only widows.

"It's just as well," Dorothy whispered.

Anna Rose fumed, practically screaming, "What's just as well, Mother?"

"Jess preyed on the weak."

Sara emerged from the children's bedroom, closing the door behind her.

"I'm not weak," Anna Rose spouted. "I know you could care less about Jessy. For heaven sake, he just died. Don't you have any compassion? You're just as ancient and frigid as the glaciers." Anna Rose's tears violently erupted. With scattered emotions, she wondered how she would ever survive.

"Old woman, it's time for you to leave," Ruby said.

Dorothy remained obstinate, standing her ground, rocking back and forth, ignoring Ruby's demand, after all this was her homestead and these were her children.

Sara tried to console her little sister while tossing their mother a disapproving look. Dorothy rejected the insult, knowing Sara felt the same hatred for Jess, knowing his death was a blessing for the residents of Hurricane County, especially for her youngest daughter, Anna Rose.

Anna Rose straightened, gushed angrily, "I realize all of you are happy that Jessy is dead. None of you cared for him, not one of you. Isn't it enough that I loved him? Couldn't you have tried to love him? He wasn't all bad, ya know. I'm a widow now and not one of you gives a damn."

Anna Rose rejected her sister's consoling offer. "Leave me alone—all of you." Without words, Sara placed a blue and white crocheted blanket next to her grieving sister and joined Ruby in the kitchen.

Dorothy stomped out of the cabin deeply burdened with her daughter's loss. Incapable of reliving the death of her own husband and experiencing the angry and self-defeating emotions that ensued, Dorothy knew that in time Anna Rose's pain would subside, making way for a different life and a new way of thinking about one's own life.

Ruby and Sara exchanged glances condemning Dorothy's wicked manners. Ruby instructed Sara on the correct dosage of herbal tea. She prepared a stronger than normal cup for Anna Rose. Steam rose from the teacup, as Ruby handed it to Anna Rose. Ruby tried to give her a warm hug. Her dear friend pulled away. Dejected, Ruby stepped outside. Walking home, guilt, secrecy and glee lay heavily upon her shoulders. The abuse was over, and a new beginning awaited Anna Rose. Ruby was pleased—another fine trade, indeed.

Anna Rose felt numb as she rocked back and forth. Feeling torn and detached, she drank her tea and soon fell asleep.

Sara drew herself a hot bath. As she bathed, she tried to forget the day's events. Jess' death was crushing, but she never expected Anna Rose's outburst of hatred. Anna Rose was right, though. No one really cared that Jess was dead. Ruby was correct, too. It was time to sever the umbilical cord, allowing Anna Rose to deal with life on her own. The explosive nature of her sister's words made it clear that the time had come. Engulfed in guilt, Sara thought, *what good am I if I cannot protect Anna Rose from harm? On the other hand, she needs to grow up. Ruby's right again, Anna Rose is a woman now.*

In the living room, Mat-Su curled up to Anna Rose. Sara overheard Anna Rose's sobs, so she quickly dressed. Approaching her sister cautiously, Sara hoped that Anna Rose would accept her comforting arms. For an instant, their eyes met. Anna Rose continued to weep, and Sara took a chance. Sitting next to her grieving sister, she held out her hand. Anna Rose's frail hand stretched to meet Sara's hand. They embraced. Once again, Sara filled her role as the older sister. *The letting go will have to wait for another time*, Sara thought. Exhausted, both women fell asleep clasped in each other's arms.

BITTER FROST

Christmas and New Year's celebrations came and went. Alone in his tiny cabin, Bryan hardly noticed the holidays. He was unable to face Anna Rose or the Tealand jurors. It had been four weeks since he set eyes on another human being. How much did Anna Rose know? Bryan was uncertain. Was she aware of Sara's accusations? By now, she must be fully informed. How could he prove his innocence? His filthy body irritated him—it itched all over. He really needed a hot shower. It would make him feel human again. *Damn Sara, she's ruined the beginnings of my work. How can I change Anna Rose's mind?* he thought.

He had finished three of the five books that Anna Rose lent him. After reading the second to last chapter in book four, another epic western, he decided to break for lunch.

He reheated leftover cornbread and navy bean soup. While eating his lunch, he noticed the stack of books sitting on the coffee table. He decided to return them, take a shower, and hopefully diffuse the gossip. Confrontations always lead him to self-destruct. For Anna

Rose, he would maintain his anger, proving his loyalty and innocence. Besides, he could not remain secluded forever.

Two days later, he started his truck. Clear skies and increasing daylight lifted his spirits. Nervously, he smoked his seventh cigarette of the day while driving into Tealand's parking lot.

With snow piled high on the outskirts, the parking lot appeared smaller. The surroundings took on a new look. Camouflaged under the white powder, the yard junk disappeared. The setting appeared peaceful. Inside Bryan, a nervous storm churned. It intensified when he noticed Sara and Anna Rose standing on the porch. *They're just women, women with power, possessions and pride,* he thought.

Without taking his eyes off Anna Rose, he uncomfortably blurted out, "Hello, ladies. Nice weather we're having." Anna Rose's fatigued face possessed an uncertain expression, though her beauty still shone through the lines of stress.

With judgmental eyes, Sara walked directly toward Bryan. "Well Mr. Smith, I had hoped that you moved out. I don't trust you. Go back to the city where you belong. You're not welcome here," she said walking homeward.

To Sara's back, Bryan hollered, "Back off, I won't be intimidated by you." Without turning around, Sara flipped him off. His chest puffed outward, his shoulders pinned back and his spine straightened. *I'm the man around here. The new man, taking charge of your sister's life, so back off bitch,* he thought.

It took every ounce of stamina to maintain a less than homicidal stance. Bryan inhaled and exhaled with a sigh. He needed a cigarette or a fifth of whiskey to calm his escalating anger. *Order up, Magpie,* he thought.

Forging a smile, he said to Anna Rose, "Hello. I brought your books back. I enjoyed all of them. You have excellent taste. I was hoping to borrow a few more and take a shower. Would that be possible?"

"You're welcome to take care of your business, Mr. Smith."

"Call me Bryan."

"No thanks." Anna Rose stiffened.

"Look Anna Rose, whatever you've heard, it isn't true. I had nothing to do with Tealand's disappearance. I came north to find peace and quiet, to forget about drinking and to better myself."

"I'm sorry Mr. Smith, but I know *enough* about you already. In fact, I know too much. Please come in, take care of your business and be on your way." Anna Rose was polite, yet distant.

Reluctantly, he walked toward her. Even with all her elegance, she had changed during the winter months. *Why am I feeling this way? Why does her opinion matter?* he thought.

Tealand's door slammed shut. Anna Rose had gone inside. Bryan hesitated before entering, taking in a deep breath, he blindly stepped over the threshold. Bravely, he looked up. The patrons stopped conversing long enough to stare down Bryan. Anna Rose busied herself behind the counter. Solemnly, he placed the borrowed books on the counter then headed for the shower stalls.

The local men whispered as he passed by their respective tables, reminding him of the prison cafeteria, whereby inmate's whispered vulgar comments, raising neck hairs and aggravating his quick temper. Bryan ignored their derogatory comments, though internally, he wanted to pummel the offensive men.

Smoke, daily grime and tension washed down the drain. The hot water boosted his confidence. He repeated to himself that he was an upstanding human being, one who could hold his head high, an innocent man ready to face his judges and speak his truth. *Who am I kidding? Committing murder is a lifelong sentence,* he thought.

Shaking off his mistaken identity, he readied himself for action. Confidently, he walked past the discriminating locals. Their piercing black eyes had no effect on him. With a sense of purpose, he swiftly strode toward Anna Rose.

Without making eye contact, Anna Rose said, "That'll be fifty cents, Mr. Smith. I replaced your books with a new selection. I hope you find them satisfactory."

He reached over tenderly, stopping Anna Rose's fidgeting hand and said, "Anna Rose, you've got to believe me. Look at me, please. I had nothing to do with Tealand. Honestly, Anna Rose, how can you convict a man without hearing his side of the story?"

She snatched her hand back and focused her vision over Bryan's shoulder. Frank, a skinny, short, grey haired man and the local mechanic approached the counter, tapped Bryan on the shoulder and said, "Pay up and leave. We all know you're a murderer."

Bryan froze then turned toward the locals and said, "Fuck you. All of you can go to hell."

"We're already in hell. Get out of Hurricane County before you become the next decomposed wildlife banquet."

"The killer's still out there."

"Wrong. He's in here. We just can't prove it," Frank said.

"Get your facts straight. Leave me alone."

"That's what we're asking of you. Now leave."

"Accusations can be painful. Keep talkin' trash an' your pain'll be delivered."

Anna Rose stepped in and said, "Frank, just forget it. I can't listen to this anymore. The truth'll come out, Mr. Smith. It always does."

Silently pleading for her trust, staring into her eyes Bryan paid his bill, gathered the books and left without saying another word. Rehabilitation wasn't working easily, and he was ready to abandon his desire to change into a model citizen. *Another little town of hell,* he thought realizing that Nurse Jackson was probably right. In one of her wicked moods and on his last day of rehab, she had whispered into his ear that he would be back, and that he would never be fit for society. Absent of witnesses, she loved to torment him.

Miserable, Bryan lit a cigarette and continued driving toward Hurks. As he backed out of Tealand's, Anna Rose peeked out from behind a half-drawn curtain window. She wondered if her tenant was the killer or if she had murdered her own husband.

The sunny day made for below zero temperatures. His truck heater worked fine, but he made a mental note to obtain a piece of cardboard from Max; placing it between his radiator and front grill would reduce the bitter cold from entering the cab. *If only it were that easy with the locals and Anna Rose,* he thought feeling the icy wedge between him and all of Hurricane County.

Ruby directed natives and whites into the tavern. *Another auction,* Bryan thought. Reminded of the bar stench, whiskey called to his subconscious. He depressed the gas pedal, increasing speed, increasing his distance from Ravens, decreasing his chances of an effortless solution though his problematic alcoholism never ceased nor did it resolve anything.

Further down River Road, a strong wind forced the truck slightly sideways, straightening Bryan's attention from liquid gold back to driving. Before he centered the truck, his eyes caught a rock formation across the frozen river. The daunting snow composition resembled a woman's face. The winter creation spoke to the spellbound driver, whispering, "She's your future." *My future retirement account,* he thought as he blinked twice unconsciously, assuring himself that he was not going crazy. *No wonder everyone drinks around here,* he thought.

He recalled hearing the native inmates speak about the spirits of the Talkeetna mountain range. He scoffed at the idea then and scoffed at it now. He shook off the incident and maneuvered into the middle of River Road. As he drove, he carefully watched the Talkeetna peaks, fearful of experiencing another spiritual encounter.

Eager to forget his roadside hallucination, he daydreamed of an *All American* meal. Grilled cheeseburger, French fries, coffee and the anticipation of fresh blueberry pie watered his mouth. *Warm pie with vanilla ice cream*, he thought.

Hurks Café was quiet. Bryan was thankful for the peace. For a few minutes, he browsed around the small store then promptly sat at the lunch counter. Customarily, he reached for the four-item menu.

"What'll it be?" Lorraine asked snippily.

Placing his order, he wondered why Lorraine was in a bad mood. *She's got four kids, a husband and a business to run. Those are reasons enough,* he thought.

"No hamburger today. Its replacement is Musk Ox. Fries and coffee are available. And canned cherry pie—sorry no ice cream."

"Musk Ox and cherry pie without ice cream will be fine."

As he sipped on piping hot coffee, the smell of the fried musk ox caused him to wonder if he had made a mistake. He missed the city. The bush lifestyle was more of a challenge then he ever imagined. The people were certainly different. The inhabitants of both existences struggled with survival; one had all the modern conveniences while the other had the constant reminder of who was really in charge. At this point, he questioned the quality of life on both accounts. However, in the city one could always procure a cheeseburger.

The burger arrived burnt. Lorraine didn't care. "More coffee?" she asked.

"Please."

"Word's out, ya know, that you killed Jess Tealand."

"So I've heard. It's not true."

"What you need to learn is that everyone around here is from somewhere else. They've done things that no human should. We all know it, but we don't talk about it. You're the latest scandal. Once the fire settles, you'll be off the hook, and another scandal will present itself. In actuality, you did us all a favor. All of us thought about killing him. A wife beater's penalty should be a violent death. I hope you got in a few good punches before offing him completely."

"I only murdered one man in my life, and he didn't live in Hurricane County."

"See, another scandal just presented itself. You better keep that information to yourself."

"Just told you."

"Small towns have no secrets."

"Small towns can't discern the truth."

"Fortunately for you, this small town justified your murdering Tealand."

"Justify it to someone else. I had nothing to do with his disappearance."

Lorraine raised one eyebrow and placed a slice of cherry pie in front of him.

Bryan's lunch turned cold. Offended, he shoved the burger aside and ate the pie, paid and left the café. He sped through Hurricane County then realized that he forgot to pick up a piece of cardboard. *I might as well be living on the glacier. Hell Town turned icy,* he thought.

Daylight vanished. Bryan smoked another four cigarettes before turning onto Tundra Rose Lane. Relieved to be home, he settled into the mountain cabin. Confused about his emotions for Anna Rose, and his resentment toward the community's allegations stirred his desire to clear his name. The cast iron stove renewed its flame as Bryan loaded it with spruce logs; a procedure that he would repeat at midnight.

That evening at a quarter past nine, he laced up his army boots and put on his wool hat. To complete the outfit, he added gloves and a heavy coat. Confidently he puffed on a cigarette, grabbed a candy bar and headed out into the sub-zero temperatures to exonerate himself. With a flashlight in hand, he met the frigid atmosphere, hoping that Ruby would help him.

The glow from Ruby's cabin hastened Bryan's pace. A glass lantern with red kerosene burned in the window lighting his way to the front door. Gentleman set off the warning that someone or something was outside. Ruby responded. "Who's out there?"

"It's Bryan Smith. I need to talk to you?"

After quieting her dog, Ruby straightened her pink, sheer robe, knowing the light behind her would shine through the thin material, showing off her robust figure. With a wide stance, she opened the door.

Holding a bottle, she asked, "Whiskey?"

"No thanks, I don't drink…anymore."

"How about a cup of hot coffee?"

"Sure. That sounds great on a night like this?"

Ruby moved delicately as she prepared instant coffee. Her hand rested firmly on Bryan's shoulder as she delivered the hot beverage. Purposely, she bent over his shoulder far enough so that her large breasts would slightly drape out of her wrap-around robe. "Cream or sugar?" she asked sweetly then sat down.

"Black's fine."

Ruby began her pursuit. "So have you had any more headaches? If you ever need more white willow, I've plenty. I also have an array of herbs if you catch a bug. There's an herb for every ailment. My cabinets are always full, so let me know if you need anything. I can work out those aching muscles, too. Massage is my specialty."

Bryan had forgotten about Ruby's insatiable appetite for one-sided conversation. "Hum, no headaches," he said. "Actually, I feel good, but I'll keep in mind your herbal remedies. Thanks." *And your whiskey*, he thought.

"I've found that living in the bush, most people stay rather healthy—well, if you can discount their drinking habits," Ruby said then gulped down a shot of whiskey. "It's a hard life out here. I dream of moving to the city—selling all of this and just move. Hot running water and heat that comes from the wall sounds better as I age. How about you, are you ready to get back to society?"

"I have to admit, today I missed the city," he said recalling the conversation with Lorraine and the cold, burnt musk ox burger.

"How's the cabin? Ever get lonely?" Ruby asked coyly.

"It's an experience for sure. It's more work than I thought it would be. I guess I'm not as young as I used to be. Chopping wood takes it out of me, and running water sure makes for a comfortable life. I haven't been lonely yet—what with all the events happening around here."

Bryan leaned in closer toward Ruby. "Ruby, I need your help. Normally, I wouldn't ask, but I don't seem to be making myself clear or maybe it's that no one's listening. Would you help me? You're the only one that can make any difference."

Ruby had hoped for an opportunity to avail herself to Bryan. Now, he was doing the asking. She sat up enthusiastically. "What is it, Bryan?"

"Well, Sara has convinced Anna Rose that I had something to do with Tealand's death. She thinks I murdered him. I need her to know the truth. Can you help set her straight?"

Ruby's face dropped. "Why is it so important to you? Are you interested in Anna Rose?"

"Ah...well, not exactly. I just want to clear my name. I'd like to patronize Tealand's without being accused of a crime that I had nothing to do with." Bryan's voice escalated. He whined, "The locals stare and whisper behind my back. I feel like I'm on trial. I'm innocent. I traveled north for the solitude. Please Ruby, you have to convince them that I'm innocent. Will you help?"

Ruby seized her chance and approached Bryan from behind. Pressing her torso against his chair, her hands slid down his shoulders. Caressing his chest, she whispered into his ear, "I usually trade for information, Mr. Smith. Do you have anything to trade?" Ruby wet Bryan's earlobe, sending a sensuous message throughout his body. He tensed then quickly relaxed. Ruby moved her tongue down his clean neck. With her fingers, she encircled his nipples. "So what do you say, Mr. Smith, got anything to trade?"

Bryan felt Ruby's breasts resting on his shoulders, and the heat of her breath on his neck. Weakened, he said, "I don't know about this kind of trade. It doesn't seem right." Spontaneously, he grabbed the candy bar from his shirt pocket then handed it over.

Ruby laughed. "Do you think I can be bought with a measly chocolate bar? Isn't your reputation worth more than simple sugar?" She pounced, straddling Bryan's lap then ripped open his shirt. Passionately, she ran her fingers through this thick black chest hair and surrounded his nipple with her lips, gently drawing it to arousal. Bryan's body arched. He winced. Confused by what his body was reacting to and what his mind was telling him, he braced himself. It had been years since his last encounter with a woman. He knew it and his body felt it.

Ruby did not stop her relentless pursuit. She kissed Bryan's neck and ears, tugging at his flesh. Her hands moved about his torso, casually passing a hardened nipple. Bryan took in a deep breath. Ruby seized the opportunity; her hand slid down into his jeans. As Ruby stroked his stiff penis, he gasped when he orgasmed. Ruby polished the weakened appendage, waiting for the pulsing to subside. "Massage is my specialty," she whispered.

Embarrassed by his quick release, Bryan said, "It's been a long time."

Ruby snickered. "I've been waiting all winter for you, Mr. Smith." Once again, she began her provocative tease.

Suddenly, Bryan could no longer control himself. He reached under Ruby's thighs, lifting her awkwardly, driving her to the floor. His hands cupped her breasts. Swirling around her protruding nipples with his salivating tongue, he passionately moved between each breast. *No more denying myself, I'm fucking her now,* he thought.

Awaiting the first plunge, Ruby slid his penis into her. Following her lead, he thrust forcefully. The connection was explosive, and they both let out a short cry of pleasure. Repeatedly, the thrilling motion penetrated their bodies. Ruby gripped Bryan's soft, round ass. With her legs, she forced his hips upward, tightening her buttocks— driving his dick further into her.

With each thrust, they drew in deep breaths. In synch, they panted as their bodies tensed. Internal heat rose to Ruby's face. She flushed, as she reached her climax then waited for the two fluids to merge. Bryan came, throbbing inside her. Exhausted, and without making eye contact, he rolled onto the carpeted floor turning Ruby on her side. Her own inner pulsating continued.

Once the brief moment of pleasure was gone, guilt set in. Bryan was on his feet. He offered Ruby a hand and helped her up. Ruby casually moved to the woodstove. A warm washcloth would clean their lustful bodies. Bryan said nothing as he bathed.

"Not bad for a man who hasn't been with a woman in years. You can trade with me anytime, Mr. Smith. Most folks around here are drunk and don't last long. They're sluggish. You have yourself a deal. I'll talk to Sara and Anna Rose. That's all I can promise you. If their minds are set on hanging you...all the convincing in the world won't change their minds. That's all I can do. Are you satisfied?"

"Deal, but please don't tell them of our trade. I don't think it would look good."

Ruby agreed. "Now, what else can I do for you on this shameless winter night?" she asked as she sat down drinking another shot of whiskey.

"I'll take some of that white willow. I feel a migraine coming on." Bryan realized that the herbs might cost him another round with Ruby, so he quickly recanted. "Never mind, Ruby, it's subsiding. I need to get back to Ol' Charlie's. I'd hate to have my fire go out on a night like this." Truthfully, what he really needed was a cigarette, a drink and to escape Ruby.

"Your fire's hard to extinguish. You better come back sooner than later," Ruby said caressing her breasts while guiding Bryan through the arctic entry.

Casually, Bryan looked back toward the open red door. Ruby caught his glance and seductively caressed her crossed legs. Bryan felt another surge of sexual energy. *Sub-zero temperatures should cool me off,* he thought as he tried to shrug off Ruby's suggestive posture. Lighting the end of a filtered cigarette, he inhaled the much-needed chemicals; an addiction he knew would send him to his grave.

"Later," Bryan said as he quickly scampered off into winter's bitter cold.

FEBRUARY WARNING

Shortly after Valentine's Day, Tealand's choked Anna Rose's every breath. She desperately needed a long walk to see the forest and to touch the snow. Drawn to the ever-changing moods of Alaska, Anna Rose prepared herself.

She stepped outside wearing heavy winter gear. In contrast to Mat-Su's gleeful stride, Anna Rose slightly dragged her feet. Despair stirred inside her, though she was ready to release Jessy's stormy influence and relieve her own murderous secret.

Contemplating her direction, Anna Rose stopped on Tundra Rose Lane. The temperatures were perfect for a southerly walk. She decided to climb Canyon Bluff at the end of the cul-de-sac.

George Creek caught her attention. In the pristine surroundings, her heart lightened. The freeing of emotions allowed the healing to begin. A heavy sigh lifted the burden from her shoulders. She listened to the hidden water trickle, imagining its clarity as it gently flowed over the rigid creek bed.

Cheerfully, Anna Rose blessed Ruby as she crossed the twisted driveway, thanking her for the support and love that Ruby showed during her misfortune. She realized that Ruby and Sara needed a personal "thank you."

Anna Rose hurried to the base of the hill where she began her ascent on the clearly cut trail. Straight up the face of the four hundred-yard knoll, she and Mat-Su climbed. Mat-Su led her up the narrow snow path. They hiked easily on the right side of the canyon. Experience warned her that the edge was a sharp drop-off. Fortunately, the snow protected her from the loose gravel.

It had been six months since her last berry-picking excursion with Sara. Clearly, Anna Rose was out of shape. Her heavy breathing caused her to stop to catch her breath.

Over her shoulder, she spotted a parcel of cottonwood, spruce and birch trees. They stood tall, open to the sky while many other tundra plants hid beneath the thick crystal covering. Mat-Su whined to keep moving, so Anna Rose pressed onward toward the lone grove where she rested under a birch tree. The sun warmed her face as she relaxed, releasing the last of her tension.

Without warning, a bullet flew overhead, exploding a tree limb. Splintered remnants plunged to the snowy surface. Instinctively, Anna Rose's arms covered her head, as she dove face first into the snow.

"Trapper, you idiot," she said. *He must be hunting rabbits*, she thought sitting up in her protective bed. Suddenly, another gunshot rang out above her head, forcing her back into the snow. This time she felt the bullet's breeze as it whizzed past. Shocked, she could not believe Trapper had such poor aim or that he would waste ammunition. Quickly, she realized the hunter was after her, and it was definitely time to leave the area.

Cautiously, she poked her head up and looked around to the four directions. She saw no one. "Come on, Mat-Su," she whispered. "Let's get out of here." Avoiding a bullet to her back, she hunkered down and dashed over to the canyon path. Anna Rose's heart beat fast as her fear escalated. Cloaking herself under a tree, she knelt down. The expanding cold air burned her lungs causing her chest to tighten. Once she stabilized her breathing, she listened intensely for signs of approaching hunters. The canyon's echo was silent.

Confident that she was out of range, she started her decent. A westbound bullet soared over her head causing her to slip on ice, spinning her legs over the canyon's crevasse. A small avalanche of snow tumbled to the calm, rocky creek bed below. Frightened, she gripped Mat-Su's collar and pulled herself to safety. Bravely, Anna Rose looked up and around the bluff.

A man wearing a long black ragged coat, knee-high leather black boots and a cowboy hat stood two hundred yards above her. She discerned Hoss' wardrobe. Now, she was truly scared. Hoss was crazy—a dangerous psychopath, a man not above murder. Certain that he had killed Golda, though no one had proven his guilt, Anna Rose knew that if he gunned her down, his own death would certainly follow, unannounced and unnoticed. He would not escape frontier justice.

Hoss had a clear shot and pointed his rifle directly at Anna Rose. Flustered, she sped up her pace, looking over her shoulders every few feet. Hoss was gaining distance. He stopped, took aim and pulled the trigger. The bullet narrowly missed Mat-Su. The dog yelped, as he high tailed it down the marked trail. Anna Rose instinctively ducked, but kept moving, as she spotted Hoss at the top of the knoll. With wobbly knees, she rushed down the steep hill.

Mat-Su waited for Anna Rose to give the command to head for the brush. *Bald branches are better than no protection,* she thought frantically. Adrenaline pumped through her body as she glanced up at Hoss. He remained on top of Canyon Bluff. Anna Rose scanned her escape route. It was a long stretch between the cul-de-sac and Tealand's. It was also a straight rifle shot for Hoss.

The hard-packed snow bank was uneven, making her passage difficult. As she plotted her safe return home, she heard Hoss yelling, "Stay off my land, woman. I'll shoot you if you don't obey my law." Two shots echoed through the canyon as Hoss set off another round.

Anna Rose instantly fell onto the snowpack, waited a few seconds and then moved out. Grabbing Mat-Su's collar, she rounded the edge of the cul-de-sac, hugging the right hand side of the road. Blind to Hoss' position, she moved toward the next set of naked brush—a distant one hundred feet away. Hoss pumped out two more shots. Darting into the bushes, she jerked her arm as she dragged Mat-Su close. Fear motivated her as she maintained a steady speed through the compact snow that lined Tundra Rose Lane.

Three hundred yards away, Hoss skillfully aimed his weapon. He had no qualms about shooting a defenseless woman and her dog. They were trespassers, and they deserved to die. Their deaths would echo through the canyon on this beautiful day, pleasing Hoss.

Without looking back, Anna Rose kept running. Her stomach churned and a dry lump stuck in her throat. Two shots flew overhead. Squealing in terror, she ran straight up Ol' Charlie's steep driveway. Exhausted, she pounded on the log cabin door. "Mr. Smith, let me in. It's Anna Rose Tealand," she yelled.

Bryan casually half-opened the door. Anna Rose shoved Mat-Su inside then pushed herself through, causing Bryan to stagger backwards. She slammed the door behind her and locked it tight. "Get your gun," she said. "Hoss is out there shootin' at me. He has gone completely mad. Please. Where is your gun?" Anna Rose's voice escalated to an unusually high pitch.

Her enlarged eyes prompted Bryan to retrieve his weapon. Quickly, he checked its cargo then frantically looked out the front window. "Get in the back room," he said firmly. Anna Rose was quick to sit on the bed. "So that's what all the gunfire's about. I thought Trapper was out hunting. If only I had known, Anna Rose."

Bryan spied Hoss. "He's coming up the driveway." Bryan cocked the gun.

Anna Rose gasped fearing for her life. "You do know how to use that rifle, don't you, Mr. Smith?"

"City folks have killed plenty. I just never thought I'd have to shoot a person. I will, if I have too. Don't worry, Anna Rose."

With a short sigh of relief, Anna Rose asked, "Where's he now?"

Hoss hiked toward the cabin, stopping at Bryan's truck. He yelled, "Stay out of range, woman. Next time, I'll kill you and your mutt."

Air heaved up through Anna Rose's lungs. She covered her mouth so Hoss would not hear her fright. "Mr. Smith, where is he? Is he coming in?"

"Get in the front room," Bryan ordered.

Anna Rose jumped to her feet and ran to the front of the cabin while Bryan raced to the rear. From the back window, Bryan saw Hoss' hat bobbing through the thick snow-covered willow trees. Hoss' shack was directly behind Ol' Charlie's, but up four hundred yards.

"He's not stopping. I think he's heading home. He isn't looking back either. He probably figures I have a gun, too." Bryan stayed on watch until Hoss' hat disappeared. Soon he laid his weapon on the bed and walked over to Anna Rose. He guided her to the dusty couch then gently put his arms around her, hoping she would not reject his genuine concern.

Relief set in and tears began to spill out from Anna Rose. Mat-Su came and sat by her side.

Bryan remained quiet, hugging and rocking her while stroking her long, soft hair. He said, "Tell me what happened. Why was Hoss chasing you?"

Petting Mat-Su, Anna Rose sniffled through her story. She described how content she had felt minutes before the intrusion, and how quickly her joy had turned into fear.

After listening to the shocking tale, Bryan said, "Someone's got to do something about him. He needs professional help—a mental hospital for sure. I thought the shots were a little too close, even for Trapper. Can I get you some coffee or tea? I have some of Ruby's dandelion herbs. She says it's a nerve tonic. It might settle your nerves, Anna Rose."

"Yes, I'd like that." Anna Rose relaxed some. Next, she realized that she was now alone with Bryan Smith. She questioned his kindness. She remembered that Ruby believed that he had nothing to do with Jessy's death, yet her sister thought otherwise. Suppressing her own guilty feelings about causing Jessy's deadly situation, Anna Rose was eager to agree with Ruby, as her safety depended on trusting Bryan until she felt safe enough to walk home. She watched Bryan prepare the tea, analyzing his every move, questioning her sister's opinion, praying for Ruby's judgment to be correct. She scrutinized her fear, blindly setting it aside. His lengthy body and appearance pleased her. He was somewhat attractive. But, could he be trusted?

The aroma of the dandelion tea calmed her anxiety. As she sipped the hot brew, she repeated Ruby's instructions, "Inhale with each sip." She smiled timidly.

Bryan felt her acceptance of him. He asked politely, "How's your tea?" *Fags ask those kinds of questions. I can't believe I just said that,* he thought.

"Just fine, Mr. Smith. Ruby sure knows her herbs."

"Please, call me Bryan." *Suddenly, I'm Mr. Polite. What a pansy,* he thought.

Anna Rose nodded shyly. Unsure if making friends with her husband's accused murderer was a good idea, Anna Rose shifted her negative thoughts toward stabilizing her emotions, hoping to return home shortly.

With a nervous tone, Bryan asked, "So how've you been these past few months? I know things have been tough for you. Are you working through your…feelings?" Bryan sounded so clinical and he backed off. "I'm sorry, I don't mean to pry. I'm just concerned."

Anna Rose scrutinized his concern. After determining his sincerity, she eased, relaxing her suspicious posture. "I haven't done much with Tealand's. My house needs a good cleaning, too. I've cried my eyes out the last three months, feeling like an ancient cottonwood tree, you know, hollow inside, craggy and withered outside."

Unsure if Anna Rose was kidding, Bryan half-smiled, glancing down at his coffee mug. He said, "That's normal when you're grieving for someone you love."

"I suppose so. I've wasted the whole winter feeling sorry for myself. I missed being out in the snow. And after Hoss chasing me, I realized how out of shape I've become," Anna Rose said with a sigh.

"There'll be plenty of winters to enjoy." *And plenty of cash too*, he thought.

Anna Rose smiled pleasantly. Her steamed face glowed with affection. After emptying her teacup, she looked to the cabin door. The uncertainty of what laid behind the door scared her.

Bryan easily read her body language. "Anna Rose, stay as long as you like. We can just drink tea and visit. Maybe if you like, we could play a game of cards. I'm getting bored winning at solitaire." He smiled encouragingly. Speaking in a western drawl, Bryan sat up and announced, "I hereby challenge you, Miss Anna Rose, to a game of Rummy or Cribbage. You choose your best card game ma'am."

She laughed. It was her first laugh of the New Year. The release felt wonderful. The pit in her stomach lifted and her shoulders shifted downward. "You're on, Mr. Smith—ah, Bryan. I'm warning you though, I've been called "Ruthless" in my card playing days," Anna Rose said with a giggle.

Her twitter awoke Bryan's protective nature. He stood up. His thighs neared her shoulder. In a smooth and gentle motion, he brushed her cheek with the outside of his curved, relaxed forefinger. "I doubt that you could ever be ruthless." He pointed her to the kitchen table and poured more tea. "Are you all right?"

"Yes. I'm fine. Still somewhat shaken, but I will relax…just as soon as I beat you in cards," she said with a nervous grin.

For an hour, Bryan sat across from his unexpected visitor. With each snap of a card, each discreetly eyed the other. Finally, Bryan said cautiously, "You have beautiful eyes."

Shocked, Anna Rose blushed. "Thank you."

"I know this is inappropriate to say, with Tealand's death and all, but I've been thinking about you these past few months."

"Impossible."

"Actually, I can't seem to get you out of my mind."

"Why?"

"It's just the way you smile or move about. I feel like a high school kid. I haven't felt like this in years." *Nor have I had anyone to manipulate*, he thought.

Not knowing how to respond, she blushed, dropping her head. Their bodies polarized as the moment continued in silence. An array of emotions passed between them. A passionate fire began to kindle.

Bryan became uncomfortable with his conflicting feelings—he liked her more than he should, making it difficult to exploit her. He moved to open the kitchen window. The fresh, cold air rushed through him. He relaxed and returned to the table. "High card deals."

His opponent stared him down. Anna Rose split the deck. Her continued glare forced Bryan to call her turned card.

"Hum, the queen of hearts—how appropriate."

A surge of excitement surfaced within Anna Rose. Uncharted territory with a man her sister despised, a seemingly gentle man though his dangerous side had yet to be exposed. Even for a timid woman this was thrilling. She felt mischievous and alive.

"Turnaround is fair play." Bryan halved the deck again. "Read the card."

Anna Rose was all too eager to read it. "The ten of diamonds earns me the deal, Mr. Smith. Just remember—"

"I know. You're ruthless. We'll see about that." Bryan tapped his fingers on the table, settling his ridiculous, useless romantic emotions. His mind turned to the familiar; plotting, preparing to move in for the kill. Losing at cards was a ploy, a confidence builder, testing Anna Rose's boundaries, aligning his plan to physically move in and steal her life.

Swiftly, Anna Rose shuffled the cards while grinning triumphantly at Bryan. She felt uneasy. Stomach butterflies fluttered within, making the unforeseen circumstances almost intolerable—a catalyst for change.

Two pots of tea and seven wins later, Anna Rose excused herself to the outhouse. "Collect yourself while I'm gone. I'll give you another chance when I return. That is, if you're feeling up to it?" She giggled.

"Oh, I'm ready for you. I was just testing your skills. I'll have my revenge, you'll see." *And your money, land and even your dog*, he thought.

They enjoyed each other's humorous bantering. Still smiling, Anna Rose slipped out the door. Bryan maintained his delighted expression until the cabin door closed. He placed another log in the chamber then replaced the teapot's water. Anna Rose's absence finally allowed him to wallow in his merriment. A calculating plan stirred within his mind. His body ached for the touch a woman; a shot of whiskey would take the edge off but a successful scheme required exemplary behavior.

Bryan warmed his hands over the woodstove. When Anna Rose returned, she joined him. The short trip outside chilled her exposed, pale skin. Trying to regain circulation, she began to rub her hands together. Bryan took over the task. Anna Rose's delicate hands lay softly between his warm masculine hands—hands that brought his children into the world, and hands that took his best friend from the world. There was no line between life and death in Bryan's world. Both merged into one meager existence.

"I've enjoyed our time together. I nearly forgot about Hoss," Anna Rose said. She relaxed into Bryan's warmth, observing his hands. *Clean and nicely shaped,* she thought.

Bryan longed to kiss her full lips. *I could seize the moment,* he thought. *No. I don't want to scare her off.* He fantasized about their first private encounter. Quickly his fantasy turned to the women with whom he had previously had intercourse with, the rapture of an unfamiliar lover. Then his mind whisked away to the men in jail who held him down, teaching him the hierarchy of prison. Neck hairs stood on end as he shook off the unthinkable invasion. Bryan shuddered, returning to the present.

"What time is it?" Anna Rose asked. Her hands and cheeks now warm.

He checked his watch. "It's twelve fifteen. Can you believe it? Where has the time gone? I think the Queen of Cards had better return to her castle. How about if I drive you and Mat-Su down...my Queen?" Bryan extended his right arm.

Anna Rose giggled and accepted the gracious offer. It was as if time had removed all notions of fear—three men, three potential disasters, leaving her free to determine her own fate, a posture foreign to Anna Rose.

Snuggled into their warm overcoats, they walked outside to Bryan's truck. He opened the passenger door for Anna Rose, Mat-Su took the lead, leaping into the cab first, separating the apprehensive humans.

Pointing toward the night sky, Anna Rose exclaimed, "Look, the Aurora Borealis. Aren't the colors spectacular?"

Just behind the frozen Talkeetna mountain range, the solar flares swirled. Endless wide bands of green and pink hues drifted silently over the earth's atmosphere as the stilled terrain of Alaska silhouetted below.

"Breathtaking," Anna Rose said.

"One of the Earth's natural wonders. They're incredible. Just think we're probably the only two watching it. It feels like this show is just for us."

"Beautiful."

He stood close to Anna Rose and said, "I could watch the Northern Lights all night, but I'm freezing."

She agreed and lifted herself into the truck. The rhythmic flutters guided them into Tealand's parking lot. Ahead, lights shined on Tealand's front door. The coming farewell caused Bryan and Anna Rose to stiffen. Uneasy about what the next few moments would reveal, their discovery edged the two toward anxiety. Bryan wanted her now.

As Bryan placed the truck into park, Anna Rose nervously blurted out, "Thanks for everything. I'm so glad you were home today. Thank you."

"Let me know if you need anything—day or night."

Without prolonging the inevitable, Anna Rose pecked him on the cheek and dashed out of the truck. Mat-Su followed.

"I'll be open tomorrow for showers."

"Shower or no shower, I'll be down."

Anna Rose blushed in the night and quietly closed the metal door. Without looking back, she and Mat-Su stepped into their chilly house. Despite the late hour, she was not tired. She was excited. Unfamiliar pleasure vibrated inside her. The evening events took her by surprise. She hoped this unusual, uplifting feeling would last forever. Carefully, she prepared herself for bed, pampering herself more than usual.

Standing on the slender deck, Bryan looked toward the northern lights. *A perfect ending for a perfect evening. She'll be mine in no time…and the land, café and rentals too,* he thought.

The following morning, Anna Rose drew back the kitchen curtains welcoming in the much-needed sunshine. Life was beginning again.

She felt the changes and their newness, although they did not overwhelm her. She felt wonderful.

"Anna Rose?" Sara hollered.

"I'm back here."

Bewildered to see her sister eating in a clean kitchen, she asked curiously, "Are you okay?"

Anna Rose patted Sara's hand and smiled. "I'm fine. I never felt better. Really, I'm fine."

"What happened? Why the sudden change? Don't get me wrong, I'm happy to see you up and around again." Sara sat down across from Anna Rose.

"I don't know, Sis. I woke up yesterday, and I wasn't depressed anymore. I can't explain it. It may have something to do with Hoss trying to kill me."

"What?"

Anna Rose ended the horrifying story with Hoss chasing her home. She hoped her lie would go undetected. She and Sara shared an uncanny telepathy. Anna Rose was not accustomed to fibbing, especially to her beloved sister, who read her like an open book. Nervously, she continued describing her change in attitude.

"With my life on the line, I just realized that time is short. That must be what snapped me out of my depression."

Sara said, "Damn that Hoss. I'm so glad that you've overcome…well, you know…Jess. Does it bother you if I talk about him?"

"It's not a problem. I'm telling you, I feel wonderful. I'm back to my old self again." *An even better self,* she thought pushing her deep-seated guilt over Jessy's death to the bottom of her subconscious.

"Thank God," Sara exclaimed. "Why don't you come over for dinner? The kids would love to see you. They've been asking for you."

"Of course, I'll come. And I'm sorry, Sara, for acting so foolish." Anna Rose reached over and patted her sister's hand. "Will you ever forgive me?"

"Don't be silly. You had every right to be upset. I love you, little sister." Sara squeezed Anna Rose's hand.

"I love you, too. Thanks for standing by me. You and the kids are all that I have now."

"I'll always be here for you. Haven't you learned that yet?" Sara stood up, hugged Anna Rose then returned home. Immediately, she broke the exciting news to her children, instructing them to invite their grandmother for dinner. Simultaneously, the youngsters jumped for joy and screamed out their delight. They quickly dressed in their snowsuits and raced each other down to the Quonset hut.

****

"One shower, please," Bryan said late in the afternoon.

Without looking up, Anna Rose said, "Okay. Help yourself."

"I like the front curtains pulled back. There's nothing like watching the sunset on a winter's day," Bryan said with glee.

Coldly, Ann Rose said, "Excuse me, Mr. Smith, but I have to serve my customers." With the hot coffee pot in hand, she scurried over to the regulars.

Bryan watched her coy behavior as she moved through the cafe. Feeling her secrecy, he followed her toward the shower stalls, nudging her with his elbow. "Pardon me, ma'am."

Anna Rose nodded inconspicuously, and then announced, "We'll be closing soon, so this is your last cup." Disappointed, the three patrons grumbled.

By the time Bryan finished showering, Tealand's was empty. Anna Rose had closed the window shades, hung the "Closed" sign and locked the door. She met Bryan in the center of the café. Anna Rose's intent was clear. As usual, Bryan cloaked his.

Gently holding her pretty face, he kissed her rosy lips. Anna Rose allowed the advance. Within a few seconds, she relaxed into his arms, filling herself with her own long lost passion. Each kiss drove the pair deeper. Out of breath, they pulled back from each other, gasping for air. Together they laughed.

"I couldn't sleep at all last night. You're all I can think about; your lovely green eyes; your long black hair; and your soft delicate skin. The way you move played over and over in my head. Your sweet voice sang to me all through the night. I'm sorry, but I just had to kiss you."

His poetic words did not surprise him. Magpie provided his material. Bryan had memorized numerous stanzas knowing they would be useful in the future. Their pirated works filtered through Anna Rose with delight. Her body responded. She surprised herself and Bryan by returning his compliments with a tender kiss.

Enamored, he engulfed her petite frame. As if it were their last meeting, he held her tight. Anna Rose laid her head against his chest. She slipped further into the romance of the moment.

"Bryan, I don't think we should tell anyone about this—I mean us. It's too soon after Jessy—"

"I understand, sweet Anna Rose. My lips are sealed." He firmed up the agreement with another long-winded kiss.

"Ouch," Anna Rose shrieked stepping backwards.

"Sorry, I didn't mean to bite you. Let me look."

Anna Rose lifted her head slightly. One precious drop of blood seeped from her lip. *Not enough, but I'll take what I can get*, he thought. In one quick motion his fingers pressed into her jawbone, squeezing her cheeks together, her lips puckered releasing one more drop, one more hint of Bryan's past. Quickly, he transferred the blood onto the tip of his tongue then released Anna Rose whose eyes had widened. *Sweeter then whiskey*, he thought.

Avoiding further intimate contact, Anna Rose quickly checked her watch, unlocked the door then hastily shoved Bryan outside. Her lip stung. Alarmed by the puncture, Anna Rose said, "I've got to be at Sara's by five o'clock or she'll come lookin' for me."

Anna Rose's nervousness caused Bryan to laugh. "It's okay, Anna Rose. Go on to your sister's house. I'll be fine. Although… I might need to take another cold shower."

His animated enlarged blue eyes and wide smile made Anna Rose laugh though she felt slightly nauseous. Pushing her intuition aside, she was delighted that the heavy feeling from depression had lifted. She allowed herself what she deserved—light-headed elation. Dabbing her lip, she unknowingly encouraged a murderer to slink into her life.

As they walked onto Tundra Rose Lane, Anna Rose said, "There's plenty of cold water."

Chuckling, they walked in separate directions. Bryan trekked home in a daze, confused by his potential future with Anna Rose, conflicted by his natural womanizing traits, all the while hearing Nurse Jackson's voice welcoming him back to rehab. Magpie filtered through his mind—another reminder of his potential future. As he ate his canned corn beef and hash dinner, he thought about his sweet Anna Rose. He realized that the relationship would move slowly, it would have to. *How can I stop myself from abusing her? Surely, she would know the signs of abuse. I wonder how long it took Tealand to start his beatings. Fuck you Magpie. Shut up Nurse Jackson*, he thought.

Satisfied for now, Bryan finished his salty, starchy meal then washed the dishes, laughed about his not wanting to read any romance novels. *Now look at me, I am a romance novel, one filled with deception, lust and greed. Is there any other kind?* he thought.

Imagining a torrid affair with a newly widowed wilderness woman, he played the lonely cabin dweller living just up the road— a road named after his secret lover. He would comfort the fragile woman, soothing her aching heart and then murder her. Running though his demented mind, the when and how to kill the widow distracted him. He laughed hardily as he pretended to write his own lethal love story. Shaking off the ridiculous, yet inspirational notions, eventually a Wild West paperback became his muse.

THE BOLD AND THE BEAUTIFUL

Clouds covered the sky on February's final day. Tealand's was full. Anna Rose busily served coffee and apple pie. Not much around the homestead had changed except the weather. Hurricane County sat idle as the dark sky encased the community. For the next seventy-twos hours, a northwest front traveling toward northeast Alaska weighed heavily on the minds of those affected. The weather report predicted heavy snowfall. Dried meat and water were stored inside the residents' dwellings. In preparation for the impending whiteout conditions accompanied with an above average snowfall-a forecasted depth of six-feet-extra firewood stacked up near front doors and along the sides of homes.

"How was your shower, Mr. Smith?" Anna Rose asked, taking his fifty cents.

"Great." Then he whispered, "Tonight?" She nodded cautiously.

Each day the pair became closer, though Anna Rose had not given into her strong sexual desires. Each rendezvous completely frustrated Bryan. Ever hopeful, he showered each day, calming his sexual cravings, yet seeing Anna Rose had the opposite effect. His pent up longing tested his sobriety, day and night, ending with a cold morning shower—a cycle that had to end and end soon. Bryan's patience was wearing thin, increasing his desire for Ruby's poisonous, life-threatening whiskey. A cure to unwind with, a lover to quench deep-seated desires, but one cure that commonly persuaded a weak mind and a weak body back into an unconscious suicide, at times, crossing over into murder.

Anna Rose told no one about her late night liaisons in Ol' Charlie's cabin. The books, the cards and the puzzles became the couple's muse. Hot tea warmed their bodies, as did the evening farewell kiss. For Anna Rose, illusions of a future together swayed the clandestine romance into the misconception of living "happily-ever-after." Her glee was authentic but reality would expose a fictitious tale.

Mat-Su's constant bark drove Anna Rose from the cash register to the front door. "Lotty? Lillian? I can't believe it," she said dumbfounded. She rushed outside, ordering Mat-Su back into Tealand's. Twelve harnessed, muscular grey and black Husky dogs barked, panting. Even when hitched together, they posed a danger to Mat-Su.

The predicted storm had yet to release its fury. Under the dark cloud mass, two heavily clothed women calmed their dog team enough to greet Anna Rose. The three friends embraced. Anna Rose was unsure whom she was hugging, as the bundled up guests' faces matched perfectly. Nevertheless, she was ecstatic to see her longtime family friends.

Bryan joined in the excitement. Proudly standing next to Anna Rose, he eagerly awaited his introduction. *Friend or foe, lover or loser, how will I be introduced*, he thought.

Astonished by Bryan's closeness, Anna Rose said, "Bryan, these are some of my dearest friends. This is Lotty and this is Lil—they're twins. This is Bryan Smith. He's renting the two-sided log cabin— Ol' Charlie's place."

As they shook hands, Bryan thought, *how could these two tiny women mush a team of twelve dogs?*

"Lotty and Lil live three hundred fifty miles northeast of here. We haven't seen them in…two or three years."

"It's been three and a half years," Lotty said. "A long three and a half years at that."

Anna Rose said, "What's kept you from your old friends? How's your Papa? We have a lot of catchin' up to do. Come inside. Let's get some hot coffee in you. You both probably need a shower. How long have you been out?"

The twins laughed. "It's good to see you Anna Rose. Where's Jess?" Lil asked looking around.

Anna Rose and Bryan exchanged implicating looks. While Anna Rose searched for a sensitive reply, Bryan searched her eyes for any hint of pain. Timidly, Anna Rose said, "Jessy's gone."

The twins exchanged a quizzical look. "We *do* have much to discuss," Lotty said. Everyone laughed. Anna Rose ushered them through Tealand's front door.

"First things first," Lil said. "We'll take our coffee outside. Let us tend to our team. Then we can relax, take our showers and have that long conversation. Is it okay to bed down the dogs in the driveway?"

"Of course, as long as you like, Lil, you know that. Look everyone, Lotty and Lil are here. How long can you stay? Oh, I know, coffee, dogs, shower then chatter. Derek, go fetch Sara. Tell her the twins are here."

Derek stopped working on a washing machine, acknowledging Anna Rose with a nod, tipping his hat while looking in the opposite direction and maintaining his distance from the mushers as he followed his orders.

Anna Rose handed the mushers each a cup of coffee. The twins promptly returned outside to care for their dog team.

"Was that Chad?" Lotty asked concerned.

"I didn't get a close look, but from what I saw, it sure looked like him," Lil said. "Did Anna Rose call him Derek?"

"I think so. Hum, let's get busy so we can visit with the Sutton's," Lotty said dismissing the coincidental look-alike sighting.

Back inside Tealand's, Bryan asked Anna Rose his questions. She answered most of them and was pleased to see that Bryan was so interested in the twins. She laughed at his confusion as to how two such small women could actually survive alone out in the wilderness. He was amazed. With great excitement, he watched through the window as the women mushers fed and watered their dogs.

"Yes, Mr. Smith, it's true. Women can lead a team of twelve dogs through the arctic and have been doing so for generations. They can camp out and survive in sub-zero temperatures, and yes Mr. Smith, they can even take out the garbage." Anna Rose laughed at her own sarcasm.

"I'm sorry. Most city girls wouldn't dream of such an endeavor."

"City folks," Anna Rose scoffed. She giggled as Bryan scanned her petite body from head to toe.

Tealand's door swung open. "…your dog team is impressive, strong, well fed and obedient," Sara said as she and the twins chattered away. Sara was anxious to hear about their lives up north.

"Thanks for the coffee, Anna Rose," Lotty said.

"You know where the towels are. There are two fresh bars of soap in the cabinet, as well. Take your time. Remember though, if one of you turns off the water before the other, you'll be scorched."

Lotty and Lil laughed recalling the numerous times that they had jumped back from the scalding water, though in reality jumping back in the three-foot by three-foot shower stall meant slamming into the sidewall and being scalded anyway. More often, Tealand's washing machines released untimely hot water, as well.

Sara's entrance cued Bryan's departure. He disappeared while Anna Rose retrieved shampoo for the twins. Sara had not said two words to him since her last outlandish threats. Disparaging looks, yes, but no words exchanged. It became apparent that she still believed that he killed Tealand. He could only imagine Sara's reaction when she found out about his and Anna Rose's affair. The accused husband-murderer turned boyfriend. Surely, she would try to convince Anna Rose to discontinue seeing him. By that time, he would have maneuvered easily into Anna Rose's life. *After Sara's tactics fail and her anger settles, she'll have to accept me,* he thought. Bryan chuckled, enjoying his secret.

"Isn't it great to see the twins?" Sara asked. "It's been so long. Tonight'll be like old times. We'll sit around the kitchen table and talk until dawn."

"Looks like closing time, boys. You'll have to take that card game elsewhere," Anna Rose said noticing that Bryan was no longer in the cafe.

"Ah, Anna Rose, it ain't even close to six o'clock," Billy said whining.

"It's close enough for me. Go on, now. Out. I'll see you tomorrow." She hustled the local patrons outside.

"Jess wouldn't cut out early if he was runnin' the place."

"Well, he's not here, Billy, so get out."

Sara sat on a bar stool stunned. "Was that my little sister, Anna Rose, saying that? What's gotten into you? Sounds like you're all grown up."

"I just decided not to allow anyone to treat me like Jessy did—ever again. I deserve better, and now I'm runnin' my own show."

"Right on, little sister, you sure have come a long way in the last few months. Whatever turned you around, I like it." "Thank you," Anna Rose said with pride.

"One of the finest inventions is the shower," Lil said towel drying her waist length, light blonde hair.

"So tell me, Lil, how's your Papa doing?" Sara asked.

"Papa is getting along just fine. He's getting old and can't do as much, but he can still belt out orders like a grizzly in heat."

Sara and Anna Rose laughed at the image of old man Evanson bossing his daughters around in northeast Alaska. He could be as gentle as a lamb but when it came to work, he had the upper hand and let everyone know it. This stout, blue-eyed man often engulfed Sara and Anna Rose, embracing them with genuine warmth and love. Sara always felt good after one of his back-aligning hugs.

Several hours passed as the four women talked about their lives: gardening, canning, chopping wood, preparing for winter and looking forward to enjoying the rare hot summers.

"It's really great to see you two," Sara said. "How long can you stay?"

Lil said, "Just for the night. We're heading up the Iditarod trail to Nome. Papa and Lotty have been training a new group of dogs. Lotty is going to become the first woman to win the 1,100-mile race. That's why we're here—to test the team. And I'm going to write about our adventure. It should make for worthy reading. But don't worry, on our way back we can stay for at least a week. Papa has everything he needs for three and a half weeks. If our calculations are correct, we should be back here in seven to ten days. Weather permitting, of course."

Sara said, "What a thrill." She looked at Anna Rose. They laughed, knowing that an excursion of that magnitude was an endeavor they would never accomplish, nor desire too. They were, however, elated for their more adventurous friends. "Oh, I can't wait to read about your trip, Lil. And I can see the headlines now: '*Lotty: Iditarod Winner…A Woman?*'"

Lotty said chuckling, "Yeah, imagine the angry men with their frosty red faces? Next thing you know, they'll be picketing in Juneau chanting: "Women should stay at home, not race to Nome." Everyone laughed.

There was nothing left of the caribou sausage, homemade cheese and wheat cracker platter. The snacks and time had slipped away. Anna Rose stood to fill her empty coffee mug and asked, "Anyone care for a refill?"

Lil said, "No thanks. We have to get up early tomorrow. I don't want to be up all night."

Lotty rose from her chair. She stretched and checked her watch. It read ten thirty-five. "We need to tend to the dogs, Lil. I could use some fresh air and a walk. I'd like to surprise Trapper. Care to join me?"

Lil pushed in her chair and said, "Oh, a walk sounds wonderful. Do you mind?"

Anna Rose placed the coffee pot back on its burner and said, "No, of course not. What time are you scheduled to leave tomorrow?"

"Six o'clock," Lotty said.

"I'll make a big breakfast. How does five o'clock sound? Sara, bring Mama up. You know if she doesn't get to see the twins, she'll be hard to handle until they return." Everyone laughed, agreeing with Anna Rose.

"I'll make up your beds. There's no sense in sleeping in your sled tonight," Anna Rose said.

Graciously smiling, Lil said, "I couldn't agree more. Thank you, Anna Rose."

Husky dogs laid in separate beds of straw, whining as the twins walked their way. Lil fed each team member a stick of moose jerky and patted each one on the head. As the caretakers started their half mile walk up to Trapper's cabin, they heard the canines chewing the leathery treats and wailing, presumably, for more food and attention.

The full moon reflected off the snow, guiding the twins to their final destination. The neighborhood was silent with the exception of George Creek's trickle and the sound of the twins' boots scoring the snow as they walked. Once they reached Trapper's driveway, Lotty announced their arrival. Taking in a deep breath, she began her call,

"Teekkekee…teekkekee." The narrow creek canyon echoed back through the valley. Disregarding the peaceful surroundings, Lotty called out again, the huskies howled, and the canyon echoed back her message each time distancing itself from its origin.

"Lotty, is that you?" Trapper asked. His ominous shadow cast over the deck onto the driveway. Towering above the unexpected visitors, excited for Lotty's return, he stood anticipating a night for reminiscing and the soft lips of a woman.

Lil raced up the half-round spruce log stairs and wrapped her arms around Trapper. He returned the affection and asked, "Where have you been?"

Lil sharply said, "It's not where have we been, but where are we going?"

"Lil, you snake. You know I hate it when you pretend to be Lotty."

"I indulge because you are my entertainment. I love to irritate you—it's so easy."

Lotty pushed her sister aside and asked, "Hey, how about a hug for me, Trap?" Quickly accommodating, Trapper forced his tongue down Lotty's throat. She reciprocated, and their hands moved freely over each other. The long-winded kiss eventually caused the two to gasp for air before another vigorous French kiss ensued.

Disgusted, Lil said, "Come on. Let's get inside before your mouths freeze together." Lotty and Trapper unlocked themselves, grabbing each other relentlessly through the doorway.

Lotty had been sneaking up to Trapper's cabin since she was sixteen. Their sizzling affair continued throughout the years, a well kept secret hidden from her father. Trapper was eleven years older, fuel for any father with a gun and a temper. At times, Lil used their covert relationship to bribe her sister—an effective tool to acquire extra rations or to hide her own misconduct. Both evaded their father's wrath, bartering to maintain their secrets and protecting each other as they developed into young women.

Trapper accommodated Lil by moving a high-back wooden chair into the tiny living room. He and Lotty sat arm-in-arm on the couch. "What are you doing here and for how long?" he asked.

"In the morning, we're heading to Nome," Lil said.

"I'm planning to enter the Iditarod race next year. We're testing the team on the trail," Lotty said.

"It's not a race for women. I hope you make it back in one piece," Trapper said dryly.

Offended Lil said, "She'll prove all arrogant men wrong. Women are smaller, smarter and have a better understanding of what their team needs. You'll see. You'll see Lotty's name in the paper. She'll go down in history as the first woman musher to win the Iditarod."

"Good luck with that."

Lil carried a low opinion of this lonely, self-righteous and now aging man. Over the years, she never figured out what Lotty saw in this gruff, wilderness man. Trapper's unjust remark caused Lil to change the subject, knowing he would talk all night about himself.

"So, tell us what've you been up too? Have you killed any large racks lately?" Lil asked uninterested.

Trapper straightened on the couch then recounted the details of the grizzly bear attack. Without missing a beat, he told the twins about the cabin robbery, describing every item missing and reciting the cabin's damage. Lotty listened compassionately. *He probably deserved it, consequences for the high and mighty,* Lil thought.

"Did Ruby take your healings out in trade?" Lotty asked with a jealous tone.

Trapper ignored the question. Over the years, Lotty's jealously caused them to fight, even fistfight, over what Trapper thought were ridiculous accusations. He thought that jealousy was a waste of time and a waste of energy. He allowed Lotty's unrefined youth to stir their relationship, as sex was amazing with her flourishing youthful body and driving passion.

Lil asked, "All of your gold was stolen?"

The twins exchanged an accusing glance using their keen telepathy communication system. Most twins develop a unique language. As adults, the twins had modified their technique, at times only a facial expression or a series of tongue clicks steered their conversations. This highly organized method affected the huskies, improving coach and team member dialogue, an advantage Lilly would use to win her first Iditarod race.

Trapper's suspicions stirred. He waited for the twins to reveal themselves. Impatiently waiting, his anger awakened inside.

"How long has Sara's workman been around here?" Lotty asked.

"Derek's been around about two years. Why?" Trapper asked elevating his voice.

"I'm sure it was him," Lil said looking toward her sister.

Lotty nodded in agreement. "If that *was* him, his name is Chad. He's the reason we moved out to the 'land of nowhere'."

"Why didn't you have your gold hidden?" Lil scolded, jabbing to stimulate Trapper's quick temper.

"It was well hidden. I told you, whoever broke in here trashed the place. My belongings looked like tossed rags. What do you know about this Derek guy? Are you implying that he had something to do with the break-in?"

"Well, we can't say for sure, but if he could bludgeon his sleeping father over a gold claim, we wouldn't put it past him," Lotty said.

"What do you mean he beat to death his own father? Sounds like something that I would do, but not Derek. How do you know this?" Trapper's voice heightened further.

"Calm down, Trapper," Lil said.

"Calm down? How can I? If Derek or Chad, as you call him, did this then that means Sara—"

"No way, Sara didn't have anything to do with it. She's in the dark about Chad's past, just as you were. Look, we were teenagers at the time. Chad's father and our Papa were close friends while they worked down at Butcher's Bay Mining Camp. Chad found a small stream and wanted to claim its gold. His father wouldn't allow it, telling his son that he was too young and irresponsible. Then early one morning while the camp was sleeping, Chad beat his father with a shovel, leaving him for dead then robbed him of his gold. No one ever saw him again—at least until today. The more I think about it, I *know* that was him."

Trapper's rage boiled to the surface. He hollered, "That son-of-a-bitch. I'll kill him." He fondled his beard, eyes wild, obviously plotting his punishment while pacing the tiny living room.

Lil quickly said, "Now you leave Sara out of this. She has two young kids to raise yet."

Derek's past was ruining Lotty's fantasy. She knew Trapper's fury would send him down the road. Abruptly, she raced up the stairs into his loft bedroom.

Blinded by his anger, Trapper didn't notice Lotty's exit. His hostile mood had taken over his senses. He reached for his loaded gun, headed toward the door, inspired by bloodshed his adrenaline surged.

Lotty distracted his temper. "Hey, Trap, come up here. I've got something to show you."

Stopping midway through the door, the image in his head switched, realizing murder required pre-meditation, perfect planning with flawless implementation. Recognizing that Lotty offered a special gift, he slowly lumbered up the staircase, placing the gun at its base.

Still clothed, Lotty laid spread-eagle on the king size bed. The 12x12-foot pitched roof created a teepee-like bedroom area. The bed and two end tables filled the space. An attractive purple stained glass lamp sat on one of the tables. On the other side sat a stack of books. A wooden dowel stretched from the rear of the cabin to the banister, exposing Trapper's clothes, which hung almost to the floor.

As Trapper neared, Lotty unbuttoned the top three buttons on her faded blue jean fly. She lifted her wool sweater exposing her lean abdominal muscles. Her white torso stood out in the semi-dark room. Once Trapper was in view, she seductively moved her fingers up and down her stomach, enticing him.

Immediately, Trapper's violent mood changed. He removed his flannel shirt, tossing it toward the clothes rack and slid off his pants, haphazardly leaving them on the forest green carpet. Abruptly, he fell on top of Lotty while jerking her tightly knitted sweater higher around her neck. Moistening his lips, he passionately sucked on one of Lotty's nipples while busily pawing the other.

Lotty rolled him on his back. Now, sitting on his waist she removed her sweater. Slowly, she slightly draped her firm breasts against Trapper's hairless chest. She swirled her tongue below his ear, and then quickly seized his earlobe, drawing the small patch of flesh into her mouth, nibbling and sucking rhythmically. Lotty teased his sensitive neck, occasionally stopping to tug at his burly skin then grazed Trapper's upper lip just enough to dampen the soft surface as she made a smooth pass to his other side. She continued to taunt him until he could lie still no more.

Suddenly, Lotty found herself on her back as Trapper groped at her firm breasts. He feverishly extended his tongue down her silky white abdomen, chilling her. Aroused, she arched her back. At the same moment, Trapper slipped his hand behind her. With his free hand, he released the two remaining pant fly buttons. He wriggled the jeans off, kicking them out of his way. Lotty laid naked on the bed, anticipating penetration; a sensation that she craved and rarely received as living in the bush allowed for no acceptable partners. Trapper stood with an erection at the foot of the bed, an enticing treat for Lotty.

Tantalizing her partner, Lotty squirmed submissively. She bent her knees and placed her hands between her thighs. She dropped her legs, still bent, toward the bed. Trapper accepted the open invitation, and in one breath, the infrequent lovers groaned with delight.

"I think I'm going to be sick," Lil hollered. "That's okay, I'll let myself out." Disgusted, she slammed the door behind her. She walked down the icy driveway trying to rid herself of the grotesque vision left in her mind. Looking up at the clouded sky, she noticed a bluish-yellow ring around the moon. *A storm's coming in,* she thought. Water traveled beneath the snow atop George Creek. As she stood over it, she discovered several small openings where the icy water made its slow decent. This tranquil setting soon replaced the unattractive picture that marred her thoughts. She was relieved to be alone.

Her footsteps squeaked against the snow and soon the dogs howled in the short distance. Lil ran to quiet them. Once the team caught wind of Lil, they stopped their malamute cries. Feeding them dried moose jerky, she promised them a long run in the morning. She patted each on the head and slipped through Tealand's unlocked door. After disrobing, she laid on the comfortable bed. *I'd better enjoy this because after tomorrow, it'll be ten days of sleeping in the sled,* she thought. Moments later, Lil was fast asleep.

Early the next morning, Lotty woke Lil. "Get up. It's four-thirty. Let's take one last shower, eat breakfast and get going. A storm's on the horizon. I don't want to fight against it. I've already taken care of the dogs. Get up, sleepyhead."

"Oh, this bed is so comfortable. Can we take it with us?" Lil said teasingly.

"Silly girl, get up. Remember, we're mushing northwest to Nome. Now get up," Lotty said tossing a pillow at her sleepy sister.

"I'm sleeping in today. Go without me."

"I'll eat your sausage if you don't start moving."

"Thought last night you would've had enough sausage," Lil giggled.

"You're one sick puppy. Get up," Lotty said stripping off the covers from her sister.

"Hey, stop that. I'm up. Just give me a few minutes, okay?"

"Anna Rose is cooking biscuits and gravy, sausage, eggs and pancakes. The kitchen smells terrific. Do you know the best part? We don't have to clean up the mess. What luxury."

Getting dressed Lil said, "Great. Enjoy it while you can because the next few weeks are going to be self-sacrificing with a basic menu of dried meat and oatmeal. Speaking of self-sacrificing, how was your visit with the self-centered mountain man?"

Lotty smiled. "It was fabulous. We made it all night."

"Oh, please, spare me the details."

Glowing with sexual pleasure, Lotty dropped her shoulders. Relaxed and starry eyed, she grinned and thought about her mountain lover, casually laughing. "You should try it sometime, Lil. It's so calming. I slept so soundly…well, in between sessions."

"Quit, Lotty. I don't want to spoil Anna Rose's breakfast before I make it to the kitchen. My stomach is churning just thinking about sleeping with that dirty bearded man. How can you stand it? No, don't answer that. Let's change the subject. Okay?"

"Come on little virgin, let's take a shower," Lotty said teasingly. "I know I could sure use one. Yes, indeed." Lotty laughed. Lil pretended to gag.

They walked downstairs, popping their heads into the kitchen. Anna Rose was placing a full plate of sausage in the oven. Lil said, "Good morning, smells great. We'll be back after a quick shower. Okay?"

"Morning, help yourselves," Anna Rose said and went back to her hot stove where the tops of her pancakes bubbled, begging to be turned over.

Fifteen minutes later, Sara and Dorothy strode into the kitchen. "Breakfast always smells better when someone else is cooking," Sara said kissing her sister's cheek. "Looks like you haven't forgotten anything. What can I do?"

"Set out the dishes and utensils, please. We can just serve ourselves. The twins should be out anytime now. How are you today, Mama?"

"I'd be better if I had a cup of coffee. It's too damn early to socialize. We even beat the roosters up this morning."

"Unlikely, Mother," Sara said.

Shrugging, Dorothy continued, "Why are the twins going out into this dreadful weather? If their father had any sense, he would stop them in their tracks. What's so important about winning a dangerous race?"

"Dorothy, you haven't changed a bit," Lotty said as she entered the kitchen. "Our Pa supports this training run with two conditions: we had to return within six weeks, and his meals had to be prepared and frozen before we departed." Lotty chuckled. Dorothy was the only mother that the twins knew, their mother died from hemorrhaging after the double birth, leaving Dorothy, George and the twin's father to raise them on the Sutton homestead. A hardship for Dorothy, as the two men, best friends since childhood, worked from dusk to dawn. The twin's father never remarried.

"Good morning, Dorothy," Lil said as she squeezed Dorothy's shoulders and then pecked her on the cheek. Lil pinned back her hair with a green and white beaded barrette, reminding Dorothy of Anna Rose—the two were similar in nature; Lotty and Sara were more headstrong like their fathers. "It's good to see you. How have you been? I guess by now, you've heard all about our journey. What do you think?"

"Well, I think it's crazy. If I were your—"

"Breakfast…," Anna Rose said. "What would you like on your plate, Mama, the works?"

Realizing that her opinion did not matter, Dorothy's shoulders slumped. "I'm not an invalid. I can serve myself."

"Get your plate then," Anna Rose said handing the twins their plates.

Everyone devoured the heavy breakfast. Lotty and Lil cleared the table and offered their apologies for having to eat and mush onward.

"We need to beat that storm. It's moving slowly now, but in a few hours, it could be right on top of us. It could affect our time trial."

The Sutton women followed the twins outside. They watched as the twins harnessed, hitched together and encouraged their dog team. Just before their departure, Anna Rose handed Lil a brown bag filled with freshly baked oatmeal cookies and two jars of smoked salmon. Thrilled with the scrumptious delicacies, the twins hugged and thanked her. The others exchanged their good-byes, as well.

"I want to see those kids of yours when we return. You can't keep them hidden," Lil said teasing Sara. Sara laughed and promised to let them out of their locked closets. The twins laughed at Sara's jousting. Dorothy's face tightened with dismay while Anna Rose giggled.

Sheba, the lead female malamute jumped, yapping at Lotty to let the team run. The other four-legged racers reacted, increasing their howling volume to near deafening decibels. Racers and humans felt jubilant, euphoric for the impending perilous trek.

Anna Rose felt a slight bit of envy, but she knew her limits. A homemaker by nature, her only desire to achieve such great feats resided deep within her, an area of the self that had recently forced itself upward into her consciousness. Jessy's death had stirred positive results.

Sara handed Lil two handwritten letters. Lil frowned when she read the envelope addressed to Frank Tealand, surmising that it contained a death notification to Jessy's brother. A letter of disappointment for Frank as Jessy had not spoken to him in over 25 years. Jessy split their mother's upper lip with his fist; Frank's condemning remarks triggered Jessy's silence. Mrs. Shirley Knatishich, a longtime friend of Dorothy's would receive the second letter. Lil placed them in her breast pocket, zipped it closed and then tucked herself inside the sled basket.

Sara yelled over the dogs, "Thanks." Proud to know the twins, thrilled for their new adventure, knowing that they would become successful as Iditarod competitors, Sara's smile beamed congratulatory sentiments though she wished her father and the twin's mother could witness the passion behind the team.

"Hike, hike," Lotty yelled commanding the team. Immediately, all twelve dogs moved out of the parking lot, leaving the three Sutton's to wave good-bye. Cautioning to keep the sled balanced, neither twin returned the gesture. Lotty had her hands full. "Haw, haw." The team turned left down River Road.

The commotion of the dog team echoed up the canyon. Trapper stood on the edge of the deck, listening and wishing his lover a safe return. Moments later, the dog team synchronized their cadence transporting the twins into the unknown.

Sara walked her mother home. After entering her own cabin, she checked on her sleeping children. With doting affection, she pondered what adulthood had in store for them, wondered if they would leave the homestead and become world explorers—possibly in search of a different lifestyle. Adding another log to the fire, reaching for a book that she previously had started, she laid on the couch and then wrapped herself in a blanket. After reading a short chapter of *Home School Mothers,* she dozed off.

Anna Rose quickly washed and dried the dishes. Feeling the lull of the early hour events, she decided to take a nap, waking just before Tealand's was due to open on this Saturday morning.

CONFESSIONS

On Monday morning, Trapper began his surveillance. The forest provided his camouflage. Cautiously, he moved among the homestead timbered boundary while Derek performed his chores. Derek's day as a workhand was typical. He ate breakfast with his boss. Then Sara sent him out on predetermined tasks. In his single room, he prepared his own lunch. He completed his day by feeding the animals and dining in the homestead cabin. Trapper observed that Derek and Sara's interaction was strictly a business relationship. Derek did not linger the evenings away in the homestead cabin.

These mundane activities continued for three straight days, boring Trapper. At times, he felt that he was wasting his time. It dawned on him that the twins could have been wrong—a case of mistaken identity or a hoax. This only frustrated Trapper further. He wondered whether to continue his watch, but intuition drove him to endure Derek's tedious daily activities. All the while being thankful that he controlled his own life, and his survival depended solely on his wilderness skills and cunning tactics.

Still there was no evidence that Derek stole his belongings. Derek seemed perfectly normal as he worked through the day. The uneventful workdays caused Trapper to question the twin's accusations.

On the fifth afternoon, Trapper peered into Derek's living quarters. He etched back a layer of ice that covered a dingy window. *Great, it's empty,* Trapper thought. He waited patiently before stepping around the corner—all clear. Taking a deep breath, he proceeded to the front door. The cold doorknob fused him in place.

"Mommy, Mommy, come quick," Mathew yelled pointing at Trapper.

"Shit," Trapper whispered ducking his head. He fled behind the shack and ran through the woods to George Creek. With shallow breathing, he cursed at the noisy little brat that spotted him. Looking back across Tundra Rose Lane, no one had followed him. He conjured a plan to eliminate his visible steps leading to Hoss' watering hole. After covering his tracks, Trapper cautiously walked on the thinning creek ice behind Hoss' shack, leaving only Hoss' boot imprints. Trapper skillfully hiked up the steep incline hillside that led to his cabin.

He hoped that Mathew would not recognize him. The chances were slim, since the two scarcely saw each other. Trapper felt that his secret vigil was undiscovered. He decided to continue his investigation tomorrow, with more caution and a different strategy.

Meanwhile, back at the homestead, Sara guided Mathew into the cabin.

"But Mom, I know there was a man," Mathew said with assurance.

"I know you did, son. I'll have Derek look into it." Without scaring him further, she left the subject for later discussions.

She looked up at the darkened sky. The day's light sunk behind the Talkeetna mountain range. It was sure to snow within the next twenty-four hours. Sara prepared an early dinner with hopes of taking the afternoon's frightening incident off Mathew's mind. He had talked about it all day. She would convince him to retire early, so she and Derek could discuss the trespasser in private.

Derek knocked twice and entered the homestead cabin. Mathew clung to Sara's leg until he recognized their hired hand. Hypersensitive, Mathew raced to Derek's side. "There was a man today comin' out of your bunkhouse. I scared him away. He took off running. Momma couldn't even catch him. Right, Mom?"

Derek looked dubiously at Sara. He picked up Mathew and said, "You frightened him away, did you? How can I repay you?"

Mathew smiled, "Awe, it was nothing, Derek. You don't need to pay me back."

"Sara, what's he talking about?"

Sara swayed everyone's attention. "We're making ice cream. Would you like to help?" She handed Derek a clean bucket and a jar of chocolate sauce.

Reading Sara's covert dialogue, Derek said, "Sure, I'd be happy to help."

Derek piled snow into the bucket then plopped handfuls of snow between the tin of soupy ingredients and the outer shell. Georgina layered the snow with rock salt while her brother turned the handle. The mixture solidified slowly as the two took turns rotating the handle. Derek continued placing snow around the frosty cylinder. Soon the children became weary and relinquished the handle over to Derek. Finally, Sara declared the ice cream finished. Mathew and Georgina filled their bowls with delicious chocolate ice cream. They thoroughly enjoyed the infrequent treat.

After ushering the kids off to bed, Sara served Derek his evening meal. Assured that the children were asleep, she informed him about Mathew's sighting.

"I was just there for the last two hours, and I didn't notice anything missing. Are you sure he was coming from the inside?"

"No, I'm not sure," Sara said glancing over her shoulder toward the children's bedroom. "Keep your voice down. I don't want to wake the kids. They've had enough drama for one day. It took me all day to calm them. Jeez, Mathew just tormented Georgina all afternoon."

Derek nodded. "It's too late tonight to follow the tracks, so I'll follow them tomorrow. Hum, it's supposed to snow tonight. Nevertheless, I'll check it out."

Pretending to be asleep, Mathew relaxed after hearing Derek confirm his search plans. Knowing he and his mother trusted Derek completely, Mathew's fear dissolved and sleep came easily.

Derek said irritably, "I can't believe that someone would try ripping off the homestead—someone's always here. My guess is that Hoss is up to no good. He's probably gone completely mad living up there all alone. Maybe tomorrow I should pay him a visit?"

Sara became worried. "Oh, I don't know. If he has gone mad—"

"Don't worry. I'll have plenty of protection. I won't let him know I'm there until he sees the end of my shotgun. I'll be fine."

"I don't feel good about this. Make sure you tell me before you go, and I'll keep an eye out for you. If you don't come back, I'll send in Trapper. Okay?"

"That won't be necessary, but okay, if it makes you feel better." Derek headed for the front door. Tonight, for just a moment, he stood over the threshold trying to sense any intruders lurking in the darkness. Satisfied with everyone's safety, he stepped outside. Large snowflakes fell on his shoulders. A candle burning in his makeshift kitchen marked his destination through the pitch-black surroundings.

The next morning, rural residents woke to three-feet of freshly packed snow. The clouds had released their hefty mass and moved east; another low-pressure system assembled behind its predecessor. It was a rejuvenating site. Pristinely the snow covered the homestead animal waste. The trail to the Quonset hut leveled, roadways sealed out travelers, rooftops weighed heavily on log foundations. Hurricane County waited as Mother Nature unleashed her impending drama.

166

Bacon sizzled as Sara lifted it from its grease. Derek strolled backward through the heavy front door. "...okay, you have fun now," he said to the children.

"Good morning," Sara said as she flipped over three fried eggs.

"Good morning. The kids are havin' a great time in the snow."

Sara nodded smiling. "Are you still considering visiting Hoss?"

Derek sat down at the table. "Yes. I want to check him out. I need to see what he's doing. I'll head up after breakfast. It's still okay with you, right Boss?"

Reaching for an antique plate with a mountain background and snowcapped cabins resting on a majestic terrain Sara placed bacon, eggs and toast on it, and then handed it to Derek. "That's fine with me, but please be careful. I can't afford to lose you."

"Don't worry, I'll be fine. It'll only take an hour or so."

Adding coffee to Derek's meal, Sara smiled apprehensively then sat down across from him and discussed his duties for the day. "Providing you come back, the walkways need shoveling, and it's time to start shoveling the roofs. The snow load is adding up. The sooner we get rid of it the easier it'll be to manage. I'll scoop the edges clear. For fun, we can throw snowballs at the kids. They love a good rally now and then."

Derek smiled as he dragged his toast crust through the remaining egg yolks. Sara poured him another cup of coffee. For the second time that morning, she cleared the kitchen table.

With a full stomach, Derek pushed his chair back and stretched. He swallowed the last of his coffee then announced that he would return in one hour.

Nervously, Sara walked him to the door and said, "Come straight back here."

Derek nodded and waved. Back at the bunkhouse, he loaded his shotgun and retrieved his snowshoes. By way of George Creek, he hiked toward Hoss' cabin.

From the levee, snow-covered branches cloaked Hoss' shack. Smoke swirled out from the open-ended stove stack. Empty metal burn barrels lined the backyard. Junk piled high shrouded the dwelling's sidewall. Derek prowled further up the frozen creek until he was directly in line with Hoss' back door. He noticed a freshly punched hole in the creek and fresh tracks leading back to the shack. There was no one in sight. Derek moved in closer.

Kneeling down, hiding below the creek's wintery ridge, he watched for signs of movement coming from inside the shack. The logs that provided Hoss with shelter were black with mold. The window condensation caused the panes to rot. The center of the roof sagged from the heavy snowfall. The dilapidated home surprisingly stood the test of the Great North. *What a dump,* Derek thought waiting patiently.

Inside, a silhouette passed by the dingy window. Derek moved stealthily and quietly, positioning himself behind the piles of garbage near the back door. He removed his snowshoes. Next, he lifted a tin can from the garbage heap then side armed the rusty metal toward the back window. It hit hard against the rotting window frame. The noise drew Hoss outside.

"Toss your gun, Hoss," Derek said pointing his gun into Hoss' temple. Hoss threw his rifle in the snow. It sank. "Good. Now, we're gonna play question and answer. Okay?"

Hoss stiffened, remaining motionless. His rotting gums stunk. Dirty teeth sharpened against each other as Hoss tightened his jawbone. Seething, Hoss recalled the first time a loaded pistol met his temple. Experience ordered him to relax, listen, accommodate the handler, and then strike back once he gained the trespassers' confidence.

"That was a question," Derek reiterated.

"Okay. What do you want?"

"I ask, you answer. Got it?" Derek pressed the cold metal further into Hoss' temple.

"Got it, you pig."

"From the looks of your humble abode, Hoss, you're the pig. Consider cleaning this dump up before it burns to the ground. I would hate to find your crispy body under all this rubble."

"Fuck you, Lackey."

"Not my brand but thanks for the offer. What were you doing snooping around the Sutton homestead yesterday?"

"I don't know what you're talkin' about. I wasn't anywhere near the place."

"I saw you comin' out of my bunkhouse. You ran when the boy screamed. Tell me, what were you lookin' for?" Derek steadied his aim.

Hoss turned slightly. "Lackey, you got the wrong guy. I was out shooting snow hare yesterday. Come see fer yourself. I got 'em hangin' in the arctic entry."

Derek was at a standstill. He allowed the filthy, crazy man to guide him inside. "If you're lying, this gun'll make a nasty hole in your head." His gun bobbed on Hoss' spine as they walked through the trashy cabin. The smell of urine and waste permeated the dwelling. Derek gagged, placing his free arm over his mouth. Fresh kill hung from the arctic entry ceiling. The skinless rabbits hung upside down, exposing their red muscles, sinew and bones—frozen and preserved in Hoss' make shift freezer.

Derek realized that Hoss was not his trespasser. He slammed the butt end of his gun against the backside of Hoss' head. Hoss' knees buckled, and he fell to the filthy floor. After Derek left the soiled cabin, he filled his lungs with clean, crisp air, managing not to vomit, despising the scent that would follow him throughout the day.

Derek found Sara rummaging through the shed searching for a second snow shovel. "If it wasn't Hoss, then who was it?" Sara asked.

"I don't know, Sara. I wasn't there. Only Mattie saw the guy. It could've been anyone. Most all of the men living here have beards and carry guns. The snow buried the tracks, so we'll just have to keep a closer eye on the place. Come on. Let's get to that roof." Disguising his anxiety by not making eye contact with Sara, Derek walked out of the barn-style shed, shovels in hand, ready to work though troubled by the intruder's identity and criminal intent.

Sara followed him. "What about the kids? Do you think the stranger will hurt them? I'm worried, Derek. It just doesn't make sense."

Perturbed, Derek turned around and said, "Look Sara, there's nothing we can do. All the clues we have are gone. So, I suggest you forget about it. Besides, if you keep worrying, the kids will notice and you'll scare them, too. All we can do is watch the homestead more. I won't let anyone hurt you or the kids. Now, come on. Let's have a little fun with Mattie and Georgina."

Stunned by Derek's upbeat mood, Sara stood watching him climb the ladder. With his shovel in one hand, he effortlessly mounted the roof. She realized that he was right; solving the trespasser incident would have to wait. She swiftly climbed the ladder. Once on the roof, she sunk deep into Derek's footsteps.

Down below and unaware, Mathew and Georgina played around their blue and red snow castle. It was customary to spray their snow creations with food coloring. Sara and Derek balled up their ammunition. Then Sara yelled, "All castle dwellers prepare for an invasion. We've come to capture your Princess, so we can force her to marry the wicked Lord of Suttonville."

The children giggled with excitement. They scattered into the castle tunnels. Their smiling faces stuck out from both entrances while their arms frantically pulled snow around the openings. Sara tossed a snowball into the air. It missed the castle wall. Another compact ball landed near the other side of the castle. Derek joined in the fun, launching a snowball.

"Castle dwellers, prepare to be bombed," Derek said with a deep voice as he rapidly fired the remaining snowballs. The children giggled and ducked inside—a winter tradition everyone enjoyed.

Still poised on the roof, the invaders further exhausted themselves by removing most of the roof's snow load. Their muscles ached. Knowing the dangers of not completing this task, collapsing rooftops killed several elders each year. Lazy or drunken homesteaders also met their death with the crushing weight of Alaskan snowfalls.

After eating tomato soup and grilled cheese sandwiches, Sara sent her little darlings off to their rooms to read. In the process, they would take a nap—a reprieve Sara relished.

Sara returned to the kitchen. To Derek she said, "You're going to have to save the rest of your strength for later. I'm going to take a hot bath, soak the pain from my aching back. Take the rest of the day off. I'll see you back here for dinner."

"You'll get no argument from me. Thanks for the lunch." Immediately, he left the peaceful cabin. Derek took advantage of his time off and strolled down to Ravens. "Give me a whiskey—straight up."

"Comin' at ya," Russell said. "I haven't seen you around much. Has that boss of yours been keeping you busy?"

"Yeah, you know, winter always adds to my list of chores. We shoveled the roof today. There must have been five-feet of wet snow. Man, it was heavy. My muscles ache. I think Sara, tough as she is, wore herself out. She gave me the rest of the day off, which was all right with me."

Russell poured Derek a second drink. "Thanks for spending your time off at Ravens. It's been quiet around here lately. Ruby is about to go crazy. Her last shipment of booze is a week late. Plus, she has the Annual Spring Break-Up Frenzy planned for two weeks from now. You know when Ruby's nuts, she makes everyone else nuts, too. I wish I could take the rest of this week off, especially if the booze doesn't make it here soon. Speaking of trades, I'll finish that roof—"

"No way," Derek interrupted. "Riddled with words that woman is. She would've driven me out of Hurricane in one day. I feel for ya, man." Derek slammed down his empty shot glass. "One more and I'll be on my way. I hate to leave you at a time like this," Derek snickered.

"Sure you do." Russell said as he filled Derek's shot glass.

"By the way, Mathew saw a bearded man coming out of my place yesterday. Have you heard anything about a trespasser?"

Russell shook his head. "No, the grapevine's been quiet on that one. But I'll keep my ears open for you."

With his shot glass raised, Derek said, "Thanks, here's to women bosses." Russell nodded. The whiskey warmed Derek as he slid off the leather barstool and waved good-bye.

Mathew woke Sara from a deep sleep. "Mommy, can we come out of our rooms now?"

"What time is it?" Sara asked groggy.

Mathew eagerly ran to the clock. He stood underneath it. "The big hand is on the two and the little hand is on the...well, it's between the four and five."

Sara could not believe how long she had slept. She surmised that her hot bath had relaxed her into a deep slumber. "The clock reads ten after four, Mathew. Go check on your sister." Chilled, Sara checked the woodstove. As she opened the cast iron door, the red hot coals expanded. She stoked the burning embers then added a birch log. The cast iron teapot used as a humidifier was empty. Its bottom had turned white, warping the thinning metal. It reminded her of her father. Many times as a child, he scolded her for not keeping the pot full of water, her only chore. His soft scolding demeanor was an attribute that she inherited, though even as an adult, she still could not manage to keep that darn pot full. She heard his reprimanding voice. She looked upward, "I got it, Dad," she said with a smile.

Mathew reported back, "Georgina is sleeping on the floor. Her Husky puppy puzzle is scattered all over the room. Why can't she..."

"Thank you. Now, could you fill this pot for your Mother?" Sara headed into the children's room, glad to be passing down her childhood chore. "Be careful to not burn yourself. Fill it with snow using your scoop and stand on your stool, please."

Mathew said impatiently, "I will, Mom." Sara smiled at her mirror image, her growing, independent young son.

Sitting on the bed, Sara gently awoke her daughter. Georgina fussed as Sara picked her up. "No, Mommy," she cried. Sara rocked the irritable child until she was fully coherent, patiently waiting for the day when Georgina needed less coddling. Immediately, she regretted her thoughts of wanting her motherhood responsibilities to diminish, knowing that one day she would miss these precious moments.

As Georgina rubbed her eyes, Sara asked, "Did you have a nice nap? I see you have a good start on your Husky friends. Aren't they cute?"

Without responding, Georgina slid out of Sara's arms onto the floor where she continued piecing together the Husky mother and her playful pups puzzle. Sara quietly left the room.

With both kids occupied, Sara removed her robe. With feelings of femininity, she put on her sexiest panties, dotted her neck with perfume then finished dressing in tight jeans and a jersey blouse. Without the constraints of a bra, her bountiful breasts swayed, her nipples rose against the silky cloth. She further indulged herself with a sexy crime novel.

****

As the Alaskan daylight hours increased, Trapper had to be extra careful. He camouflaged his remaining facial features for his sixth straight day of surveillance. Dusk came and went; darkness saturated the canyon. He loaded his gun, placing extra shells in his coat pocket. He grabbed a baseball cap, headed out of the log cabin, then strapped on his snowshoes. In his mind, he devised a reasonably safe escape route, but was unsure that any plan would work in such tight surroundings. The new snow prevented a quick retreat. He started his descent toward Derek's home. Minutes later, Trapper stood near a back window. Candles lit the bunkhouse, shadows shifted on the far inside wall. The recent snowstorm left a steep edge around the wooden house, creating a slippery vista in which to spy.

Trapper leaned his weapon against a cottonwood tree, unlaced his snowshoes then strapped them to his back. There were no obstacles, no metal traps, no signs for discovery, so he confidently grabbed his gun and stepped underneath the four-paneled window, the eave providing a slim, yet stable lookout point. With his ear close to the wall, he heard Derek and a woman laughing. Surprised that Derek had a female companion, he listened closely trying to identify the voice. Trapper repositioned himself so he could see the woman's face.

Shocked, Trapper's eyes widened and his mouth dropped open. "Sara?" he whispered. *How long has this been going on? That bitch. I don't care if she does have two kids. She's dead. They both are,* he thought. Trapper closed his mouth and eavesdropped further.

A yellow sheet draped over Sara's hips and buttocks, covering Derek's legs. Straddled on top of him, her full breasts bounced, moving back and forth as her pelvis thrust against Derek's midsection. The couple laughed periodically then became serious as their sweat-glistened bodies synchronized and each stroke intensified their climax. Their pleasure became Trapper's amusement.

As Trapper watched, he became aroused. His hatred plagued his senses triggering his erection to fluctuate between hard and soft. While covertly investigating, enjoying Sara's robust bounty and the live entertainment, he allowed the distraction.

The lovers soon arched and moaned with relief, decompressing, resting their bodies as one. Soon they once again became playful. Derek motioned for Sara to close her eyes and hold out her hands. Still seated on top of him, Derek dangled a gold nugget necklace in front of her. She opened her eyes. Astonished by the generous gift her face lit up. Derek placed the shiny gold piece around her neck. Their lovemaking commenced again.

"Thief," Trapper whispered as his passion to kill rose within. His father's condemning voice screeched through his mind. While Trappers' thoughts burned with murderous desire, he readied himself to rush into the shabby bunkhouse, seize his property and slay both naked lovers. He focused his blurred vision. *I've got to think*, he thought. He continued to mull over a plan of attack, but became increasingly interested in scanning Sara's body as she fucked Derek.

After the long session ended, Sara dressed. With a sheet wrapped around his waist, Derek walked her to the door. Trapper knelt below the window, listening closely. Sara stepped outside and said, "I need you to drive to Hurks tomorrow after breakfast. The kids' homeschool package has arrived."

"No problem."

"Thanks for the necklace. It's lovely."

"No, thank you. Sex with you is awesome."

"Of course it is," she teased then turned, returning to the homestead cabin.

Trapper imagined that both Sara and Derek were smiling from ear to ear. As soon as Trapper heard Sara close the homestead cabin door, he trekked back through the woods toward his cabin. With a new plan and somewhat sexually satisfied, Trapper was pleased.

Early the next morning, Trapper packed a few tools in a backpack and parked his rig in front of George Creek. He followed the trail back to Derek's home and waited.

As scheduled, Derek left the homestead after breakfast. Anxious to get started, Trapper wedged his crowbar between three back wallboards. After crawling into the warm shack, he locked the front door and began his search.

First, he looked under the bed. There was nothing but dust and an old pair of black boots. He ransacked the kitchen cupboards, tossing canned food and cereal out onto the floor. Next, he targeted the chest of drawers, throwing the clothes onto the scattered food items. Erupting, Trapper smashed his hand on a drawer then realized that his anger was getting him nowhere. He sat on the bed to collect himself. Disappointed, he hung his head low. *It's got to be here somewhere,* he thought. A minute later, he kicked the multi-colored braided rug away from his feet. Sure enough, there was a loose floorboard. Skillfully, he removed the stained piece of wood and stared into the obscure narrow cache. Furs lined the hidden stash. Trapper retrieved a lantern, lit the oily wick then placed it on the floor. He removed one of the furs. Surprised by its heaviness, Trapper unrolled the beaver pelt. "Bingo" he said. "That crook is gonna pay."

He loaded two backpacks to full capacity. After replacing the board and lantern, he unlocked the door. Trapper hiked back to his truck, devising plan two. Once securing his property in his cabin, he carefully returned to Derek's home.

Inside the bunkhouse, Trapper positioned a wooden chair in the far corner, sat down propping his feet up on the bed. Carefully, he loaded sleek, silver bullets into his six-shooter then spun the barrel. The sound of the metal bearings raised his adrenaline. Resting his method of justice on his lap, he waited patiently. An hour and fifteen minutes later, Trapper heard Derek's truck pull into Sara's driveway. When the vehicle door slammed shut, Trapper peeked out of the front window. He saw Derek hand over the package to Sara. She greeted him with enthusiasm while fondling her necklace. They waved each other good-bye. Trapper bolted back into the chair, pointing the revolver directly at the front door. "Revenge always leads to someone gettin' killed," Trapper said with a demonic smile.

Mindlessly, Derek entered the bunkhouse. Trapper pulled back the hammer, startling Derek.

"What the hell...Trapper? What have you done?" Derek said stepping on the mixture of scattered food and underclothes. "What do you want?"

Casually, Trapper stood up, pointed the gun at the roof just above Derek's head. He pulled the trigger three times. Derek instinctively ducked. The bullets splintered the old roof and wood fragments fell to the floor. Dust powdered Derek's sandy-brown hair and his red and black flannel shirt. Without words, Trapper waited gleaming with pride as his plot unfolded.

Just as he planned, Sara came running into the bunkhouse, armed. She hollered, "What the hell's going on here? Derek, are you hurt? Trapper what are you doin' here?" The whole scene confused her.

"Thanks for joining us, Sara. Derek has a few things that he would like to tell you. Isn't that right, Chad?"

Trapper added another bullet to the roof. Ancient lumber crumbled onto the bed. Startled, Sara flinched and screamed, "Trapper, stop."

Trapper pointed his gun at Chad's heart. "Tell her, or the next one's goin' straight through you. You know what I'm talkin' about. Tell her how you murdered your own father."

"What?" Sara asked grabbing for her gold nugget.

Chad dropped his façade. "It's true, Sara. I killed my Pa. That was a long time ago. I've regretted it ever since. My real name is Chad Westler."

Disappointed and confused, Sara looked at Trapper. "Trapper, why are you here? Did you come just to ruin Derek's, I mean, Chad's life?"

Waving his gun Trapper said, "Tell her Chad. Tell her about how you've been ripping people off."

"Just put the gun away. I'll tell her everything."

"No chance of that, Chad."

Chad sat Sara down on the bed. He held her hands. "I'm sorry, Sara. I never meant to hurt you. You know how I feel about you, the kids and the homestead. I need you and working here has made me feel...whole. We're a family."

Dumbfounded Sara abruptly stood up and said, "So, I guess this belongs to you, Trapper." Remorseful, she handed over the gold nugget necklace, staring death into Chad's eyes. "I'm sorry for all the trouble that we've caused you."

Trapper nodded as he placed the final article of stolen property into his pocket. "Look Sara, all I wanted was my stuff, and to find out if you had anything to do with the robbery. Now I know you didn't. You didn't even know who you were screwing." Trapper laughed. "I got what I wanted. Do you want me to throw this piece of trash in his truck and send him on his way?"

Painfully fuming, Sara looked deep into Chad's eyes and firmly said, "No. I'll take care of him myself." With vengeance, she pointed her gun at the man who had fooled her keen and astute instincts. Livid, her eyes filled with madness. She held steady aim.

"Well, it looks like my work's done here. I hope Sara doesn't rough you up too much." Trapper laughed as he squatted, crouching through the three missing wallboards.

Angered by Trapper's ego, Chad hurled a can of green beans across the room, shattering a stained-glass mirror, the mosaic pattern seemingly resembled Chad's colorful past, his hidden schemes destroyed. Shards of truth glistened on the wooden floor.

Pressing her gun into Chad's back, Sara said, "Gather your belongings and get the hell off my land. I trusted you. You've betrayed my family and me. Get out of here, and don't ever come back. If I ever see you, it'll be a good excuse to shoot you. And believe me, I'll put the word out that you're a thief and murderer. All of Hurricane County will know who and what you are. You'll be a trespasser throughout this territory, Chad Westler."

Chad defended himself. "Who'll take care of the homestead? You can't possibly do it all by yourself. Who'll protect you and your family? Tell me, who'll get rid of the next Jess Tealand?"

"Ah," Sara gasped. "Old man Kurtz knew—"

"That's right. I made damn sure that Tealand never hurt Anna Rose again. I did it for you. I'm the best thing that ever happened to this family of widows."

"You cold blooded murderer. Get the fuck off my land, you deceitful, ungrateful, son-of-a-bitch. Get moving," Sara yelled.

Sara and her rifle escorted Chad to his truck. Exasperated, she watched with hatred and disbelief as Chad sped out of the driveway.

Infuriated, she returned to the inside of the homestead cabin, unloaded her weapon and placed it back in the gun rack. For a moment, she supported her head on the glass door, not allowing herself to cry. She locked the gun cabinet while two frightened faces watched her. Immediately straightening, Sara said, "Everything's all right, kids. Derek and I just had…a disagreement."

"Why were you yelling, Mama?" Georgina innocently asked.

Sitting down on the couch, Sara patted the seat cushions. Her children came to her. Georgina crawled up onto Sara's lap while Mathew sat next to them.

Gently, she announced that Derek would no longer be working on the homestead. She sheltered her children from the full truth; an arrow of pain impelled her heart, though convinced her decision was fitting, yet a bullet through Derek's heart seemed more apropos.

"Couldn't he just say he was sorry, and we could forgive him? Aren't we supposed to forgive?" Mathew asked.

"Yes, Mathew. We are supposed to forgive. In time, I will forgive him. But for now, I feel it is in the best interest of our family if he worked elsewhere. It's important for me to trust whoever works for us. I have two little ones to protect, you know?" Sara ruffled Georgina's hair. "Does that answer your question?"

The children nodded. Georgina wrapped her arms around Sara's neck and squeezed it tight. "I'm sorry Derek made you mad, Mommy."

Sara returned the hug. "Thanks, baby. I'm okay."

"Yeah, I'm sorry too, Mama." Mathew said with compassion.

Sara huddled her little darlings together and said, "Well, we always have one another. I love you both very much." Sara kissed her kids' foreheads and scooted them off the couch. "Now, go play. Why don't you invite Grandma Sutton up for dinner? I'm cooking up a big pot of spaghetti."

"She loves spaghetti," Georgina shouted. Excited, the children layered themselves in snowsuits and raced out the door. Sara took a few minutes for herself and then followed them outside. Informing Anna Rose weighed heavily on her mind; a step backwards could crush her delicate sister, as she reluctantly walked into Tealand's café misery overwhelmed her posture.

"Are you killin' chickens out of season or what?" Anna Rose asked jokingly.

Sara glanced over to the locals drinking coffee, watching for perked ears, she pointed Anna Rose toward the kitchen to speak in private.

Anna Rose refilled their cups then entered the kitchen. "What's up, Sis? You look upset?"

"I'm furious. I had to fire Derek or Chad," Sara said depressed.

"Why? What are you talkin' about?"

Sara held back her tears. No one knew that she was romantically involved with Derek. Now, her lover just turned murderer—murdering her only sister's husband—was a fate that even Sara could not have predicted.

"Sit down, Anna Rose. Chad is Derek's real name. He stole Trapper's belongings and...he killed Jess."

Aghast, Anna Rose sat stunned, processing the unbelievable account, her mind spun in every direction.

"Are you all right?" Sara asked.

"How? Why? I can't believe this. This is too unreal. I'm shocked. I don't even know what to say."

"I'm so sorry, Anna Rose. I feel responsible," Sara said holding Anna Rose's hands.

"Derek or Chad killed Jess?" Anna Rose repeated in disbelief. "Maybe we should move to the city? Hurricane is becoming dangerous."

"It's always been dangerous. The city is no place for us. I would never raise my kids there. We have better odds living in the bush. I have to tell Mama. She's going to come unglued."

Anna Rose thought for a moment. "She'll probably cheer for Derek, I mean, Chad. We'll never hear the end of it when she discovers that we both made bad choices. Let's keep it simple. We tell her *only* about Trapper's robbery. By the way, how did Trap find all this out?"

"Everything happened so fast, I didn't think to ask him."

Anna Rose turned her dismay into concern for Sara, "What are you going to do about the homestead?"

"I don't know. I'm so outraged and so confused I can't think straight."

Anna Rose seized her opportunity, "What about Bryan Smith? He might be willing to work for trade."

"Bryan Smith? How could you think that I would hire him?" Sara asked astonished.

"Well, he is available."

"I don't like him. He's hiding something. I can tell."

"Like you could tell that Chad was hiding something?"

"Don't turn into our Mother," Sara scolded. "Chad and I were…involved romantically, so I might have mistaken lust for honesty." Appalled by her misperceptions about Chad, hiring a murderer sickened her. The fact that she had placed her children and family in jeopardy horrified her. Embarrassed, Sara hung her head.

"No way, you and Chad had a fling? That's news." Anna Rose asked, thinking about what a great scandal this would make in Hurricane County. Sara read her thoughts.

"Don't you dare tell Mama or anyone else for that matter. Promise me that you won't."

"This is big, Sara. Telling Mama might take the pressure off of me."

"Promise me, right now. I would be mortified if she spouted off in front of the kids. They'd be so confused. I don't want to expose them to 'romantic relationships' just yet."

"Good one, use the kids against me. Of course, I won't tell her. I'm just teasing you. So… we have a deal: you don't tell her about Chad killing Jess, and I won't tell her about your affair. Deal?"

"Deal. Thanks, Anna Rose. I feel just awful. You're taking the murder of Jess far too well. What gives?"

"It's a terrible thing, Chad murdering Jess and all, but I'm so much happier without him. Please don't mention *that* to anyone. I don't want to appear insensitive, but he was a brute. I can admit that now. My life is so much better without him. My ribs have healed. My mind is in a good place. I feel strong inside."

Sara half-smiled and said, "Okay. But that makes it two of your lies to my one lie. You'll owe me later."

"I'm in and I'll pay you back when you most need it."

"I'm so thankful that I have you Anna Rose."

"I love my big sister and couldn't live without you either."

Taking a deep breath, the sisters embraced, mentally grasping for their dependable past and grappling with their uncertain future.

Cautiously Anna Rose asked, "So what about Bryan. He might be a good worker?"

Suddenly, Sara realized she wrongfully convicted Bryan for slaying Jess. At this point, despondent and hardened, she withheld an apology. As man's physical strength was imperative for the homestead's survival, Sara counted Bryan among the weak and unreliable.

"He's a nice guy, Sara. Just give him a chance. Would you like me to ask him?"

"Shit, after all this business with Chad, how can I trust my own judgment? This horrible incident has completely unnerved me."

"Oh, you'll trust again. Somehow, we always do."

Sara sighed and released her anger toward Bryan. "He seems kind of weak. Do you think he can do the work? I guess I don't have much choice." Incoherently, Sara left the kitchen. Before leaving Tealand's, she turned around and said, "We're having spaghetti tonight. Mama will be there. You're welcome to join us. Please, don't leave me alone with her." Sara's eyes pleaded with Anna Rose to attend.

"I'll be there. Six o'clock?" Anna Rose asked.

"Thanks." Sara said. Walking heavily into the homestead driveway, she noticed Georgina with her head sticking out of the snow castle. Mathew stood on a pile of snow beating his chest proclaiming to be the King. His sister countered back stating that she was King. Sara walked up to the red and blue snow castle. "Did you see Grandma Sutton?"

"Yep," Georgina said. "She doesn't like spaghetti, Mama. Maybe we could fix her a hot dog instead?"

"She'll eat spaghetti."

"I told her that you and Derek were fighting, and that he tried to shoot you. Grandma said that Derek was a no-good son-of-a—"

"Georgina," Mathew yelled, "you weren't supposed to tell." He looked at his mother waiting for her to scold them.

"You kids have fun. I'll be inside." A good mother, a fair and just employer, Sara reprimand herself. Sickened by deceit, her confidence shaken, the children's discipline would come another day. Once inside the cabin, she checked the woodstove. The heat warmed her face. Grabbing the cast iron poker, she stabbed and turned the red glowing hot coals. Thoughts of her deceased husband returned. His sudden death in the swift river and Georgina's premature birth, both simultaneous events, had cheated her. She crushed a burning ember pulverizing angry energy toward two absent men. Sparks exploded in the metal chamber reminding her of her loveless existence. In private, Sara unleashed her pain. Finally, tears began to flow.

The evening dinner conversation lacked substance. Clearly distraught, Sara picked at her food, wondering what damage she had caused; her heart, her children and the homestead would suffer greatly.

Troubled by her sister's mood Anna Rose said, "Sara, you can't do anything about it now. You did the right thing by firing him. By now, he's long gone. Forget about it."

"I always knew he was rotten," Dorothy said smirking. "He just seemed too quiet. You've gotta watch the quiet ones. They have the deepest secrets, ya know. Your Papa would have shot him on site. You let him off easy, Sara."

"Pa would have never committed murder, Mother. I can't help feeling deceived. Two years was a long time. I'm shocked. Usually I'm a good judge of character, but after today, I'm not sure of anything. Now I'm out of a worker, and faced with putting my trust in someone else. I don't know who to trust anymore."

Dorothy spouted, "Men don't come in packages like your father. He was a good man, never cheated and always provided. You youngsters just want it all right now. Toughen up, Sara. Forgive your mistake and move on."

Sara rolled her eyes. "Anna Rose suggested hiring the man living in Old Charlie's cabin, Bryan Smith. What do you think, Mama?"

"Well Sara, I think what you need is time. You'll feel differently in a few weeks. Don't let this one man shake you. After all, we all have skeletons hanging in our closets. As for this Smith person, I don't know him. You'll have to decide for yourself."

"That's a big help, Mama."

"Okay. You can't trust anyone. Is that better?"

"Mother," Anna Rose scolded.

Dorothy waved her second daughter off. "How did Trapper find out about Chad?"

"I don't know. I had my hands full. What's wrong, Anna Rose?" Sara asked.

Anna Rose stiffened, her head slightly bent, she listened to the great outdoors. "It sounds like a pack of wolves moving through." Everyone listened to the howling wolves. The sound bounced off the canyon walls obscuring the packs' numbers as they migrated closer to the homestead. Free-range chickens risked survival. Sara retrieved and loaded her rifle.

"Wait a minute," Anna Rose said. "That's no wolf pack. The twins are back." She quickly put on her coat.

"Take a gun," Dorothy scolded.

Anna Rose disregarded her mother's warning and walked home unprotected. Sure enough, she found her twin friends unleashing the dog team from their respective harnesses. Anna Rose waved anxiously. "You're back. You're back." She engulfed both bundles of thick clothing not knowing whom to greet first or who was beneath the winter gear.

"Anna Rose, it's good to be home. What a ride. We have so much to tell. But first, let us finish with the dogs. Would you fetch two pails of water?" Lotty asked handing her a collapsible cloth bucket.

"I'd be happy too," Anna Rose said admiring her adventurous friends.

From a nylon dry bag, Lil dug out frozen meat and fed each team member. The twelve dogs barked and howled until Lil finished feeding them. Once Lil had completed her caretaking tasks, she sighed with relief, feeling glad to be safe, and ready for a hot shower. Anna Rose said, "Come polish off the rest of Sara's spaghetti."

An hour later, Lotty rubbed her expanded stomach and said, "I can't eat another bite. It was delicious. Thanks, Sara."

"We're all glad that you're home," Sara said.

"So how were your last few weeks?" Lil asked.

The cabin fell silent, as the Sutton family looked at one another. The silence affected the children's game. They stopped to listen.

Sara said, "Kids…"

"We know, go to bed," Mathew said disappointed. He grabbed his sister's wrist and reluctantly guided her to their shared bedroom. He closed the heavy door, leaving it ajar.

Dorothy said wickedly, "Sara had to fire her workman, Derek. Apparently, he was using an assumed name. Derek is really—"

"Chad Westler," the twins said in unison.

Shocked, Sara and Anna Rose turned away from the dishes. Dorothy's mouth dropped open. Everyone stared at the twins. Mathew eavesdropped.

Sara stood leaning against a high back chair and asked, "Now, wait a minute, how did you know?"

Casually, Lotty said, "Chad killed his father when we were at Butcher's Bay. Our fathers were good friends. Our Pa cleaned up the bloody mess after Chad had bludgeoned his father to death. We were surprised when we saw him at Tealand's."

Frightened, Mathew ducked under his covers, wishing he had completely closed the door.

"Why didn't you say something?" Anna Rose asked.

"At first, we weren't sure it was him," Lotty said.

"We did mention it to Trapper after he had told us about his cabin being robbed. Seeing Chad earlier that day, we put two and two together and became more suspicious, though we shrugged off the incident."

Sara said, "Apparently, Trapper can add as well. He has been watching Derek or Chad. Wow, this is too much. You two knew all along. Just think, if you had visited sooner, we would have already known about his lies."

"We're sorry," Lil said.

"Oh no, don't apologize. I just find it so ironic," Sara said hiding their romantic involvement.

Dorothy and Anna Rose sat listening to the accounts of Chad Westler. Lotty and Lil shared plenty of titillating stories. Everyone agreed not to inform the twin's father, leaving the past of Chad Westler to rest with his uncertain demise.

"It's enough to give an old lady a heart attack," Dorothy said. "I'm beat. Anna Rose walk me home. I've got to lie down."

"We're all tired. This has been a long day. Let's go, Mama. Lotty and Lil make yourselves at home. I'll see you back at Tealand's." Anna Rose gave Sara a hug. "Try to get some sleep. Things will look better in the morning."

Sara returned the sentiments. The twins followed Dorothy and Anna Rose outside. Unsure of what to do next, Sara stood alone in her kitchen. Tears would not emerge. Hatred persisted. Aware of her children's distress, she tossed a dishtowel across the room. Leaving the remaining dirty dishes in the sink, Sara reconciled her emotions by soaking in a hot bath.

JADED TRUST

The threat of severe weather persisted into the beginning of April. Hurricane County enjoyed twelve hours of daylight. With each new day, daylight increased by five minutes. Snow gradually transformed into running water. Soon it would wreak havoc on the roadways. Saplings scented the crisp air. Dogwood, Devil's claw, rose hips, and watermelon bushes inched upward, pressing against the thawing soil, sprouting and eventually blossoming to full capacity with the soon to arrive twenty-four-hour daylight. Alaskans prepared for spring runoff, their spirits high as daylight progressed toward the next solstice.

Anna Rose stood alone in the woods near George Creek. The trickles of water no longer whispered. They now spoke in mellow tones. Mesmerized by its flow, Anna Rose said a prayer, "Papa, it's been a long and weary winter. I wish you were here. I miss your smile and strength. I think Sara and Mama could use a dose of your good humor now, too. Everything has changed so much and so fast, I can hardly keep up. I'm tired, Papa. I'm really so very tired."

She relaxed her mind and allowed her father's creek to soothe her soul. His words cascaded, hypnotizing her. With her sixth sense, she saw her father's image standing in the middle of the creek. With outstretched arms, he spoke to her, "Life's about change. With change, you have growth." His image disappeared. Anna Rose sighed, accepting her father's simple wisdom. Promptly, she drifted back into reality.

As she reflected on her father's message, she continued on her way to visit Bryan. It had been a full week since they had spoken candidly. The twins had taken most of her time. During that long week, Bryan managed to slip in a few showers. The sun approached the horizon when Anna Rose entered Ol' Charlie's cabin. Bryan eagerly wrapped his arms around her. He asked, "Did anyone see you?"

"No."

"Good. Come sit down. I've missed you. Tell me, how are the twins?"

"They'll be on their way tomorrow. I already miss them."

"You had a nice reunion, then?"

"Yes. The twins are awesome. They could inspire the dead. I was amazed how they handled the life-threatening situations on the trail."

"What happened?"

"Remember that awful storm? The twins had to race against it. They said that for at least one hundred miles they never saw their shadows. They mushed right into a blizzard and had to hustle to make a snow den for the dogs and themselves. They were buried all night under three-feet of snow. Only a piece of pipe kept them alive. Can you believe it?"

"Wow, they were prepared."

"Standard procedures for mushers, I guess. But still, the threat of a cave-in and suffocating…scary. Then on the way back, they had to fight off a mother moose and a yearling. While Lotty and Lil were scouting the trail ahead, a yearling attacked the dogs. They had to snowshoe back about a half-mile to camp. The dogs were so distraught that a few became unharnessed which antagonized the yearling more, not to mention the mother moose. They scrambled to harness the dogs, but Lil fell, the mother moose charged her. Lotty took a clean shot through the moose's heart—it dropped dead right in front of Lil. Never a moments rest…immediately they had to harness the team and race to Shalktoolik, as the moose meat needed to be harvested before the birds and wolves started in on it."

"You're right that is an amazing story. Hope they don't have to relive it during the Iditarod race."

"Tough and smart, their Papa will be proud when he hears their report."

"They need to be tough if they're going to compete."

"Better them than me. They promised to return this fall. But, I've news that's even more exciting," Anna Rose said beaming.

"Really?"

"How would you feel about working for Sara? You could trade your work for rent. It would give us more time together without making excuses. So, what do you think?" Her enlarged eyes showed her enthusiasm.

Bryan rose from his chair and peered out the kitchen window. His mind swarmed with unanswered questions. An opportunity for a new beginning was presenting itself, disturbing his proverbial lack of confidence, stirring his notion to become completely honest, reminding him of his botched life, a lifestyle which he had grown accustom to. Working for Sara could work to his advantage, giving the appearance of a natural transition toward his plan to overtake Tealand's and Anna Rose's assets.

Anxious, Anna Rose asked, "Well, what do you think? I know it sounds like a lot of work, but it's really just general maintenance. I think it's a great idea, because in time, we could become more open about our relationship."

Bryan turned away from the window. With his eyes, he caressed Anna Rose's dainty features. "What? You know Sara doesn't like me. Her resentment will prevent us from having a working relationship. What about Derek?"

"You haven't heard?"

"Heard what?"

"That's what you get for staying cooped up in Ol' Charlie's. The gossip mill is outside."

"Spare me the lecture."

"Derek was fired last week. His real name is Chad." Anna Rose acquainted Bryan with the unsettling news about Chad. Dismayed, and for the first time, Bryan connected with the Hurricane County residents. The accounts of Chad Westler were unbelievable for the naïve, though common in Bryan's world. His deep-seated thoughts elated him; he was no longer a suspect. Chad was the newest small town controversy and scandal, relieving Bryan, if only for a few weeks, of suspicious comments, undermining his true motives.

"Sara is outraged and Chad has shaken her confidence. The homestead will fall apart without support. I think her heart aches some, too," Anna Rose said not being completely honest, and not wanting to break her promise of secrecy.

"Oh, so your sister does have a heart after all?"

"Come on now, Bryan. You two just need some time together. I'm sure you'll find each other less…callous. Who knows, you may even grow to like each other. So, what do you think about her offer?"

"Her offer? I didn't realize that she was making this offer. It seems very unlikely."

"Well, I might've had my hand in making the suggestion."

Undecided, Bryan changed the subject. "Where do you think Chad went? I mean, how long can he keep running? His actions were brazen at best. What's the bush coming too?" Bryan chuckled.

"There are a lot of outlaws up here. It's easy to lose yourself in Alaska. Men hide out in the bush all the time. Hurricane County has been lucky to get rid of them as soon as they enter. Alaskans implement their own laws and punishments. Do you remember when you first arrived in Hurricane? We all thought you were escaping the authorities. Your common name, your reclusiveness, your standoffish behavior screamed *convict*."

Nervously Bryan laughed. Much to his surprise the laughter settled his troubled stomach. How much Anna Rose knew about his past, he was uncertain. Meticulously, he hid his murderous past. "Let's play cards," he said abstaining from the potentially damaging discussion. Anna Rose shuffled the soft deck then dealt twenty-two cards. "Bryan, stop staring," Anna Rose said uncomfortable. "Are you having second thoughts about tonight's card game?"

Naïve girl, he thought while tapping his fingers. Bryan diverted his eyes toward his cards. "You don't scare me, my sweet Anna Rose. Keep talking. It'll just distract your concentration. And when you least expect it, I'll call out *Rummy.* You won't know what hit you." *You won't know until it's too late, all that is yours will be mine*, he thought smiling while tapping his thumbs.

Anna Rose blushed enjoying Bryan's soliciting tone. Their competition lasted until just before midnight.

"Well, it appears that you got the best of me tonight, Mr. Smith. Your crown won't last long," Anna Rose said stretching. "I better get home. I'm exhausted."

"You want a ride?"

"No. Will you walk me halfway?"

Victorious, Bryan pushed himself away from the table. "Fresh air sounds good."

He switched on his flashlight as they stepped out into darkness. Anna Rose slid her arm through his. The cosmos hid behind the clouds. The narrow flashlight beam guided their muted stroll. Bryan lit a cigarette.

Higher elevation ice and snow melted, canyon rocks relocated which echoed through the peaceful valley. George Creek's inexhaustible water supply gushed, drowning out Bryan's deep cough, flushing his deceit down to the glacial rivers below.

"You have yet to respond to Sara's job offer."

"I need some time to think it over." Bryan gently kissed Anna Rose good night. When their lips became over-impassioned, Bryan forced her hand onto his bulging zipper, squeezing her hand over his dick. Instantly he came, moaning. Shocked by Bryan's forcefulness, Anna Rose pulled away.

"Good night. I'll see you tomorrow," she said bashfully.

"Sleep well, sweet Anna Rose." As usual, Bryan's arousal subsided as he walked home. Tonight, he did not mind his sexual frustration or his quick release. He was just relieved that the evening was over.

Bryan's sponge baths were a clear sign that he was avoiding Tealand's and Anna Rose. By the fourth day, the inevitable desire for hot water drew him into the cafe. He managed to dodge Anna Rose, only winking at her with his back turned to the all-consuming patrons. His self-induced stress lured a migraine to the surface.

Returning to his cabin, he stoked the fire and fell onto the musty yellow and brown couch. Once he was able to relax, he fell asleep.

Four hours later, Bryan awoke feeling worse. As he bent down to refuel the woodstove, he groaned, the migraine had obstructed his sinuses. Ruby's white willow was sure to relieve his pain. "Shit, I'm out. What am I gonna do now," he said. "It's either Tealand's or Ruby's—either way I'm trapped." He opted for canned chili.

That evening, Bryan could no longer endure the migraine. He stood outside near the creek, waiting for Ruby to return home as Gentleman barked inside.

Ruby appeared behind him. "Well, if it isn't Bryan Smith. What brings you here? Are you lookin' for some action? You've come to the right place," Ruby rambled on. "Your shame won't last. I have to admit, you are unwavering. Most men come at least once a week. Pardon the pun." Ruby's flirtatious skills arose. As she continued, she touched his shoulders and chest. "I was hoping you would come back. What took you so long? I know you're a disciplined kind of guy—controlling your every move, never allowing intimacy. Am I right?"

Bryan's head swirled with the perpetual array of questions. He said, "You hit the nail right on the head, Ruby. And speaking of head—"

"That'll be extra, ya know? I don't like dirt around the rim, so it better be clean."

"No, no, Ruby. What I meant was I have a splitting headache. I was wondering if I could purchase some white willow."

"Well, it won't be as much fun. Come in anyway. I'll prepare my special blend. It'll speed your recovery. You're not going to rush off, are you? We haven't spoken for some time. I enjoy your company."

Gentleman bolted out the cabin door as Ruby and Bryan entered. He growled and sniffed Bryan. Ruby patted the German Shepherd's head, reassuring him that Bryan was a trustworthy customer. Satisfied, Gentlemen raced to the nearest bush.

Ruby hung up her coat, motioning Bryan to sit down. "It'll take a few minutes for the water to boil," she said placing the teakettle on the lit propane burner. Next, she built a fire and soon the cabin warmed.

The heat forced Bryan to remove his jacket. With his security blanket removed, he nervously fidgeted in the chair hoping that Ruby would ease off on her sexual advances—an unlikely expectation. Bryan steadied himself, ready to decline her skilled trading abilities.

The teapot whistled. Ruby stuffed chamomile, white willow and dandelion into a metal tea ball and placed it in a ceramic mug. She drenched it with hot water then handed the brew to Bryan. She ended her chores by loading the woodstove. Now, she was ready to sit down and visit with her patron.

"How much do I owe you?"

Ruby swallowed a shot of whiskey and chuckled. "I'd be happy to trade. We could…start where we left off the last time you stopped by. I'm sure I can get rid of that headache. There'd be only one thing throbbing when I got through with you." She laughed, feeling loose from the alcohol.

"You're too much, Ruby. I'm gonna miss you."

"What? You're not committing suicide on me now, are you?"

Bryan laughed. "No. I've already seen my suicidal days. I felt like it every time I had a hangover."

"So, what's up?"

"I've decided to move back to the city. I've had my fill of the bush. Besides, I'm sick of canned food. I hate cooking for myself. I crave fast food. And that hot water you're always talking about, it sounds better and better every day now. The road's calling me. I've even considered locating my kids to see if they'll have anything to do with me. I came out here for peace. What I found was just the opposite. Although, I'm sure I've beat my drinking problem."

With a raised eyebrow, Ruby questioned, "Do you actually think you can survive without alcohol?"

"Don't get me wrong, I'm still under the opinion that not everyone can rehabilitate. Once I get back to the city, I can test my theory, proving that I am one of the lucky ones. Now, I feel I can move on with my life. I need a paying job first, and the city's full of them. There's the possibility of working for the North Slope. They pay big bucks, ya know."

"They work twelve-hour days for weeks at a time. Are you sure you're ready for that kind of hardship? It's more isolated on the slope than here. There won't be any luscious blondes to take care of your aches and pains—no alcohol either."

"I can handle it."

"I'm not convinced. When are you planning to leave?" Ruby asked infatuated.

"In two weeks. I prefer clear roads—breakup should be minimal. It's a long drive, and I can't afford any mishaps. My truck'll appreciate easy travel. I've worked hard to maintain its immaculate condition."

Ruby removed her calendar from the vertical log wall. She opened it to April, which had a picture of a mother moose and her triplets standing near a flowing river with an Alaskan mountain backdrop. "That would make it April…"

Bryan pointed to Tuesday, April 17, 1975. "I should hit Anchorage by Wednesday. I want to stop in Talkeetna and spend the night. A big breakfast should carry me through until I reach the north end of Anchorage."

Ruby internalized her plan. *Here's my chance,* she thought. Her second shot of whiskey went down smoothly. She stoked the fire then reached for Bryan, massaging his knotted neck and shoulders. "How does that feel?" she asked pressing deeper each time.

"Great." Bryan's eyes rolled backward. He allowed his neck to go limp. *Here she goes again. Don't fall for it,* he thought.

Ruby grinned behind him. "I'll take care of you," she said softly caressing his shoulder blades and lower back.

Bryan relaxed as his headache subsided. Snared again, he fell into Ruby's trap. Sex without commitment was man's weakness. Ruby knew this, and Bryan felt it as his faithful promise to Anna Rose slipped through Ruby's massaging fingers. Guilt had never entered his mind, and it never stopped him from mistreating others. A game he played well, a game of hide the truth from those you are swindling created a proficient conman. *Practice makes perfect,* he thought as Magpie entered the back of his mind quoting another cliché.

Observing his weak posture, Ruby's trained hands swiftly reached around to his thighs. Her imagination turned to the city life, her plan not quite a scam, but clever strategy to exile herself from Hurricane County. She could sway anyone to her side, bedside or her opinion.

Always easy prey and a trap for men, sex was always the key component.

With her hands, Ruby seized his face and pressed her body hard against his. She vigorously kissed him—deeply submerging her tongue.

Bryan pushed her back. "I can't let this happen again."

"Why not? You want it. I want you. So relax. Let's have some fun. It's not every day you have your brains fucked out."

"Ruby, stop."

She continued to taunt her target. Slowly, she unbuttoned her cotton dress then placed Bryan's hands over her breasts. Quivering, he closed his eyes as Ruby manipulated his fondling touch. Again, she snared Bryan into submission.

He swatted her hands from his and engulfed her body, simultaneously jamming his tongue down her throat. Bryan was out of control. Zealously, they groped each other. Bryan was in practice mode once again. The two suited one another, plotting and using each other for personal gain. This game would take just a few minutes, and in those few minutes, they would destroy friends, family members and lovers.

Ruby stopped to catch her breath. With lust in his eyes, she guided Bryan into her tiny bedroom, unzipped his pants then grabbed his penis. He moaned faintly. Ruby tugged his hardened appendage then devoured it.

Bryan gasped. Falling backwards, he reached out. The bed broke his fall. Anxiously he attempted to pull up Ruby, but she would not budge. He ejaculated. Smirking, she withdrew her mouth, stroking the rush of milky fluid until it dried.

Sweaty, Bryan lie half-naked on the bed. His pants surrounded his ankles, making him feel awkward. Ruby did not allow him time to feel anything except pleasure. She began her relentless pursuit once more.

She stood up. With Bryan's full attention, she seductively removed her dress, swaying back and forth, lifting her breasts then caressing her inner thighs. Her robust figure undulated with each sensual movement.

Ruby's erotic dance captivated Bryan. His eyes never left her body, a second erection materialized. He tried to remove his boots. Ruby would not allow it. She pushed him backward then climbed on the bed like a cat stalking her prey, standing, she straddled above him, stooping downward, hovering above his body. With strong legs, she activated her hips.

Bryan supported her ankles as she sat on his chest. She raised herself, stepping above his shoulders, stroking her inner thighs. Bryan widened her stance then looked deep inside her. The dark passage thrilled him, and his caress became aggressive.

Expertly, Ruby stepped backward. She squatted onto Bryan's waist. Then she pressed her blonde bush down, gliding over Bryan's dick. His hips rose, and he groaned with each pass. Ruby savored the initial plunge, sliding his penis into her vagina. United, they moaned. Bryan latched onto Ruby's hips then swiveled them back and forth. Ruby synchronized their movements. Beads of sweat surfaced as Ruby and Bryan neared orgasm. *Just a few more...*, he thought pressing his fingers deeper into Ruby's hips. In unison, they came, sighing and relaxing every muscle. Ruby collapsed onto Bryan's chest.

"Whew. Now, wasn't that fun?" she asked breathless.

Pushing her aside, Bryan looked at her with disgust and pulled up his pants. After brushing clean his sweaty brow, he gulped down two shots of whiskey, slamming the bottle back on the table.

Ruby whispered into his ear, "Consider your debt paid in full." She laughed. "Take the bottle with you. You'll need it to finish your rehab." Realizing that she had broken another man, she laughed.

"Fuck you slut."

Ruby laughed again as she closed the red door. Alone, she settled into the cabin. Immediately, she started writing a list of personal items to move, sell and trade. *Finally*, she thought elated. She was moving to the city, though she could tell no one. Her excitement brewed deep within. Sleep would not come on this shameless, conniving Alaskan night.

Leaving the bottle behind, Bryan solemnly walked home. Wishing for one more drink, wishing he had never moved north, wishing for peace of mind, he knew Ruby was right. So was Nurse Jackson. Dismissing their opinions, he concentrated on justifying intercourse with Ruby. He thought, *I'm not gettin' anywhere with Anna Rose. I'm a man. I need sex. Anna Rose had better give it up soon. Once we're married and away from her family, she'll have no choice.* He washed himself with cold water, freeing himself of Ruby's manipulative ways, her sexual advances and hoping she did not transfer any diseases. The distasteful memory of his latest interaction with Ruby repulsed him; blindly unaware that he and Ruby were equally guilty of using and profiting from others. He felt dirty and dishonest, relieved and relaxed, finding comfort in his familiar pattern of falsehoods.

****

The next morning, Bryan performed his usual chores thinking of Anna Rose—tormenting himself with becoming a trustworthy man. Before incarceration, life had taught him well. His abusive stepfather modeled his life as a user. His second instructor, Magpie, influenced his life as well. Convicted of fraud, embezzlement, domestic violence and an array of other petty crimes, mostly against wealthy, aging women, Magpie had a con for every scenario. An excellent student, Bryan absorbed Magpie's techniques easily. The odds were against both men. The halls of jail and rehabilitation would greet them frequently.

Outside, another Alaskan spring cycle was in full force. The sweet aroma of cottonwoods filled the morning air. Their shedding, tacky leaf remnants stuck to the thawing snow, staining it yellow. Pussy willows stretched toward the deep blue sky. Sap moved up the towering spruce trunks. Hurricane County came out of hibernation, only to ready themselves for next year's winter.

Setting out for Hurks, Bryan noticed that the snowpack was receding quickly. River Road was muddy and slick, creating precarious driving conditions. Mud splattered onto his cherished vehicle. Glacial silt connected with the polished brown paint. Irritated, he tapped his fingers on the steering wheel, hoping the damaged metal would erode slowly. Cursing his bad habits, he pulled into Hurks near the flashing roadside sign. It read: *WINDSHIELD WIPER FLUID $2.99 gal.*

Eager not to miss the eleven o'clock out-going mail, he placed two envelopes into the mailbox. Nervous, Bryan hoped the correspondences would not raise too many questions about his past, though he was confident that the intentional inaccuracies on his resume would prevent such dialogue. What worried him was a criminal background check. This would exclude him from most employment. *I should've falsified my name,* he thought damning himself for his stupidity.

With a deceptive smile, he greeted Lorraine at the lunch counter. "I'm back for another musk ox burger," he said tapping his fingers on the counter.

With her hand on her hip, Lorraine chomped down hard on her gum. In her usual snippy mood, she asked, "What'll ya have with it? Come on, you know the routine chips, French fries or coleslaw? And I suppose you want coffee and pie?"

Bryan smiled, tapping harder. *It would be so easy to take her out, shoot her, it would be nice to do Max this favor*, he thought. Lorraine's attitude was not going to change his upbeat mood. "I'll have fries and apple pie. And as you know *my* routine, keep the coffee comin'. I've gotta long day ahead of me."

"Try working here all day then going home to four kids." Lorraine spun around and called Bryan's order into Max. As a veteran husband, Max half-smiled at Bryan, seemingly apologetic, then complied with his wife's request.

Unaffected by her harsh tongue, Bryan sat gloating. He sipped his coffee and thought about how his evening would culminate. *Perhaps tonight we'll play strip poker, have sex on the table, solidifying my plan,* he thought. Ever hopeful, Bryan smothered his crispy fries with catsup. Eating heartily, he scooped up another week-old newspaper then drove back to Ol' Charlie's cabin. Wanting to catch a glimpse of Anna Rose, he slowed down near Tealand's driveway. His futile reconnaissance caused him to accelerate. Twitching, his mind raced back to his insecurities as he wondered how he could be successful at any relationship—faithful, unfaithful, abusive, non-abusive, honest or deceitful, it didn't matter to Bryan. *Success is based on acquiring assets. Continue with the plan, success will follow,* he thought.

Two days passed and Bryan had not seen Anna Rose. Aggravated, he grabbed his shower bag and hustled out of the cabin. His urgency prompted him to drive. He bolted through Tealand's front entrance, sending the newly installed door chimes flying from the doorknob, scaring the locals into silence. They watched him intensely, distrusting his every move, hoping that he would reveal another morsel for their daily gossip.

Bewildered by his abrupt entrance, Anna Rose said, "Hello, Mr. Smith. Are you in a hurry? You look a bit ruffled?"

Tapping his thumb on the counter, eyes bulging, he said, "Yes, I am. I need a shower."

"Fifty cents, please. I think stall number two is available. Watch for temperature changes. Billy's using the washer." Anna Rose leaned in closer to Bryan as he handed over two quarters. She whispered, "It's good to see you. I should be able to make it up tonight."

Her words relaxed him, and he smiled back in acknowledgement. Overcoming his impatience, he entered his assigned shower stall, undressing slowly in hopes that Billy's laundry would complete its wash cycle. *That bitch had better make it tonight. I'm runnin' out of time*, he thought.

That evening, Anna Rose rapped three times on Ol' Charlie's door. Within seconds, she was embracing Bryan. Confidence restored, he continued to manipulate this naïve woman.

"Where have you been? Why haven't you come up? I've missed you."

"I'm sorry. I've been helping Sara in the evenings. We really have our hands full. We could really use your help. I can't possibly care for Tealand's and the homestead. I love my sister, but these long days are exhausting me." Anna Rose fussed all the way to the couch.

"Here, let me take your jacket." Anna Rose removed her nylon coat, handing it over to Bryan. Draping it over the recliner, he affectionately held her supple hands, locked his eyes onto hers, yielding for a moment then said, "Anna Rose, I've made up my mind. A few days before you came to me with Sara's offer, I had decided to move back to the city."

Confused, Anna Rose said, "Why didn't you tell me?"

"Before you get upset, let me say this: That night, I had planned on telling you, but you were so excited about me working for Sara. I lost all of my courage, and I knew that I should at least consider the offer. It's been an emotional roller coaster of a week." Bryan paused, knowing it added drama to his speech. He took a deep breath. "Anna Rose, I love you. I've come to realize that my life would be miserable without you. I want you to come with me."

Anna Rose's face waned. Tears filled her eyes. "I can't leave."

"I've already sent out job applications and found a few nice rental houses in Anchorage. I can provide for you. You won't have to work. We could start a new life together—just the two of us. We could have a large family, as many children as you want." Bryan gently squeezed Anna Rose's hands. Again, Magpie's teachings added to his performance...*be kind, touch lightly, speak softly, use warm and inviting words, and then ambush your prey, stealing her heart and belongings.* "Come with me, my sweet Anna Rose. I love you. Please say you'll come."

Astonished by his sudden decision and announcement of love, her intuition ignited, she broke free from his grip, recalling Jess' last promise of children and everlasting love. Defending her vow not to trust men, she needed time to assess the situation. Apologies would have to come later; possibly, they would come too late.

"My whole family lives here. How can I leave them? I've lived here all of my life. Mama's aging. Sara's raising the kids and trying to keep the homestead from falling apart. Both need my help."

"But I need you, too. We deserve this chance. I thought we had something special. You're not in love with me, are you?"

Anna Rose smiled through her tears. "I do love you. But, I don't see how I can leave. Can't you stay here? I'm sure by next year the family'll accept you. Then, we can start our life together—start a family. It's just too soon, Bryan. Jessy hasn't even been dead a year. What would people think of me? If I moved, what would I do with Tealand's?"

Unprepared for her response, Bryan looked away. Life without Anna Rose would be a hardship, financially devastating as he would have to conjure up another plan, find another victim, all of which takes time, planning and effort. He knelt down, pleading. "Anna Rose, I want you beside me. I didn't mean to spring this on you. I didn't realize...I guess I was being selfish. I'm a fool. To think that you would just drop everything and come with me was crazy. At least say that you'll give it some thought."

Confused, Anna Rose rested her head on Bryan's shoulder and began to sob. Unsure about speaking her truth, her mind drifted from Jess' similar words back to Bryan's kind words. *Were his words just lies?* she thought. Somehow, his proposal had shaded her thinking. Buried deep in her heart was the truth. She knew she would never leave her immediate family and the forest that surrounded them.

In one graceful motion, Bryan stood Anna Rose on her feet. Not wanting to part, they held each other tightly. Eventually, Anna Rose stopped crying. The woodstove smoldered, chilling the air as they embraced in silence. *A fine performance, indeed,* he thought.

****

"Hey Russell, this box goes outside," Ruby said. "Oh, and these bottles can go, too. Thanks."

Russell nodded obeying his boss. Yearning for a shorter workday, thinking of his elk rib steaks simmering in the crockpot at home, he would endure the ten-hour shift pondering whether he had forgotten to add anise to his late evening dinner. Ruby's auctions proved to be a long and a grueling day.

Inside the cardboard box were three brass candleholders, two handmade Eskimo dolls, a scrimshawed ivory handled Ulu knife and three, four-inch carvings: a polar bear, a seal and a whale. Russell was surprised. Deeply concentrating on Ruby's motives, his curiosity stirred.

"The black plastic bag in the office can be auctioned off, as well," Ruby said directing Russell.

Picking up the heavy garbage bag then placing it under the auction table, he took a quick peak inside. *What's Ruby up too, now*, he thought heading back into the office.

"Ruby, why are you auctioning off your favorite items? What's going on?" Russell asked towering over her desk.

"Today's your lucky day, Russell. Sit down."

Sliding a barstool over, he sat down and readied himself for one of Ruby's long-winded talks, thinking about how he could get home early.

"I can trust you, right?"

"Of course."

"What I'm about to tell you doesn't leave this room. Okay?"

"Whatever you say, Ruby."

"It's time for me to move on."

Russell sat in shock. "Move on to where?"

"Anchorage."

"The city? You won't last, Ruby."

"I'll manage. Your luck comes into play the day I leave. I can think of no one else that I'd rather leave Ravens too."

"What?"

"You heard me. I want you to manage Ravens. There are enough supplies until your next order arrives. You'll have plenty of cash to pay for it and then some. I want you to stay at my cabin, as well."

"Manage Ravens?"

"Yes. Eighty percent of the profits go to you—mail me the twenty percent until I settle into city life. You have a good understanding of how I run this place, right?"

"Well, yes but—"

"I, of course, have one condition. A contingency plan so to speak."

"Of course."

"I've never lived in the city. And if for some reason, I need to return, I'll take back control of Ravens and my cabin. I don't foresee anything bringing me back to this dump."

"This is way too generous."

Ruby laughed. "That's exactly what I'd expect to hear from you. That's why Ravens and the cabin are yours. At least, you appreciate me. I want you to have them. I know you'll keep the property up, and Ravens will continue to prosper. Change whatever you like. It's all yours after tomorrow."

"Are you sure you want to move out? Where will you live? How will you support yourself? Have you really thought about this?"

"Thought about it? I've been dreaming of it for as long as I can remember. I don't want to live like this anymore."

Russell rose from the barstool and then hugged Ruby. "I'd be happy to take over for you. I'll run Ravens just like you. You can be sure of that. You taught me everything. Ravens will be intact when you return, assuming that you will. You gave me a chance when no one else would. I'm grateful. Now, how will you get to Anchorage?"

"Another secret, Bryan Smith is leaving tomorrow, and I'm going to hitch a ride. I have it all planned out."

Russell cocked his head. "I'm sure you do. What does this Smith guy think about your plan?"

"He doesn't know…yet."

"You mean you're selling everything on impulse? What if he refuses to take you?"

"He won't. I've yet to meet a man who refused me. He's no different." Confidently, Ruby disappeared behind the curtain door, leaving Russell to digest her intentions in private. *She'll be back in a month*, he thought chuckling to himself.

A small crowd, comprised mostly of men, gathered outside Ravens. Russell had roped off the staircase to protect the more valuable items. Mocking their bids, two traders pointed at the fox furs hanging from the exterior wall. In thirty minutes, the crowd had doubled in size. Their clamor rose in volume. Ruby's watch marked the noon hour. She and Russell stepped out of Ravens arctic entry.

Yelling over the crowd, Ruby said, "Good afternoon everyone." They simmered, lowering their voices.

The traders quieted anticipating a sound day of trading. The spring auction consistently offered interesting and unique items. Ruby knew their value, as did the traders standing below her. Both of which prided themselves on buying low and selling high.

Ruby lowered her voice. "Thank you. Now, before we get started I want to show you several real treasures. These items are from my personal collection. I'm sure there's something here for each of you." She turned to Russell asking for the garbage bag. He removed its contents then unfolded an unusually large black bear hide, in mint condition.

Together they stretched out the heavy hide, displaying it to the crowd. The traders admired its size. Someone hollered, "Twenty dollars." Then another hollered, "Thirty."

Ruby dropped her end of the bearskin. "Wait. Stop the bidding. I want to show you all of my trinkets, first. So don't get ahead of yourselves. You might find something you can't live without. You may even need to pool your trade goods together. Please, be patient."

The next items that she exhibited were the brass candlesticks, the Ulu knife and the ivory carvings. Russell assisted Ruby. The group appreciated each article. The handmade Eskimo dolls stirred some interest, as well.

Eager to expose her final piece, Ruby waited for silence. "I've one final commodity. I'll accept only cash or gold. As all of you have heard, whether from your elders or at Ravens, this precious stone has had many tales. In your minds, these stories became surreal." Ruby paused as the crowd mumbled, questioning her intent, trying to recall what tale she was speaking of. She waited for their full attention.

"Today, I stand before you to present the mythical…Russian Jade Stone." Dramatically, Ruby unveiled the flawless, oversized rock.

The crowd gasped as the transparent green stone glistened in the afternoon light. Their comments jumbled together. The traders livened with excitement. No one, including Russell, had ever actually seen the stone. For forty-seven years, Golda and Ruby had kept it well hidden.

To acquire such a treasure was sure to bestow great honor. The clans grouped together, combining resources. Money and gold piled up in the middle of each circular patch of traders. Others stood in awe, admiring the jade. This was a historical day. Golda's true legacy resurfaced, exciting all spectators.

Anticipating large sums of cash and gold, Ruby patiently waited for the united traders. Excited, she basked in Golda's tale, knowing that she revived the myth, stirring great curiosity among the spring auction crowd.

"Are you sure you want to trade the stone, Ruby?" Russell asked in shock.

"It's Golda's day to shine. Let's see how much we net."

"Ruby, this is a mistake. All of this."

"What do you mean? I know what I'm doing."

"Yes, but—"

"You worry too much, Russell."

The traders set aside individual egos and compiled their collective bargaining tools. Unspoken and clearly understood between the clans, the eldest would return with the jade in hand, proudly adding a new chapter to the stone's and clan's history. The crowd quieted, turning toward Ruby. Exuberant, she addressed the traders.

"I'm ready to hear your bids. The highest will take home the illustrious Russian Jade Stone. Begin bidding."

The Eagle clan eagerly spoke first, "We offer, seven hundred dollars and seven ounces of solid gold."

A small group of white merchants gathered closer, one man hollered, "Eight hundred dollars, six ounces of gold nuggets and three ounces of dust."

Next, the Raven clan leader spoke, "One thousand dollars and nine ounces of river gold and four ounces of gold dust."

"One thousand fifty dollars and four ounces of gold dust," the white merchant countered.

Ruby laughed at the naïve bidders. "You must be joking. Look at this magnificent piece of earth. I should've made it clear—minimum bid starts at three thousand dollars."

Discouraged, the traders grumbled. Shattered hopes filtered throughout the crowd—a disappointing spring auction, the first of its kind.

"We need more time."

"Yeah, let us come back tomorrow afternoon."

"How do we know that it's the real Russian Jade Stone?"

Ruby laughed. "Come now, when have I ever betrayed you? Tomorrow afternoon will be too late."

To Russell she said, "What was I thinking? Someone with much more capital will have to purchase it. Forget about the jade. Pass me the ivory carvings." To the discontented crowd below, Ruby said, "Your families and clans will be disappointed as well, but at least you can verify the jade's existence. Keep the legend alive, for this is the last time anyone will set eyes upon this extraordinary green stone. Now, who'll start the bidding for this ivory carved polar bear? Let's start with fifty dollars."

Each trader retrieved his share then settled into bidding on less luxurious items while guarding the classic tale of the Russian Jade Stone—some shamelessly conspiring to heist the stone, acquiring prestige and new wealth.

Ruby felt a sense of the extraordinary; it was a nostalgic day. It proved to be profitable as well. On the auction table three items remained—a beaver pelt, a whiskey bottle and the Russian Jade Stone. She gave Russell the fur and placed the whiskey behind the bar. Carefully, she wrapped the legendary rock in a silk cloth then placed it in its leather pouch. *Your time will come*, she thought patting its protective cloth.

Today, an old photograph hanging above the office caught Ruby's attention. Mesmerized, she dragged a chair beneath it and removed it from its rusty nail. Wiping the dust from the glass, she steadily stepped off the chair and sat down. Her fixation aroused her childhood memories, a time of innocence, home studies and life lessons only Golda could have exposed her to. "Russell, bring me a shot. Better make it a bottle." She stared into the photo.

Russell sat across from her and poured her a shot of whiskey. "Are you having second thoughts?" Ruby did not answer. "Ruby?" he prodded.

"What?" she asked still focused on the black and white framed image.

"Are you having second thoughts?"

"Heavens no," Ruby said with certainty. "I was just looking at this old picture. The light in here is awful. I can hardly make out these men's faces."

"Ruby, the lighting has been this way for years. You never complained about it before. What gives? Who's in the photo?"

Saddened by retrospect, Ruby said, "You know, I never knew my father. It could've been any of these men." She slid the framed picture over to Russell. "I guess I'll never know. He's probably dead, anyway. I'm just another bastard child running around Alaska." She swallowed the whiskey, filled the shot glass again and hastily ingested it.

She reached for the bottle a third time. Russell intercepted. "Slow down. I understand the importance but Golda made a choice long ago. You have no control over her decision. You never will. Whiskey isn't the cure. So relax, huh?"

Russell's frankness did not surprise Ruby. She expected it. She examined his hairless face. Tiny lines stretched across his brown, leathery features. Lush black lashes surrounded his deep-set dark brown eyes. His long black hair added to his attractiveness. She had come to love this man, a platonic relationship that surprised even

Ruby or was it Russell's clear boundaries that surprised her more? "What is it, Ruby? Why are you staring at me?"

"I'm going to miss you." Ruby stood up smiling then approached Russell. She placed her thumb and index finger around his mouth, gently cupping his chin. She bent over and kissed him on the lips. Realizing her life-long ambitions were ahead of her, she buoyantly walked out of the dimly lit bar.

Ruby's excitement mounted as she made her departing preparations. Unable to sleep, she lit all of her candles and sat watching the flames flicker shadows onto the vertical cottonwood log walls. As she glared into the natural light, she knew it was time to say her final good-byes. She reached for a pad of paper and her finest ink pen. She wrote:

Dear Sara and Anna Rose,

I hope you'll forgive me for not saying good-bye in person, but I wanted to leave without any hoopla, nostalgia or tears. By the time you receive this note, I'll be halfway to Anchorage. As I get on in years, my dreams seem to be slipping away, so I must act before it truly is too late. The timing could not be more perfect, another sign that the time for me to move on is now. Bryan Smith has offered to take me to Anchorage. You know, I think he actually likes me. I've given Russell my cabin, Gentleman, and of course Ravens. He has been my constant strength over the years, and I am sure he'll keep Ravens running smoothly.

Since I'm the last of the white healers, I leave you two my recipes for healing. Remember to always use them in good faith, and ask the Great Spirit to assist you whenever you need help. The Great Alaskan Spirit's power is limitless, as is yours. If all else fails or you're not comfortable with these teachings, I'm sure that elder Ken Kurtz will assist. You must summon him properly. Respect their healing abilities. Don't be frightened by their powers.

And to Dorothy, you've been a thorn in my side since the day I was born. Even through our differences and over the years, I must admit that you've been right about whoring. It isn't proper, and it's most degrading to a woman's soul. I've found no honor, only emptiness. Your scornful words have kept my dream alive, and I thank you for that. Now that you're an old woman, you've become more condemning. I'm glad I won't be here to watch you pitch your final disparaging words. Remember, your tongue will have a lasting impression on your children and grandchildren until their deaths. Be thankful each morning that you have one more day, for life is a gift.

If by chance you see the almighty Trapper, give him my regards. He will not be receiving such a gracious good-bye.

My shoulders have lightened, and my bags are packed. I bid you farewell.

Love,
Ruby

ONE FOR THE ROAD

"…there's not a single cloud hanging over the entire state. My car was pelted by mud and sand this morning, folks—break-up's here," a radio weatherman said. "Temperatures are on the rise. It must be that global warming those radical environmentalists have been screaming about—those leftover hippies from the sixties. Okay, okay, now don't send the station any letters, please. You wouldn't want to put a Republican out on the streets, now would you? If you are traveling this week, the weather is on your side. The roads will be messy but hazard-free, though watch for early morning patches of fog. Much of the snow has melted creating ponds in nearby ditches. So…my advice to you: Stay sober and stay on the road. Stay tuned for more great rock-n-roll...comin' at 'cha from K-W-A-V, the station that's always on your wavelength…."

Bryan turned off the radio. *Anna Rose is too slow, a proper goody two-shoes. No more delays. I'm leaving. Maybe tonight she'll spread those legs*, he thought. The subject of his departure turned his stomach. Even with no sexual benefits, he felt something for Anna

Rose. Nervous or not, his time had run out, a conviction he could no longer dodge—a life sentence without sweet Anna Rose or her sweet assets. Frustrated, Bryan impatiently tapped his fingers on the kitchen table, finding it ironic that Anna Rose should ruin his life when his plan had been to ruin hers.

Anna Rose planned each step carefully, mud slowed her stride as it squished between her waffled-boot tread. As scheduled, she and Mat-Su walked up Tundra Rose Lane. The late evening stroll eased her aching back. The thought of Bryan's company motivated her up the incline.

"Anna Rose," Bryan said throwing his arms around her. "Come in. How are you?"

"I'm tired, but better now." She squeezed his neck and kissed his cheek. "What should we do tonight: play Rummy, Cribbage or should we finish that thousand-piece puzzle?" Despite being tired, Anna Rose was in a sporting mood.

The pressure mounted inside Bryan's mind. *Cards'll make a nice distraction,* he thought trying to put off the inevitable. "Whatever you like, my sweet Anna Rose."

Sitting at the kitchen table, she shuffled the cards. With his back turned toward Anna Rose, Bryan occupied himself by preparing two cups of tea. Then he placed them on the table. Sitting down, he watched Anna Rose intensely. *How can I leave? I should give her more time. I want her...and Tealand's...and the rights to the homestead,* he thought.

"I'll warm up the cards with a round of twenty-one," Anna Rose said cheerfully.

Bryan stopped her in mid-shuffle. "We have to talk."

"Bryan, what is it?"

"I can't stay here, Anna Rose."

"But—"

"Listen. I can't live with the vindictive locals, your suspicious sister and without water or heat. I just can't take it anymore. I'm leaving tomorrow."

"Tomorrow's too soon."

"I've got a job. South Anchorage is building a new high school. I start next week." *Okay, maybe I don't have the job yet, but I will*, he thought.

"Oh Bryan, this is so sudden." Tears welled up in her eyes.

"Anna Rose, I never expected to fall in love. Please, come with me. I'll rent a nice house while you arrange things with your family. I've weekends off, so I could come back to move you south. We deserve this opportunity, Anna Rose." *I deserve her inheritance. That would really burn Sara*, he thought.

Anna Rose began to cry. Bryan reached out to her. *Great, more tears. It's like babysitting a five-year-old*, he thought. Finally, the tears stopped. Bryan pushed back Anna Rose, looked into her heavenly green eyes and said, "I don't want to leave without you. I realize this is sudden, but I need a job. I couldn't provide for you while working for Sara. You deserve the best of everything. We can work this out, Anna Rose. You can visit your family anytime. And they'd always be welcome in our home. Aren't you tired of this lifestyle?"

Blurry eyed, Anna Rose tried to focus. Bryan handed her a tissue. Dabbing her eyes, she said, "This is my world, my life. I belong here. Sara needs me more than ever. And there's Mama and Tealand's to consider. I can't leave."

"Not even for…say a year or two?"

"I'd miss so much. I'd miss my niece, nephew and everything that my family has worked so hard for. It's just impossible." Anna Rose threw herself back into Bryan's arms.

The evening passed by slowly as the broken pair shed their emotions, holding each other close. They rarely spoke. When they did, they talked adoringly. Each soft-spoken phrase spun them back, reminding them of their loss, of their non-existent future together, of the unattainable. The cabin became too cozy as the hours ticked away. Sadness overwhelmed Anna Rose, meanwhile Bryan wanted to take the easy route and have Anna Rose comply with his request to move. Magpie taught him that patience was crucial in deception. Even through Anna Rose's ridiculous crying spells, Bryan waited: patiently, impatiently, calmly, irritated, struggling with wanting to knock some sense into his victim, expediting his trap. Completely drained at one o'clock in the morning, Anna Rose wiped her tears from her face. Thankful that she had finished processing her grief, Bryan was proud that someone actually liked him enough to sob for hours and considered him a good suitor, even though he had misrepresented his true intent. His confidence rose.

Through swollen eyes and into Bryan's ear, she whispered, "No one has ever been this kind to me." She kissed his cheek and darted out of Ol' Charlie's cabin.

Bryan raced after her. "Let me drive or walk you down."

Dispirited, Anna Rose hung her head low. "No. I'll walk. But thank you."

Rushing in for his last chance, Bryan said, "Anna Rose, I'm so sorry. I didn't mean to end it like this. I had hoped—"

Anna Rose stopped his words by placing her index finger over his lips. "I guess it's just bad timing."

Bad timing for me, not you, he thought thinking about how much time and effort he put into manipulating her. Now the process would have to begin again, a new place, a new person and under a new set of circumstances.

Desperately, they enveloped each other. The painful heartache smothered the fragmented couple though Bryan's mind was already on fast forward, thinking of where he might find his next wealthy victim.

"It doesn't have to end," Bryan said tenderly, trying to convince Anna Rose.

She nodded, knowing that it would be their last embrace. The finale to a seemingly warm relationship, one that might have satisfied her dream of having children and maintaining a happy marriage, her confidence for acquiring a loving husband spiraled downward.

Bryan released his grip, stepping backward. For the last time, he scanned Anna Roses' features, etching them in his mind. Sensing his intent, she fled down the driveway.

Watching his target disappear into the morning dew as moonlight lit her distraught path home, Bryan's stone heart sank, knowing that his wallet would remain empty.

After a sleepless night, Bryan clicked on the radio hoping to hear an updated weather report. Quickly, he realized that it didn't matter. He was driving south. Today. Radio reception echoed static throughout his brain. Annoyed and becoming progressively frustrated, he abruptly turned it off and proceeded to disengage from Hurricane County.

His last week spent in Ol' Charlie's was unlike rehab. He was the one giving the orders, assigning the departure date, depleting his food supply, all the while dreaming of what could have been. Broke, with no income prospects, he loaded the last box into the back of his truck. Returning to the cabin, he stripped the bed down to its mattress, folded the blankets neatly, placing them at the foot of the bed. The bare room felt like his former jail cell. The cabin was ready for inspection. The woodstove cooled, reminding him of the first time he had entered Ol' Charlie's cabin, and the first time he met Magpie. Both days seemed so long ago. Standing in the doorway, looking back, he felt the cabin's emptiness. A deck of cards sat alone on the table—left there deliberately to manipulate Anna Rose's emotions. *She deserves it. I hope she cries for a week*, he thought.

Tealand's offered one last shower, one last chance to change Anna Rose's mind. When Bryan entered the café, the sound of chattering patrons ceased. Anna Rose unconsciously stopped pouring coffee;

her patrons took notice. Bryan lowered his stare and walked toward the cash register.

Anna Rose cautiously approached the counter. "Can I help you?" she asked jittery, fighting back her tears.

Her appearance captivated him, catapulting him into depression, and wondering if more time would allow him future gains. Solemnly he said, "I need to pay my final month's rent and take a shower."

Sadly, and with discretion, Anna Rose sighed. "Take your shower while I tally your bill."

Nodding, he walked over to the shower stalls. Anticipating a different response, it appeared that Anna Rose was ready to be relieved of him. *Maybe that bitch Sara said something to her. Life never changes, people remain the same and unforeseen circumstances never falter, and I'll always have nothing... I'll always have something to hide. Now, that's something to hold on to. Not like a soft woman with assets, but something nevertheless.* The likelihood of a relationship dissipated with the shower's steam— vaporizing opportunity into nothingness. Bryan felt his old lifestyle creeping back, derailing any chance for positive change. He felt the chill of the sterile corridors of rehab, an existence familiar and comfortable, but never transformational. Disappointing Magpie and pleasing Nurse Jackson, the potential to return to jail or rehab strengthened his desire for freedom, no matter the cost to others.

Enjoying the hot water running down his back, he purposely allowed the shower timer to complete its cycle. *I could change my mind*, he thought. The words from a book he read while incarcerated popped into his head, *'Isolation breeds separatism, yet a unique individual inevitably emerges.'* Living in the bush proved that philosophy, or had it? The city life would test his sobriety, as would the loss of Anna Rose. *I need to prove it to my kids, to myself and to Nurse Jackson*, he thought, knowing that the odds were against him. The effort of fighting against himself was a hardship, alien and confusing, a straight life complicated matters.

Slowly he dried his body, combed his hair and repacked his shower bag. With closed eyes, Bryan stepped out of the stall. He felt his face turning red. Drops of water beaded and dripped from the ends of his curly hair, like tears from an alienated conspirator.

With a level head, he managed his emotions: lust, anger and disappointment. Now, he and Anna Rose stood across from each other at the till. As the clock ticked, the local customers skillfully eavesdropped. Anna Rose and Bryans' nerves twisted inside, their sense of longing permeated the moments, though common sense would form their outcome.

"How was your shower?" Anna Rose asked solemnly.

"Just fine, thanks." Bryan said without conviction.

She scanned his tab. "Your bill comes to eighty-five dollars. I have it itemized. Here's your receipt." With hope in her heart and pleading eyes, she slid his final bill across the counter.

Reaching into his front pocket, without lifting his eyes, embarrassed by his bad habit, he pulled out a wad of crumpled up bills and handed over the scrunched cash.

Nervously, Anna Rose counted the bills. "Out of ninety dollars." She handed him the correct change. Bryan squeezed her hand, then kissed the other side. He whispered, "I'll always love you, my dear sweet Anna Rose." *At least until I find someone else—an easier target with a heftier financial portfolio. I deserve it after all this bullshit*, he thought. With her features etched into his mind, Bryan released his tender grip and walked out the door. *Another fine performance…thanks to Magpie's influence, she'll be running after me in no time*, he thought smirking.

Anna Rose watched absent-mindedly, as the door gently met its frame, the chimes resonated faintly. There was so much to say, yet her feet would not move. Run. Tell him that you love him, she ordered herself. Her body malfunctioned; her motor skills disarmed. Her hands grew cold. She felt a huge vacuum pulling her back into the present. Hearing a cry for more coffee, she spiraled back to

Tealand's and retrieved the coffee pot. As she served her customers, she wondered if she had made the right decision. The empty porcelain cups mirrored her feelings.

****

Scolding her from the heavens, denouncing her offspring, Golda condemned her child's plot, as Ruby's broken promise surfaced. Casting aside unearthly judgment, erasing disparaging personal thoughts, Ruby filled her final liquor order. "Russell," she hollered from her office.

"What's up, Ruby?" Russell asked pulling back the curtain door.

"It's time for me to leave. I wrote out your first order and my last. I just wanted to say good luck and thank you. In addition, I need you to give Sara and Anna Rose this note. I couldn't just leave without saying good-bye. Deliver the letter tomorrow, no sooner." Ruby stood up and hugged her trusted friend. "Thanks for everything."

"Good luck, Ruby." *You'll be back*, he thought.

Tossing her duffel bag over her shoulder, she walked out of her office and stood in the middle of Ravens. "I don't think I'll miss this place," she said. Russell held open the front door, and she walked out for the last time. They exchanged good-bye waves. Uncertainty laced Russell's eyes while conviction gleamed from Ruby's. They were no longer partners, no longer sharing paralleling thoughts or business goals. Without looking back, Ruby walked down the stairs.

An eighth of a mile down River Road, Ruby heard a vehicle coming from behind. Her plan ensued. Excitement sprinted through her veins as the man of her dreams rolled to a stop. Bryan pushed open the passenger door. "Get in," he said gruffly.

Ruby threw her bag into the truck bed and jumped in the cab. "Oh thanks, Bryan. Luckily you came along. My feet were starting to ache. Wow, from the back it looks like you're moving out. Is this the big day?"

Depressing the gas pedal, he said, "Yes, it is. I've a job lined up, and from the looks of the rental market, it won't take long to find a decent place to live." He surprised himself with his chipper voice because inside he was thinking only of Anna Rose, needing her to secure his future and fulfill his lust. Right now, what he really needed was a bottle of whiskey.

Bryan pulled into Hurks. "I've got to have one more charred musk ox burger before Hurricane County becomes a memory. Then, I'm filling up the truck, and I'm out of here."

Meanwhile, struggling to maintain speed and balance, Anna Rose raced to find Bryan, hoping it was not too late. Potholes impeded her progress as she sped down River Road. Jess' old truck had no power steering and one shock was broken causing the truck to bounce off line.

"A musk ox burger sounds great. Mind if I join you?"

Hesitantly, Bryan said, "Sure, why not?"

Heading straight for the lunch counter, he placed his order. Ruby stood next to him and said, "Make that two." She walked over to Nico and paid for Bryan's fuel. Pleased with her covert activity, she smiled mischievously then returned to the lunch counter.

"I just love this meat," she said tasting the blackened burger.

Bryan disagreed then devoured his lunch anyway. Anxious for the long drive, he finished his cherry pie in three bites and washed it down with the last of his coffee.

"Slow down, you'll get indigestion," Ruby ordered.

"I've had enough of Hurricane County."

Failing to negotiate the turn at the Nugget Inn, white-knuckled Anna Rose gripped the steering wheel and counter corrected the old truck. She zipped through the abandoned town of Hurricane. Her mind reeled with unsettled questions, flustered emotions and an overpowering craving to become Mrs. Bryan Smith.

"More coffee?" Lorraine asked.

"No thanks. I've got to be on my way. I'll take the check."

Lorraine totaled his lunch ticket, then ripped the thin piece of paper from her pad and snidely handed it to Bryan.

"Thanks," he said checking the addition and then left a crumpled dollar tip. He slid off the barstool. "Well, Ruby, I'll be leaving now. Nice knowin' ya."

A mouth full of food prevented her reply. She swallowed, panicked that Bryan might depart without her.

Bryan paid Nico forty dollars for fuel and walked away. Nico placed the cash in his jean pocket. Max called Bryan back, shooting his son a disappointing look.

"Ruby already paid for your gas. Here's your money back."

"What?" Bryan said perturbed, giving Nico the evil eye. "Ruby, what's going on? Why did you pay for my gas?"

"Well...I, uh...thought that I'd pay for the fuel. Our trip to Anchorage is a long one, so I'm pitching in. In fact, this whole trip's on me."

"Just what do you mean *our* trip?"

Max and Lorraine stood back to watch the drama, hoping for juicy gossip to share with their next patrons. They listened intently, as rumors were their major source of entertainment.

Ruby wiped the mustard from her face. "You don't mind giving an old gal a ride to Anchorage, do you? I'm relocating, too. I cashed in all of my treasures; gave Russell Gentleman, Ravens, and the cabin. Now I'm ready for the big city lights."

Bryan pushed open the front door and stomped out. Instantly, Ruby followed him, staying close behind.

"Wait just one minute, Ruby," he hollered swatting at her. "That was a dirty trick you played on me. What gives you the right to assume that I'll *even* take you to Anchorage? I should leave you right where you stand." His body shook and his stomach pitted. *Unbelievable*, he thought, rushing to his truck.

Dust flew into the air as Anna Rose skidded into Hurk's parking lot. Not noticing Ruby and Bryan, she put the truck into park and jumped out. That's when she saw her neighbors arguing face-to-face.

"Oh now, just calm down. All I asked for was a ride to Anchorage. How much trouble can that be? I'll pay for everything. When we arrive in Anchorage, you can just drop me off at the nearest shelter. I won't be any trouble. In fact, I'll keep you company."

"What makes you think I want company?"

"What's goin' on here?" Anna Rose asked confused.

"Anna Rose," Bryan said with glee. "You've changed your mind?"

"Thinkin' about changin' it again—Ruby, what the hell are you doing here?"

Ruby smiled, "Headin' south, Anna." Ruby got into the truck and rolled down the window. "It's a long drive. Come on, let's get this truck fueled and be on our way."

"You're really pushing it, Ruby."

Shocked Anna Rose said, "You're leaving together?"

"He wasn't always cold this winter. Isn't that right, Bryan? We had our fun."

"Shut up, Ruby."

Aghast, Anna Rose threw her keys at Bryan. Rage rattled her emotions into overdrive. "How could you? Sara was right—never trust city folks and apparently not even your lifelong neighbors."

"Anna—" Ruby started to explain.

"Golda's bastard child all right, you were born a whore."

"That may be. Hey, I had no idea that you and Bryan were an item. During those lustful nights, he never mentioned it."

"Well Ruby, here's an idea for you. You take 'im. You screw 'im. And you keep 'im."

Bryan hollered, "Ruby, keep quiet. Anna Rose, this isn't what it looks like."

Shaking her head in disbelief, Anna Rose said, "Really, you preyed on a widow? Nice work, asshole."

"It was nothing like that. Please, calm down. Let me explain." As Bryan picked up Anna Rose's keys, a migraine began to pressurize near his temple.

"Ruby, did you sleep with him?"

"Don't recall sleeping."

"Shut up, Ruby," Bryan yelled.

Exasperated, Anna Rose spouted, "Stop joking."

"Okay, we got it on...three maybe four times."

Shaking his head in disbelief, rubbing his forehead, visualizing slapping Ruby to stifle her incessant chatter and hoping to cover up his lies, he handed over the keys.

"Unbelievable." Anna Rose stormed off and jumped into her truck. "Have a nice life. You deserve each other." Red faced, she flipped them off and punched the gas pedal. "Bastards," she hollered.

Face-to-face with Ruby, Bryan said, "I ought to jam my fist down your big mouth."

"Hey, you never said that you had a thing for Anna Rose."

"Well, you sure put an end to that."

Bryan maneuvered the truck to the gas pumps. Jumping out of the truck, he gave Ruby a reproachful look and then slammed shut the metal door. Suddenly, the sound of the metal prison bars clamored inside his mind. Trying to shake off their influence, he tried to clear his aching head, wishing the migraine and Ruby would disappear— before the bars once again offered to lock him behind them.

Ruby sat in the cab and sighed with relief. Freedom was several hundred miles away. Making herself comfortable in the stiff bench seat, she untied a leather pouch from her waist, placing it in the center of the seat. The pouch contained her precious jade stone. Unzipping her jacket and with a slight struggle, she removed it then laid it on the armrest. From her belt loops, she unleashed two, eight-inch long satchels filled with gold nuggets, placing them next to the legendary jade piece. The sun shined on her shoulders, relaxing them, maintaining her sound decision to move south. She regretted nothing.

Outside she noticed Bryan tapping his thumbs on the gas pumps while smoking. She considered reciting the dangers of smoking near a gas pump but decided not to push her luck.

Without saying a word, Bryan revved up the truck and sped off. The truck reached ninety-five miles per hour. As if he were serving another jail sentence, Bryan could not wait for the drive to end. Slowing the vehicle down to the legal speed limit, he felt as if he were crawling toward Anchorage. *This trip'll last forever. Ruby and Magpie are one-and-the-same,* he thought rubbing his temple. Nurse Jackson raced through his mind, *"Smith, you're coming back to us, just wait, you'll see."* *Never!* he thought.

An hour had passed and neither traveler had spoken. Bryan was busy shutting out Magpie and Nurse Jackson, who had continued to infiltrate his mind. Not allowing himself the luxury of sightseeing, tapping his fingers, Bryan tried to focus on the road. To be alone, to think about Anna Rose and to plan his future was all he wanted—besides a good stiff drink or two, sex and money. His thoughts constantly bantered between his anti-social behavior and the ever-elusive conventional lifestyle.

Ruby shifted her position, straightening her torso while yawning. "Do you want me to drive?" she asked. "I'd be happy to."

"No way." Bryan said firmly, fingers tapping harder.

"Well, it sure is a beautiful day. I just love these clouds. The winds stretch them to their limits and then poof, they're gone. I can always find a creature lurking in the sky. Hey look, there's one now."

"I'm driving." Bryan said curtly as he lit a cigarette. Now, the other side of his head pulsed, swollen blood vessels pressed on nearby nerves.

"It looks like a dragon. Just wait a few minutes though, it'll change into something else." Ruby began to ramble. "When I was a kid, I used to sit on the bluff and watch the clouds roll in. I'd try to separate them with my imagination. You know it worked, too, when I concentrated hard enough."

Only a few seconds lapsed when Ruby hollered, "Look. It's a bald eagle." She pointed to the west. "Oh, how graceful they are. Did you know that they mate for life? Just look at that six-foot wingspan. I'd love to ride the winds like them. I hear they can see a meal from two miles away. Have you ever watched them when they've spotted their prey? They quickly turn vertical. Then, they rush in for the kill. It's amazing. They free the spirit, ya know?" Ruby took in a much needed breath.

"I'd like to free your spirit," Bryan said as the truck came to a screeching halt. He jumped out and slammed the door. He hiked over to a group of spruce trees, peed while rubbing his forehead. Magpie squawked in his head, pushing Bryan into a murderous frame of mind.

Fearful that Bryan would leave her behind, Ruby quickly relieved herself in front of the truck. Quickly, she zipped up her blue jeans, jumped back into the cab then struggled to tuck in her favorite white button-up, lace-collared shirt.

"Thanks, I needed a break," Ruby said as Bryan entered the cab.

"Whatever. I should've left you behind in Hurricane. What was I thinking?" He knew what he was thinking: concrete floors, sterile walls, rehab, Magpie, Nurse Jackson, a sentence for another murder.

"You made the right choice, Bryan." As he turned the ignition key, Ruby hollered, "Look." She pointed to the opposite side of the road. Fifty-feet ahead, two cubs and their sow strolled rifling for food along the highway.

"Look how cute. The cubs are so uncoordinated," Ruby said. "Boy, the mother sure is thin. By September though, they'll be plump. Oh, there they go off into the tundra. Happy hunting."

"Why me?" Bryan asked rhetorically, pulling back onto Highway 1 with Magpie and Nurse Jackson cheering him on.

"Lucky for you, I'm here. Wow, first we saw the powerful eagle and then the bears. I wonder what else we'll see today. Probably a moose, wouldn't you think?"

"And anytime now, you'll be quiet?" Bryan said tapping his thumbs on the steering wheel, puffing away on another cigarette. Daylight over-sensitized his eyesight. The migraine worsened. He felt Magpie's presence. *Don't even think about, Magpie. You're nothing but trouble, certainly entertaining, but trouble*, Bryan thought.

"It's too long of a drive for silence. Hey, did I ever tell you about this hunk of stone?"

Bryan gave her a hateful look, emphasizing silence, like the persona of the stringent nurses of rehab, condemning and forbidding all conversation.

"Well, I guess not. I rarely expose it to strangers." She removed the transparent green rock from the leather pouch. "The story goes like this: My mother, Golda, traded a gold wedding band, worth virtually nothing, to this desperate young Russian man. You see, he was in love with a fellow Russian woman. He wanted to marry her. He was very poor, but in love. He came to Mama and traded what he thought was a worthless piece of jade. Little did he know, at the time it was worth fifteen hundred dollars. Back then, that would've been enough to buy a ring and place a down payment on a cabin."

His thumbs continued to tap harder, smoke swirled out of the truck's cracked window, he whispered under his breath, "It's too bad your Mama didn't trade you."

"What?"

Extinguishing his cigarette, Bryan ignored Ruby. Trying to relieve the pain in his head, hoping the cause would jump out of his rig, he lit another cancer stick. Unfortunately, Ruby continued with her story.

"I guess it was unfortunate for the young man and his bride. I mean, having to live in poverty. But, that's business. I often wondered about their fate. This precious stone has been my ticket out of the bush. I've always known it would bring me freedom from Hurricane County. In fact, Mama always said, 'Don't trade the jade.' Of course, I promised not to, but I knew that one day I would. Just as soon as we get to the city, I'm having it appraised. I can't wait to see the shopkeepers face. Then, I can't wait to see the cash that flows my way."

"I wish you'd flow out of my truck. Your incessant talking is driving me crazy. Your raspy voice isn't helping my migraine either."

"Anyway," Ruby said discounting Bryan's rude comments. "This rock became a legend in Hurricane. Traders still ask me about it. Ravens became quite popular as the story spread. Eventually, most everyone believed the story to be a myth. Only those who witnessed the actual trade remained believers—they're all dead now. Boy, it seems like yesterday, but it's been forty-seven years." Ruby sighed, placing the stone back on the seat.

Poor Hurricane County—forty-six years and three hundred sixty-five days is too long with ol' chatterbox. Oh my head, when will it stop? When will Ruby stop talking? he thought in agony.

Bryan's eyes watered from the high-pitched tones. The multiple wavelengths rippled each brain cell, sending spiked currents down through his nervous system. Suddenly, Bryan heard Magpie and Nurse Jackson squawking inside his head. The half-ton truck crossed the centerline.

"Bryan," Ruby screamed.

With intense hatred, Bryan leaned toward Ruby then hollered, "Ruby, shut up."

This scared her back into her seat. She sat erect with her eyes opened wide, heart racing, but confident she could break him again, taming his frazzled spirit.

Bryan countered his steering back to the southbound side of the road. Adrenaline surged, overloading his severed nerves. His heart rate soared which increased the gnawing, pulsating beat in his temples. Static raced through his head, disabling his senses. Unconsciously, he tapped his fingers as he heard Nurse Jackson recite the twelve steps and Magpie recite his proven techniques. Bryan's mind burst, blurring his vision. *Shut up everyone, just shut up, leave me alone*, Bryan silently screamed trying to command his imagination.

Ruby relaxed, as she continued, "So, one day Golda took the jade to Homer..."

Bryan's raw anxiety caused him to yell, "Yeah. I know, your precious ticket out of here, we'll see..." Alarmed, Ruby's eyes widened. In his mind, Magpie applauded while Nurse Jackson snickered.

"Calm down. This is supposed to be a fun trip. Anyway, once in Homer..."

Ruby's voice rattled Bryan's nerve fiber. His right hand slid off the steering wheel, landing on the ancient jade. Unfamiliar with its texture, he glanced downward, clenching the stone. Ruby's incessant chatter depleted his common sense. *Do it, do it, do it*, Magpie chanted. *Fuck off, Magpie, stay out of my mind, stay out of my life*, he thought, and then he shouted, "For the last time, Ruby, shut your fuckin' mouth."

"Calm down. In no time, we'll be in Anchorage living happily-ever-after. So just relax."

He lifted the jade. His jagged nerves shortened Ruby's last longwinded, one-sided conversation. "Didn't I tell you there *is* no happily-ever-after." With great force, he struck Ruby's temple, smashing her head against the side window. Her last breath was a shocking gasp. At last, Ruby was silent. Magpie cheered, stirring the other inmates; Nurse Jackson laughed hysterically—laughing, laughing, laughing. Bryan's brain fizzled and all logic dissipated.

"Back off, Magpie. Go to hell, Nurse Jackson. I'm not goin' back. Both of you, shut the fuck up," Bryan spouted. Tension pressed against his temples as his co-conspirators continued taunting him.

Ruby's body slumped in the stiff seat. The window supported her tilted head. Her eyes rolled backward, and her mouth involuntarily fell open. Moistened with her blood, Ruby's golden blonde hair hung over half of her face. Her most cherished possession had crushed her skull. Ruby was dead.

"That'll keep you quiet," Bryan said repulsed, pulling the truck over, then securing it in place. His hand shook as he released his grip; the jade fell onto the seat, human flesh meshed with stone, an eyebrow pressed firmly into a thin crevasse—the evidence of a life. *You're on your way back...*, Nurse Jackson said shading his mind with confusion. "Stay out of my head, bitch," Bryan countered. His body ached; the call for whiskey was overwhelming, adrenaline overflowed coursing through his veins, his heart raced from the excitement—his second murder, his second chance to escape, his first chance to hide the evidence, freeing himself from Magpie and Nurse Jackson forever.

From the outside, Bryan opened the passenger side door. Ruby fell limp into winter's slush, splashing mud on his boots. Blood trickled down the window. He tried to wipe it clean, but it was too late. The blood had already seeped down between the rubber seal and the glass.

"Damn it, my truck. You bitch, you ruined it." His beloved truck withstood time but not Ruby's fatal, final conversation. Appalled, he estimated Ruby's numerous sexual partners, and for the second time, he vacillated over the possibility that her blood was tainted. The succulent smell awakened his senses. Memories of his best friend's blood spraying his face, Magpie's gushing wrist and the sweet smell of Anna Rose came rushing back. No longer could he resist a taste.

Each crease of his chapped hands filled with blood—Ruby's essence. Fearless and satisfied, he looked up and down the highway.

Seeing nothing but pavement, he hoisted Ruby over his shoulder. He struggled with her weight. After hiking over to a grove of birch trees, he haphazardly dropped her.

Vigorously, he scrubbed melting snow between his bloodstained palms. To Ruby's dead body, he said, "I told you, not everyone can be rehabilitated. You should've listened." Suddenly, Bryan heard Nurse Jackson laughing and wolves howling. Ignoring Nurse Jackson, he followed the hungry cries. Two wolves stood atop a nearby hillside sniffing the air. "An easy meal, now that's a happy ending—no evidence left behind," he said with a smirk. Once satisfied with clean hands, he returned to his beloved truck. Without looking back, migraine free, he drove away in peace.

EPILOGUE

CALM BEFORE THE STORM

Why is my body distorted, bloody and cold? My hyper-extended legs almost touch my rear end. (I've never been that flexible.) I'm not moving. My left arm's positioned over my head, hand open to the sky. My right arm sprawls outward, hand open, facing downward, into the soggy earth. I'm confused. Mud and ice adhere to my lovely face. My open, sparkling blue eyes have turned grey. Teeth exposed, my facial tissue droops. (How interesting.) Why are my best clothes wet? What happened to me? I feel without the familiar sensation of my senses.

I'm dead.

There's no light, no tunnel, no one to greet me.

Why does my soul keep tugging at me to stay? Certainly, I'm not going back to Mother Earth so soon? Don't drag me backwards, drag me upwards. I'm already free. Why would I return? Take me.

I hear someone whispering 'retaliate...validate these untimely circumstances...retaliate.' Why does my ascending essence command retribution? This doesn't seem natural. Yet somehow, I'm compelled to return. My unearthed psyche prods me into submission. (I'm familiar with that!) Is this my destiny or someone else's?

From above I mentally rewind, seeing the path to my death...Oh, that bastard murdered and robbed me! Certainly, I will stay to reclaim my soul! I wasn't ready to go anyway. It's my fate, fulfillment of a contract written so long ago. I surrender and return to avenge my death.

Promptly, a chain reaction occurs, awakening those closest to my previous life—even those whom I've hurt or deceived. I send a message. In a nanosecond, it's received. Oh, the power I have!

My cells cringe. I hear them. The four-leggeds, I'm certain. They howl into the wind. Their cries resonate out toward faraway relatives, extending an invitation to other packs. Now, I cower.

My favorite white, lace-collared shirt shreds and thousands of soiled, bloody fibers rest into winter's slush. Sinew tears away from my cartilage. Bones splinter and break apart. My marrow's still warm. Yet I feel nothing as wolves devour my flesh and bones. Coyotes surround the feast. They must wait; nature's hierarchy is patient, providing for all. Crows caw above. Their hungry spirit engages. I'm pleased they have arrived. They'll clean up the carnage, my remains, leaving but one clue as to my existence.

All is as it should be.

****

Old Man Kurtz awoke startled and chilled, gasping for air. He knew. The message was clear—Ruby was dead.

Never before, had he been disturbed over a message from those who had gone to the other side. As he lit dry spruce in the woodstove, he checked his intuition to understand the messenger's intent. His mind wandered back to his teachings: Owls fly during the night delivering sound advice, bestowing lessons and were the messenger of the Great Spirit. Riddled with ambiguous teachings; you must listen, ever so closely; open yourself to the lesson; filter out the literal; bond with reality. Owl interaction is a blessing; it's influence asks of you to: find your dark side, delve into it, work with it, understand it then go forth.

Flames flickered, sending Old Man Kurtz into a deep trance. Once on the edge of light and dark, nothing distracted him. Suddenly catapulted into an array of colorful white light, translucent flashes of energy surrounded him. Pink light over his heart, warmed him, soothing his trepidation. His stomach relaxed as yellow balls circled around his torso. Spheres of blue and purple encompassed his crown, pulsing downward and around his throat. Orange and red discs encircled his waist and pushed through his pelvis. Whirling energy spiraled down to his toes. The blessing of Silence allowed logic to disappear, allowing truth to reveal itself, slowly, methodically, undeniably.

A gushing vision swooned through his forehead. Kurtz saw the blow to Ruby's head, the blood dripping down a window and heard the wolves cry. The finale left him sad. An Albatross swooped down and carried his emotions upward. Silence returned.

Boom!

He was back and staring, eyes watering, at the blazing fire. He sat shocked, dumbstruck with grief, overwhelmed by the truth, as he once again had become a messenger. Delivering a white woman's message was unacceptable according to tribal customs. His clan would test his leadership. What would they think? Would they allow this? Would Ruby's spirit influence them? He would have the final say, even if it became his last decision as Chief.

As the woodstove blazed, a fire burned in his heart, a sensation that had been stored away for war. Tucking it deep into unseen cells, he hoped it would have never again rule his world. Squelching it, it now tore at him like a caged animal hell-bent on lashing out, striking its offender, devouring its essence. Old Man Kurtz fought it, held it at bay, struggling with this demon from the past. He let out a roar of pain as revenge burst through his heart, revealing Ruby's intent—revenge and vengeance. Kurtz became apprehensive over Ruby's power.

A coffee cup rattled, tipped over and shattered.

Ruby, thought Kurtz. She was warning him. Her powerful spirit rose ready to avenge her murderer. Would she also avenge those left behind?

He shuddered to imagine Ruby's vengeful side. Recalling their time together; both had been respectful, teachings and lessons for both were meaningful and spiritual. No, there would be no retaliation from Ruby toward Kurtz.

Warming to the fire, a spark ignited. His mind returned to the morning message: thinking, deciphering, making clear assumptions as to Ruby's intent—her message of death. Who killed her? Where was her body?

He drew in a breath, slowly exhaled, then repeated. Relaxed, he drifted off into meditation. In darkness and alone, he forced his attention deeper. Emptying his mind, he waited. Like a hot arc, lightning struck his mind, allowing the truth to unfold. Upon awakening, he understood. The message was clear. Ruby's body rested some place in the south. But where?

Slightly dazed, Kurtz made coffee, ate smoked salmon then dressed in ancient regalia—his best spring attire. Without warning, the front door blew open, breaking the hinges. This was clear confirmation—Northerners built their front doors facing south, never facing north, never opening themselves to freezing temperatures or biting winds—that south of Hurricane County was where Ruby took her last earthly breath.

A nearby wolf cried out, stirring the clans' dogs to howl back. *Damn, Ruby,* he thought as a red streak flashed through his mind.

Again, red for the south, not blue for the north or yellow for the east or indigo for the west. Red. Kurtz saw nothing but red!

The village clamored with morning chores and a dozen howling malamutes. Undistracted, Kurtz moved through it, paying no attention to the clan. Red snow slushed beneath his beaded caribou boots. Walking steadily, Kurtz grew angry. Ruby needed to step aside, let him handle this his way. He received the message, received her warnings, received a broken door, a shattered coffee cup and now, he was seeing red—everywhere. This was not his usual path of leadership. Ruby was controlling him. Irked and inconvenienced, Kurtz didn't have time for this intrusion. He reached the village entrance and forced himself, grudgingly, to walk to Ravens. Or was it Ruby leading him onward?

Ruby, you have no right, he thought. She had always done things her way, and now she was powerful, even more powerful than him. He chuckled to himself. As he did so, his ego dropped away, diffusing his anger. And, the red disappeared along with it, correcting his vision.

From above, Ruby was teaching him: reminding him of his own teachings regarding laughter, stress, being at peace, creating inner wars, embracing positive forces and releasing negative ones.

Breathe, Old Man. This won't take long, he heard her say.

The wolves let out one last howl, leaving Kurtz to walk in silence. Settled with delivering Ruby's message, he surrendered, allowing Ruby her final request. Or was it her final request?

Gentleman whined, dancing around Russell's feet as Ken Kurtz entered Ravens. His presence surprised the patrons into silence. Never before had he stepped into Ruby's drinking establishment. Russell felt a harpoon impale his heart.

Gentleman continued dancing. "Hush, G'man," Russell ordered struggling with what Kurtz would announce; what Russell already knew; what was to be one of the worst days for everyone. Ruby's spirit filled the tavern. She rattled several tables and tumblers, scaring Wally into taking another gulp of whiskey. It was a sign from spirit, and Ruby's way of announcing her newly found power.

Kurtz didn't look around. He understood economics and addiction and withstood both tests: ninety-proof beverages had stolen his true love and their marriage. Denying the damaged souls—drunken Brothers of Spirit from spirits—he cast his black-brown eyes directly at Russell. The exchange penetrated Russell's core, twisting the imagined harpoon.

The two native men and Gentleman stepped outside. Reaching solid ground, a gust of silt abruptly lifted then forcefully flew up and over Ravens, then at full speed hurled over miles of Alaskan tundra. Ruby was mad. Russell felt her then ignored her. Gentleman sensed her and cowered. Old Man Kurtz was more than ready to unload her message.

Chief of the Eagle Clan spoke, "Great Spirit has sent a message."

"Why bring it here? Who sent this message?"

"I see that you can feel her. Acknowledge her."

"Old man, don't speak in riddles. Tell me and be on your way." Gentleman whined, prancing and pawing at Russell's leg.

"Ruby's dead."

"How do you know this?"

"I know."

"Old man, you're out of your mind."

"In my last dreamtime, Ruby crossed over. She's full of revenge. Wolf has tasted her blood, eaten her flesh and delivered her soul to the Universe."

Gentleman howled toward the sky.

From out of nowhere, another gust spiraled across the parking lot. A black, grey and white wolf appeared in its wake. Gentleman cautiously sniffed the air. Hunched down submissively, he slowly walked toward the wolf. No hierarchy, no posturing transpired; an understanding passed between the two breeds, and they stood in harmony.

"See there, Russell. Ruby's essence is *in* the wolf. Even the dog knows it."

Gentleman and the wolf disappeared. "You have no proof."

"You're a fool not to believe. Her message is clear. She needs something from you, maybe from all of us. Ruby's power is unlimited."

The sky crackled with thunder.

"Look around, feel the air, smell her scent."

"Enough. Old Man, go back to the clan. Tell your brothers, 'free shots tomorrow.'"

"Killing your own is disgraceful."

"I eat well." Russell cringed, as Ruby's voice faded from his mind. This was her standard response—her choice of words. Russell shrugged, once again ignoring her spirit.

Gentleman bolted through the brush, knocking Russell to the ground. Deafening wolf howls and blankets of swirling dust surrounded Russell, kicking silt into his mouth. His eyes and nose clogged. Coughing the fine silt from his lungs, he became aware that something supernatural was to blame. *Ruby?* He questioned with uncertainty.

After Ruby's tornado ceased, Kurtz laughed at Russell's indignant look, his obstinate behavior, and his stifled pigheadedness. "You'll see—a man will come. Beware. Ruby's impatient."

"Even after all your teachings, I still believe in nothing."

"You'll believe soon enough." Relieved that Ruby's message had been delivered, Ken Kurtz proudly smiled and walked away.

Russell dusted off. "Gentleman, what's gotten into you? Is Ruby back?" Missing his long-time caretaker, Gentleman whined then bounded back into the brush, no doubt to play with the lone wolf. As Russell entered Ravens, it was vigorous with patrons stealing drinks like mad men without water in the wilderness.

Wally piped up, slurring his words, "You dis…respected the Chief of…our clan. Dis…respectful, I tell you, dis…respectful."

"Gotta have respect in order to disrespect," Russell replied. "Get your hands off my booze, you drunken thieves. You're all going to hell!"

"As are you...," Wally said in a quiet voice, "...as are you."

From out of Wally's thick head of hair, Ruby's spirit plucked a single black hair. "Hey!" Wally said swatting the air. Embarrassed by his drunkenness and his confusion, he scratched his head. He rotated his shoulders forward, hung his head low sinking closer to his best friend—a shot of stolen whiskey.

PREY BE FOUND

Glacial winds blew north to south. Easterly winds had quieted while the west winds held the truth, awaiting discovery. Hurricane force weather relentlessly beat the residents of Hurricane County for nine long days. Ruby had summoned the strong winds. Through each crisp gust, her powerful spirit-wolf howled. The ominous sound multiplied as it echoed through the forest.

Dry ground turned to solid clay. Hollow cottonwood trees cracked then snapped, falling to the ground. No longer able to fight the hurling debris, Sara shut down the chainsaw then walked to the Quonset hut to check on Dorothy. Waiting out the twisted winds, Raider hunkered down, safe from predatory wolves. Anna Rose placed uneaten pie into the freezer and stopped making coffee. She hadn't given Bryan Smith a second thought. *Done was done,* as Ruby would say, *D-O-N-E, once a woman was on the "E," the relationship was over.* Besides, it was the first day of May—a special day. It was *Freedom Day*; Ruby had dubbed this date a day to free oneself from the confines of winter and any personal or business relationships that weren't working. *Move on*, she would announce waving her hands above her head. Waiting out the unusual storm, Anna Rose replaced the memory of Bryan Smith with books and family.

Anxious to hike up the bluff for a spring hunt, Trapper wrestled with cabin fever. Hoss stayed home, pissing into empty coffee tins and tossing hollow food cans aside. Evergreens split, falling to the Alaskan soil, spooking Hoss as he feared his own karma for killing Golda. Under the circumstances, he refused to haul water—a futile task anyway as George Creek was a mixture of dirt and foliage.

Russell had had no customers. The onus was placed on him to address Ruby's vengeful needs. Stubbornly, he dismissed his responsibility, and Old Man Kurtz refused Ruby's second request to talk to Russell again. Hence, the raging winds continued. Ruby was furious.

Downed trees and brush scattered the valley as Ruby's message went unheard. After ten days of crying wolves and high winds, temperatures began to rise. Rivers flowed, freeing ice and snow, flooding the dry soil.

Finally, the man came. And the winds stopped, quieting the forest. Stroking his grey and tobacco-stained mustache, he read the menu then neatly placed his hat on the counter. "Give me a musk ox burger, cheese, tomato, lettuce—no onion. Coffee, cream and sugar," he said confidently.

Lorraine spouted, "There's no cream. We had to toss it out. Sugar's on your left. We haven't had a customer in thirteen days."

With a tentative smile and a pot of hot coffee, Max greeted the short, thin uniformed man. "What are you doing this far north?"

"A life gone bad," he replied twisting on the tip of his pinky finger a single diamond gold nugget ring. The way he rotated, polished and fondled it continuously was odd. He appeared to obsess over it. Did anyone else notice?

From behind the grill, Max shook his head, "Life's a riddle. Are you committing suicide?" No response.

The man's badge, and his lack of conversation made Max nervous.

Sipping his coffee, he looked at Max, then at Lorraine, "You toss anyone out in the last thirteen days?"

Lorraine didn't take a liking to his question. "Look Mr. State Trooper," reading his nametag, "Crane is it?" Lorraine started to lay into him. "We don't like city folks comin' around here asking a bunch of questions—law included."

"Like I asked before, you toss anyone out in the last ten or more days?" Crane pressed, neither gently nor hard. Patiently, he waited for information, anticipating the moment when they would trip up. While rotating the ring, he listened intently, observing their body language.

In her normal tone, Lorraine said snidely, "Just a drunken native."

"Male or female?"

"I think a female. She looked to be about eight months pregnant. You want her DNA?"

With finesse, Max swept the burger from the grill and said, "Simmer down, Lorraine. He might blow his own fool head off." He piled fries into a basket, topped them with an open-faced bun then placed the wild meat on top.

"It wouldn't be a first. Just do it away from here. I don't like the bears sniffing around the garbage—assuming that's where you'll end up."

Max gave her the *hush* look. She gave it right back with a firm, pronounced facial expression strong enough to scare a grizzly. Max knew the look well. He also knew not to push his wife of twenty-two years. Her mother must have been a mean old bear, he often thought, because that's what Lorraine turned out to be—mean and old. As always, his second thought followed: maybe she's just mean because, at six-months old, her mother dropped her off at a nearby cabin in Chugiak, Alaska. The cabin was filled with men who sold her to a desperate native woman who had not conceived in her thirty-eight years. That's when the baby was named, and that's when the baby became a burden. The mother drank heavily, divorced then departed, following a penniless man half her age. Raised by several aunts, Lorraine was abused, in the worst possible ways, by her uncles. Fleeing the Chugiak natives, she hitch-hiked north trading dried meat and lust. Lorraine knew when to tease and when to disappear. At the age of fourteen, she was dropped off in Hurricane County. This had been her first adult decision. Max became her first and only real lover, then husband. Four kids later and with a wavering business, Lorraine grew cold and resentful. Max understood. He dealt with it the best any uneducated man could, though he never gave up trying to please her. To protect himself from her wrath, he kept his benevolence to a minimum. Happiness wasn't in Lorraine's design, so he let it be. He let her be. Most importantly, he wanted their children to understand the give-and-take of a relationship. It was the best he had to offer, and he had no regrets.

"Order up," Max hollered for what seemed like the one-millionth time.

Under the overhead lighting, gold glistened, stopping Max in his tracks. "You gonna pay for this with that ring?"

"So you've seen it before." State Trooper Crane made a statement of fact, not posing a question. Often he implemented, easily and effectively, one of the oldest interrogation tricks, known as *Street Cop 101*, which he had learned 21-years ago. Criminals commonly dragged evidence around like a dead weight, and with time, their lies became distorted—embellished tales of their evil deeds. Crane enjoyed trapping his prey.

Max replied, "Might have."

"Whose finger does it belong too?"

"Can't say for sure."

"Or won't," Crane said as a fact, not a question.

"I don't need the hassle."

"Max, what is he doing with Ruby's ring?" Lorraine asked.

"Lorraine, you should mind your own business."

245

"This is my business, Max. A strange man wearing a woman's ring, asking questions—you can be sure this is my business."

Max rolled his eyes. Crane raised one corner of his thin, dry lips.

With her hands pressing against her bulging hips, Lorraine barked, "Now, what the hell are you doin' wearing Ruby's ring?"

"Who's Ruby?"

"I asked first."

No response.

Crane ate slowly as Lorraine watched him. It was a stalemate between two stubborn, demanding people. Max bounced back from the eyes of two devils, though he wasn't sure which set of eyes held the most spite. Lorraine had the background. Crane had the experience. Lorraine had four children. Crane had a wealth of training in negotiations and standoffs. Lorraine dipped one knee, dropping the opposite hip then repeated with the other knee, as if she were an impatient child waiting to pee. Steadfast and looking straight ahead, Crane continued to eat. Tension saturated the diner. Crane motioned for more coffee. Not moving one inch, Lorraine's red eyes discharged imaginary heat down Crane's back.

Max felt the air around him compress, its heaviness unbearable. He couldn't take the stress. He poured the coffee giving his wife an apologetic look then stepped aside.

"So, what's it gonna be, Mr. State Trooper? Are you gonna tell me why you have Ruby's ring? Or do I have to toss you out myself?"

No response.

Crane wiped his mouth then pressed the napkin back onto the counter, making sure each corner was flat as if it were clean. Casually, he looked up at Max, who was waiting impatiently for the shit to hit the fan. Crane turned to Lorraine. In the calmest of voices, he said, "Ruby appears to be dead."

Lorraine straightened, stiff as a washboard, and in the calmest voice she could muster replied while walking away, "So I've heard."

Max relaxed, releasing his shoulders away from his ears. His mouth dried into a paste, and his lungs held no air. Crane didn't flinch but his mind was working overtime: *Interesting response...How did she know? Did she kill Ruby? Does she know the killer?* Planned to perfection, his counterattack waited to be unleashed. He would interrogate the weaker of the two.

Crane looked squarely into Max's worried blue eyes, "I'll be arresting your wife now. Apparently, murder doesn't faze her. She'll do fine in jail."

Up went Max's shoulders. His eyes glazed over. He needed to sit down. *A foolish move*, he thought as he didn't want to appear guilty and wanted very much to step up for his children's mother. With his wife's back to him he said, "Lorraine, get over here, and tell this State Trooper that you didn't kill Ruby."

She didn't move.

"Right now."

She didn't move.

"I won't have my children thinking you're a killer."

With attitude overflowing, Lorraine turned around and said, "Your children?"

There, now Max had her attention.

Crane watched the family dynamics change—the alpha male ruled over the female. *Nice work*, Crane thought.

Lorraine said, "Ruby's the slut of Hurricane County."

"Lorraine, quiet," Max said lowering his head, ashamed of his wife's words.

"Truth is truth. Between her and Golda, they wouldn't have known the first name of the last man they had slept with—let alone Ruby's father's name."

"Who's Golda?" Crane asked.

"Ruby's mother. Golda taught Ruby whoring and herbal medicine. They were good at both." To Max, Lorraine said, "Is that better?"

Max gave her the traditional marital look that asked, *Really?*

Crane covered his thick sand and salt-colored hair with the tall, and wide brimmed official Alaska State Trooper hat then paid his tab. "How do I find Golda?"

Lorraine huffed, "Right about now, the permafrost has her pinned down about eight-feet underground. Your scrawny arms would never survive the dig."

Max stood still as his wife bantered with the law. *When did she get so mean?* he thought.

"I could just take her in for obstruction. What do you think, Max? Get her out of your hair?"

Max half-laughed, "A few days without Lorraine would feel like…" he looked over at his wife with her hands back on her hips "…a hundred bad days. I'll have to pass."

Crane nodded, thinking about the hierarchy of marriage. He found the hassles of marriage to be reinforcement for his divorce. The lies, the days of wanting to run for the closest border, sexless days and nights waiting for the woman he had married to return—marriage was incarceration at its best. Before considering getting married again, Crane promised to lock himself in a jail cell—just for the practice, just to remind himself of matrimonial limitations and constraints. Marriage was about the only subject that made him shudder.

"You're still leaving me empty-handed. I could take you both in."

"You bastard," Lorraine said stepping forward as if to strike. Max intercepted.

"Try Ravens—it's the watering hole that Ruby owns. It's about twenty-two miles east. Turn left at the Nugget Inn."

"That's better. Now, I can feel the love."

Max held Lorraine tight. "I feel it too," Max said, pecking Lorraine on the cheek. She about broke her neck trying to dodge his lips.

"Don't leave town."

"Where the hell are we gonna go?" Lorraine spouted.

"South. To purchase cream," Crane made another statement, not a question. He rubbed his stomach. Coffee without cream was second to marriage—sour and volatile.

Queasy from the bumpy road, Crane pulled into Ravens parking lot, took note of the aging totem pole, the tavern's plywood construction and faded red door. *Not so much a watering hole, but a hole in the Alaskan landscape,* he thought. No surprise to him, as most bush communities had few resources and no need for permanent structures. In the bush, a man's way of living was always temporary. Vulnerable to the elements, they adapted accordingly. Bottomless milky-green rivers had taken many men to undisclosed graves. High winds crushed the unsuspecting. Wildlife raged from out of nowhere to maim or kill those hunting or those being hunted. Bears and wolves were known for tracking the trackers, then killing them. Crane admired those living without the comforts of the city. He never had any desire to join them, though he still respected their choice of lifestyle. Which reminded him, he needed to pee.

Unzipped behind the Raven Clan's totem pole, Crane's butt felt the cool May air. As his bladder emptied, he relaxed, until he heard growling. Simultaneously, he turned and zipped up. A wolf showing its fangs and raised hackles readied itself for an attack. Two choices flashed though Crane's mind: make a move for his gun, which offered potential deadly results or stare down the wild beast, which offered potential deadly results.

Taking two steps forward, the wolf gracefully moved in closer. It let out a howl to the heavens so robust that it prompted even Crane to cower. He remained perfectly still. A German Shepherd bolted through the brush. Now flanked by the canines, his potential deadly results turned into imminent deadly results. *Shit*, he thought. Gentlemen cautiously sniffed his leg, nudging Ruby's ring.

"Easy boy," Crane said befriending him. With his teeth exposed, Gentleman growled. Crane froze. His eyes scanned for the wolf's position. Like an Alaskan winter ghost disappearing into a stilled arctic night, it was gone. With skin crawling, Crane remained stationary. Was the wild beast behind him? Would it attack from the side? Where did it go?

After a few tense moments, Trooper Richard Crane relaxed. Thankful to have missed a good mauling, and with Gentleman leading the way he entered Ravens then sat next to Wally.

Like an absent old friend, Wally coddled his drink. His afternoon drink had arrived just before his liver demanded liquid sugar, just before the blues set in and just before his hands began to shake. Alcoholism took the lead, directing Wally's daily activities that consisted of waking up, drinking two pots of sweet coffee and eating a half slice of toast, making ready evening firewood, and if creek drainage was suitable, he'd pan for gold. All this before noon and before the shakes took over. Staring into his drink, full bottles rattled as Russell skirted past without a word, leaving the old man alone to enjoy his caramel-colored friend.

Russell recognized the hat. His lips parted slightly as he whispered Kurtz' words, "'A man will come.'"

Wally looked up. "Nice watch. You wanna make a trade?"

"Maybe." State Trooper Crane placed his hat on the clear lacquered bar. Gentleman nudged his pants pocket. Crane removed the ring, concealing it in his palm.

Russell braced himself for the sharp, painful blow. He didn't like cops nor did he have the stomach for what this cop was delivering. "Plenty of drinks are served south of here."

Spinning the ring around his pinky finger, Crain said, "Not much of a drinker."

Wally slapped the bar, "Then what the hell are ya doin' here?" The ring's single diamond caught Wally's eye. "Russell," Wally whispered, nodding toward the ring.

After seeing the ring, Russell stopped restocking the shelves. "What are you doing this far north?" Russell asked perturbed.

"Just checking things out."

"Bullshit. That's Ruby's ring. How'd you get it?"

"Give it to me," Wally said reaching for it.

Crane pulled back. Gentleman growled.

Wally asked, "Trade ya for a generator—perfect condition?"

No response.

Russell said, "Ruby would've never parted with her mother's ring."

"Golda," Crane stated without posing a question.

"Yeah, Golda. You know her?" Russell asked baiting the trooper.

"Hard to know a dead person."

Again, Wally tried to snatch the ring. Crane was faster, stronger.

"Ouch," Wally cried out struggling as Crane bent his hand back, touching it to the bar.

"Leave the old man alone. What do you want?" Russell's patience had evaporated. "See that sign? That means even you can be tossed out of here."

Not intimidated, Crane pressed Wally's hand down harder.

"God damn you," Wally cried out.

From beneath the bar, Russell drew his .357 magnum.

Crane released Wally. "You sure you want to use that?"

"Just needed to free an old man," Russell said as he shelved the gun, positioning it for a quick draw. "But don't test me because I will use it, if I need too."

WORD TRAVELS

The fire smoldered after Russell tossed water into Ruby's old barrel woodstove. Haphazardly, he shoved into a backpack: a pair of socks, wadded-up boxers and toiletries—obviously planning a short stay. Gentleman whined as Russell loaded a pistol, spun the barrel twice and then placed the gun in a side pocket of the backpack. What remained of Ruby—hair, her skull and a shredded blouse—waited in a sealed plastic bag. Crane solicited Russell to perform the dreadful task of identifying the remains. Russell wondered if Crane was setting him up—law enforcement was tricky that way; setting up innocent people to close a case, making the investigator look good. Russell didn't trust Crane. Annoyed, Russell hushed Ruby's dog, now his sole responsibility, as was Ravens. Uneasy, he walked Gentleman down to Tealand's where Dorothy waited. A grim look stretched across her weathered face.

Gentleman greeted Raider with the usual round of sniffing. Anna Rose and Sara tossed their overnight bags into the truck bed. Dorothy spouted off about being careful in Anchorage, driving safely and returning home. God forbid if she ended up raising Sara's two young kids, not to mention maintaining the homestead. Regardless of the results of Ruby's murder case, she needed her daughters back.

The news about Ruby's murder had reached the Hurricane County gossip mill. The community buzzed with theories and joking references about her demise. Sworn to secrecy, they all thought they knew what had happened. Eventually, the conversation led to what Rubys' life savings could purchase. Anger stirred as the Russian Jade, the mythical treasured stone brought back to life during Ruby's final auction, rightfully belonged to Hurricane County. It was a priceless piece of Hurricane's history. However, some had already set their sights on stealing and trading it then disappearing into Alaska's vast landscape. They had better disappear because frontier justice would eventually catch up to them, resulting in a harsh punishment—death, the painful way. Guaranteed.

Bryan Smith, the only logical suspect, not revealed to State Trooper Crane, was on the lam. Russell wanted Smith for himself. Ruby was annoying, but was a good friend and a big part of Hurricane County. Knowing Crane would be following him, Russell intended to retrieve Ruby's life savings and the Russian Jade then guide Bryan Smith into the hands of the law, sending him back to jail—hopefully for life. But if things got messy, the deciding factor would end with a bullet.

Regulars cheered as the three drove past Ravens full parking lot. Anna Rose and Sara waved. Russell half-smiled worried that he'd return to an empty bar, robbed of inventory. Silently, he asked Ruby to protect what was theirs. Bound to their verbal contract, Russell mindfully remained loyal. Russell's fantasy about what had happened to Ruby played in his mind: Ruby must have bailed on Bryan or he left her on the highway; she wasn't dead—just missing among the living in the enormous state of Alaska. Now seeing Old Man Kurtz on the roadside, Russell's stomach dropped. His intuition fluttered, dispelling his version of Ruby's status.

Ken Kurtz stood, raised staff in hand, as Russell intersected Pearl Street. A translucent wolf crossed in front of the Jess Tealand's truck, then disappeared into thin air. Feeling Ruby's afterlife energy, Kurtz smiled. He understood wolves, their power, their prowess, their stalking behaviors and their go-for-the-jugular killing techniques. *Ruby would be successful*, he thought grinning.

After Russell fueled Tealand's rig, Max shook his hand, "Fuel's on the house. Go get the bastard that stole Ruby's life. Better yet, return the Russian Jade."

Only a stranger to the bush would think Max's remark cold and calloused. Russell understood. Hurricane County didn't have much except their stories, legends and the prospect of wealth. The loss of life was a given in the harsh northern territory. Mourners easily put death into perspective, knowing the Alaskan elements were real, alive and the majority of the time, triumphant. As they pulled away from Hurricane County, each grappled with Ruby's presumed death, the accuracy and cruelty of it, ultimately leading them toward vengeance. They owed Ruby that much. Eager and highly motivated, the trio drove in silence. How would they find Bryan Smith? Was he the killer? Was it really Ruby lying in pieces at the Anchorage Morgue? All three knew how to take a life. But could they find one? Anna Rose broke the silence, "How—?"

"I don't know," Russell cut her off.

"Let's wait until we determine if it is Ruby," Sara added. "Russell, watch out!" she yelled. He slammed on the brakes, swerving to the right.

In the middle of the road, a wolf stood glaring at the trio. Sara's neck hairs stood on end. Goose bumps traveled over Anna Rose's body.

After his heart rate slowed, Russell smiled. He understood. Ruby was watching, guiding them into a successful hunt. "'Listen to the cry of the wolf,'" Old Man Kurtz had said. Russell had shunned the Elder. Another failed demonstration of listening to Spirit and learning from his clans' beliefs. Russell wondered if he might one day accept their philosophy. Equally important, he wondered if he would ever participate in his native Alaskan heritage. Kurtz thought the same. Soon Russell would force himself to apologize.

Driving past milepost two hundred seventy, Russell felt the spirit of the wolf—Ruby's spirited essence. Not wanting it to become a point of reference for Hurricane County, he hadn't shared the milepost information with anyone. For now, there'd be no place marker for Ruby. Only the Troopers, Russell, Bryan and the wolves knew of Ruby's gravesite.

It was a Tuesday afternoon when Crane announced Ruby's death. Hurricane County had calculated thirteen days to be more accurate. Bryan had departed on April 17th. After a hard winter and hungry, the wolves hadn't allowed her body to decay, warm blood served them well.

Bryan Smith was starving too. He hungered for peace and quiet. And, he hungered for wealth. Ruby's incessant chatter had driven him mad. A silent ride into Anchorage had been his plan. Ruby had ruined it with her trickery and conniving. He faulted her. Occasionally, frontier justice had to be executed. Similar to a daunting movie scene etched in his mind, he remembered the moment the jade had struck her skull. In one fell swoop, Ruby became silent, and Bryan became rich. No one could possibly find the body. Alaska was too remote and uncharted. He felt secure in knowing that if Ruby was found the Troopers wouldn't bother to open a case. They didn't care, nor would anyone else. Troopers didn't know about the Russian Jade, and Ruby's gold was undocumented. She was a nuisance, an annoyance and a manipulator. She deserved being left to the wolves. Bryan's fate had blossomed into freedom and prosperity.

****

In Anchorage, the *Black Market Pawn* shop came into view on Fourth Avenue. After long periods of trapping, hunting and gold panning this was the first stop for many traders.

"That's him!" Anna Rose shouted, pointing at a tall man wearing army issue boots and a pea-coat.

"Where?" Sara looked around feverishly. Russell doubled back. There was no one. *Black Market Pawn's* neon sign flashed "Closed."

"I swear it was him."

"It's been a long drive. Maybe you just thought you saw him," Sara said.

"No, I know it was him."

"Let's get to the police station," Russell said. "They're expecting us. Afterwards, we can search on our own." Anna Rose's sighting, if it were correct, would have been sheer luck. He didn't believe in luck. He was calm though ready to combat the untrustworthy law. He pulled into the Anchorage Police Station parking lot. Their bodies demanded a good stretch, but no one moved. Neither could fathom the end of this meeting. Would Ruby be classified deceased? Would the Troopers declare no foul play or declare a murder investigation?

Dismal, boring hallways and the stench in the antiquated elevator stifled the trio and State Trooper Richard Crane. The elevator left them in the basement, an even more sterile environment permeated with the dreadful odor of formaldehyde. Slowly, they headed into the frigid morgue where the dead hid behind stainless steel doors. Two other men were already inside standing next to a stainless steel examination table.

The plain-clothed man appeared to be the Coroner—a fat, older man with hunched shoulders. He was bald yet sported a full, silver beard. The other was a slender, oily-skinned man wearing an Alaska State Trooper uniform; his fingers tucked into his wide leather belt, both hips shielded by unlatched holsters—guns ready to be drawn. He looked bored, as if another dead person had interrupted his day. The assignment to *Corpse Identification* was for lower ranking personnel. He hated the over dramatized, emotional part of the process: people dwelling over a deceased family member, the tears, the cries of, "*No!*" and "*How can this be?*" He just wanted to sign his name on the five pages of paperwork and get back to eating his tuna sandwich.

Crane strutted around with an egotistical attitude. Strategizing to manipulate their emotions, he snubbed compassion. After tossing in a few harsh, morbid statements, Crane would be on his way to closing this investigation. "There wasn't much left. Wildlife ate her flesh and most of her bones, but most of her skull was found intact."

Holding onto Sara, Anna Rose gagged. "Anna Rose, you've seen many dead carcasses. This is no different."

"It's Ruby!"

"Can you confirm that?" Crane asked.

Sara spouted, "No. She's just upset."

Russell remained stoic, watching and listening for Crane's inferences.

"The Coroner," Crane indicated the bearded man, "labeled cause of death to be by a blunt object. Her skull's flattened on the left. She bled out as the wolves had a tasty meal."

"The stone!" Anna Rose exclaimed.

"Shush," Sara said while Russell shot Anna Rose the *hush* look. It was too late. The first secret was out.

"What stone?" Crane demanded moving in.

Formulating a lie, Sara stepped between the law and her sister. "It was one of Ruby's healing stones—a blood stone, I think."

Anna Rose added, "Yeah, it's red. She said it was good for circulation."

"Her mother gave it to her. She carried it everywhere. It was small enough to fit into her pants pocket," Sara added thankful that her sister followed along with her fib. Although Ruby did carry a blood stone, given to her by her mother, every day.

Crane emptied a manila envelope. A stone fell out, clanked against the shiny steel gurney, and then rolled to a stop. "Like this one?"

Anna Rose started crying, "That's it. That's it. Ruby really is dead. Oh, no. No." Sara hugged her tight, whispering in her ear not to say another word. Beyond upset, Sara's words went unnoticed. "How can this be?" Anna Rose sobbed further.

In his head, the armed trooper mocked her reaction wanting just once to throw up his arms and scream melodramatically, *"how can this be...how can this be?"* Maintaining his unsympathetic stance, shutting out Anna Roses' sobs, he wondered if his wife had added extra mayonnaise to his sandwich.

Sara addressed her sister, "Stop this. We haven't determined that these...these parts are Ruby's. This crushed skull could be anyone's."

Russell nodded, observing the drama and Crane's posture.

Ignoring her reminder to be quiet, Anna Rose said, "Poor Ruby, taken out by her own medicine. He got it all."

Sara shoved her elbow into Anna Rose.

"He?" Crane asked. "Who got it all?"

Sara gave Anna Rose the death stare.

Russell shifted, knowing the jig was up. Disappointed, he said, "Ruby caught a ride with a tenant of Tealand's."

"Why didn't you tell me this before?"

"You didn't ask."

"So you know the murderer?"

Russell missed challenging the law. He replied fervently, "Was Ruby murdered? Is that even conclusive? There isn't enough evidence to determine Ruby's identity. Sara put it best: 'this could be anyone's skull.'"

Sara added, "We're basing all of this nonsense on assumptions. You have no real proof that these remains are Ruby's. She could be alive and well."

Crane desperately needed a cigarette, hot coffee and a nightstick. These people were hiding something or someone, and he wanted to beat it out of them—wasting time never sat well with him. Methodically, he opted for the weaker suspect. Obviously, Anna Rose was the only one he could manipulate to achieve the truth.

"Anna Rose Tealand, you're under arrest for the murder of Ruby Steffis."

"Hey stop...ouch." Anna Rose cried out as Crane cuffed and ushered her into the hallway.

Sara made a move for the door but the witnessing cop stopped her from leaving the room.

They heard Anna Rose holler, "Sara? What's happening? Stop this. I didn't kill Ruby. Let me go. Sara!"

Face-to-face with the cop Sara said, "She's no murderer. You have no grounds on which to arrest her." He appeared to be of Italian or Greek descent with thick black hair, shiny skin and bushy eyebrows. He towered over her with oily pores glistening. His intimidation tactic didn't stop her from spouting off. "You think you have it all figured out. You're nothing but a bunch of—" "Sara, let it rest," Russell ordered.

"Rest? They just arrested my sister. My innocent sister," she said fuming.

"Let's go."

"Now? We can't leave Anna Rose in jail. She's too...delicate for that."

"Sara. Now. We're leaving before they assign you a bunk next to her." Russell took the pigheaded Sara by the arm, lightly shoving her into the hallway then escorted her to the elevator.

Jerking her arm free, she demanded, "Russell, what are you doing?"

"Later. Let's get a hotel."

"What you are doing?"

"Hush."

Once inside Tealand's truck, Russell divulged his plan. They checked into the historic Captain Cook Hotel. Silently, they rode up the second tower elevator then stepped out into the lush golden-hued hallway. Filled with lavishly framed oil paintings of past owners and famous guests, they walked through the east wing then separated as they entered their adjacent rooms.

Sara didn't agree with Russell's plan. Worried sick about her sister, she tossed her purse onto the plush queen-sized bed. She needed her own plan. Springing Anna Rose weighed heavily on her mind. Each idea came up empty: creating an alibi for Anna Rose would be difficult and hard to prove, demanding that the charges be dropped would be a waste of time, and posting bail would have to wait for an arraignment. That left her dear sweet sister in jail until Monday. Needing a distraction, she grabbed the hotel information booklet and started to read the history of the Captain Cook Hotel.

Whether she wanted to or not, this was what she learned: The 1964 earthquake had leveled the hotel's original building. Walter J. Hickel reopened the first tower in 1965. As Alaskan prosperity grew, dignitaries and celebrities unknowingly paid for the second tower. A grand celebration was held during the start of the 1972 Iditarod Race. From the tower's fulcrum point, one could envision the HMS Resolution anchored in Turnagain Arm, where in 1778, Captain Cook and his crew stood astounded by Alaska's vast, untouched landscape. They watched seawater lap against her peninsulas and admired her majestic jagged, snowcapped mountains. Sara tossed the tourist information across the room.

Frustrated and unannounced, Sara swung open the adjoining door. "Russell, I'm—" Russell stood stark naked in front of her. Fully embarrassed, she rushed back to her room.

Speechless, Russell closed the door. It had been many years since anyone had seen him without clothes. He recalled that day. After one of Ruby's Spring Auctions, she had asked Russell to trade a bulk of the goods. Pleased to get away from Hurricane County, he headed south. After a brief encounter with a drunken white man and a swift encounter with the man's hunting knife, Russell's sliced abdomen required stitches. Claiming to be a doctor, a Talkeetna man had stitched him up. For a man with little or no training, he turned out to be proficient using catgut and a fishhook. The last time a woman had witnessed his naked body was beyond countable years.

Sara sat on the bed. Images raced through her mind. Burying her face into the pillow, she giggled as she compared Russell's body to Derek's. They were complete opposites. She missed Derek's muscular build. Yes, she missed each facet Derek had to offer, though not to the point of shedding any tears. Robbing Trapper, lying about his identity and murdering her sister's husband was unacceptable. She forced her feelings aside and knocked on Russell's door.

****

Bryan continued monitoring the television. So far, there had been no local news stories about hunters finding a dead body. He was certain the wolves had removed all traces of Ruby. Relieved, he settled into the furnished one-bedroom apartment near the airport. His plan was to keep a low profile, acquire nothing and be prepared to escape Alaska unscathed. Discreetly, *Eagle River Pawn* traded six sizable gold nuggets for cash and a fake driver's license. Next, Bryan had purchased an open-ended airline ticket. Alaska Airlines was more than happy to take his cash then issue him, Frank DeLong, a one-way ticket. If necessary, he'd fly to Arizona, hitch a ride further south and cross over the Mexican border. If necessary, Frank DeLong would disappear forever. Ironically, he'd have to drive through the town of Ruby before entering Tijuana. That's where he would give thanks to the ol' gal that he used, screwed then murdered. This made him laugh. Obviously, his court-ordered rehabilitation dollars were wasted. This also made him laugh. He was feeling good, good enough to have a drink.

****

Dorothy's homeschooling taught Anna Rose nothing about confinement. Nor did it prepare her for a concrete cell surrounded with bars, filthy floors and prostitutes for cellmates. Dressed in platform shoes, black tights, mini-skirts and gaudy, jersey tee-shirts two prostitutes stretched out on the two dirty mattresses. Bra straps exposed, they slept, smelling like old sex and rum. Afraid to awaken them, Anna Rose remained silent. Sitting on the stained, cold grey floor, she wrapped her arms around her bent legs. Starving and exhausted, she rocked her tailbone against the concrete floor, resting one eye at a time.

"Hey. Hey little lady," whispered a voice. A scraggly looking man stuck his arm through the bars with a stick of gum in hand. "Hey there, no need to be frightened."

Both eyes peered over her wrapped arms. She shook her head then dropped her forehead back onto her forearms.

"Hey, I can't hurt you."

"Shush. You'll wake them."

"They won't hurt you. They'll sleep until they smell breakfast. If you can call dehydrated eggs and surprise meat breakfast."

"Leave me alone." Anna Rose heard the iron gates open and close. She perked up, hopeful that Sara was coming for her.

"Back off Magpie," Trooper Crane said. "Anna Rose and I have some unfinished business. Are you gonna tell me who you're protecting?"

"What are you going to do for me? Are you going to let me out of this dump?"

"Give me what I need, and I'll see what I can do for you."

"That's not good enough. I want to call my attorney."

"You don't have an attorney."

"My constitutional rights are being violated." That much her homeschool lessons had taught her. Anna Rose knew her rights. What she didn't know was how to get out of jail and out from under a murder charge. What she did know was the Alaska State Troopers would do as they please.

"You have no right to hold me."

"Let me see…a missing husband and a missing friend. I've done my homework. You'll be here awhile. This lovely establishment…" gregariously, Crane spread his arms like a game show host displaying potential prizes, "…is just your first stop toward life in prison."

"Can't you see that you're scaring her? Leave her alone," Magpie said. Rule number one: *gain their confidence.*

"Shut up, slime bucket. Now, Anna Rose…that's such a sweet name. I'm sure the courts will show pity on you for your delicate nature. But then again, most statements from neighbors of murderers read: *She was so nice. She never bothered anyone.* That's the irony of justice, sweet Anna Rose."

"What did you just call me?"

"A murderer?"

"No, sweet Anna Rose. That's what he called me."

Magpie smiled. That was rule number two: *before robbing them be kind.*

"Give me a name before I recommend to the judge to gavel you into prison for life."

"Stop threatening me. I know my rights."

"Good for you. But there are only two people on the outside who know you're here. And they can be arrested too. Give me a name."

"By now, he's probably long gone."

"You say that Ruby was a good friend. Why do you protect the person that killed her?"

"First off, we don't know that Ruby is dead. Until we do know, this arrest, interrogation and murder charge is moot." Anna Rose sat back down, crossing her arms around her bent knees.

"Nice work, sweet Anna Rose," Magpie said. Rule number three: *always take your victim's side.*

"Shut up, Magpie," Crane's voice escalated, waking the sleeping street workers.

Groaning, they rolled over smacking their pasty mouths while adjusting their risqué wardrobe. Anna Rose stood up. Her eyes gave way to fear. Crane took notice and capitalized on it.

"They'll be your first opponents. What do you think, Magpie? Will they beat her? Will they tear her clothes from her? They do need new outfits. Maybe rape her once they see her vulnerabilities."

Magpie softened his eyes, giving Anna Rose a look so gentle and pleading, it caused her to relax her shoulders, dropping her hardened posturing. That was rule number four: *melt their hearts then steal their lives.*

Crane took notice of both prisoners and let the game play itself out. Time was on his side. He knew Magpie's tactics. Magpie was a regular with a rap sheet as long as Crane's arm. Concrete blocks were home to repeat criminals. Magpie was no different. Years of intermittent jail time and counseling had not changed his lawbreaking behavior. Schooled in crime as a teenager, Magpie knew the boundaries of the law; petty crime was his game. Tonight, Crane used it to his advantage.

"If you let me out now, I'll tell you his name."

"You know I can't let you out. You're accused of murder," Crane said shaking his head, needing a cigarette.

"We both know it's a false accusation."

"Just tell me his name, and I'll see about dropping the murder charge." After a short pause, the real situation dawned on him. "Oh, I get it. You're in love with him."

Anna Rose blushed with embarrassment. "No, I'm not in love. He was there for me when I needed him. And now, you ask me to hang him when we don't even know if that's Ruby's skull."

"Jail looks good on you. Good night." It was 10PM; Crane had had enough, and he was starving. Anna Rose would crack by morning. He was sure one night in jail would be enough for this fragile, homestead, homeschooled woman.

"Lights out," Crane instructed the guard.

Concrete corners nestled Anna Rose as all went black. Trying to orient herself in total darkness, she listened to the women snoring. Next, she heard a whisper so sympathetic it almost made her cry.

"Morning'll come sooner than you think. Rest your eyes, sweet Anna Rose," Magpie said counting on subtle reminders. Refining his act was rule number five: *thoughtfulness lead victims into his deceitful arms.*

****

The wind blew past Bryan as he strolled home sober from *Simone's Bar and Grill*. From behind, footsteps stalked him; someone was following him. Covertly, he stopped to light a cigarette, turning slightly to scan the empty streets. Across the damp road, the shadow of a longhaired dog appeared on the cinderblock wall of the *Mirror*

Lake Print Shop. With an open mouth, exposing its fangs and stretching its neck to the full moon, she howled. *Wolf?* Bryan thought, questioning not only the siting of a wolf in the city but his ability to discern a wolf from a Husky. Nevertheless, a shiver ran down his spine. The spirit wolf howled a second and third time. As it shook its head, a silhouette of saliva splattered the walls. Bryan nervously puffed the cigarette, quickening his pace homeward.

Ruby was watching, stalking her prey.

Stepping inside his apartment, he locked the door behind him. Leaving the lights off and from behind a dusty window curtain, he peeked outside just in time to see someone running across the street. The shadow of a man disappeared behind the closed *Yukon Music Store*. Someone was out there. Bryan needed to know whom before killing him.

Bryan turned around only to trip and fall over a chair. Getting to his feet, he stepped toward the kitchen. He stumbled over something, he wasn't sure what. Lunging for the stove, he flipped on the hood light. The sight of his ransacked apartment stunned him. There was nothing left in its original place, and food was scattered everywhere. Whoever was following him was looking for something. *The jade*, he thought. Bolting into action, he stepped over the overturned kitchen table, slipped on a *Playboy* magazine then fell banging his head against the short hallway wall, triggering a headache. For a moment, his eyes blurred, and his head felt ready to explode. Using the wall for stabilization, he forced himself onto his knees. Standing, he guided himself into the tiny bedroom then flipped the mattress back onto the box spring. Lying on the stained, orange shag carpet, he picked up the cheap poly-filled pillow; it was soft as soft could be. That's not what he was expecting—the key was missing.

****

With the exception of Magpie, no one slept that night. Crane had stuffed himself with a greasy cheeseburger and fries, giving him an all-night dose of heartburn. Ruby would have said that was his karma for treating Anna Rose so shamelessly. Poor Anna Rose's body felt frozen to the cell floor, causing her bones to ache. Sara was worried about what terrible things her sister was undergoing in jail. Tossing and turning throughout the night, Sara tried to punch down the overstuffed hotel pillow, increasing her aggravation. Russell had his own personal issues that kept him from sleep. Nervous about the demise of Ravens, he wondered how much booze to purchase before heading north. Unsettled about how Crane would end this ordeal, he struggled with the possibilities: Would Crane charge all of them with murder? And perhaps add Jess Tealand's death to Anna Rose's charges? Or would the three Hurricane County residents be allowed to leave Anchorage unscathed? The eerie wolf, the stranger running across the street, and the break-in agitated Bryan into a restless, sleepless night, escalating his headache into a full-blown migraine.

****

"How do you feel about the color orange?" Trooper Crane asked. The guard escorting him grinned tucking his yellow teeth behind his overgrown mustache.

Anna Rose stood slowly, stretching her aching muscles. "Are you talking to me?" she asked Crane.

"These Fourth Avenue professionals don't wear orange. In fact, they're lucky to wear anything."

"Fuck you," said the prostitute with matted jet-black hair.

The cell door automatically opened. "Come on ladies, your pimp posted your bail. I'm sure you'll be working for free at least a week." "Asshole," grumbled the blonde prostitute.

Magpie whistled. "See ya on the outside. If you get cold…" "You can't afford me," the blonde prostitute said flipping him off.

Now, Anna Rose was alone with Crane and in earshot of Magpie.

"You'll look good in orange. How was your night? Comfortable, I hope?" Crane asked sarcastically.

"You have no right to hold me. The Sixth Amendment states—"

Crane chuckled, "You won't last three minutes in a high-security correctional facility. A delicate flower such as yourself will be beat up the first night, raped the second night and then become someone's life-long lesbian bitch. I suggest using caution before eating the food—due to lack of funding, rat meat helps to supplement government protein requirements. Just tell me what I need to know so I can end this nightmare."

"You're full of shit, and you don't scare me."

"Such language from a delicate flower, it doesn't suit you. Now stop delaying the inevitable."

Thinking for a moment, Anna Rose conceded, "If I tell you his name, will you release me?"

"That's always been the deal."

"Do I need to get that in writing?"

Frustrated he spouted, "Damn, are you a lawyer or what?"

"I need to be sure."

"Why? So you can jump on a plane?"

"Really? How can you believe that I killed my dear friend?"

"I've seen and heard all the bullshit that I ever want to hear. Like you, I need to be sure."

Anna Rose looked over at Magpie, "Should I trust him?"

Magpie smirked, shaking his head and said, "He's a cop. Bullshit's bullshit—no one's exempt."

Anna Rose looked Crane in the eye, "It doesn't appear that your word has value."

"Value? Look lady, I don't know what you read or who educated you but you're in here on a murder charge. Apparently, you don't understand the *consequences* of these charges. Stop wasting my time. Tell me your lover's name."

"Heaven forbid, he's not my lover."

"Then roll the dice, and take your chances."

A quick glace toward Magpie told Anna Rose what to do. Magpie had those pleading eyes that no woman could resist. Shortly after midnight, Anna Rose had shared her secret. Magpie knew the truth and the name Crane was seeking.

"Bryan Smith."

"A generic name? There could be a few thousand of those walking the planet." Crane shook his head condescendingly. "Description?"

"It's not generic. He's tall, brown hair, full beard and drives a Chevy pickup."

"That's it? You make out with a guy, and that's all you know about him?"

"We didn't make out. We played cards, nothing more."

"Right. Come on, let's go."

"You're releasing me?"

"Immediately." Crane looked over his shoulder and hollered, "Guard."

Relieved, Anna Rose brushed off her shirt, straightened her posture and stepped outside of the cell. "Crane, you must know where Sara spent the night. Can you take me there?"

"Unlikely on both accounts," Crane lied.

"What? You owe me that?"

"You wasted my time. I don't owe you anything. The guard'll take you."

"Thank you."

Crane handed her off to the guard. "Make sure she eats and showers then issue her regulation clothing. She'll look good in an orange jumpsuit."

"What? You liar!" Anna Rose struggled, releasing the guard's grip.

"I didn't lie. I'm releasing you to the arraignment cell. Your appointment with the judge is on Monday."

Escorted out of the holding area, Anna Rose cursed, "You bastard."

Crane smiled back hiding his need for a cigarette. "Magpie, don't get too lonely."

"Crane, I know the guy you're looking for."

"Sure you do. Everyone knows a *Bryan Smith*."

"Check my records. We bunked at Dayton Pass. Let me out, and I'll take you to him. I know all of his hangouts."

"Did you and Anna Rose have a coming to Jesus conversation?"

"I got her to talk. She told me everything."

"You're a marvel to society, Magpie. It must be your body odor."

"Better be nice. I know he has the goods. And it's highly probable that he killed the woman."

Departing Crane said, "Lying is your forte. You better sit in here a while longer, maybe a new profession will strike your fancy."

Magpie yelled, "Check my records. I *can* find him."

****

Spring had Saturday morning looking like a mountain tributary. Run-off was still in full force, creating wet and muddy roads. Winter was no longer a threat, and the sun remained up through late evening. Summer solstice was seven weeks away. Shorter days meant winter was approaching. Alaskans were in a perpetual cycle of preparation: growing and storing food, chopping and stacking cords of wood, ordering supplies, rotating and replenishing survival provisions. Given the reality of two short and unpredictable seasons—summer and winter—there was no time to waste.

"We really should check on Anna Rose," Sara said during breakfast.

"No, remember the plan? Let them think she killed Ruby. We need to find Smith first."

"But—"

"No, Sara. She's a liability and our only asset. Let's get the jade back, turn Smith in then we'll collect Anna Rose from jail."

"Do you think they'll really let her out?"

"They have no grounds. Once we hand over Smith, they'll set her free before she even gets near a judge."

"She'll never speak to me again."

"You worry too much. This'll become just another Hurricane County story."

"I hope you're right."

"We have a lot of tracking to do. Let's go."

Russell parked in front of the *Black Market Pawn* shop. Sara remained in the truck while Russell spoke to the manager. She scanned the streets hoping to get lucky, hoping that Bryan Smith would appear from out of nowhere. Restless, she got out of the truck and walked down the street.

"Sara, what are you doing?" Russell asked perturbed.

With a wide stride, Sara hoofed it back to the truck and got in. "Sorry, I can't just sit around. What did you find out?"

"Word on the street is that a white guy's been cashing in gold nuggets at several locations. The first time was up in Eagle River where he cashed in big and purchased a fake driver's license."

"What for?" Sara asked not thinking.

"To flee the country. Wouldn't you if you had just murdered someone?"

"Leaving doesn't fit his pattern."

"Now you're a detective?"

"No. Anyone would surmise the same MO." Sara chuckled at her choice of words. She did sound like a detective. Maybe it was because she read a fair amount of homicide paperbacks. Unlike her sister, she loathed romance books. They bored her to tears. Besides she had had a real-life romance with Derek—Hurricane County's hunk. Even though his lies had shattered her reality that ended their relationship in heartbreak and disgust, still she missed him. She asked, "What's next?"

"Let's head up to Eagle River. It's only twelve miles from here."

"Yeah, but it's north of Anchorage. The only time I want to head north is when we're ready to go home."

"Sara, if we can find out what name he's using…"

"Why don't you go? Drop me off at the nearest bar, and I'll start asking around."

"Are you joking?"

"No. If we split up, we can cover more ground."

"What makes you think that anyone will talk to you? And just what are you going to ask? *Have you seen a tall, bearded man?* That fits just about every man in Alaska."

"Just let me out. We'll meet back at the hotel around noon." Before Russell could protest, Sara jumped out of the truck, walked away and never looked back.

"Dorothy's daughter all right—bullheaded as an ox," Russell said as he merged onto Highway 1 North.

Crane had assigned an undercover cop to follow Magpie. Next, he checked in with the cop that had been following Russell and Sara. Trooper Watson reported that they had split up. This was a good sign and a bad sign: good because Crane could pursue Sara, the weaker suspect, and bad, because Bryan Smith hadn't been located. *More time wasted*, Crane thought popping another calcium-rich tablet.

NON-CONFORMING
NORTHERNERS

Staring at his former lover, Bryan rubbed his aching temples. Red faced and with bloodshot eyes, he counseled himself over the ripple effect his beloved had on him. *Should I or shouldn't I delve into this golden, long awaited relationship?* he thought. She was luscious. She was satisfying. She was warm. And, she was dangerous. It would take only a moment to feel her pleasure. Becoming hooked again would also take only a moment. She was like a satisfying drug: addictive, delicious and faithful. They had been the best of friends for a long time. Bryan's body ached. He needed her. She was the only one that could settle his internal disputes. Knowing what a migraine and what her influence had caused him to do in the past, he waited, hoping that the pain would subside, clearing his vision and backing off his yearning to reenter this timeless relationship.

After leaving *Simone's Bar and Grill*, Bryan frequently looking over his shoulder as he traversed his way through the heart of Anchorage. The wolf was never far behind, sniffing the air, tracking and making him even more nervous. He would kill the wolf later, after dark, luring it to an empty alley then shoot it.

You've already killed me once, Ruby laughed.

Rain began to fall hard and fast, soaking his clothes. Sweeping winds lifted Bryan's hair. He wiped water from his aching forehead and blurred eyes. As his vision cleared, a wolf materialized directly in front of him, stopping him dead in his own tracks. Fangs dripped with saliva. Rain matted its fur. The wolf growled, pulled back its hips then sprang forward. Bryan fell to the ground as the wolf disappeared into transparent sheets of rain, not unlike a phantom disappearing behind its illusive cloak. Shaken, he stood up wondering what had happened.

Without warning, a rock soared through the air striking Bryan in the stomach. Stunned, he ran toward its trajectory. He sprinted toward the edges of two, three-story buildings. A dark potholed alley separated the two businesses. The alley was empty. Another rock hit him in the back of the head. He spun around. No one was there. The rain stopped. Pooled water rippled down the dark cavern. Cinderblocks crumbled downward, falling block-by-block, splashing into the potholes below. Bryan ignored his heightened instincts; curiosity guided him to walk between the buildings. Two rusty garbage bins flanked the alley's lofty walls. He heard beastly snarling as the buildings echoed with rage. The vibration amplified, gyrating off the towering cinderblock buildings. The pulsating caused Bryan's head to pound incessantly. With great force, a palm-sized rock struck his back. Winded, Bryan spun around splashing water up under his pants. No one was there.

Blurred vision halted Bryan. Unclear what was happening and as the echoes grew louder, rocks from all directions pelted him. Head throbbing and chest pounding, he ran toward the alley entrance. He gasped as the wolf blocked his escape. With raised hackles and projecting coal-black eyes, its glare penetrated through to Bryan's marrow. Petrified, he shook his head achieving clear sight. Street lamps illuminated dry streets. No rain had fallen. Yet, his clothes were wet, and his heart rate erratic. No wolf stood growling. Stepping forward, he looked down the empty road. There was no one.

From above, he heard faint laughter—a woman's voice. Something was familiar about the voice but he couldn't place it. Nor could he make sense of the last few minutes—logic had eluded him. Spooked, his skin crawled, and he shivered as his hair stood on end. He tried to focus while scanning the two buildings—they were intact. Instincts moved him to sprint to the other side of the street. He turned to see that the illusive wolf was indeed following. *Shit*, he thought. Panting, he wished for his gun. He'd kill that bastard wolf with one clean shot. Raised spine and teeth showing, the wolf stared Bryan down. Steam rose from its snout as the wolf moved closer, one slow step at a time, growling a subtle yet menacing guttural sound. Bryan froze, as if paralyzed, knowing that his life was about to end. With the exception of his own strength, he had no protection. Would he fight or let the wolf take him? Life had often scrutinized how Bryan lived his life. And now, death was scrutinizing how he would die. He would fight for a life that in the past wasn't worth anything until he had stolen Ruby's gold and the Russian Jade. His future was just around the corner. If only he could cross the street and duck into an open business, his life could be saved. He tried to move to the left. The wolf followed, furling its brow. Bryan centered himself, ready for action. The wolf stood steadfastly two-feet away, growling and drooling. Suddenly, it sprang upward, pushing Bryan into a brick wall, puncturing his jugular. Powerful legs and paws clutched Bryan's shoulders pressing him backwards. When Bryan resisted, the wolf vanished into thin air, leaving Bryan holding his neck, drenched in sweat and fear. It was over as soon as it had started.

As if playing the cello, Ruby struck a chord with lightning. *Karma's on its way,* she bellowed with laughter. Streetlights flickered as streams of high voltage connected with Alaskan roadways. Coinciding with flashes of lightning, the mysterious laughter continued. Shaken, Bryan took off running.

By 10:30PM, Bryan had not eaten nor had he slept. With wet clothes and ruffled hair, he looked like how a man on edge looks—worn and wild. Evading his stalker, he managed to crisscross through Anchorage until he reached *Koots Tavern*. Famous for its chili, hard rock bands and loose young women, *Koots* offered good times, good drugs and good trading. Three muscular bouncers, two posted at the front door and one at the back door, guarded its patrons as they sat in the low-level lighting devising schemes, constructing false promises and bartering for easily acquired sexual favors. Finally, Bryan felt at home. Tonight was the night…his night to kiss an old friend. She was already waiting for him behind the bar.

It wasn't the wet jeans that irritated Bryan most. It was the soggy cotton socks that clung halfway down his calves; not so much the sponginess of them, but the reminder of what he had seen and heard earlier. Was the wolf real? Or was it just his imagination? The rocks were real, he was certain, because his back ached. He could discount the wolf attack, but he couldn't dismiss the vandalized apartment and the bruises from the rocks. Someone was still out there, following him, watching him and now attacking him. Nevertheless, one kiss from his sweet lover, and he would easily slide into heaven, the unknown, a world of denial. And soon he would dismiss the familiar, yet undecipherable laughter and then disregard the entire alley incident as a migraine side effect. He was ready for his first kiss.

Koots was hopping. Loud music played for singles and couples as they danced the workweek blues away. Regular drinkers were well on their way to oblivion and the newer, younger patrons pounded down drinks like pros. Bryan summoned the busy male bartender and ordered a whiskey sour. Ice rattled against the tumbler. The cubes quickly melted as the alcohol met with them, warming it, diluting Bryan's drink and judgment. A coaster and a ten-dollar bill completed the beginnings of this reunion. The band danced Bryan right into good old times. This time, would it end with a nagging hangover or with another murder?

Two men staggered into the bar. The skinny, scraggly looking one sat two seats away from Bryan, tilting his red baseball cap low, just above his brows. The other a brawny, clean-shaven man settled into the bar's dark hole, presumably needing to be alone with his booze or with his woman of choice—both arrived simultaneously. Hard alcohol and time would uncover this man's story.

More dancing, more drinks, and more loud music skipped time forward to midnight. Hoping to prevent drunks from killing themselves and keeping the roads safe, Cops waited in the parking lot. Like clockwork, they ticketed the inebriated midnight patrons then came back for the professional 2AM drinkers. *Koots* simmered around 4AM, however remained open for afterhours bashes. On slower nights, the Troopers easily made their quotas by raiding these promiscuous, drug-infested parties.

The red baseball-capped man finally made his move, sliding over onto the barstool next to Bryan. His arm nudged Bryan's as he waived the bartender over. "Buyin' you a drink, Asshole," the man said keeping his head low.

Impaired, Bryan slowly rotated his head toward the asshole calling him an asshole. Then he proceeded to give him the *fuck you* look. His free drink arrived just in time before Bryan had the chance to mock the jerk sitting next to him.

"You're welcome."

Rolling his eyes, Bryan looked away and straight ahead—fingers tapping.

"I'm just trying to gain your trust."

Remaining silent, Bryan focused on the bar's mirrored wall, but five shelves of booze prevented him from identifying the man.

"That's rule number one, Asshole. Or did you forget?"

Bryan turned toward the faded red ball cap. Sure as a bear shits in the woods, Magpie tipped his hat to him.

Unimpressed, Bryan asked, "What the fuck man, how'd you get out?"

Magpie smiled and said, "All that good behavior significantly reduced my sentence. More accurately, all that not getting caught and playing the game significantly reduced my sentence." Magpie laughed.

Toasting, Bryan said, "Balls to you, Magpie. You playin' someone here?"

"Sure am, Asshole."

"Who's the bitch?" Bryan asked looking around the bar.

"No bitch this time, it's you Asshole."

"Stop calling me that."

"Drink up, Asshole. We need to talk."

"Stop calling me that."

"What should I call you, Frank DeLong?"

Bryan burrowed in real close, flicked Magpie's hat from his head and asked, "You've been following me?"

"I'm no follower, man. Word travels."

The man from the bar's deep, dark hole handed Magpie his hat and walked onward.

"What do you know, Little Rat Dick?"

"Well, I know you need me to fence the jade."

"What jade?"

"You know what I'm talking about. Let's get this over with. I'm in for fifty percent. You take your share and head south. I'll take mine and head further north. I hear there's a lovely, sweet Anna Rose that needs my attention."

Bryan's blood boiled as his fingers drummed the bar. His murderous twitch intensified. He was not even sure he could control his rage. Alcohol and the words *sweet Anna Rose* would indeed drive him to kill. "Fuck you, Rat Dick. You better leave while your shrew-like legs can still carry you back into your hole."

"Gonna kill me too?"

Like a dragon breathes fire, Bryan breathed death into his former cellmates' nostrils. He stared Magpie down. The alcohol from six whiskey sours evaporated, clearing his head. He almost felt sober. Yet, he was angry enough to kill Magpie—an annoying, mouthy rodent. Bryan chuckled, thinking how much Magpie and Ruby had in common. "No problem. Shall we step outside?"

"You know you've been made, right? Let me help you get away. I'm just asking for a cut, that's all."

"You gonna share my jail time too? I mean really—fifty percent? You should have at least killed the bitch. You know, she messed up my truck. Blood dripped below the window seal. But I quieted her, real fast."

"Look, we got us a situation."

"We?"

"They're looking for you. Your sweet Anna Rose squealed on you. Let me unload the product, split the dough and ride off into the sunset."

"We're not in Hollywood, and this ain't the movies."

"But we could be...Hollywood, with all that sunshine and all those rich bitches ripe for the takin'." Magpie held out his hand. "Shake on it."

"Fuck you, Rat Dick. I'll take my chances alone."

"What are you gonna do with all that gold? Come on, cut me in."

"Some days, criminals need to be selfish, and today's my day. Drink up, then get the fuck out of my face."

"I have someone waiting to trade the jade for cash. Let me take it to him. You could be heading south tonight."

"It's already morning, Dumbshit. I don't need your help. Disappear before I make you an afterthought—a bad memory that no one's ever cared about."

"Come on, this guy's got a boat load of cash. He'll pay you whatever you want."

"Pipe it before I slam your face onto the bar."

"I should let you just hang yourself, but I'm trying to help you, man. Sixty-forty then? You take the bulk of it. And I'll stay clean away from your sweet Anna Rose."

"Mention her name one more time—"

"Asshole, your time just ran out. Look." Magpie nodded toward the front door.

Russell ushered Sara up to the side bar, ordered her a drink then headed to the restrooms. Boldly Sara slammed the straight tequila, sucked on a bar-cut lime then ordered another all the while scanning the bar through the reflection of mirrors and bottled booze. A red hat caught her eye.

Magpie stood up, exposing Bryan. He said, "I'm out of here, Asshole. I know where you hid the gold and the jade. I'll be on my way to collect it. You're out of chances. My offer ends now."

"You don't know shit. Move on, Magpie, before my fist makes your face even uglier."

As her second shot moved smoothly down her throat, Sara caught sight of Bryan. She slammed the shot glass on the bar and stood up. Walking toward him, she casually lifted a beer mug from an empty, unbussed table. Gripping the handle tightly, she walked straight up to him and slugged him in the back, exactly where the stranger had landed the rock earlier. Bryan winced, quickly turned and punched Sara in the jaw. She fell flat out onto the sticky floor. Bryan followed her, kneeling and rearing back his fist. In mid-swing, his downward thrust was intercepted two inches from Sara's face, and his arm bent backwards, snapping his collarbone, forcing him to spin face up. The man from the bar's dark hole stood over Sara, repeatedly punching

Bryan's face. Blood splattered her blouse as patrons shouted, "Fight. Fight. Fight."

Russell rushed over, lifted Sara up and placed her in a chair. Then he pulled the winded man off Bryan.

"That's enough," Russell ordered.

Stunned and holding her swollen face, Sara stood up.

"Quick, take the back door," Russell instructed as he propped Bryan up then casually sat at the bar.

Sara and the winded man exited arm and arm. Sara wasn't sure if he was holding on to her as a hostage or because he was breathless. She wasn't sure why she was holding on to him as if nothing had come between them. Her face and heart continued to swell.

Recognizing Crane as he entered the bar, people scattered, finding their way outside using the back door or becoming lost in the darkness of *Koots*. A code of silence filtered through the bar as Crane assessed the situation. Those seated back at their tables wondered whom he would be arresting. And why? The finale of the fight became just as interesting as the fight itself. There was something behind the beating. But what? Of course, *Koots'* patrons would adhere to the code; keeping the unknown man, and Sara's physical description to themselves. After all, the man propped up did punch a chick and was rearing back for more. It only seemed right that the unknown couple be permitted their due freedom—that's how Alaska's frontier justice worked.

Russell nodded at Crane and said, "That's him on the floor."

Magpie confirmed with a nod then bolted through the front door into the throes of his next victim.

"Looks like I'm a little late. What happened?"

"Shit if I know. He was lying there when I walked in," replied Russell.

Disbelieving the same old *shit if I know* story, Crane shook his head. He took one good look at the bloody man resting against a table leg and asked, "Bryan Smith?"

Bryan replied, "Frank DeLong."

"Bullshit. We know about your fake ID. We know about the gold and the Russian Jade. We also know about the woman you murdered. In fact, Bryan Smith, you're under arrest for the murder of Ruby Steffis." While quoting the Miranda Rights, Crane forcefully applied the cuffs then tightened them.

"It's Frank DeLong. And he didn't murder anyone."

"That's right, but Bryan Smith did. Come on, Asshole." Crane jerked the cuffs upward forcing Bryan to his feet.

"There's no proof."

"Right now, your truck's on its way to forensics. You can thank Magpie for that."

"Fuck you and Little Rat Dick. I'll kill both of you."

"By the time you get out of jail, I'll be in an old folk's home wasting my time and wishing for death to arrive. I'll be waiting. Don't be late. Where's the jade?"

"It's right next to the gold, Dickhead."

Crane jerked Bryan around hard so they were face-to-face. "Really, Asshole? You're not gonna talk to me that way. I could leave you here and let the beatings continue. Tell me where they're at."

"When I get out of jail, I'll dig it up, come for you, kill you slowly and then be on my way."

"A slow killing's not your style. You've a short fuse. Better to be consistent—kill me fast, like you did Ruby."

"No loss there."

"Do the right thing; return the jade to the natives."

"I already did do the right thing. They're free of Ruby."

"So you admit killing her?"

"No confessions. Get me a lawyer."

Before Crane removed Bryan Smith from *Koots Tavern*, Russell nodded satisfied that Ruby's death was vindicated and without him having to inflict pain on anyone, except Anna Rose.

"I'll be picking up Anna Rose in thirty minutes," Russell said.

"Make it forty-five, paperwork, you know."

Russell nodded. He was happy to be driving north within the hour.

The bouncer opened the door for Crane allowing him to shuttle Bryan toward the patrol car. The back door bouncer opened the door for Russell as he joined the unknown man and Sara.

"You knew?" Sara questioned Russell.

"I needed a tracker."

Suspicious, Sara asked, "So what am I supposed to call you, Chad or Derek?"

"Derek. I don't know Chad Westler." Holding her hands, he said, "I've missed you."

"I've missed you too. But I'll never forgive Chad." Sheepishly, she added, "Though I might have to forgive Derek."

"I understand. I also understand that you don't understand the depth of my commitment."

Russell interrupted, "Where's the Russian Jade?"

Derek looked at Russell, then at Sara. "If Sara tells me that she loves me, I'll tell you."

"Bartering for sex is considered prostitution."

"I've killed for her. Prostitution's easy."

Impatiently, Russell asked. "Sara?"

Squeezing Derek's hands, she said, "I've never stopped."

Smirking, Derek asked, "Anyone need a vacation?"

Russell and Sara exchanged a perplexed look.

Derek reached into his pants pocket and pulled out an airport locker key. Excited to have Ruby's legacy returning home, they smiled.

Allowing Derek and Sara a few minutes alone, Russell walked to the front of the tavern to retrieve Jess Tealand's truck. On his way, he nodded and smiled as he passed the spirit wolf.

You're welcome. I'll be watching, Ruby taunted.

Sara held her jawbone, probing, "Are you asking to come back?"

"I am."

"Why should I take you back?"

"Because it's what you want. It's what I want. And it's the right thing to do."

"Really? What do you know about doing the right thing?"

"When the right choice presents itself, I act accordingly."

Sara was silent.

"Besides," Derek prodded, nudging her shoulder, "Ruby would approve."

The spirit wolf howled in agreement.

Sara chuckled, relaxing her posture, "Ruby always did live on the edge."

Heavy black clouds parted. The lone wolf rose to the heavens. The clouds converged, sealing the gap between heaven and earth, angels and killers, friends and lovers. Ruby was free.

Sara squinted, stiffening her stance and said, "Promise me…no more killing."

Derek looked away. "Protecting you is all that matters."

Impatiently, Russell revved the truck.

Grabbing his shirt, Sara repeated her request with gusto, "Promise me!"

He kissed her forehead then opened the truck door. Before getting inside, Sara stood firm, "Promise me, right here, right now."

For a long moment, Derek looked down the lonely streets of Anchorage. Slowly, he turned to look at Sara. The Alaskan morning sunlight played with his soft eyes, penetrating her heart. With sincerity, he looked lovingly into her eyes. Another long moment passed, and he firmly said, "I can't."

ABOUT THE AUTHOR

Living in Alaska for 18 years, Cie Marchi experienced a great many sights, sounds & encountered an array of wildlife. Her writing stems from these unique events, compelling her to write & teach. Her work is poignant. Her teachings build confidence, self-reliance & understanding among youth & adults.

Now living in Eastern Washington, she participates in all seasonal activities. She enjoys co-facilitating the Chelan Rebel Writers Group, being a personal trainer & creating healthful meals. Cie writes children's books, movies, novels & inspirational teachings. One of her standing philosophies is *Teach Where You Can*.

www.cmarchionline.com